FRUIT OF THE DRUNKEN TREE

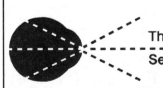

This Large Print Book carries the
Seal of Approval of N.A.V.H.

FRUIT OF THE DRUNKEN TREE

INGRID ROJAS CONTRERAS

THORNDIKE PRESS

A part of Gale, a Cengage Company

GALE
A Cengage Company

Farmington Hills, Mich • San Francisco • New York • Waterville, Maine
Meriden, Conn • Mason, Ohio • Chicago

Thorndike Press® Large Print Basic.
The text of this Large Print edition is unabridged.
Other aspects of the book may vary from the original edition.
Set in 16 pt. Plantin.

LIBRARY OF CONGRESS CIP DATA ON FILE.
CATALOGUING IN PUBLICATION FOR THIS BOOK
IS AVAILABLE FROM THE LIBRARY OF CONGRESS

ISBN-13: 978-1-4328-6032-5 (hardcover)

Published in 2019 by arrangement with Doubleday, an imprint of The
Knopf Doubleday Publishing Group, a division of Penguin Random
House LLC

Printed in the United States of America
1 2 3 4 5 6 7 22 21 20 19 18

Para ti, Mami.

CONTENTS

1.
THE PHOTOGRAPH

She sits in a plastic chair in front of a brick wall, slouching. She is meek with her hair parted down the middle. There are almost no lips to be seen, but by the way she bares her teeth you can tell she is smiling. At first the smile seems flat but the more I study it, the more it seems careless and irresponsible. There is a bundle in her arms and a hole for the newborn's face, which comes out red and wrinkled like an old person's. I know it's a boy because of the blue ribbon woven into the blanket edge; then I stare at the man behind Petrona. He is afroed and striking, weighing his cursed hand on her shoulder. *I know what he's done,* and it turns my stomach but who am I to say whom Petrona should allow into a family portrait such as this?

On the back there's a date stamp of when the photo was printed — and because when I count back nine months it falls exactly on

11

the month my family and I fled from Colombia and arrived in L.A., I turn back the photograph to look intently at the baby, to register every wrinkle and bulge around the dark hole of his gaping mouth, to decide whether he is crying or laughing, because I know exactly where and how he was conceived and that's how I lose track of time, thinking it was my fault that the girl Petrona was just fifteen when her belly was filled with bones, and when Mamá comes back from work, she does not yell (even though she sees the photograph, the envelope, the letter from Petrona all addressed to me) — no, Mamá sits down next to me like taking off so much weight, and together we are quiet and sorry on our dirty stoop on Vía Corona in East L.A., staring at that fucking photograph.

We were refugees when we arrived to the U.S. *You must be happy now that you're safe,* people said. They told us to strive for assimilation. The quicker we transformed into one of the many the better. But how could we choose? The U.S. was the land that saved us; Colombia was the land that saw us emerge.

There were mathematical principles to becoming an American: you had to know one hundred historical facts (*What was one reason for the Civil War? Who was the president during World War II?*), and you had to spend five uninterrupted years on North American soil. We memorized the facts, we stayed in place — but when I elevated my feet at night and my head found its pillow I wondered: of what country was I during those hours when my feet were in the air?

When we applied for citizenship, I rounded the hard edges of my accent and that was one tangible way in which I had changed. We heard nothing for a year. We grew thin. We understood how little we were worth, how small our claim in the world. We had no money after our application fee, and nowhere to go. Then, we received the summons for our interview, the final background check, the examination, the approval.

At the ceremony, they screened a video filled with eagles and artillery and all of us recited a pledge. We sang our new anthem and once it was done it was said we were American. The newest batch of Americans celebrated, but in the open courtyard, I let my head hang back. I watched the sway of palm trees knowing here was where I was supposed to think about the future, and how bright it might be, but instead all I could think of was Petrona, how I was fifteen like she had been the last time I saw her.

From Mamá's old agenda I got her address. But it wasn't a real address, just a set of directions Petrona had dictated to Mamá back when we lived in Bogotá: *Petrona Sánchez at the invasión between Street 7 and 48. Kilometer 56, the house past the lilac bush.* In our apartment, I locked myself in the bathroom and turned on the shower, and as the bathroom steamed I wrote the letter. I didn't know where to begin, so I followed the form I had learned in middle school:

Heading (*3 de Febrero del 2000, Chula Santiago, Los Angeles, Estados Unidos*), respectful greeting (*Querida Petrona*), body that uses easy and exact vocabulary (*Petrona, cómo estás? Cómo está tu familia?*), each new paragraph with first line indented (*Mi familia está bien./ Estoy leyendo* Don Quixote./ *Los Angeles es bonita, pero no tan bonita como Bogotá*). The closing line was next, but instead I wrote about what it was like to flee from Colombia; how we boarded a plane, Bogotá to Miami to Houston to L.A., how I prayed for no immigration officers to stop us and send us back, how I could not stop thinking about everything we had lost. When we first arrived to L.A. it was impossibly sunny and all I could smell was the salt from the ocean. *The smell of salt burned my nose when I breathed in.* I wrote paragraph after paragraph about salt, like I was crazy (*We washed our hands with salt to reverse bad luck./ Salt was the one thing Mamá bought when she was afraid to spend our money./ I read in a magazine that packaged salt has crushed animal bone in it, which disgusted me until I realized that so must the ocean's. Beach sand was part bones too*). In the end all the talk about salt came to feel like some type of code. *It's gotten so,* I wrote, *I can't even smell salt anymore.* It became my closing line, not because I meant it to be but because suddenly I had nothing more to say.

I never asked the one thing I wanted to know: *Petrona, when we left, where did you go?*

When Petrona's reply arrived, I tried to find hidden messages behind the ordinary information she volunteered: the nice weather, the newly paved road to her house in the invasión, the lettuces, the cabbages in season.

In the end it didn't matter her letter back to me was so ordinary, because all the answers I could ever hunger for were printed on that photograph, which she creased in half and placed in the folds of her letter before licking the envelope and pressing it shut, before handing the letter to the postman, before it traveled just like how I once did, Bogotá to Miami to Houston to L.A., before it arrived bringing with it all this wreckage to our doorstep.

2.
THE GIRL PETRONA

The girl Petrona came to our home when I was seven and my sister Cassandra was nine. She was thirteen and had only gone through the third grade. She stood with a tattered brown suitcase at the gate of our three-story house in a yellow dress that dangled at her ankles. Her hair was short and her mouth was hanging open.

The garden yawned between us like an abyss. Cassandra and I gazed at the girl Petrona from behind the two left-most columns of our house. The white columns rose from the porch and supported the overhang of the second floor. The second floor stuck out like an overbite. It was a typical Bogotá house, made to look like the old colonials, white with wide windows and black iron bars and a clay roof with red-blue half-moon tiles. It was part of a row of identical houses linked one to the other by the sidewalls. I didn't know then why the girl

Petrona looked at our house that way, but Cassandra and I gaped back at her with the same kind of awe. The girl Petrona lived in an invasión. There were invasiones in almost every tall hill in the city, government land taken over by the displaced and the poor. Mamá herself had grown up in an invasión — but not in Bogotá.

From behind her column Cassandra asked, "Did you see what she's wearing, Chula? That's a *boy* haircut she has." She widened her eyes behind her glasses. Cassandra's glasses took up a great deal of her face. They were pink-rimmed and oversized and magnified the pores on her cheeks. Mamá was waving at the girl Petrona from the front door. She sprang forward into the garden, clicking her heels on the stepping-stones and bouncing her hair on her back.

The girl Petrona watched Mamá as she approached.

Mamá was a natural beauty. That's what other people said. Strange men on the street stopped her in order to pay compliments to the dramatic breadth of her eyebrows or the pull of her deep, brown eyes. Mamá didn't like going through pains for her beauty, but she woke up every morning to apply thick black liner to her eyes, and drove monthly to the salon to get her toenails done, arguing all the while that it was worth it, because her eyes were the well of her power and her small feet the mark of her innocence.

The night before the girl Petrona arrived Mamá made three stacks with her tarot cards on her breakfast table and asked, "Is the girl Petrona trustworthy?" She put the question in a number of ways with a variety of tones until she felt she was asking the question with one mind; then she picked the top card from the middle stack. She flipped the card over and laid it in front of her and saw that it was the Fool. Her hand froze in midair as she regarded the upside-down card. The card depicted a white man smiling caught in a half step looking dreamily to the sky, in one hand a white rose and over his shoulder a golden satchel. He wore leggings and boots and a princelike flouncy dress. At his feet a white dog leaped. The man wasn't looking, but he was about to fall off a cliff.

Mamá collected the stacks in her hands, reshuffling. "Well, we've been warned."

"Should we tell Papá?" I asked. Papá worked at an oil site far away in Sincelejo and I was never sure when he was due back for a visit. Mamá said Papá had to work far away because there were no jobs in Bogotá, but all I knew was that sometimes we told

Papá about things, and sometimes we didn't.

Mamá laughed. "It's all the same anyway. *Any* girl you hire in this city will have ties to hooligans. Just look at Dolores down the block — *her* girl was part of a gang and they robbed Dolores's house, imagine: they didn't even leave the microwave." Mamá saw the worry on my face. Her eyeliner ran thickly and ticked up at the corners. The tick wrinkled as she smiled. She dug her finger in my ribs. "You're too serious. Don't worry."

In the front garden Cassandra said from behind her column, "This girl Petrona won't last a month — look at her; she has the spirit of a mosquito." I blinked and saw that it was true. The girl Petrona shrank back as Mamá opened the gate.

Mamá always had bad luck with girls. The last girl, Julieta, was fired because Mamá had walked into the kitchen at the wrong time and saw Julieta form her mouth around a drop of spit, and as the girl Julieta looked up the spit plunged into Mamá's morning coffee.

When Mamá demanded an explanation, the girl Julieta said, "Maybe the Señora's eyes are seeing things." A second later Mamá was throwing the girl Julieta's belongings on the street, and grabbing the girl Julieta by the collar saying, "Don't come back, Julieta, don't you bother coming back," pushing her out of the door and slamming it shut.

Mamá hired girls based on the urgency of their situation. She sought out girls employed at other houses and gave them our telephone number in case somebody they knew needed a job. Mamá heard sad stories of families struck by illness, pregnancy, displaced by war, and even though we could only offer five thousand pesos per day, enough for some vegetables and rice at the market, many girls were interested in applying. I think Mamá was always hiring girls that reminded her of herself in her youth, but it never turned out how she wanted.

One girl had almost stolen Cassandra when she was a baby. Mamá didn't know her name, only that she was infertile — except how Mamá put it was that the girl was *barren like beach sand in a drought.* Most people we knew got kidnapped in the routine way: at the hands of guerrillas, held at ransom and then returned, or disappeared. The way Cassandra almost got kidnapped was a fun twist on an all too common story. There was a photograph of the infertile girl in question in our family album. She looked out from behind the slick of the plastic sheet with frizzy hair and a missing front tooth. Mamá said she kept the girl's photo in our album because it was all part of our family history. Even the photos of Papá as a communist youth were there for anyone to see. He wore bell-bottom jeans and dark sunglasses. His teeth were clenched and his fist was in the air. He looked sophisticated, but Mamá said not to be fooled, because really Papá was as lost as Adam from the Bible would be on Mother's Day.

Ours was a kingdom of women, with Mamá at the head, perpetually trying to find a fourth like us, or a fourth like *her,* a younger version of Mamá, poor and eager to climb out of poverty, on whom Mamá could right the wrongs she herself had endured.

At the gate, Mamá extended her hand firmly to the girl Petrona. The girl Petrona was slow so Mamá scooped her hand in both of hers and moved it rigidly up and down. The girl Petrona's arm undulated free and loose like a wave. "How do you do?" Mamá said. The girl Petrona merely assented and locked her eyes on to the ground. Cassandra was right. This girl Petrona would not last a month. Mamá put an arm around the girl Petrona and led her into our garden, except instead of going up the stone steps to our front door they veered to the left. Together they walked toward the bed of flowers at the edge of the garden. They stopped in front of the tree closest to the gate and then Mamá pointed at the tree and whispered.

We called it el Borrachero, the Drunken Tree. Papá called it by its scientific name, *Brugmansia arborea alba,* but nobody ever knew what he was talking about. It was a tall tree with twisted limbs, big white flowers, and dark brown fruits. All of the tree, even the leaves, was filled with poison. The tree drooped half over our garden, half over the neighborhood sidewalk, releasing a honeyed scent like a seductive, expensive perfume.

Mamá touched one droopy, silky flower as she whispered to the girl Petrona, who watched the flower as it swung lightly on its stem. I guessed Mamá was giving her the same warnings I had received about the tree: not to pick up its flowers, not to sit underneath, not to stand by it too long, and most important, not to let the neighbors know we ourselves were afraid of it.

The Drunken Tree made our neighbors nervous.

Who's to say why Mamá decided to grow that tree in her garden? It may have been that long mean streak in her, or it may have been because she was always saying you couldn't trust anyone.

In the front garden Mamá lifted a fallen white flower from the ground, pinching it at its stem, and threw it over the gate. The girl Petrona followed the flight of the flower and her eyes lingered on it as it landed on the neighborhood sidewalk with its two o'clock shadow. Then the girl Petrona stared at her hands holding the suitcase.

Just after she planted the Drunken Tree, Mamá laughed like a witch and bit the side of her index finger, "The surprise they will get, all our curious neighbors who stop to spy in our windows!"

Mamá said nothing would happen to our neighbors, except if they dwelled for too long the perfume of the Drunken Tree would descend on them and make them a little dizzy, then their head would feel like a balloon, and after a long while they would want very badly to lie down right there on the sidewalk to take a little nap. Nothing too serious.

Once there was a seven-year-old girl who ate a flower.

"Supposedly," Mamá said then. "But do

you know what I told them? I said maybe they should watch their young girl more closely, eh? Keep her from poking her dirty nose in my front yard."

For years the neighbors had pleaded with the Neighborhood Administration to make Mamá take her tree down. It was, after all, the tree whose flowers and fruit were used in burundanga and the date-rape drug. Apparently, the tree had the unique ability of taking people's free will. Cassandra said burundanga was where the idea of zombies came from. Burundanga was a native drink made out of Drunken Tree seeds. The drink had once been given to the servants and wives of Great Chiefs in Chibcha tribes, in order to bury them alive with the Great Dead Chief. The burundanga made the servants and wives dumb and obedient, and they willingly sat in a corner of the underground grave waiting, while the tribe sealed the exit and left them with food and water that would have been a sin to touch (reserved as it was for use by the Great Chief in the afterworld). Many people used it in Bogotá — criminals, prostitutes, rapists. Most victims who reported being drugged with burundanga woke up with no memory of assisting in the looting of their apartments and bank accounts, opening their wallets and handing over everything, but that's exactly what they'd done.

Mamá, however, showed up at the Neighborhood Administration with a stack of research papers, a horticulturist, and a lawyer and because the fruit of the Drunken Tree was something the experts had little interest in, and because the small amount of research there was didn't agree on defining the seeds as poisonous or even a drug, the Administration decided to leave it alone.

There were many attempts to damage our Drunken Tree. Every few months we woke up to see out of our front windows that the branches hanging on the side of the gate over the sidewalk had once again been sawed off and left on the grass around the tree's trunk like dead limbs. Our Drunken Tree flourished nonetheless, persistently, with its provocative white flowers hanging about it like bells and the wind forever teasing out its intoxicating fragrance into the air.

Mamá was convinced la Soltera was behind the attempts. We called her that because she was forty years old and single and still lived with her old mother. La Soltera lived to our right and I often saw her wandering around in circles in her garden, wearing too much purple eye shadow and enveloped in a day-old-coffee-and-fresh-cigarette smell. I often put my ear to the wall we shared with la Soltera to hear what she did all day, but mostly what I heard was bickering and the television left on. Mamá said la Soltera was the only kind of woman with enough time on her hands to go attacking someone's tree. So in retaliation, when Mamá swept our front red-tile patio, she swept the dirt through the sides of the tall ceramic planters and the pines, *toward* the patio of la Soltera.

Back in the garden, Cassandra said, "Quick, Chula, before they see you!"

Cassandra shuffled her feet and slid her hands clockwise around the column to remain hidden as Mamá and the girl Petrona came up the stone steps to the front door. I did the same, but kept my head out the side to watch. Mamá had her arm around the girl Petrona and the girl Petrona was staring down.

"These are my girls," Mamá said as they came to our red-tile patio. The girl Petrona did a curtsy, her long sandaled feet together and her knees out to both sides, stretching the lap of her dress like a tent. It was odd to see a girl six years older do a curtsy. Cassandra and I remained hidden behind the columns and stared back at her and said nothing. She looked at us, her eyes a spot-lighted brown, nearly yellow. Then she cleared her throat, yellow dress to her ankles, tattered suitcase in hand.

"They're shy," Mamá said. "They'll get used to you."

They walked inside together, Mamá's voice fading slowly, like an outgoing train saying, "Here, let me show you your room."

Cassandra and I always felt strange when we had a new girl in our house, so we stayed in Mamá's bedroom and watched Mexican soap operas until they were over and then *Singin' in the Rain* on the English channel with subtitles.

The movie was interrupted twice an hour by a news flash. We were used to it, but Cassandra and I groaned all the same. I let my face stretch and droop against my hand, and the reporter talked about that mysterious ocean of acronyms that seemed to always be close at hand — FARC, ELN, DAS, AUC, ONU, INL. She spoke of things the acronyms had done to one another, but sometimes, the reporter spoke of one name. A simple name. First name, last name. *Pablo Escobar.* In that confused ocean of acronyms, the simple name was like a fish breaking the water, something I could hold on to and remember.

Then our movie would begin again. The singing would return, the yellow raincoats, the white rosy faces. North America seemed like such a clean, pleasant place. The rain was sleek on the black-tar street and the police were well-mannered and filled with principles. It was striking to see. Mamá always got out of tickets by batting her lashes, begging, and slipping policemen bills of veinte-mil. The Colombian police were easily corrupted. So were the officials at the notaries and the court, whom Mamá always paid so she could be ushered to the head of the line and her applications put at the top of the stack. Cassandra held her nose in front of the television and spoke like Lina Lamont, the beautiful blond actress cursed with the horrible, nasal voice. She said, "And I cayn't stand 'im," and we giggled. She said it over and over until we quivered with laughter and we lay on our backs overcome.

3.
MOSQUITA MUERTA

At our house Petrona received her first instructions in washing, ironing and mending, scrubbing the floors, cooking, making the beds, watering the plants, dusting, fluffing the pillows. Petrona didn't look thirteen, though that's what Mamá said. Her face was ashy and her eyes bitter-old. Her hair was cut short like a boy's and she wore a white apron with border lace like a fine tablecloth. She always had flushed cheeks and red knuckles.

Petrona left every day at six in the evening, but there was a room in the back of our house, past the indoor patio, that was all her own. There, when Cassandra and I got back from school, we would find Petrona, sitting on the bed and listening to the radio. We could see her plainly through the clear window of her bedroom. She sat motionless, hands clasped against her chest, the muffled sounds of men singing over soft guitars escaping from under the crack of her door.

Cassandra and I pressed our noses against her window. We watched Petrona as she rocked, but most of the time she remained very still sitting there, like a lifeless rag doll slumped against the wall. I wondered what Petrona thought about as she closed her eyes. I imagined that something hard was swelling from the inside of her, and if we left it alone, Petrona would turn to stone. At times I was sure it was beginning to happen because the light began glowing gray on her cheeks and her chest wasn't moving with her breath. To me, Petrona looked like one of those smooth plaster statues on display in private courtyards and public squares all over Bogotá — Mamá said they were saints, but Papá said they were random people who had done something good and remarkable.

In our house Petrona wore a cloud of silence wherever she went. Her footsteps had no sound. She deliberately lifted and placed her feet one after the other on the carpet, inaudible like a cat. Then, the only noise announcing Petrona was the sloshing of soapy water, which she carried in a bright green bucket to the second floor, holding the handle with both hands, advancing one elephant step at a time.

I could hear her panting as she carried things up and down the house. She carried trays with food, mops, bags of clothes, boxes with toys, cleaners, disinfectants. When I heard the first murmurs of her panting, I left my half-done homework on the bed and stood at the door of the bedroom that I shared with Cassandra. It opened to the left at the top of the stairs. As I watched Petrona, she looked up at me and smiled weakly. Then she cleared her throat and went down the hall toward Mamá's bedroom.

I always imagined the silence in Petrona's throat like dry fur draping over her vocal cords, and when she cleared her throat, I imagined the fur shaking a little, then settling, smooth like hair on a fruit.

Petrona's silence made Mamá nervous.

Mamá put all her energy into making Petrona speak. Mamá shared countless stories about our family in the northeast, her childhood, her Indian grandmother, seeing ghosts, but Petrona never told stories of her own. Petrona only punctuated Mamá's stories with "Sí, Señora Alma," "No, Señora Alma," and shook her head when she wanted to convey surprise or disbelief.

Cassandra and I were intrigued by Petrona's silence. We hung around to see if she talked with Mamá. We decided it was just like a street cat when a cajoling stranger offered a bowl of milk. We made it a point to count the syllables Petrona used each time she spoke. We pressed our fingertips to our thumbs and pronounced her syllables in our head. We counted obsessively and slowly we realized she never spoke more syllables than six. We started to think that maybe Petrona was a poet or maybe someone under a spell. I didn't tell Cassandra that in a certain light Petrona looked to me like a statue, that when she was still and quiet the folds of her apron seemed to me to harden into the stone draperies of church saints. I knew Cassandra would find the idea ridiculous and she would laugh at me forever. Privately, I came up with saint names for Petrona. *Petrona, Our Lady of the Invasiones. Petrona, Patron Saint of Our Secret Girlhood.*

At night, when Petrona was gone, we looked for clues in her room. There were fashion magazines stacked next to her bed and a red lipstick standing erect on the windowsill. Her room smelled like laundry soap. On the white wall of the bathroom she had drawn little hearts by the toilet paper dispenser in black ink. The black hearts floated up in a smoky pattern until they disappeared behind a beehive painting Mamá had hung before Petrona arrived. I thought the black hearts were proof Petrona was a poet, but Cassandra said that the magazines and the lipstick weren't something a poet would own. None of the items seemed like they would belong to a saint either.

At home, Mamá watched Petrona closely. Her eyes hovered over Petrona like two bright-as-the-moon planets, deep with death. Cassandra and I sat on the floor with our homework on the coffee table. From time to time we glanced from our books and just over the top of the living room couch we could see Mamá smoking her cigarettes at the dining table and following Petrona with her eyes.

That meant she was looking for incriminating evidence. It happened the same way when Papá came home for vacation and she thought he was cheating on her. "His thing smelled like fish, it's not normal," she said while Cassandra and I stared at her wide-eyed. As Papá made breakfast, read the newspaper, played solitaire, Mamá followed him with her eyes and said, *"Sucio,"* under her breath, until one day she stopped doing it altogether, and I had to wonder how Papá had managed to convince Mamá to stop.

In the living room, I tried to keep my eyes on my math book, but as I looked at the numbers I couldn't understand them, and looking at them I only remembered Mamá's eyes, felt them, the darkly set eyes deep with death hovering over Petrona. Petrona felt them too, and this made her run into things and topple over Mamá's pretty vases with the stick end of her feather duster.

Mamá petted her widow's peak. She drew a breath from her cigarette and said, "Petrona, how is your mother?" The white smoke of her cigarette climbed in a winding trail to the ceiling, where it widened in circles. Some of the smoke trailed out of Mamá's mouth. Petrona looked up. She looked shocked, then relieved. "Well, Señora, thanks," she said, the *s*'s in her words carrying the most volume and burying everything under their hiss. She slinked to the swinging door and sighed a long sigh before going into the kitchen.

If the tarot cards had called Petrona an upside-down Fool and Mamá didn't trust her, I wondered then how come Mamá didn't fire her. Instead she became the girl whose name bubbled up beneath our hours.

Staring at my math book in the living room, I thought it must have been Petrona's saintlike qualities that stilled Mamá's distrust.

Mamá put out her cigarette. "God knows how she survives the invasiones."

"Shh, Mamá." Cassandra stared at the still swinging door. "She'll hear you."

Mamá waved the air. "Hmph. Ella? Ella no es nada más que una mosquita muerta."

Because Mamá grew up in an invasión she prided herself in being openly combative, so people who pretended to be weak disgusted her. That was why she called any nonviolent person *a little dead fly,* someone whose life-strategy was playing dead while pretending to be highly insignificant. Other mosquitas muertas included our schoolteachers, our neighbors, the newscasters on the television, and the president.

Mamá yelled at the television, "Virgilio Barco thinks he's fooling this country with his little mosquita muerta act, but I know he's nothing but a snake! Who does he think he's fooling? 'He has no ties to Pablo Escobar'? I wasn't born yesterday."

When Papá was home, he too yelled at the television, except he said: "Are we mice or men, no me joda?"

I wanted to yell at the television like Mamá and Papá, but I had to learn how to properly do it. I gathered that being a mouse was better than being a mosquita muerta, and being a snake was better than being a man, because flies pretending to be dead could be crushed, mice were shy, and men were persecuted; but everybody always avoided snakes.

Mamá had been yelling increasingly at the television because of a man called Luis Carlos Galán. Galán was running for president and Mamá was a complete fanatic. She said that Colombia's future had finally arrived, and it had arrived in the most beautiful package possible. *Am I right, princesas?* We were watching the presidential debates in Mamá's bedroom.

Petrona sat on the floor. She didn't seem to have much of an opinion, which was fine because neither did I. I told Mamá Galán didn't seem to me to be different from any other man on the television and Mamá pretended to spit into the air, saying, "See this? This is what I think of what you just said." She clicked her thumb on a key on the remote until Galán's voice boomed in the bedroom, and then she raised her voice over the television, asking was I blind, was I not able to see how all politicians were salt statues compared to Galán?

Mamá was making a reference to the Bible

— that much I knew. Cassandra and I went to a small Catholic school where a priest visited each year and told us the basic stories, but our knowledge of the Bible was spotty at best. I knew there had been a woman fleeing her burning town who had looked over her shoulder and God had pulverized her into a pile of salt — but I didn't know why she was punished, and I didn't get what that story had to do with politicians. It didn't matter anyway. Mamá was always coming up with weird metaphors. One time she said, "Trust is water in a glass; if you spill it, it's gone forever," as if she had never heard of mops or the cycle of rain and evaporation. I liked what Papá said better — that Colombian presidents were all of them salados, all of them unlucky. I caught Petrona's eye and smiled, but she didn't respond. I made circles with my index finger at the side of my head and pointed at Mamá. Petrona pressed her lips together and looked away in a grin.

Papá was interested in the war like Mamá was interested in Galán. When he was home, he clipped articles about the civil conflict, turned up the volume when the news came on, and ran to the phone to gossip with his friends afterward. "Did you hear the latest?" He talked about the most recent political scandal and then exploded into accounts of the 1980s, which was his favorite decade in Colombian history.

That's how come I was interested in politics myself. Someday, I wanted to be just like Papá. Papá was like a walking encyclopedia. He boasted that he could name at least a third of the 128 paramilitary groups in Colombia: *the Begrimed, Black Eagle, Antimás, Alfa 83, the Crickets, Magdalena Cleansing, Menudo, Rambo . . .* He also said he knew some of the names of the groups within the death squadrons, the narco-paramilitary (*Death to Revolutionaries, Death to Kidnappers*), the regular guerrillas (*FARC, ELN*), but his specialty was the paramilitary. I tried hard to be like Papá, but no matter how much of an effort I made, I couldn't even grasp the simplest of concepts — what was the difference between the guerrillas and the paramilitary? What was a communist? Who was each group fighting?

Mamá wasn't ashamed to admit she knew nothing about politics. "Look at me," she yelled, winking, "I'm learning. Have you seen the way Galán fills his red shirt? I'll learn *all* the issues you want."

Cassandra shook her head, then Mamá said, "He is *all* a specimen, no?" Cassandra

39

shushed her because she couldn't hear Galán's speech, but Mamá ignored Cassandra
and begged the television, "Teach me to
care, Galán, querido!"

Galán shook with vigor on the screen, yelling into a mob of microphones: *The only
enemy I recognize is he who uses terror and
violence to silence, intimidate, and assas-
sinate the most important protagonists of our
history!*

Mamá inched forward on her seat. "Isn't
he beautiful when he says '*our* history'?"

Cassandra rolled her eyes.

Mamá's bedroom windows were completely covered in red half-tone posters of
Galán. The very air in her room was tinged
red from the light coming through the row
of Galán faces — all of them turned up,
frozen in mid-yell, his hair up in a tempest.
I glanced at Petrona, who was now folding
white napkins into triangles, and saw as her
right eyebrow floated up and tensed a crease
on her forehead.

I decided that presidential debates were
tiresome.

I slipped underneath one poster and
pressed my forehead against the window. I
gazed down at the empty sidewalk and spied
on the neighbors. To the right, la Soltera
held a watering hose to her dying bed of

flowers. To the left, small children flipped pails with dirt onto the ground. An old man was making his way across on the sidewalk. When he saw me, he leaned on his cane and stared. It only occurs to me now how symbolic it must have looked — a seven-year-old girl gazing out below a row of Galán faces, giant and feverish, trumpeting some kind of future.

I told Cassandra about Petrona's eyebrow going up during Galán's speech later when we were alone in our bedroom. Cassandra said it was too little to go on, but probably Petrona was *apolitical.* That's what people who didn't like Galán were called — that's what we learned from Cassandra's home-room teacher, Profesor Tomás, who said if you didn't like Galán you were either apolitical or in a coma. When we told Mamá, she didn't question Cassandra's theory and explained that Petrona was apolitical because of her background. Mamá lowered her voice and told us that the girl who had recommended Petrona said that Petrona was the main breadwinner in her house. "Imagine, a thirteen-year-old — the *breadwinner* of a house." Mamá said that when you had that kind of responsibility, it was difficult to be interested in abstract things like politics.

Cassandra nodded. I didn't know whether to agree or disagree. What I knew was that I felt sorry for Petrona, so I told Cassandra it was in our best interest to get on Petrona's good side — because not only did Petrona control the candy, she also had the power to cover for us if we did something wrong, and she could spit in our drinks and food without us knowing. So when Cassandra and I went to play in the park, we brought Petrona along. We thought Petrona would join us, but instead she sat alone on the swings, saying nothing, doing nothing. When we invited her to build a sand mountain, she said she was resting her feet, and when we grew tired and went to her side to make conversation, our efforts fell flat.

"What's your favorite color?" Cassandra said.

"Blue."

The silence after her one word was deafening. "Mine's purple," I said. "What's your favorite television show?" This was the conventional, two-step procedure for making friends, but Petrona blushed, and her eyes teared up, then became frosted in what seemed like anger. I didn't know what to do, so I ran away to climb a tree, and Cassandra followed. From far off, high in the branches we watched Petrona. Petrona rubbed the sleeve of her sweater on her nose. She sneezed. Cassandra said maybe Petrona didn't have a television. I shrugged.

We knew what it was like to feel different. There were kids who didn't play with us because their parents forbade it. There were rumors that Mamá had *Sold It.* One parent said, "Poor women don't rise from poverty with their wit *alone,*" and when we went to Mamá to tell her, Mamá had been so angry she fumed right into the park yelling at the top of her lungs that she had had *no* occasion to sell *anything* — *It* being made of gold, *It* bringing men to her feet before she could even *think* about lifting a finger to charge.

Cassandra knew what *It* was, but she wouldn't tell me, and the tightness of her face kept me from insisting. That was why Cassandra and I played alone. We chased each other around the swings, we played tag, we made castles in the sand pit and trampled them underfoot. We ignored the other children who skipped hand in hand and sat in tight circles, making believe Cassandra and I weren't even there.

PETRONA

In Boyacá, we had a plot of vegetables and some cows. My older brothers killed rabbits and I roasted them. Mami kept us all in school and out of trouble, the farmhouse tidy, and the table full of harvested vegetables.

In the Hills, in Bogotá, we had no plot, and there were no animals to hunt. We got our food from the market. I made a small indoor fire to cook for us. I kept Mami comfortable in the only plastic chair we owned and when the cooking was done, I boiled eucalyptus leaves to help with her asthma. But I was not good at watching children. The little ones skinned their knees under my watch. They bloodied their hair from throwing rocks. They got black eyes. Mami wanted to know what was I doing, her children falling apart under my watch? I tried to keep them clean. I kept a bowl of water in the corner and a rag to pass over their cheeks, but I often forgot to look at them, the little ones.

The day I bled and stained our mattress Mami had said, *You're a little woman now. Marry or go to work.* I did not have suitors. I knew women in the Hills worked in cleaning. Mami said I had been doing housekeeping since I was five, cleaning for a rich family would be easy. I stood on the main path in the Hills and waited until the women returned from their day at work. They filed out of a city bus at the bottom of the hill. All the women looked worn and tired, except for one. Gabriela was a few years older than me, maybe eighteen. She was energetic, carrying big bags of groceries. I stood in her way. I asked if she knew of any work a girl like me could do. She studied me from head to toe. *A girl like you . . .* When her gaze came to rest at my eyes again she seemed to have made up her mind. She said she would come visit me, and asked if I did not live in the hut held up by the old electricity pole.

When Gabriela came around, I wanted to show I was capable, so I gave her gaseosa. When my little siblings came in, I complained loudly about how unpresentable they were. I pretended it was my habit to drag them to the bowl of water when they came in. I scrubbed at their cheeks. Gabriela turned to Mami, *Petrona tells me you suffer from asthma.* I did not tell her, but everything was known in the Hills. All of us lived so close. I shooed my little siblings away and sat on a stone. Gabriela said she knew of a family in the neighborhood where she worked who needed some help. *All Petrona would have to do is make some beds and meals.* Mami gave her blessing, and in a few days I was getting ready in my best dress to meet the Señora. Gabriela rode with me on the bus. *Try not to look shocked, Petrona,* she said, *these people live in a big city house.* The last time I had been this far out into the city was when my family first arrived and we had to beg for coins at stoplights. Gabriela said, *The woman's name is Alma, but it's Señora Alma to you.* She pulled on my sleeve. *Are you listening?* Gabriela's curly golden hair was tied in a knot at the top of her head. Her cheeks were round and dusted in freckles. I looked into her eyes. Gabriela continued, *Don't worry, I've told her all about you. You just say you're good at taking care of a home because you do it for your family. You'll most likely be hired right away.*

I had been so nervous then. The Santiagos' neighborhood was clean and there was planning, even around the trees. They made them grow evenly in rows.

Mami said I had to train little Aurora so she could do the house chores. We were the only women in the family. The boys were older, but Mami wanted the boys to focus on their schooling. Mami said if just one of them became a doctor or a priest, it would be our ticket out of the invasión. All the mothers in the Hills said something of the sort, but I hadn't seen it work out for anyone.

I taught little Aurora to watch her brothers. I taught her how to clean all her brothers' clothes and wash them in a plastic tub. I gave her knives so she could cut the vegetables. I taught her to prepare unripe papaya for her brothers when they had worms. *This is how you hold the papaya to spoon the seeds out,* I told her, holding the long glove of the halved papaya in one hand, posing the spoon ready to rake against the fruit's flesh. Aurora took the spoon from me and dug.

Sometimes my mind went to places I wanted to forget. Like the look of our farmhouse in Boyacá after it was torched by paramilitary. All the walls of the farmhouse fell.

Now chop, I instructed. Little Aurora pressed her knuckles down against the table like I had shown her. She seesawed the knife slowly on the slimy black seeds. They broke apart into smaller and smaller pieces. When Aurora was finished, I collected the seeds into a napkin and wiped the knife on my pants and put it back in the plastic cup where we kept our cutlery.

The only thing left standing of the farmhouse was the staircase. Even the wood of the banister had turned black.

4.
THE PURGATORY SPOT

It was after the once-a-month big city blackout that the mystery of Petrona began to lift. In our neighborhood blackouts were like carnaval. Cassandra and I fished out our flashlights from our sock drawers, filled balloons with water, and ran howling into the streets. We pointed our lights at trees, at houses, at each other, up at the sky. We found kids without flashlights and threw balloons at them and ran away. We hid from our unsuspecting victims among the adults, who congregated on the sidewalks complaining and dancing. We ducked behind men playing checkers. There were improvised lanterns on the ground, brown lunch bags half filled with soil, a candle buried in each and burning steadily inside. Then, we strained our ears toward the unlit park, trying to locate kids with no flashlights by sound. A woman put her hand on my shoulder and informed Cassandra and me that smoking was disgusting and warned us not to become like "yonder lost youth."

She had one hand on a baby carriage and was pointing her flashlight at a group of older kids huddled in the park who were making the tips of their cigarettes burn bright at their mouths. They wore jean jackets and boots. I was about to tell the woman not to worry; older kids weren't what we were after — when just behind them, sitting on the swings, past all the teenagers, I spotted Petrona. She held on to the ropes of the swing and leaned forward with a cigarette between her lips, bowing her head into a girl's cupped hand where an orange flame flickered.

"Is that — ?"

"Ohh," Cassandra said. "She's like — a teenager."

"Oh my God," I gasped. "You're right." I nodded. "How did we miss that?"

"Come, Chula, let's take a closer look." Cassandra pulled me to her, advancing on tiptoe, and the mother called behind us, "What did I tell you? Don't go near! You'll fall into sin!"

We trod softly into the darkness of the park, letting the dancing red tips of cigarettes guide us. The sky was a dull, dark blue. The tips were like flying embers. Suddenly we were engulfed by a riot of children who ran in circles around us, pointing their flashlights and screaming in delight. I turned on my flashlight and then I discovered the same face twice.

Cassandra and I were so surprised we forgot where we were going. We shone our lights from one face to the other — unbelieving of the identical noses, the identical squinting eyes. Their names were Isa and Lala and they had the power to read each other's minds on account of having once shared a placenta. They had flashlights too, and while we spoke, we pointed all our flashlights to the ground. Our beams spotlighted one pair of black strappy shoes, one of Converse sneakers. Kids yelled in high-pitched laughter all around us, but I heard Isa clearly as she said, "It's like I know what Lala is thinking before Lala even thinks it."

"But we can only do it by looking into each other's eyes," Lala said. There was no moon and though I could tell where each of their voices came from, I couldn't see their silhouettes. Isa lowered her voice. She said that on the next blackout she and her sister would break into some houses to test their power. "We're shaping our career like Houdini — the magician?" Lala said.

"Except," Isa remarked, "instead of breaking out of a chest, we're going to break into a house and then we'll get out unharmed and unseen — it's called *Escapology.*"

"And even if we *are* seen, it will be dark and nobody will be able to identify us," Lala explained.

Cassandra said breaking into a house was criminal, but I argued it was only criminal if you took something, and Isa said I was right and Lala added their intention was just to look. "Anyway," Isa said.

Lala continued, "Our plan in case somebody is about to discover us is just to shine our flashlights in their eyes and then they would be blinded." Cassandra pointed out that while it would be dark enough that nobody could see them, Isa and Lala also wouldn't be able to see each other's eyes, so there was no way they could use their telepathic powers. I shifted my feet in the awkward silence, and then the electricity came back on.

I had to shut my eyes it was so bright. The grass seemed blue. The sidewalks white. Teenagers reeled, one girl reached for another's shoulder. An adult woman was wrinkling her eyes and stretching her mouth. Then I saw Petrona standing at a distance, not weak on her feet like everybody else, but staring at us. I blinked rapidly, trying to see; she was motionless in her below-the-knee woolly coat. Her legs were bare. She looked slight, but then her stillness amidst such confusion made her seem pointy like a blade. I wondered if I was just imagining her.

Lala grasped my arm. "Does everyone see that girl standing over there?"

Cassandra batted her lashes and rubbed at her face.

"Blessed Souls of Purgatory, save us," Isa said. "It's a ghost."

Cassandra cackled when she saw who it was. "It's the girl from our house! You thought it was a ghost."

Isa clasped arms with her sister. "We did *not.*"

Cassandra pulled me by the hand. "Let's go, Chula. She probably wants us to follow."

"Be careful!" Lala called. "She could *still* be a ghost!" and just as Cassandra and I started toward Petrona, Petrona turned around and began the walk toward our house. Cassandra and I looked at each other, then at Petrona walking ahead. "Petrona, wait up!" Cassandra called, but Petrona didn't slow or turn around.

"She's so weird," I whispered, hooking my arm through Cassandra's. "Who do you think she was smoking with?"

"She has a friend," Cassandra said.

We walked the rest of the way in silence, staring ahead at Petrona as she shuffled her feet in the alternating pools of lamppost light.

The next day Isa said that if we wanted to discard the possibility that Petrona was a ghost, we were going to have to ask the Blessed Souls of Purgatory. Isa reached for a salty cracker and fit all of it in her mouth and Lala nodded once but with great reverence. We were sitting in Isa and Lala's bedroom. It was the weekend, and Cassandra and I had spent every waking second since yesterday with them, but we had not invited them to our house in case their mother realized who our mother was and forbade Isa and Lala from being our friends. I took a cracker and bit at the edges. Lala asked if we knew who the Blessed Souls of Purgatory were and then Isa explained that Purgatory Souls were people who had sinned a little but not enough to go to hell. They were stuck on earth and had to drag heavy chains, but if anybody prayed for them — especially a child — their chains got lighter. That was why the Blessed Souls of Purgatory were eager to carry out any request put to them. Isa said we would negotiate the terms for them telling us what or who Petrona was, but it would probably cost five recitations of the Lord's Prayer — ten at most. The only problem was we had to find them.

Isa said she had heard that somewhere in the neighborhood there was a place where you could see the Blessed Souls of Purgatory making their way from *who-knows-where* to *God-only-knows.* Isa said Purgatory Souls had see-through skin and that you could only see them in one spot, which meant that as you stood there watching you were constantly seeing one Purgatory Soul come into being in one step and then disappearing into the next.

We walked along each street in our neighborhood looking for the Purgatory Spot. The streets were lined with identical white houses. Some streets spidered out, connecting to each other like a maze, while others led into the park, and still others dead-ended in guard booths and gates. The guard booths were wooden. They stood at the middle of the street with gate arms coming out of their sides. The gate arms opened and closed like powerful crocodile jaws. They were steel and long, and striped like candy canes. Our neighborhood was patrolled twenty-four hours by guards who sat inside the wooden booths in their full uniform, two guns strapped to their belts. Every time we came to the small window, we heard boleros or the sound of salsa, and we saw the guards fiddling with their two-way radios. "Red alert," we heard one guard say, and at first I was excited because maybe there was a murder under way, but then I saw the guard was staring at a woman in a red skirt coming out to water the plants in her garden.

The guards we talked to hadn't heard of the Purgatory Spot. I was surprised they didn't laugh at us, and Cassandra said it was because Mamá knew all of them by name and gave them food baskets on Christmas and the New Year, and they would be fools to mock us.

The only guard we all liked was Elisario, the afternoon guard on our street. Elisario carried lollipops in his pockets and he told us stories about shoot-outs in the neighborhood.

On Monday after school, we asked Elisario about the Purgatory Spot, and he said we should forget the whole thing because if we ever found it, the Blessed Souls of Purgatory would haunt us. Then to distract us, Elisario gave us sour candy and told us jokes. He looked both ways before lifting the brown jacket of his uniform. He held the side of the jacket bunched up by his ribs so we could see. There, by his hairy belly button, a scar rose in a knotted, pale ridge. He was hit by a bullet a year ago defending a neighborhood house from burglars. He could make the scar jiggle by pumping his stomach. Elisario said burglaries happened all the time. He had a gaunt face and a mole above his lip.

We were about to give up our search for the Purgatory Spot when we came upon a large house. I thought all houses in our neighborhood were the same, but this one was as big as four regular houses combined. We stood before the house in silent appraisal of it until Cassandra said, "*That* is a mansion," and then we looked at the house with this new language for what it was.

The mansion stood four floors high, and had a single tower jutting out the side. It was the only mansion I had seen besides on a television screen. It sat alone at the meeting of three streets, encircled by a wide garden with long grass. There were old pines in the garden, beds of roses, and everything was hush and still.

Isa was surprised we hadn't seen the mansion before. She said nobody was sure how many people lived inside, but Isa and Lala's mother had once seen a woman. She was a woman who no one had heard speak, Isa and Lala's mother thought, because she was a Nazi with an accent.

"What's a Nazi?" I said.

"The same people who burnt witches at the stake, don't you know?" Lala said.

"That's not all," Isa said and told us their father had said that he had it on good authority that the woman who lived in the mansion was not a Nazi but a former stripper who, having outwitted a drug lord and made away with his money, was now in hiding posing as a German woman concealing her Nazi roots.

"Either way the woman is an Oligarch," Isa said.

Cassandra said being an *Oligarch* meant having *blue blood.*

"What color is our blood?" I asked, but nobody answered.

We were standing across the street looking at the mansion when we saw Petrona walking down the block talking to a girl I instantly recognized as the girl she had been smoking with during the blackout. Now in the daylight I saw all kinds of new details about the girl that I had not been able to make out in the dark: there was the hair so startlingly yellow growing out from the dark brown roots of her scalp. And then there were her eyebrows, which looked like they had been shaved off and then penciled in in the wrong place. Both she and Petrona wore the white dress that was like a cross between a sleeping robe and a lab coat, which nobody called a maid's uniform, but that's what it was. They wore the same peach-colored lipstick and were giggling, looking down at a stack of money Petrona's friend was fanning out.

We waited until they were near and then Cassandra spoke up, "What are you two doing?" Petrona paled. She wiped the lipstick off her mouth with the back of her hand.

"Are these your girls?" Petrona's friend smiled. Petrona nodded and her friend walked up to us, smirking. "It's Monopoly money, look, someone tried to pay with it at the grocery store, can you imagine?"

"That looks like real money," Lala said.

"It's Monopoly money," Petrona's friend repeated, squaring the bills, rolling them and tucking them into her bra.

Isa tilted her head. "You weren't at the grocery store: you have no grocery bags."

"Because it was too funny — we had to leave the store laughing, both of us, isn't that true, Petrona? Petrona, do you really have to watch four girls?"

"No, just the two," Petrona said. Four syllables. Petrona glanced at Cassandra and me, flinched her lips into a smile, then looked down.

Petrona's friend examined the face of her watch. "Well, I've got to run, Petrona. Walk with me so I can give you that thing you wanted to borrow."

Petrona's friend walked away and Petrona caught up with her in a quick jog. Then they rounded the corner, holding their hands over their stomachs like they were nuns out for a walk. As we watched them go, Isa said Petrona was definitely not a ghost. Cassandra said she agreed. She was not a ghost, not a poet, but was she a saint, or under a spell?

PETRONA

Mami said, *Wasn't life unfair, a patilimpia like
la Señora Alma with an Indian grandmother,
skin the color of dirt, ending up in that large
house with proper bedrooms. And us sharing
blood with the Spanish, here in this dump.*
Mami liked to share the story of our famous
ancestor. He was the one history books
talked about when they said Spaniards came
in a boat bringing civilization. We didn't
know his name, but our ties to him were
clear by our white skin and our fine black
hair.

When I came home from the Santiagos'
my family knelt around me in a tight circle.
They wanted to know about the kind of
wealth my employers had. My siblings
wanted to know what the family ate. I talked
to them about the house. *There is a large
rectangle of grass in front and they've planted
stones so that la Señora's heels don't sink
into the grass.*

61

The second floor has to be supported by tall beams, the house is so large.

They have a room on top of their house where no one actually sleeps, but which they fill with the excess of their stuff.

I didn't tell my family I had a bedroom of my own and a shower too. It felt cruel because our bathroom was an outhouse, and our front door a curtain. At the Santiagos' there were all the doors you could imagine, to the bedrooms, closing the bathrooms, but also there were doors with no purpose. There was a swinging door dividing the kitchen from the living room. There were double doors in the kitchen and inside there was a boiler that heated up water. Anyone could take a hot shower whenever they wanted.

I told my friends in the Hills, *My employers are rich. They have breakfast every day with milk.*

In the Hills, everyone's dinner, lunch, breakfast, snack was pan con gaseosa. The bread was filling with a taste you couldn't get tired of, because the gaseosa could be Pepsi, Sprite, or the orange one called Fanta. The many options of fizzy drink dressed up even the stalest bread. You could break the bread in half and dip the sponge in the different colors and it could seem like a different meal.

In the Hills I laughed to myself remembering one thing or another about the Santiagos. I told Mami about how the little Santiago girl asked me to teach her to wash. Mami laughed and laughed. *A rich girl, wanting to learn to wash!* Mami prompted me to tell the story to every person from the Hills who stopped by our hut to say hello. Every person laughed at the part when Chula insisted on learning, saying someday she would go off to college and there would be nobody there to wash her clothes. *Ask her if she wants to learn to plow the field,* people in the Hills joked. *Nobody in college will do that for her either!*

Chula reminded me of little Aurora, even though Aurora was a year older, and there couldn't be more differences between two girls. But they both had a habit of staring off into space, daydreamers.

Steal for us, my little brother begged. *Bring us a little taste of what they eat.* But I was too proud and I told Ramón, so little and his cheeks so red, that the day I brought back meat it was going to be because I earned it with the hard labor of my own two hands. I tried to impress in him the pride of labor, which I still remember from

Papi, who refused the government handouts, the paramilitary handouts, the guerrilla handouts, and on nights when we went hungry because one group or another had taken our harvest, he would tell us that it was better to sleep alongside your own clean conscience than to be a parasite of the state or of the militarized groups who were also just a different version of a state.

With the sweat of my brow I will provide for you, I told little Ramón, which was also what Papi told me when I came aching and crying from my stomach twisting with hunger, asking how come he hadn't accepted the aid of one of the groups, all similar to each other in his view with their weapons and excuses for violence.

But it wasn't the same. I couldn't keep my family together the way he could. One day when I came home early from work, I saw little Ramón sharing a sausage with one of the encapotados. The guerrillas stay up in the mountain but every once in a while they come down. They hide their faces with bandanas, that's why we call them the hooded ones, but most of the time we recognize their voices and we know who they are. The encapotado had given Ramón a stick with a sausage and I saw little Ramón's face as the sausage cooked in the bonfire. The sweet smell filled my nose, and I understood his weakness, but later I told him not to do that again. My little boy spit into the ground and he told me my pride didn't feed his stomach, that it was my fault his three younger brothers were skin and bones, that I could starve if I wanted, but he was in line to be the man of the house, and the power wasn't mine anymore.

5.
THE DEAD GIRL'S SHOE

On Thursdays after school we called Papá at the oil site in Sincelejo. He spoke to us through a crackling radiophone and his voice came out broken up and filled with static.

"How is my favo . . . te?" he said.

"Well, Papá."

"An . . . school?"

"They give us a lot of homework."

"A lot of wh . . . ?" he said, and then there was dead static, like the tuning dial before a radio station.

"A lot of homework."

"A lot of wh . . . ?"

"Homework," I repeated. I tried to enunciate my vowels and consonants as plainly as possible. I could never have real conversations with Papá when he was away because the radiophone swallowed up our words. He always asked about school and then he asked to talk to Cassandra.

"Oh. Wh . . . re is your sist . . . ?" Static erupting at the heels of his voice.

"I'll get her," I said, but didn't move. "Papá, when are you coming back?"

He was quiet for a moment. "Soon."

"*How* soon?"

"Ver . . . soon, Chula, I pro . . . ise."

"Okay. I love you, Papá."

"Lov . . . you too," he said.

On Fridays we watched television. I loved Fridays because they were the only days when I could really observe Petrona. Fridays were a half day at our school, so Cassandra and I were home by noon. Then, we all got together in Mamá's bedroom. Petrona sat on the floor near the bed, with the excuse of folding up laundry or balling up socks but she never got very far and Mamá didn't care. Cassandra and I lay on our stomachs on the bed and Mamá sat under the covers with her back against the wall. I often forgot to watch the television program and stared instead at Petrona's mouth.

It was pink and thin and closed in a line. A light mustache grew under her nose. I stared at her lips, thinking how great it would be if the lips parted and words suddenly came out. I wondered what Petrona would say. Maybe she would tell stories of her childhood. Maybe she was heartbroken and the heartbreak had stolen her voice. Looking at her, I grew convinced this was the reason behind her silence. Whole television shows came and went as I thought about Petrona, until, when I least expected it, her lips parted and suddenly the vowel sounds of laughter came out. The sound made me jump and Cassandra turned to me with a puzzled, guarded look. Petrona teetered forward with laughter.

When Mamá changed the channels we were regularly disturbed by the graphic quality of the news reports. I could piece some things together from the news — massacres in the countryside, common graves found in farms, peace talks with the guerrillas, but I didn't understand who was responsible for what or what any of it meant. The name I had heard so often was on every newscaster's tongue. When I asked Mamá who Pablo Escobar was, she sat up. "Pablo Escobar? He's the one responsible for every shit that happens in this country." Cassandra stretched her lips down and I raised my brows at Petrona and Petrona cleared her throat.

I decided to commemorate the dead I had heard about in the news by walking around the house, opening and closing cabinet and closet doors. But there were so many massacres and common graves and disappeared and kidnapped persons, that after a while, I lost interest.

The television lit our faces pale blue. Death was such a common thing.

Sometimes a detail would make me feel again. Once there was a line of bodies in a field covered with a white sheet but *red* wetted through only at the sixth body. Another time there was a common grave, and the camera lingered on the feet sticking out: everybody wore shoes but one person had bare feet.

I knew that there was no gate surrounding the invasiones where Petrona lived, no iron locks on the doors, no iron bars on the windows. When I asked Petrona how she and her family stayed safe, she laughed. Then because I was embarrassed she shrugged her shoulders. She thought for a moment then said, "There's nothing to lose." Five syllables.

I thought about all the things I had to lose. There was Cassandra, Papá, Mamá, all my tías and uncles, Abuela María, all the cousins. We had a house, I had school friends, I had a lot of pretty shoes and many plastic bracelets, there was the small television, my box of colored pencils, the radio with the big plastic knobs in the living room.

War always seemed distant from Bogotá, like niebla descending on the hills and forests of the countryside and jungles. The way it approached us was like fog as well, without us realizing, until it sat embroiling everything around us.

One Friday we recognized a street.

Cassandra and I sat up and reached for our hearts. Cars were upside down, billowing smoke. The buildings had giant shark bites out of their sides. And the fountain, where Cassandra, Mamá, and I had so often thrown pesos and made wishes, was now leveled to rubble and the water and a thousand people's wishes drained on the street. The reporter entered the scene, leading with the black foam top of his microphone. "This is the site of our latest tragedy. A car bomb exploded in Bogotá just two hours ago, leaving seven dead and thirty injured. Among the dead is a seven-year-old girl who was waiting in the car next to what officers believe to have been the car carrying the bomb. She is survived by her father, who went into this building," the reporter said, pointing behind him at a blackened structure missing its front walls. "He was buying tickets for the circus. And here," he pointed among the rubble on the ground, "is the young girl's leg." The camera zoomed its shaky lens at a heap of burnt car parts and then a blackened red shoe and a smoky white sock filled with leg came into focus.

"This night the murmur of people praying with the girl's father is a constant as officials try to discover who was behind the attack. The father was the last to see her alive. Officials struggle to unearth the rest of her remains, but this," the reporter said, lifting his hand holding something small and golden between his fingers, "is the girl's ring." The camera zoomed steady like a tunnel to the gold ring. It glimmered in the reporter's fingertips. Then the camera zoomed out and the reporter put the ring into his breast pocket. "Officials believe the guerrillas are responsible for the car bomb, as the target appears to have been a bank."

Cassandra and I turned away from the television and crawled to Mamá. I couldn't believe we had just seen a *recently dead girl's ring*. Mamá was calm and she received us in her arms. I said, "Mamá." Cassandra said, "They killed a little girl." "There's no helping what happened," Mamá said. "When it's time, it's time. There's no escaping death." Mamá combed our hair with her fingers. They vanished within our hair. I looked up at Mamá's nose, the eyebrows curving up and sweeping down.

Petrona spoke from her corner: "The girls are frightened, Señora?" It was more a statement than a question. I counted, automatically, the syllables of her sentence, pressing the tips of my fingers against my thumb. Eight. I stared at Petrona in the corner, her legs tucked under to a side, her black short hair, her skinny arms supporting her weight, her body leaning forward. "Things like that scare my little sister too," she said. Ten. I tried to catch Cassandra's eye but she was lost in thought.

Mamá snaked her arms to the back of our necks. Mamá always said — *the life she knew was a last-minute tsunami that could sweep away fathers, money, food, and children.* You were never in control, so it was better to let things run their course. Petrona came and knelt near us by the side of the bed.

"Niñas." She reached and rubbed Cassandra's back. "Don't worry. That little girl probably didn't even know she was dying."

I tried to count but lost it, then Cassandra rose up on one elbow. "Wasn't their target a bank? Why kill a little girl? She was little, like she was Chula's age, Mamá."

Mamá put her hand over my ear. "When

it's time, it's time. There's no escaping death," and then she repeated the first thing. She repeated the two things like a poem. Petrona twirled the lace of the bedsheets in her fingers. Then she gripped the sheet in a fist.

"But did you see," I said, "her leg wasn't with the rest of her."

"She didn't feel a thing," Mamá said, and said again the thing about never escaping death.

I rested my head on Mamá's chest and stared at the white comforter. I followed its cloudy seams down to the end of the bed, to the television, snug in its cream armoire between Papá's and Mamá's separate closets. It blared colorful commercials: lime green, purple, and red.

I imagined the dead girl just minutes before, sitting alive in the backseat of the car, her father leaning back, saying whispery, "This will only take a minute." Opening the car door, swinging it shut. Then —

Then the blast. Unhinging things. Sending each limb off into different directions, each part of her soaring away with car parts.

"Could we drive to see it?" I asked.

Mamá's hand froze inside my hair. "Why?"

Cassandra turned her head away from the

television, with effort, and followed Mamá's eyes to me. Petrona let the bedsheet drop out of her fist and it floated down and lay on top of the bed like a wrinkled hill.

"Just to see," I said. "I want to see how the street is."

"On a day like this, Chula, it is better to stay indoors, where no one can see you."

"But you just said when it's time, it's time. You said there's no escaping death. So why not go see it? If it isn't our day, nothing will happen, Mamá."

"You won't die if it's not your day, it's true, but remember: curiosity killed the cat. You might end up paralytic. That's what happens when you go looking for what you didn't lose, Chula. Why go looking for trouble?"

"It's true, niña," Petrona said. "Listen to your mother."

I let my head drop and thought of the dead girl's leg wearing its red shoe. Of all the years of watching the news and all its images of death, this was the worst by far. The girl's shoe, like my size shoe, glimmered in my mind. I blinked and saw it, glowing eerily, on the backs of my lids.

I *really* wanted to know what it was like to be dead but nobody would tell me.

The only dead person I knew was Tío Pieto. One Christmas Tío Pieto was there, snoring in the folds of a hammock; the next Christmas Tío Pieto was gone. At the funeral the priest said Tío Pieto was still alive — we just couldn't see him. Tío Pieto had been a drunk and he lived in Barrancabermeja, so we rarely saw him. Mamá said when you died, you became alive elsewhere, but your body was put underground. You stayed underground and the worms ate your skin and eyes, but left behind your hair, your nails, your teeth, and your bones. In the car ride to the hotel where we stayed the night, Papá said the opposite and told us nobody really knew what happened after you died. He said it was possible that you just stopped existing. You stopped having thoughts, you stopped feeling, you were erased off the earth, and others lived on without you.

"But how?" I asked.

"Look, it doesn't matter, Chula. If you stop existing, you won't have the presence of mind to *know* you've stopped existing."

Mamá said, "Stop teaching the girls Western philosophy, Antonio, you're scaring them."

Papá shrugged his shoulders. "They're going to know, they might as well know now."

In the car, Cassandra bit her nails and

75

wiped them on the chest of her black dress. I stared at the lap of my own dress and imagined what ceasing to exist would be like. I held my breath and tried not to have thoughts. I stared at the shape of my thighs, past them into a yawning void of nothingness, where I was unthinking and breathless, nonexistent and nonfeeling. For a few seconds, I was a big roaring nothing. Then I gasped in air and sprang back into fearful, rushed thoughts about not existing. *How horrible it was to die!* I breathed in deeply and let the air out slowly. My heart was beating fast. Blood thumped into my fingers. I tried forgetting about death, but still I wondered, so I held my breath and tried again. I paid close attention to nothingness so that I would always remember — so that when the moment came, in the split second of my waning presence of mind, I could recognize what was happening to me. I went forth into my un-thoughts and back to my anxiety, on like that, until night fell and I slept in tired terror, tossing and turning in the strange bed of the hotel.

Lala claimed to know somebody who had found the Purgatory Spot and had seen the Blessed Souls of Purgatory walking. If the Blessed Souls of Purgatory had been seen, it meant that Papá was wrong and Mamá was right, and you became alive elsewhere after you died. Of course, Lala could be lying.

Mamá was right about us playing it safe. We could end up paralytic. It could've happened. It might have happened if we weren't careful. There was a lot to lose. There was a lot to protect in life.

When Petrona left and night came, we closed our curtains and shut our windows. Mamá got on a stool and tied some rope around an aloe plant living on a little clod of dirt and then hammered a nail into the ceiling. White powder floated down. Mamá hooked the end of the rope to the nail on the ceiling. "If you hang an aloe plant it will absorb all the bad energy that comes to your doorstep. When it falls rotten to the ground, that's how you know it's working."

I didn't know that bad energy could come looking for you at your doorstep. I thought about this type of inhumane persecution as I stared up at the aloe plant, turning on its rope, twirling its spiky edges, animated by a ghost wind.

Cassandra and I went early to bed. Mamá burned sage bundles at every doorstep of the house. She went around the house shuffling her feet and muttering things under her breath. She held the chains of her brass pot of incense and swung it just above her bare feet. It followed her turns and kept in rhythm with her muttered prayers. It trailed puffs of white, hazy smoke behind her that made our mouths taste like lavender. I stayed awake for some time, watching how the creamy smoke dispersed and fogged everything in the house, and I thought about Petrona, how she had nothing to lose and how she was not touched by the tragedy of the girl and her red shoe as Cassandra and I were. I thought about what she had said — that the girl with the red shoe didn't even know she was dying — and how she had meant it as comfort, but how the thought only filled me with terror. Mamá's prayers hung about me and I went to sleep.

PETRONA

The thing is they found a boy's body in the trees behind the playground. The encapotados said that's a false positive, that's the police taking our innocent people, and I shook little Ramón. *Now you see why I say keep your distance?* But little Ramón brushed my hands off and said I was of no use to him with my heart of a woman.

When little Ramón disappeared, I cried behind the bushes by our hut.

There was an old man in the Hills. We called him Abuelo Andrés, but he was nobody's grandfather that we knew. Abuelo Andrés told me he saw little Ramón join up, that he was in the mountains receiving guerrilla training. Abuelo Andrés with his white stubble said nothing would happen to little Ramón there. *Worry later,* he said. *Worry when he comes back.*

Since I had memory, our young boys had been leaving the Hills with nothing on their back but a shirt. They returned in jeeps, wearing leather jackets and nice Nike shoes. We knew they had been in the mountains, training. Then the Colombian army came and shot them. Or they left and never returned.

Once a young boy came home carrying a large television. I was not working for the Santiagos then, and little Ramón still listened to me. We saw the boy climb the path, bent backward bearing the weight of a brand-new television. It was tied up in a red bow and everything. Everybody in the Hills came out to watch. We followed as the little boy walked to his grandmother's hut. The old woman came out and clapped her hands. *Mi nieto, what's this? What elegance!* The boy set the television down on the dust. *For you, Abuela, to thank you for all the hard work of raising me into the man I am today.* The boy was barely fourteen. *How many batteries does it take?* the abuela said, and then some rowdy boys in the crowd whistled. *Abuelita no tiene electricidad!* I was afraid for the whistling boys. They didn't realize who they were making fun of. The abuela pretended not to hear and told her grandson. *Bring it in, mi'jito, you have made me proud. I have just the place: in the center of* the living room. *That way when the comadres come by and see what my big muchachito has brought home, they'll be green with envy. Gracias, mi'jito, gracias.*

Little Ramón and I had laughed about it. But later Ramón said, *I want to return home like that one day,* and I had to slap the back of his head. *Don't you know that boy was guerrilla?* I prayed for Ramón, there were so many things he did not understand.

Leticia consoled me when little Ramón left. She lived in a shack in the north end near the bottom of the hill. We sat on one flat rock that was near the road. Across the muddied street, people lived in actual buildings. Leticia rubbed my back. I cried into a handerkerchief. *Ramón is a real bobo, doesn't he know there are other ways to make money?* Leticia shook her head, anchoring her eyes to the ground. Then she inched closer to me on the rock and dropped her voice. *I know you said you don't want to do what I do, but when your family's hungry? Extra money is extra money. Maybe it'll bring little Ramón back. And what's the big deal, anyway? No one's ever been caught.*

I thought about what Leticia had told me the day we were walking together in the neighborhood, Leticia showing me the money that was her payment for passing information: *All you do is wait at a corner and pass an envelope to a man on a motorcycle, nothing to it, all of us girls do it.* It was hard to believe that it was possible: triple what we were paid, just for handing on a piece of paper.

I turned to Leticia, who was so close I smelled the scent of mangoes coming off her hair and the sour mustiness of her breath. Her brows were thin, drawn with a reddish color. Her hair was dark near her scalp and then blond. I inhaled. *Leticia, you know, I am not the kind of girl to do anything illegal.* She angled back to look at me. *Perdón, but I am not that girl either.*

I thanked Leticia for watching out for me, but I wanted to do things as Papi would have done, and Papi would have not stood in the middle of the street delivering an envelope. Leticia shrugged. *I am only trying to help you, Petrona.* I patted her knee. *Gracias, Leticia, gracias.*

Mami said, *What did I tell you, only women survive this.* She begged me to look after the boys, but most of all, to take care with Aurora, our youngest. Mami was wheezing

82

because it was cold that day, a light coat of dust on her cheeks, but still I could hear the disappointment in her voice.

Mami was right. I had to protect Aurora. I ran to the playground and found little Aurora there, sitting on a patch of grass drawing in a notebook. I wanted to slap her, how could she be humming in the same place where the army shot that boy. The blood had drained into the dirt, but a few days ago, before he disappeared, little Ramón crouched before the stain, saying the dead boy was his friend, the Colombian army shot him and dragged him to the back of the hills and dressed him in fatigues, planted a gun in his arms, took photos so they could say he was guerrilla. I said, *Why would the army do that, Ramón, don't you see it's all a story made up by the guerrillas to get new recruits?* Ramón insisted the army really did kill innocent people and pass them off as guerrillas for bonuses and vacation. The Colombian army had killed his innocent friend, what more proof did I need? *Those sons of bitches.* He scoffed. *Those are the people supposed to defend us.*

I wanted to drag little Aurora away from there by the hair, but when I got close I saw she was so thin, so little, and I draped my sweater on her. *Don't worry, Aurora.* I gathered her to my chest. She tried to wriggle free, *Petrona, what are you doing?* but then she saw I was crying. *Petrona, what's wrong?*

I'll get you out of this place. I looked at the dry earth, at the tall retaining wall built by the government for the rich people who lived on the other side, to keep them separate and away from us. The rich people who had so much money they had hired security and hired help. I closed my eyes and smelled the scent of Aurora's hair, and tried to forget how I had lost Papi, then one brother, and another, now another. *God help me we'll all die in this hill, is there anything I can do to prevent it.*

6.
Hola Padre, Hola Madre

There was a flurry of preparations the day of Papá's arrival. Fresh meat was bought and placed in the freezer, coffee was sent for, Papá's aguardiente was replaced, his shirts were handwashed and refolded in his closet, the bookshelves were dusted, and Petrona was trained.

Mamá and Petrona went over what Petrona was supposed to say and not supposed to say.

"So if el Señor asks, Petrona, if there are any men that telephone the house when he's away, what do you say?"

"I say that I never answer the phone, Señora."

"And what if he says, 'Well, what about the time I telephoned and you answered, Petrona?' What do you say to that?"

"I say that it was the one exception, Señora."

"Good. Petrona, and you remember: you

listen to me. I'm the one who runs this house. El Señor, he knows nothing."

"Sí, Señora Alma."

Cassandra and I were excited to see Papá. We kept a lookout for Emilio's taxi from the second floor window, knowing that's who would give him a ride home. Emilio was Papá's friend from high school. Emilio had a hooked nose and high arching eyebrows and garlic-rosemary breath. Mamá said Emilio and Papá had been communists together, but while Papá was no longer a communist, she thought Emilio still was. We could spot Emilio's taxi from a distance because a small flag of Cuba unfurled in the wind from the hood antenna. Papá had once made Cassandra and me memorize all the flags of the world. He pointed at each flag with a pen. He tallied our points on a separate piece of paper, each flag worth one point except for the flag of Cuba, which was worth twenty. It was a full fifteen minutes before we spotted the taxi, but when we did we ran down to the door. In two seconds Emilio would pull up, Papá would open the cab door, walk to our front gate, and look up.

When Papá came home from work, he often looked different. Once he wore thin silver glasses instead of his black-framed ones and his whole face was thrown off balance. Another time he arrived without his mustache, and there was nothing to justify his thick, black brows. He had looked like a stranger then, like somebody else's father.

When the cab pulled up, Papá stepped out and Emilio drove off honking a friendly goodbye. Papá opened the gate and walked toward the house. At the moment of lifting his eyes, his face lightened and he smiled brightly and said in English, "Oh, gad. Wat a welcome!" His tie was loose and the top buttons of his shirt were undone. He staggered up the stone steps, his face clumsy and slack.

Cassandra said, "You smell like whiskey."

Papá said airplanes made him nervous, and bringing his face close to Cassandra's he added, "That's what the smell really is, Cassandra. It is fear."

Cassandra recoiled from him and Mamá appeared at the door. Mamá surrounded Papá's waist with her arm. She stood on tiptoe and pressed a kiss on his cheek: "Hola, Padre." Papá smiled at her from his height and returned the salute: "Hola, Madre."

Hello, Father. Hello, Mother. It was a tradition that Papá said dated back to the grandparents of past generations. Husbands and wives had saluted each other just the same way and the salute had traveled down from generation to generation like an heirloom.

At the door, Cassandra and I pulled on Papá's sleeves and bounced in an orbit around him as he went up the stairs, down the hall, and into his bedroom, asking: "What did you bring us, Papá? What did you bring?" I wondered for a moment where Petrona was hiding. Then in the bedroom, Papá smiled and opened his bag. "All right, chicas, see if you can find them." He lay down on the bed and rested his neck against the headboard.

Inside his duffel bag, there were colorful barrettes for our hair hidden in the roselike pockets of his bunched up socks. Tucked in the white arms of his button-up shirts there were colored pencils, stickers, and gum erasers that smelled like grapes. We smelled the erasers, rubbed them, and pressed them on our cheeks. At the bottom there were two books of maps, one for Cassandra and the other one for me. They had raised, colored mountains and veined rivers that climbed the hills and the dips of the paper.

When we looked up, Papá was sleeping. We stood there looking at him until his head fell to the side but his glasses remained balanced on his nose.

"Is he sick?" I asked.

"He's drunk," Mamá said.

Mamá said that Papá couldn't drink at work, and he had so little self-control, he was so weak of spirit, he didn't have the decency to wait and drink when he got home; he had to go and drink whiskey on the airplane.

Petrona left at the end of her workday, looking relieved. Maybe she was glad she hadn't met Papá, or maybe she was relieved she hadn't had to lie on behalf of Mamá — I mean, I didn't know if Petrona would be lying. *Were* there men that called the house while Cassandra and I were at school? I knew Mamá had many friends.

That afternoon and evening swelled with Papá's snoring. Even from the bedroom I shared with Cassandra I could hear him. When he inhaled there was a wheezing, choking sound, and then three consecutive, short snores, and then silence. Papá's sleeping was a habit carefully teased and maintained by his work. The hours of sleep he knew were erratic and depended on the whims of the drill at the oil site, so he had learned to give himself to sleep entirely and quickly. When he slept it was as if a small death overcame his body, but his mind was alert and careful not to go too far away, just in case it was needed to share its expertise on drills, the trigonometry of its angles, or the landscape of the earth plates. But the snoring was always worse when he fell asleep drunk.

Close to midnight Cassandra and I stood at the closed door of Papá and Mamá's bedroom: "Mamá, we can't sleep." Mamá opened the door and turned on the night-stand lamp and the three of us hovered over Papá, watching him snore, trying to decide how to stop him. We moved his shoulders, stuffed pillows under his head, turned him over, plugged his nose, raised his feet, put pillows on his face, raised his arms, scissored his legs, covered his mouth, until finally Papá sat up with a bolt, looking at us in half terror.

"What's happened? Is there a fire? Has something happened?"

"Nothing's happened — we can't sleep."

"Should I go sleep downstairs?"

"No, let us move you. Go back to sleep."

Then, at once, Papá closed his eyes and fell back on his pillow, and just like that he was off to sleep. His snoring started up again, like the rumbling of a century-old machine.

In the morning, Mamá made Cassandra

and me a big pot of coffee. Mamá wasn't watching, so Cassandra and I drank three cups and then we jumped in place and ran up the stairs, then down, then up. Papá was in Mamá's bedroom ripping Galán posters from the window. Mamá was stomping her foot. "Do you think I'm painted on a wall, you hijueputa? What if I leave? What will you do then?"

Mamá was always threatening to leave. You'd think Papá would realize it was all a tactic, but in truth, no one could bluff like Mamá. All of us practiced bluffing when we played cards. When Cassandra bluffed her jaw hung slack, even when her lips were closed. Papá wriggled his eyebrows both when he had a good hand and when he didn't, so it was hard to tell which one it was — but Mamá, Mamá didn't do anything to her face and her face became, of a sudden, blank. You had no idea what she was thinking. I was bad at cards because I couldn't remember the rules and I was constantly giving my hand away through my questions. "What does the ace do again?" "You need five of the same suit to do what?" Papá said I had beginner's luck.

Cassandra and I knew without having to follow the fight that within an hour's time, Papá would apologize, back down, and hang

91

Mamá's posters up again. So we ran up and down the stairs, careless, free, nothing more normal than Mamá and Papá fighting.

Always when he came home Papá upset our kingdom of women.

He was a bully, for one. "Well, tell me then, who is the one that makes money in this house? Your hair will not be short for the simple reason that I would pay for the haircut."

Papá had strange rules about hair and how long it should be. Mamá said it was all part of a sordid belief system called *machismo.* Mamá said Papá was a *machista.* On the other hand, Mamá, Cassandra, and I were *feministas.* Meaning, if I wanted to have short hair, Mamá would let me and Cassandra would like it (none of us, however, was sure about Petrona — was her short hair convenience or was it rebellion?).

As feministas, Mamá said we had to choose our battles: "With your father, only fight the really important battles, which are: profession, love, money, and the right to go out in the world unhindered by him. Hair is not an important battle." Cassandra nodded meaningfully. Her hands folded primly in the lap of her school skirt and her right leg crossed carefully over the left.

For another, Papá was a master manipulator. One day, he won a stack of American one-dollar bills in a game of pool. When he came home, he dangled the American dollars in front of our faces, asking whom we loved best — him or Mamá. I didn't want anything to do with the American dollars. I made it a point to snatch Papá's dollar and rip it in two whenever it was offered because *that* was a money battle.

Papá would yell, "Ey! Stop! That's a perfectly good dollar!"

He made me sit at the dining table and looked over my shoulder as I aligned the bill perfectly. Then he gave a little grunt of approval. Making sure the bill pieces remained aligned, I taped the two pieces together. Sometimes I had to redo it until Papá was satisfied.

Every time he promised not to, but he always reripped the bill after I was done with it. He said it was a lesson. "Do you see, Chula, that is exactly how I feel when you rip a dollar I've worked for." Papá said I didn't understand the value of money, and furthermore, I didn't understand consequences because I was spoiled.

When Papá dangled dollars in front of Cassandra, Cassandra never answered if she loved him or Mamá best; instead she took the dollars and let him think whatever he wanted.

Cassandra told me her strategy was that of deception. If she never answered but took the dollar bill, Papá would think she was answering she loved him best, but in reality, Cassandra had not said a word. Cassandra said those were the rules of politics: you pretended to answer questions without actually answering them.

"Look, Alma!" Papá always called when Cassandra snatched the dollars from his hand.

"Look how the eyes in this one light up with the money. Come look! Like little stars in a cartoon!"

Mamá came and watched as Papá repeated the whole exercise, except the part about whom Cassandra loved best. Mamá watched Cassandra's eyes attentively as Cassandra snatched up the dollars, and then Mamá and Papá laughed knowingly and in between gasps they said, "Yes, you can really see it! How the eyes dance with real happiness!"

Meanwhile, Cassandra was getting richer and richer.

Petrona watched us from the corner of her eye. Petrona didn't like Papá. I could tell because Papá and Petrona were rarely in the same room together. I didn't blame Petrona for not warming up to him. Sometimes Papá got into a mood and put on his bathrobe when it was still daylight. It meant Papá would be in his bathrobe all day, with his nose buried in a book, emerging only to talk in some language none of us could speak.

Then, Papá would walk right by Petrona arranging flowers in a vase as if she were in a different dimension. Papá didn't even see me, and I was standing right next to Petrona pulling petals from one flower, telling her, "He loves you, he loves you not, he loves you, he loves you not." Papá looked up and said a few strange things, of which I caught — plebiscite, plutocracy, Weltgeist. I had no idea what any of it meant, but I liked Weltgeist. It sounded important and big like *Poseidon, god of the Oceans.* I told Petrona Weltgeist was god of the mountains. She was a bearded woman riding a magical goat. Petrona seemed impressed.

"And what does the bearded woman do?"

"She spreads the seeds of flowers, and she helps lovers meet." I waited a moment, then asked, "Petrona, do you have a boyfriend?"

Petrona giggled. "No, but. Maybe someday."

At home, I was transfixed by Petrona's

quiet elegance. I liked the way she said words. I liked how she looked in the sunlight in the living room — the tidy white bow of her apron vibrating just slightly as she hummed in her pretty alto voice, dusting the windowsills, motes rising up and dancing in the light.

Mamá was loud and grating by comparison. There was nothing subtle about the way she moved or talked, and she was lazy and wanted everything done for her.

I liked Petrona's changing moods too. It was like she was an unstable planet. In seconds she went from being peaceful, like she was watching things from above, to her muscles stringing up her neck and palpitating with tension. It only drew me to her. I found her waverings mysterious and alluring.

I practiced moving like Petrona. When I reached my finger to flick a light on or off, I did so at half speed. Petrona moved so slowly, it looked like a ballet. I didn't know why I was the only one really seeing Petrona, but it seemed like a gift.

After the weeklong struggle for power and territory came the day when Papá and Mamá would make peace and go out for a date. They asked Petrona if she could sleep over to watch us. Papá wore a tie and Mamá looked like a bejeweled bird, her shawl with small black feathers hanging down from shiny beads. Papá said they were going to a fancy restaurant, then to a party to dance.

Once they left, Cassandra was under the illusion that she had been left in charge and she told Petrona to bring us a tray with two oranges, four cans of Pepsi, two bags of nuts, and plenty of bread rolls. Cassandra and I were getting ready, as we did every Thursday night, in case of a bombing.

Every Thursday since the dead girl's shoe, we repacked our emergency backpacks and set them down ready by our beds. Our lives could be so close to ending it was better to be prepared. When Petrona realized what we were doing, she said it wasn't a good idea, the food would spoil, and Cassandra said she was right — that was exactly why we had to repack our bags every week because the food got mushy and wrinkly and started to give off smells. We gave the spoiled food to Petrona and then we knelt in front of our beds stuffing our backpacks. Petrona gazed into the tray of rotting food, and when she finally left, Cassandra and I sat with our backs to one another using our beds as working tables.

That Thursday I packed my spare toothbrush, toothpaste and soap, the orange and bread and nuts, a change of clothes, and a diary to write nostalgic things. Cassandra packed her crossword puzzles, four new cans of Pepsi, a bag of straws (because she didn't like touching things that were "public"), and a novel she had to read for school, *The Bell Jar.* I asked wouldn't it be better to leave her school book out so she could actually read it, but Cassandra turned and asked if I would carry her toothbrush, and if worse got to worse would I share my food with her, and the toothpaste, and the soap, because as I could see, there was no more room in her bag. She tilted her bag and opened it wide. It was full and at the top things stuck out in sharp angles.

"Chula, remember. I'm the older one. The older one tells the younger one what to do." The bridge of her pink-rimmed glasses slid down her nose.

Cassandra had a hard time getting the right perspective on things.

"I'll do it porque quiero, not because you're telling me." I offered her my open palm. Cassandra twisted and grabbed her toothbrush on her bed. Her long ponytail swung out as she twisted back, beaming, toothbrush in hand. She slapped the toothbrush on my hand and turned to rearrange her belongings. I stared at her long ponytail shaped like a dark, upside-down tear.

"You're welcome," I said. She didn't say anything and zipped and unzipped her bag.

I looked at my hand. Cassandra's toothbrush was pink and had plastic wrapped around the brush-end held together by a rubber band. My toothbrush was blue, and had gone in unprotected because I liked going against things. I stuffed Cassandra's toothbrush deep in the bag, up to my elbow. I thought about the dead girl's shoe. The sock filled with leg. I knew I was supposed to know who was responsible for her dying, but I kept forgetting. Cassandra said, "Don't you know, Chula, it was Pablo Escobar. They said it like six times on the television." I remembered something vague about the guerrillas, but maybe they were one and the same. I shook my head. My mind was always up in the clouds. The sound of Cassandra's backpack zipping up sounded with finality behind me.

"What do you think Pablo Escobar thinks about?" I asked.

"Money." She threw her bag a few times in the air, testing its weight, before setting it down on the floor and stretching out on her bed, yawning. Between us there was a long line of masking tape, from the left wall down the middle of our night table and the night lamp, down the brown carpet floor between our beds, and up between the middle wall between each of our closets. On her side was the writing desk with the boombox. On my side was the wall-to-wall window that looked down on an empty grassy lot and two cows. I had chosen that side of the room so I could look at the cows.

Ever since the car bomb, I knelt on my bed at least twice a day to pull the lace curtains out to both sides and stare beyond the plastic roofing that sheltered our indoor patio, beyond the broken glass cemented to the top of the wall, to the empty lot. I watched the two cows practicing the swing of their tail and listened to them draw out their lonely mooing for anyone who would listen.

I named one cow Teresa and the other cow Antonio, after Papá. I didn't know what gender the cows were or how you could tell them apart, so I referred to them in plural, as in *las vacas. Today las vacas lay down at opposite corners of the lot like they were strangers, even though they're the only cows they know in the whole world. Why do they do that, Mamá?* Papá said maybe my cows had been reading Sartre, whatever that meant.

When there was no one around to see me,

I opened the window and mooed at las vacas. They perked up their ears and stopped the swing of their tail, frozen in attention, listening; but they never mooed back.

I played at being the security guard and stared beyond the cows to where there was a wide sidewalk, and after it the street with the cars speeding past. I watched out for any kind of suspicious behavior and made notes in my diary. Every once in a while there were pedestrians hurrying down the sidewalk, but I was too far to see their faces, to see if they were dangerous. I decided that walking outside by the highway was suspicious enough and jotted down the words "Suspicious pedestrian," then the time, the day, and the year. Cars left abandoned were also suspicious, because they could hold bombs. I told Mamá or Papá when a car was left unattended, and sometimes they called the police.

Cassandra asked, "What do *you* think Pablo Escobar thinks about?"

I sighed, zipping up my bag, and glanced out the window before lying down like Cassandra.

"Monstrous things."

When Mamá and Papá got home, we made popcorn and cuddled together in

Papá and Mamá's big bed, even though it was late, and we watched the story of a robot who was also a cop. I nestled my head onto the side of Papá's chest, watching explosions on the television as I fell asleep. The paper with Galán's outline was lit through by the lamppost light outside. Galán lifted his fist three times across the window.

The next day when I woke up, Papá was gone.

PETRONA

In our hut made of trash we mourned little Ramón leaving. It brought on Aurora's blood. A streak ran down her leg. Mami told me to calm myself, Ramoncito would return, but I was crying for Aurora. It was only a matter of time before Mami would think of Aurora as a burden, and little Aurora would have to go to work. Mami and I fought.

Little Aurora did most of the cleaning in our hut now. Mami so sick with her breathing, Aurora so little, but still Fernandito, Bernardo, and Patricio, all older than Aurora, refused to get water from the well because that was woman's work, even though it took that little girl half an hour to drag the water back.

Bringing water from the well used to be my job. I filled the buckets and carried them on a yoke back to our hut. I splashed the water with an easy swing of my torso. Water fell over the stamped-down dirt floor of our hut. It kept the dust down so Mami could breathe.

Aurora was not strong. She set the buckets at the entrance, kicked them over, and then on her knees and hands went after the trail of water, drumming her flat palms on the puddles to make it absorb down.

That was Aurora's life now. The care of others.

My life was cleaning and cooking and more cleaning and cooking when I got home to our hut in the Hills.

My life was tossing and turning at night in the mattress I shared with Mami and little Aurora, my three little boys sleeping like sardines on the mattress next to us.

I was not good at living a life of honor like Papi. I planned to get groceries for the Santiagos when I knew Leticia had the habit of going. I waited for Leticia at the corner by the house where she worked. I saw her come out, running her fingers through her hair, and I caught up to her like it was a coincidence we were meeting, and then before I could stop myself, I told her I would do it, I would pass the envelopes, I had changed my mind — when could I start?

7.
Fruit of the Drunken Tree

Isa and Lala said now we knew beyond the shadow of a doubt that Petrona had been under a *black magic spell* — how else could we explain the fact that what had broken Petrona's silence had been something violent like the dead girl's leg wearing its red shoe? Only black magic worked that way.

Even though the others put the question of Petrona to rest, I still had the feeling that something hounded her. On the last day of the school quarter that September, Cassandra and I ran home in our newfound freedom. Cassandra went to take a shower, and I went to the kitchen to see what Petrona was up to. I found her carefully placing the broom with the bristles pointing up against a corner like she was putting a baby down in a crib. I went to touch the broom, and Petrona yelled to leave it alone, and when Mamá asked about it, Petrona said it was there to keep witches from landing on the roof of our house.

I was afraid of witches. How could you protect yourself against one? They could make you bleed from the nose by just staring. I heard a man on the radio say, *Pablo Escobar is so slippery, the man probably has the protection of a witch.* I found Mamá painting her nails pink at the edge of her bed. "Mamá, what witch protects Pablo Escobar?" She looked up. "Pablo Escobar?" She looked to the ceiling thinking for a second. "Probably a witch from the Amazon. That's where the strongest witches come from." She extended her right hand and brushed the last bit of pink polish on her pinkie and hummed as she started on the left.

Cassandra's and my birthdays came and went, and we spent our whole vacation playing with Isa and Lala. As I went in and out of our house, running into the kitchen yelling for a snack or cold water, Petrona jumped. Soup spoons clattered to the floor, plates broke. I kept track of what Petrona snacked on in my diary in case one day it all made sense: apple with honey, fried plantains, sunflower seeds, chicken breast.

One day the four of us dozed off watching television. Mamá and Cassandra and I were at angles on the bed, and Petrona was sitting on the floor, resting her head on the edge of the bed by my feet. I stirred awake when Petrona got up. She stood at Mamá's door. I saw the slow motion with which her hand reached for the knob, the way she turned it trying to keep it from clicking, the way she braced against the door with one hand and opened it slowly with her other hand so it wouldn't creak. It was so striking I waited until she made her way downstairs, and then I snuck into the hall. I peeked over the banisters and saw Petrona brace the front door like she had done with Mamá's door, and then she walked out into the front garden.

Her behavior was so suspicious I rushed to Mamá's room to watch from under the Galán posters. In the garden, Petrona ran dirt through her fingers. She squatted, then zigzagged across the garden, inching closer and closer to the gate. I hid when she looked over her shoulder. I counted to ten. When I lifted again, Petrona was kneeling under the Drunken Tree, holding a flower over her nose taking deep breaths.

She swayed. I searched myself for a feeling of alarm, but there was nothing. I watched Petrona reach her hand to the gate to steady herself. I thought she would come inside the house now, but instead she stood up and plucked a fruit from the tree. I thought to myself I should probably move now, or in the least say something, but I did not. I looked on as Petrona broke the shell of the fruit and her hand became full with seeds. I watched as Petrona put a seed in her mouth and chewed. I watched as she fell to her knees.

"Mamá, Mamá!" I ducked under the poster and jumped on the bed. "Mamá, wake up! Petrona is possessed!"

Mamá sat up, "What?"

"Petrona, Mamá! She's eating from the tree."

Mamá flung the sheets aside and we ran down the steps and into the garden and there we came upon Petrona, rolling from side to side, laughing, clawing at space, Drunken Tree flowers lying on the ground all about her.

Mamá dropped to her knees and gripped Petrona's wrist. Petrona growled like an animal, and I fell back. Mamá held on fast to Petrona's hands and Petrona tossed her head and laughed long and maniacally. In the few seconds before Mamá next spoke, as I gripped the grass, recoiling from Petrona, I saw, for the first time, objectively, that she really was thirteen. She was thin and rosy, and stuck somewhere between woman and girl, alive with secrets.

"Petrona, calm down," Mamá commanded, and instantly Petrona smiled and hugged the dirt, her legs twitching. She became again the Petrona I knew. I reached my hand to her and Petrona lifted her face. The black of her pupils was large in the amber of her eyes. I did not touch her. Mamá placed the back of her hand on Petrona's forehead. The touch of Mamá's hand seemed to soothe her, and Petrona shivered now like a puppy.

"That new girl of yours is no good." It was la Soltera speaking to us. She leaned over our planters at the front porch, holding a cigarette, closing her white bathrobe at her breast. "Serves her right, that girl."

Mamá told Petrona, "Let's go inside." Petrona sat up. When she was on her feet, Petrona gave me a ghastly grin. I shrank back. "Come along, Petrona," Mamá said, and Petrona got under Mamá's arm and they walked to the porch. I stayed in place, afraid to go after them, afraid to stand too near the Drunken Tree flowers that looked so delicate and white against the grass. Mamá said, "Keep walking, Petrona," and I saw Petrona was frozen in place at the red-tile patio, her breath coming in little convulsions through her nostrils. She pointed and stared at la Soltera like la Soltera was a spook. Mamá said, "Nearly there, just a few more steps," and Petrona kept pointing, but she let herself be pulled into our house.

La Soltera scoffed. "What *ever* is the matter with that girl?" She ashed her cigarette over our planters and I made a run for our house.

Inside, Cassandra stood by the stairs. "What happened?"

In her bed, Petrona's breathing was fast, then slow. Cassandra knelt down next to me, and we stared at Petrona twitching, dying, we didn't know. Since Petrona's family didn't have a telephone, Mamá called the corner store near their house and left a message with the clerk. She told the clerk to tell Petrona's family that Petrona had fallen ill with food poisoning, and that she would be recovering at our house over the next few days. The clerk said he would pass on the message no problem; Petrona's brother came every night to pick up some soda for the family. After it was done, Mamá got a bottle from her closet and poured its contents into a glass. She gave it to Petrona to drink and told us it was a special drink that would absorb the poison. The glass was filled with a black liquid tar.

Petrona tipped it back and swallowed,

black streaking down her chin. She tossed and turned. Mamá said Petrona was intoxicated. Mamá held a wet towel on her forehead. Petrona sat up after a while, saying she had misplaced her bowl of soup in the sheets, and asked me to help her look. Mamá nodded so I pretended to look with Petrona. We dug around her sheets and I wondered who in their right mind would sniff from a Drunken Tree flower and then eat from its fruit? Mamá said it wouldn't be long now, the black liquid would clean Petrona out. She told us to go to our room, Petrona was about to be very sick. Cassandra and I half obeyed. We set up camp in the living room. We were quiet, lying sideways on the couch together with our blankets hearing Petrona retch. I didn't think of anything, just wordless worry, the feeling pulsing through every heave and moan and whimper coming from her bedroom.

Once it was dark, it got very quiet and Mamá emerged from the kitchen. She put on a coat and told us she had to go to the pharmacy and get some serum for Petrona's dehydration. She came back with a bottle for Petrona to drink and Cassandra and I finally fell asleep.

The next day Petrona was normal, except she didn't remember the day before at all. It was just like when Papá drank too much and he didn't remember the stories he told. She listened mystified as we told her about the way she stared at la Soltera, all the time that she knelt in bed looking for the bowl of soup. "I wonder what I was seeing," she said, and Mamá waved the air. "The important thing is you leave stupidity aside and do as I say, Petrona — didn't I tell you to stay away from that tree?"

Petrona seemed to be completely recovered, but Mamá insisted she stay in bed and drink as much water as she could. Mamá didn't say anything about Petrona playing, so Cassandra and I brought down our Barbies. We had a box deep with Barbies. Our Barbies had blue eyes and short, jerky bobs because Cassandra had cut it, swearing their hair would grow back. They had no legs or arms because Cassandra had chewed them off. Cassandra had a habit of chewing the limbs when she watched television or took long showers or did her homework. She would hold the Barbie head of hair with her hand and sink her teeth into the rubbery fingers, ankles and wrists, calves and thighs and forearms, until her saliva and teeth broke the pieces of vinyl off. She entertained the feel of them in her mouth, the squishiness between her teeth, the taste like old gum, and then she would swallow, and start anew on another limb.

We thought it to be a real tragedy.

At first we invented elaborate stories about how our Barbies had come to their paraplegia. But later, our favorite game became pretending they were war veterans and victims. And this is the game we invited Petrona to play.

Cassandra's Barbie, Veracruz, had lost her arms and legs running from the guerrillas. She had run a million miles for a thousand days until her feet grated off against the road, and then she ran with her hands, but her hands rubbed off too. My Barbie, Lola, had been the boss of guerrillas in Putumayo, but her men revolted against her and chopped her up and left her for dead in a jungle. She had a red bandana around her forehead and penciled-in bags under her eyes.

When she saw our Barbies, Petrona covered her mouth and laughed. She was sitting up, looking paler than usual, but she laughed violently, leaning and slapping her thigh. Petrona wiped a tear from her eye and, sighing, she reached her hand in the box, Barbies piled on each other. She pulled out a Barbie wearing a shiny blue dress. The dress was close-fitted and stopped just after the separation of her thighs.

Petrona caressed the short blond hair of her Barbie and then looped her index fingers under the Barbie's hard plastic armpits, and dangled the torso with stubbed legs and stubbed arms in front of her like a baby.

"I'll call her Bianca," she said. "And she was born like this."

"Really, Petrona?" I said. "With no arms or legs?" It was an interesting problem.

"Sí, niña, of course, it's common," Petrona said. "Her mother smoked and drank during pregnancy. Plus, she was dropped on her head when she was a baby."

On Petrona's bed where the light waned from warm yellow to gray and we had to turn the overhead light on, we bounced our limbless Barbies and flipped their hair. Veracruz and Bianca became friends when they sat next to each other on a bench. After all, what were the odds of meeting another woman who was only a torso like you, and who like you, had to get around by doing somersaults?

Bianca was on her way to the supermarket, when she spotted Lola. Bianca was so excited to see a third like them, armless and legless, that she rolled to befriend Lola right away; but Lola didn't want friends, she wanted more people for her guerrilla army.

Petrona's Barbie Bianca bounced on her stubbed thighs and said she already had a guerrilla army of her own. Lola wanted to start a war against Bianca's army, but Bianca said that wasn't how guerrillas worked. Their real enemy was the rich.

"Oh," I said. "Like the Oligarch."

"Kill the rich!" Lola said.

Cassandra joined in and raised Veracruz's stubbed arm. Veracruz chanted, "Kill the rich! Kill the rich!" Bianca sang, " *'Tis the final conflict, let each stand in his place. The international working class shall be the human race.*" Cassandra lifted her eyes from her Barbie. "What is that?"

"Just a song," Petrona said.

Mamá opened the bedroom door. She was carrying a tray with a large bowl of soup and juice. "Go on," she told Cassandra and me. "Leave Petrona alone, she has to rest."

Petrona smiled at me and put Bianca facedown on her bed and sat up to receive Mamá's tray. Cassandra picked up our Barbies and threw them into the box with all the others. She picked up the box and said, "Hope you feel better."

"Feel better," I echoed and we went out. Mamá was asking Petrona something quietly and then Cassandra said, "That song was weird."

"Why?"

"It's probably nothing."

As we made our way through the kitchen I noticed that the broom with the upside-down bristles was not in the corner. I wondered if a witch had landed on the roof and made Petrona eat the seeds of the Drunken Tree. A shiver ran down my spine. I looked around but everything else seemed to be in its usual place. I followed after Cassandra as we went up the stairs, staring at the white ruffle of her socks, too scared to say anything out loud.

PETRONA

Little Ramón had been at the coast packing freight trains. He brought back money and Mami bought juice and poured us all a glass and said what a godsend, our family still our family. I was angry at Abuelo Andrés for saying our little Ramón was guerrilla. But I couldn't stay angry because Ramón was a little man now — his chest was wide, his back strong, and even his knuckles had grown new, rougher skin. I daydreamed about Ramón on the coast. I imagined him hoisting boxes, filling train cars, finally a good son for Mami. I sang to myself. Ramón was working with the same train company but in Bogotá now and overseeing packages. I stopped passing the envelopes. If Ramón kept working, I could go back to school. I could take a class or two, and become a secretary.

Mami and Ramón talked on the phone every day at six in the afternoon. Mami went to the corner store. She walked up and down the mountain to be there for the phone call in spite of her asthma. Mami talked to Ramón about the weather, then she talked to him about the future: the house they would own, the food they would have in the fridge. Then Ramón said, *Mami, la bendición,* and Mami gave him her blessing. Mami was worried the train company was working Ramón too hard, and I told her as long as they paid.

One evening Ramón didn't call and Mami nearly went out of her mind. The corner store owner, Señor David, felt so sorry for Mami he got out of bed at three in the morning when Ramón's call finally came in. He climbed the mountain to our hut and helped Mami down to the store. When Mami picked up the phone, Ramón sounded dead tired. *Is everything all right, mi'jo?* He sounded cheerful for a moment and Mami relaxed. *La bendición,* he asked, and Mami gave it, *Dios me lo bendiga, mi'jo.* They were quiet and then Ramón said he needed to go rest. The next day some kids hunting turkeys found his body, dumped in the Hills, like the other body, except people said it wasn't the army this time but the paras, because everybody knew Ramón was guerrilla, that he had been packing dynamite and explosives, that the money he gave us was guerrilla money, that when he called to ask for a blessing it was before going on missions, and we were stupid not to have seen it.

We kept the casket inside our hut for two days. It was everything we could afford. I looked at Ramón dressed by Mami in a T-shirt and jeans she had scrubbed clean. He was not a little man. He was a boy of twelve. His skin was like clay, his eyebrows wiry, his face like a mask. I knew where the bullet holes were, our little Ramón, how they climbed all over his back. I took his hands in mine and swore I would prove he had been doing honest work. When I wiped my face clean of tears there was the smell of gunpowder. I smelled my shirt, but my scent was just dust and sweat. I smelled little Ramón's hands, fell on my knees, and cried. Mami looked at me with so much hate. *His hands don't smell like anything, you liar, liar, liar.*

The people of the Hills knew what had happened, but nobody stopped by our hut. I imagined they wanted the whole thing to go away, but we had nowhere to bury the casket so we put it in front of our house.

Leticia came with a bunch of flowers. They came in a plastic cover so I knew she had spent money on them. Leticia held a little piece of cloth to her nose. The smell of Ramón filled the air. There was a young man next to Leticia. He'd known my brother. People called him Gorrión. Gorrión looked at me. Leticia said something but I could not hear properly, because there were Gorrión's eyes in front of me, attentively watching, pools of brown sucking me up, from which I could not look away, but I did, to look at his hand coming forward to meet mine. It was soft and gave me a jolt of electricity when I touched it. He grazed his afroed hair with his fingers, and then I looked into the glow of his eyes again. I felt seen in a way I didn't know was possible and it quenched something in me, and so I uncovered the casket for this man who had the power to see, because I wanted him to see what was happening to little Ramón too.

Leticia staggered back, *Dios mio.* She gagged by a tree, but Gorrión did not move, and I was thankful. His dark cheekbones bounced off sunlight. I read on his face that he was sad, but not surprised like most people, who did not expect Ramón to be deflating like a busted balloon. Gorrión smiled sadly at me and I smiled in sadness too. He spoke. He said he wanted to pay for Ramón's burial. *How?* I asked, holding on to his voice that seemed to go under my feet, but I meant to say, *Don't.* Gorrión pulled out an envelope from inside his jean jacket and he put it in my hands. He said it was his savings. I stared at the thick white envelope resting on my palms not able to understand such kindness from a stranger; then the envelope was slapped to the ground. It was Mami who had come out of the hut. Leticia was gone. Mami threw dirt and rocks at Gorrión, who dodged her attacks and then lunged for the envelope and ran away. Mami called after him: bestia, animal, atrevido, desgraciado, how dare he give us his dirty money, she knew where that money came from, of course he was black, black like the dirt he was. Mami yelled at me, *I never want to see you talking to that black man again.*

At night I went to throw out the dirty dishwater and Gorrión came out of the shadows. *Stay away,* I whispered, but he came forward and put an inhaler in my

121

hand. I stared at it, dumbstruck. *Where did this come from?* There was a rush of wind through the trees. Gorrión stretched to look over my shoulder. The front door curtain of my family's hut was bright from the candlight inside. *Ramón was my friend. He told me to take care of you, so I am.*

Inside the hut there was a small clattering sound, and I glanced back and then at Gorrión. He stepped back into the shadows. *Can I visit you where you work?* he whispered. *Maybe we can have more time to talk.* I stepped toward his voice. I found his hand then I kissed his cheek. It was too dark to see his face, but he lingered next to me for a few more seconds before he ran away, rustling the trees where he went. It brought on a sweet kind of pain, his leaving. I didn't want Mami to destroy the inhaler, so I told her it came from the Santiagos, that they sent their condolences and Mami frowned but she took it.

The next day Abuelo Andrés came saying we could put Ramón in the same plot with his wife. I didn't know Abuelo Andrés had had a wife, but in the Hills we don't ask too many questions in case we end up knowing something we're not supposed to. We hauled the casket by mule to the cemetery. The hole was already dug. The caretaker helped us put the casket on top of the one that was there. The stone read *Diana Martínez, beloved wife.* That was Ramón's resting place. We threw dirt down into the hole, the little ones and Mami and me, and my eyes filled with tears. I looked everywhere around me, wanting to feel something else. I glanced at the bushes, the trees, between the cemetery stones, but there was nothing to shore me up.

I felt light, even though la Señora had said I could die, taking big breaths off the flower of that tree in the Señora's garden. I lay one seed on my tongue and bit into it even though I tasted bitterness. I must have grinned, or at least it felt like it. Things blurred and my knees went weak. Then my pain became small. My life opened up clean and clear before me.

I dropped to the ground.

It was like falling asleep.

8.
GALÁN! GALÁN! GALÁN!

When school started again for the final quarter that year, I felt it in my bones that something bad was about to happen. My stomach tensed and fluttered. At school, I smelled blood. I thought I had a nosebleed but when I went to the bathroom to check there was nothing wrong with my nose, just my skin paler than usual and my hands all worked up. I couldn't figure out where the smell was coming from. During recess, Cassandra patted my back and said I was just excited to see Galán, because Mamá was taking us to Soacha to see Galán give a speech. It was possible that it was just nerves, or maybe it was because we were withholding the fact we were going from Papá since he wouldn't have allowed us to go. Cassandra gave me her soda pop and took me to see the horses the guards kept at the back of the school. We sat together by the small stable under the eucalyptus trees, and somehow seeing the horses chew grass made me feel better and I forgot about the whole thing.

When we got home Cassandra and I drew fat hearts on our cheeks with Mamá's red lipstick and then we traced huge letters on a white posterboard spelling, "Galán!" Cassandra was good with grammar so I mainly filled in the letters of our poster with red, because that was the color of the Liberal Party. "So-a-cha," I murmured. "So-acha." *Acha* sounded like ax, but *so* didn't sound like anything, and neither did *cha.*

Mamá clicked on her seat belt and we dropped off Petrona at a bus station and then we were off. I couldn't believe we were going to a political rally. In the car, I sang along to everything that came on the radio. We were the first car in a caravan of seven driving from Bogotá as the sun went down, all of us obviously making the trip to see Galán. The cars sported posters, banners, and stickers. Mamá bounced in her seat and said she was clearly the strongest driver. "I am the *Alpha.* Oh, look!" she said, decelerating. "I almost lost a subject in the heat of that curve."

Mamá's first subject, directly behind us, was an old man wearing a hat and a vest. Behind him, there was a car filled with girls letting their arms hang out of the window. I could see them at the curves when the old man swept slightly to one side. The one girl in the passenger seat made waves with her arm, while the ones in the back just let their hands hang down. That looked like the thing to do, but Mamá wouldn't let me put my hand out, even though I pointed to the girls and asked how come they could.

When we got to Soacha it was getting dark. We were late and Mamá parked the car in a hurry and yanked us so hard she didn't allow us to get our posters and I nearly fell. Mamá took no notice. The town was small and there was only one main street. She did not slow down until we reached the crowd. People on second-floor balconies hung on to railings yelling down at the crowd, but others sat on stoops silently.

I didn't understand what the hurry was. The street where the parade would take place was empty and lit with the amber light of streetlights. The sidewalks were full of people. There was salsa playing from overhead speakers and I was hemmed in by smelly adults who jumped and danced and squished me every which way. The adults chanted and waved little red plastic flags. When I heard drums, I decided I would jump. I looked and looked, but in between seeing the dancing barricade of adults and the street, there were no clowns, no beauty queens, no confetti, no funny hats. I couldn't find the drums. Mamá had completely forgotten about us. She was jumping in the air, waving a little Colombian flag, laughing. "Ga-lán! Ga-lán!"

"What kind of a parade is this?"

Cassandra wrinkled her eyebrows and the red hearts on her cheeks glinted dully. "It's a political parade, don't you know anything?" Cassandra was looking at the political parade through a little tunnel formed between a man's raised arm and a woman's hat. If we stood on the base of a street lamp we were tall enough to see through the tunnel. Mamá stayed close. I hung on, encircling the lamppost just under Cassandra's arms. It was difficult, but at least it was a constant sight into the street. Through the little tunnel I saw a man with a wide-open mouth singing, a woman with green eyelids, a man with a trumpet, and a boy dashing by, blowing on a gaita and shaking a maraca.

"Ga-lán, Ga-lán!" Mamá shook us by the shoulders. "That's Galán! Galán! Chula! Cassandra!"

We looked through our tunnel, but it opened and closed as the man with the raised arm jumped up and down and the woman took off her hat and waved it in the air. There was a white truck and then, on the truck bed for a few long seconds, there appeared, in our small tunnel, in flesh and blood, Galán. He seemed to be staring right at me. His hair curled upward like it was charged with static. He smiled, in a dark blue suit and red tie, lifting his hand and waving. And just as quickly he was gone. He was followed by tall white banners that said *Galán Presidente* and men in suits jumping. We didn't even have time to think about what we had just seen when everyone closed behind the float and Cassandra and I were swept away in the crowd.

"Chula! Chula!"

The crowd carried me away like a strong current. "Help! Cassandra!"

"Ey! Ey!" a young man cried, seeing I had been separated. Nobody listened and he fought to remain in place but still we got carried further. "Cassandra!" I screamed. The man saw where I was going and said, "Okay, just climb, ready?" and then he threw me and I was up in the air, scrambling on top of people's heads. Everyone was upset and pushed me aside on top of somebody else until I landed on a large white banner and scratched and kicked over it until I got back close to Cassandra. I threw myself over people until I fell into her arms. Cassandra and Mamá stood still hugging a lamppost. I couldn't tell if it was the same one as before. The young man was gone when I looked and Mamá wrapped her arms over Cassandra's arms and yelled to not let go and we all got into the crowd and allowed it to move us. That's how we found our way to the back of the crowd where people had standing room. Just in time too, because the next thing that happened was that they were announcing Galán on the stage.

"There he is, Mamá!" He was walking to the front of the stage, both arms raised in salute to the crowd, while on the podium a man was saying, "Here he is, the man we've all been waiting for, el *Señor* Luis Carlos Gal—" Then gunshots splattered into the air and I threw myself, flying, toward the ground. I noticed there was a crack in the pavement. I could see it even by the amber light from the street lamps. I was screaming, but everything lagged — there was a thought in my head, *Am I going to die?* The words crawled over the splatter of gunshots, suddenly in slow motion, over a hundred people screaming, and then when I hit the ground, everything was happening quickly again, and I heard one clear voice as it said: *"Lo mataron! Lo mataron! Hijueputa, lo mataron!"*

There were no more gunshots, just people wailing and running. I clawed at the ground, littered with bottles and flags, yelling for Mamá. I started to run but tripped and my hand was nailed under someone's boot. I screamed and then Mamá was there, suddenly plucking me up by the neck of my sweater, skinning my legs on the ground, and then I was in her arms with Cassandra, my hand hanging limp and burning. "Dios mío," Mamá repeated. "Dios mío, Dios mío, Dios mío, Dios mío."

Cassandra was crying and people were jumping over walls and running down the alleys and climbing over cars and then Mamá hurled us in through the driver's car door and then we were driving. Men and women were crawling over the hood of our car, trying to get away. Mamá drove into people, honking. I covered my ears, but my hand hurt terribly when I moved it and Cassandra held me close.

"Move!" Mamá yelled. She drove on the sidewalk, then we were around the corner and there was no one in the street. Mamá was out of breath, speeding out of Soacha.

130

Cassandra and I sat together clutching each other.

As time passed, I realized I couldn't see the mountains, but I knew they were there. We traveled in absolute darkness. We didn't speak. Mamá's silence was forbidding. At times beams of cars driving in the opposite direction flushed our car, and I could see Mamá and Cassandra. Mamá's temples and overlip gleamed with sweat and her eyes were alert and glanced at everything. Cassandra's lipstick-hearts were faint and her whole face was reddened slightly with the rubbed-on shade of them. I felt like we were traveling in an invisible vehicle. We were souls speeding up a mountain we could not see, floating in the dark.

Maybe Galán was dead. Maybe they had shot him. Maybe he had made it out alive. Maybe his soul was now traveling.

In the distance hanging in the black space a pair of headlights appeared, then they moved right, and disappeared again. That was how I knew we were driving on a winding cliff road.

After a while, Mamá remembered to turn on her lights. She was less forbidding, so I said, "My hand hurts." Cassandra said, "Mamá, I think Chula sprained her arm." Mamá said, "Mierda." Then, "Cassandra, hold Chula's hand still."

We were all quiet again. Mamá's headlights lit up the yellow fluorescent lines of the road. They were curvy and it seemed like they were being traced out of nothingness by the invisible hand of God — like God was bored, drawing hills and lines with a highlighter.

Mamá turned on the radio and that was when we heard Galán had been shot but he was in a hospital fighting for his life. Those were the announcer's words: *Galán is in a hospital fighting for his life.*

I thought we were going to the hospital because of my hand, but Mamá pulled into our driveway. She didn't turn off the car and remained very still. Then she dipped forward. She was crying. "Mamá, are you okay?" Mamá never cried about anything. I didn't know what to do, but Cassandra said, "It's okay, Mamá. Take a deep breath." Mamá tried breathing, the headlights of the car shining eerily into the first floor of our house. This was a new thing — Cassandra comforting Mamá, like Mamá was the child and not the other way around. I don't know how long we sat there, but suddenly Petrona came out.

I was shocked to see her, because hadn't we dropped her off at a bus station? Petrona shielded her eyes at the door. Then she ran and opened my door. "Señora? Niñas? What happened?" That was when pain exploded in my arm and my arm pulsed like it was a heart. "Does it hurt, niña?" She took me inside. The living room was bright. Petrona was asking me to move my fingers, but I couldn't. It almost killed me when I tried and they didn't even move although I thought it. Everything was strange with the pain of my throbbing arm and I heard the disembodied words of the announcer again, *fighting for his life.* Petrona lifted my jumper to look at my legs. My thigh was bruised dark green, as if I was rotting from the inside. I could move my toes. *Fighting for his life, rotting from the inside.* Petrona came back with slices of raw potatoes and placed them flat on the bruise then wrapped my thigh with plastic. Outside Cassandra was telling Mamá I needed to go to the hospital because my arm was not sprained, but broken. Mamá came rushing into the living room and knelt by my side. "It's not broken!" I yelled over Petrona, who was saying that it was. Mamá gave me aspirin and water and was about to get us into the car again when Petrona snatched Mamá's keys away.

We stood in stunned silence.

Mamá's keychain charms — an amethyst

133

stone, a golden flower — dangled out of Petrona's fist. Petrona held Mamá's eyes. "Señora, forgive me, but you're not thinking straight." I closed my mouth. Nobody in the history of *ever* had dared to do anything like that to Mamá. I turned to Mamá to defend Petrona — to say she was young, she was good at her job, she could swear never to question Mamá again — but as soon as I was facing Mamá, I saw Mamá stood clasping her hands at Petrona like how she clasped her hands in front of the saints inside the churches we occasionally visited; like she was praying, and her eyes were even wet.

Petrona put the car keys down on the mantel. She announced she was coming with us to the hospital and turned away to call for a taxi. As I watched her dial, I wondered why Petrona was at our house. I looked down and noticed she was wearing Mamá's house slippers.

In the emergency room Mamá didn't leave me for a minute. Petrona was with Cassandra in the waiting room. The doctor said my arm was sprained. He told me to not move as he rolled a great wet bandage on my arm. It felt like my arm was trapped, pulsing inside a cloud. *Fighting for his life, rotting from the inside.*

"Are you okay, Chula, mi cielo?" I nodded. After a while, Mamá said, "Galán is dead." I knew Mamá was right even though we would not know for sure until the next day. *Fighting for his life, rotting from the inside.* Mamá hugged me close and I thought about how when Galán had waved from the top of the stage, those had been the last moments of his life. He had been waving goodbye.

9.
PAÑUELITOS BLANCOS

Gunshots were frightening. But the horrifying thing was that you didn't know if they were headed in your direction. The not knowing, that was what made them chilling. You heard a shot and then you waited to see where it would strike. I thought about how on the platform Galán first saw a welcoming crowd of people yelling his name, and then the opposite — as he lay dying, people running away.

I thought every second about telling Mamá of how I had smelled blood, but every second I remained quiet. Mamá said the country was under a State of Emergency. Everyone on the television called Pablo Escobar *The Brain*. Cassandra said it meant Pablo Escobar had ordered Galán's killing. I couldn't understand how someone could wake up and order a killing, so I studied the photograph of Pablo Escobar that they showed on the television: his black and white smile, his eyes a little close together, the collar of his Hawaiian shirt starched and wide-angled. His demeanor led you to believe he was in a photo booth at a party, but he was in fact at a police station holding a plaque of numbers with the label *Judicial Department of Medellín Prison*. I wondered if Pablo Escobar had shot Galán himself. The news played a tape Pablo Escobar had sent to the radio, except it wasn't him speaking but one of his men: "The fight is now with blood. Every time one of us is extradited, ten judges die."

Cassandra didn't know what extradition was either. I poked at my deadened arm. The pain was dim, like an echo. I told Cassandra I was confused and she said it was simple: Pablo Escobar was the King of Drugs.

On the television, the Colombian police, dressed up in blue fatigues, confiscated farms, weapons, airplanes, yachts, ranches, and everything inside Pablo Escobar's mansion, even though Pablo Escobar wasn't there.

Cassandra lay on her back and covered her eyes. "You mean they knew *exactly* where he lived all along? How can one government be so stupid?"

Pablo Escobar's mansion was like an

amusement park — there were giraffes, elephants, peacocks, ostriches, antelopes, lions, luxury cars, faucets made of gold. The reporters said it was the biggest narco-raid in history. I shifted in my seat. I knew enough to know that just as when people said los Paras, it was short for *los Paramilitares,* when people said los Narcos, it was short for *los Narcotraficantes,* and when people said los Narcos who they were really talking about was Pablo Escobar. Pablo Escobar was like the King Midas of words. Everything he touched, the word was transformed: narco followed by a dash — narco-paramilitary, narco-war, narco-lawyer, narco-congressman, narco-estate, narco-terrorism, narco-money. Petrona turned the television off.

I went to my room to get the book of maps Papá had given me. I knelt on my bed and opened the book to the map of Colombia. I closed my eyes and concentrated. *Wherever I point my finger that's where Pablo Escobar is hiding.* I found out Pablo Escobar was hiding in Pasto, Buenaventura, and Valledupar. But then I kept pointing at cities close to Bogotá: Suba, Chía, Anapoima, Usme, Zipaquirá.

Papá was yelling at Mamá on the telephone: "I forbid you to go to Galán's funeral! Alma! Do you hear me? Don't take the girls out of school!"

He was very nice to Cassandra and me. He purred against my ear: "How is your little hand, my little doll?" Even though Papá had gone to the local phone company, it was still a bad connection and his voice came forked. One Papá spoke in full sentences, and the other was weak and echoed odd things: *hand, doll.*

"It's okay."

Papá laughed. "Uy, what a pretty little soldier."

"*. . . pretty,*" whispered the second Papá.

"Papá, did Galán know he was going to die?"

Papá sucked in air, but the second Papá was quiet. "I don't know, Chula. I think he knew there was that possibility." There was radio static on the phone line, and then the second Papá was saying, "Possibility," and then the first Papá said, "We all have to die *some*day."

I stared at my sling. Papá asked to talk to Mamá again, but he didn't yell at her like the first time. They must have been talking about me, because Mamá gave short grunts in agreement and looked at me through the corner of her eye. When she hung up Mamá rubbed my back and said she was going to

139

the funeral and taking Cassandra, but not me. Mamá said it was because my arm was sprained and she didn't want it to get worse, but in our bedroom Cassandra told me it was because I was traumatized. "I am *not* traumatized, I am not *traumatized*!" I ran to Mamá. "Mamá, I was there when they shot him! I have to go say goodbye!"

"Say goodbye here, say goodbye there, it doesn't matter, Chula."

"If it doesn't matter then why are *you* going?"

Mamá clicked her tongue. "Chula."

"Why are you going, why are you going, why are you going?"

Cassandra and Mamá snuck out. I only heard the motor of the car starting up and then driving away. I kicked the walls in the closet until Petrona came. She carried me in her arms to the kitchen and pressed ice cubes wrapped in towels on my eyes. I told Petrona it was absolute betrayal to be left behind, and she said yes, it was, and my eyes felt swollen. I felt the hot of tears and the cold of ice mixing and wetting my skin.

"Don't cry anymore, niña." Petrona took the ice away and looked into my eyes. "The important thing is I'm here. Right? I wouldn't leave you." There were pretty gray

140

speckles in the amber of Petrona's eyes. She pressed me close and I nodded. I held the ice to my cheek.

I wondered what possible reasons Mamá and Cassandra could have to betray me. Maybe it was something I said. To Cassandra I had said, "Face of a bat! Face of a bat!" To Mamá I had said, "No, Mamá, you can't play Barbies, you don't know *how.*" To Cassandra I had said, "See how Mamá always braids *my* hair better?" To Mamá I had said, "Mamá, don't try. You can't make hot chocolate like *Petrona.*"

I started to feel better. Petrona was making flan just for me. She was burning sugar in a pan, making it dark and thick. The air smelled like vanilla. She put the concoction in the fridge and then I asked Petrona if she would watch the funeral procession with me on Mamá's television. Yellow light from the fridge brightened her face until she closed the door. She hardened her jaw. She didn't protest as I grabbed her hand and pulled her up the stairs.

We sat together on Mamá's bed. On the television, I saw how the flag-draped coffin made its way across Bogotá's main plaza. It was topped with a beautiful flower arrangement. In some ways, it was better to see the funeral from home, because it was like you had many eyes — some swerving overhead, others close-up on the crowd, always following the action around the coffin. I started to think that the coffin was like a black hole, and the mouth of the black hole was Galán and down his throat was the great mystery: a heart stopped, a body decomposing. I wondered if Galán would become a Blessed Soul of Purgatory. He didn't seem sinful, but you never knew. It was like that saying: faces we see, hearts we don't know. Maybe he was already walking somewhere in our neighborhood in that endless procession of Blessed Souls.

On the screen, the streets were filled with people waving things — white handkerchiefs, white shirts, Colombian flags, red plastic. Galán's face was printed on posters, flyers, cloth. His face fluttered everywhere. His face also on Mamá's bedroom window.

Petrona didn't know who the men carrying the coffin were, but they looked important. There were fancy soldiers marching at their sides. The soldiers had a rigid march. Their hats had a golden point. Police with guns held the crowd in place, but they allowed people to throw red and white carnations on the black limousine trailing behind the coffin. The flowers fell on the roof and hood. Petrona said that's where Galán's family probably was — sitting down while people struggled. I told Petrona I guessed it would have been nice for them to walk instead of being in a car, but they had just lost someone. "I wouldn't want to walk if Mamá had just died."

"But you have a choice, niña," Petrona said.

I was looking on the television for Mamá and Cassandra, but there were so many little faces. There were thousands of people hanging from trees, from lampposts, out of windows, boiling in the crowd, men weeping, women chanting. "Who *doesn't* have a choice?" I couldn't take my eyes off the television. All throughout the crowd people were beating white handkerchiefs into the air. It was an ocean of beating white cloth. People were chanting, *"Se vive, se siente, Galán está presente!"* and the white-gloved hands of the fancy soldiers moved rigidly up and down by the coffin.

Then the doorbell rang. "I'll get it!" I pushed off the floor and sprinted down the hall and down the stairs. There was a young man at the door. He had short, afroed hair and sharp cheekbones. His eyes and ears were small, but his lips were large and brown. "Hello," he said. "Is your mami home?" When I didn't answer, he smiled

143

and lifted his eyebrows. "I'm here to fix the carpet." I cocked my head to the side and looked at him. His knees showed through frayed holes in his jeans. He was no carpet guy. I could tell. He was too young, didn't have any tools, not even a duffel bag. I wasn't about to let him in, but Petrona grabbed the door handle behind my back and said Mamá told her somebody was stopping by to measure the carpet. She beheld the carpet guy, pursing her lips to keep a smile from her face. Petrona welcomed him. I didn't stand aside but he pressed in. I grabbed the tail of his flannel shirt and pulled him back, pointing to the welcome mat. "Are you going to wipe your boots? You'll ruin the carpet." His nostrils flared. He set his jaw and wiped his boots. He was grim. Then he smirked.

"Will you sit in the living room?" Petrona asked, but the young man didn't answer and walked into the house in a self-important gait. I didn't know what part of the carpet he was fixing, but once inside, he wandered through the living and dining room and let his small eyes roam over everything — the lights, the paintings, the furniture, the little plates in display easels — everything in fact, except the carpet. He made his way into the kitchen, the indoor patio, Petrona's room, and turned back. He seemed impressed but in a moment his tone changed. "It's cramped like a tuna can in here."

"If you'll have a seat —" Petrona insisted, but the young man paused, suddenly absorbed in studying the stairs. He knelt. When he saw that over the carpeted steps there was a runner, he laughed. "A *carpet* over *another* carpet." Petrona giggled shortly into her hand. The carpet guy knelt at the third step and ran his finger along the golden rod holding the runner in place. His finger was slow along the length of the rod — then he gripped and pulled it with force. He held it in his fist and showed it to us, smiling. He sat on the steps and took out a knife from his pocket and, bending over his work, he scraped the metal. After a while he seemed satisfied and rose to his feet to show me. "It's garbage, look." He scraped the rod with the blade and I saw how gold powder stripped away. He sneered as he placed the crooked rod back in place. Then he bounded up the steps. Petrona and I looked at one another and started behind him. He was lifting a painting that hung on the hall at the top of the stairs, peering behind it like he was expecting a safe to be there. I scoffed and he bowed and swept his hand in front of him like this was his house he was welcoming us to. Petrona frowned and cleared her throat and passed in front of him. As she did, his hand came up and caressed her behind, absentmindedly, like Papá sometimes did with Mamá. Petrona didn't even notice. I was so confused I stood in place, thinking about what I had seen: the knees through the frayed jeans, the rod, his palm caressing Petrona. When I lifted my eyes there were noises in Mamá's room and I raced to see what it was — I passed Petrona, oddly standing halfway up the attic stairs, and then I sprang into Mamá's room, where the carpet guy was crouching and looking under Mamá's bed.

I crossed my arms. "Who are you *really*?"

His voice came muffled. "I told you, little girl. I'm the carpet guy."

"How are you measuring the carpet without measuring tools?"

"I don't *need* measuring tools on account of my lifelong experience in measuring."

"Then why would you grab our maid's behind if you are really just a carpet guy?"

He cackled, laughing into the darkness under Mamá's bed. He shot up. "I didn't touch *your* maid's behind." He spoke close to my face: "Eh? Are you threatening me? Little girl?"

Petrona ran into the room, getting between the carpet guy and me, keeping him back with one arm. "You must have not seen right, niña! We were just walking by each other like normal. You think I would let a stranger grab me?" She turned to the carpet guy, waving the air with her hand, tittering. "Can you imagine?" The carpet guy was instantly appeased and then Petrona said, "Listen, I think it's time for you to leave." He shrugged and said he was done measuring anyway.

His dark caramel eyes bored into me.

Petrona told me she was going to tell Mamá about the carpet guy and that he was surely going to get fired, so I should forget about the whole thing. I nodded. When Mamá and Cassandra got home, I refused to talk to either of them. Cassandra wanted to tell me about the funeral procession, but I didn't want to know. I sat on my bed and sulked and hugged my bandaged arm. I could hear Mamá tearing her Galán posters down.

At night, Mamá knelt by our beds and told us we weren't allowed outside the neighborhood. Which meant Cassandra and I were no longer allowed to pass Elisario's gate and cross the street and go to the stores that sold candy and milkshakes. Mamá said you could never know where there would be a car bomb or men on motorcycles. Men on motorcycles is how Pablo Escobar killed his targets. Bystanders died every day. Mamá seemed sad but I was upset, and I refused to feel sorry for her.

"For how long?" Cassandra asked. Her voice hung in the dark. The moonlight fell on the end of her bed and I saw her feet shift under her blankets.

"Until they find that damned Escobar," Mamá said.

I bit my lip, unable to remain upset after all. "Are we telling Papá?"

She ironed our sheets with her hands and sat cross-legged on the floor between our beds. "He's coming home. We've decided that what you girls need is a little vacation. Won't that be nice? We're going to visit your abuela and spend the holidays there!" Mamá placed each of her hands on our chests. "I heard Abuela has baby rabbits now."

"What are you talking about, Mamá?" Cassandra said. "Final quarter just started."

Mamá laughed. "I talked to the Principal. She's giving us permission to skip it. You'll have make-up work to do when you return, but. You can go."

"But what about my friends, Mamá? You

want me to just *leave*? I'll miss everything!"

"Grow up, Cassandra. Not everything is about you. We're a family. We have to take care of one another."

"That's so typical, every time something happens you run to Abuela."

"What about Petrona?" I asked. "What is she going to do?"

"She's going to her own home, Chula. She has a family of her own, you know. Now go to sleep. I want you to get some rest."

My lids felt heavy. I tried to imagine Petrona's family, but the best I could do was picture a row of little children standing in front of a father and mother, all of them with a Petrona face. Mamá said Petrona's family was twelve total, so I imagined Petrona splintered in eleven. I imagined eleven Petronas mopping the floors, eleven Petronas stirring a pot with a long wooden spoon, nothing in the house because there was nothing for them to lose.

The weight of Mamá's hand on my chest was comforting. Her green veins pulsed under the light of the moon. I felt my mind growing dizzy and heavy. I didn't want to be dead. All it took was a little bad luck. Mamá's veins and their outlines rose in the air and floated there like green branches, and then turned into the waves of a green sea where a lost ship sat bobbing, and where sharks shot up at all sides, their white bellies glistening in the sun. They stayed suspended in the air, their gray tails dripping seawater. Their lips curved down in sadness and parted to mutter incomprehensible things.

PETRONA

I was upset about how Gorrión had behaved at the Santiagos' but the nearness of his body took the air out of mine. *Don't hate me, cielito, I get protective sometimes. I wanted to make sure they're treating you right.* I couldn't stay angry. I didn't tell him in a few days it'd be my birthday, but Gorrión took my hand and brought it to his lips like he knew. *Petrona, how can you stand to be so pretty?*

I stared at my tennis shoes climbing the Hills with Gorrión. *These are the shoes of the girl that could have kept little Ramón alive but did not.* I was not a good person and after thinking about Ramón, I thought about Gorrión and the soft way his lids fell over his eyes. Lids like night, the white of his eyes moonlight. I saw Gorrión clearly in my imagination. I could not remember how Ramón's lids fell over his eyes.

Gorrión wanted justice. *Why do you think*

some bodies are worth more than others? He wanted me to see all the ways I was taken advantage of. He liked to list the things the Santiagos had as opposed to what I had. I listened to him.

We avoided the playground at the top of the Hills where little Ramón was found. Gorrión took me down the path and around to the north end where there were a few trees, and there we sat on a stone. Birds sang and Gorrión stared at my lips. Gorrión had the power to make everything disappear. When I tasted him the only two things in the world were the grit of sand on his lips and his muscular hand at my waist.

Little Aurora covered for me. She sat by the well a few paces away. She did not hear what we did. Gorrión made me tremble and I came back flushed full of the possibility of a future.

Later, Little Aurora cried for her brother. I consoled my girl. I told her what la Señora Alma said to her girls. *When it is time it is time,* though it wasn't true, not for us. I could have kept Ramón safe, had I earned more, had I been able to buy us anything other than pan and gaseosa. I carried the water on the yoke and as we went back to our hut, I wondered if it was an injustice that Ramón had died, and if it was, then who was to blame.

I could not keep a secret in the Hills. Somebody told Mami I had been with Gorrión, and when I entered our hut Mami threw our pots and plastic dishes and plastic plates at me. *How dare you, Petrona, did you forget your brother is dead? He's dead! Your brother is dead! I don't want to see you, go away, I can't even look at you.*

10.
SAFE ROUTES

To visit Abuela María we had to get our driving directions from the newspaper. The headline had read "Safe Routes for the Holiday Break" in boldface and capitals, but when Papá tore out the map, all that was left was a string of illegible half letters. The letters spread ornamentally atop the birdlike map of Colombia. In the car Papá said the reason there were safe routes was because of Pablo Escobar and his men, or as they called themselves, *los Extraditables.* I didn't know Pablo Escobar had a group. I asked Papá if they played instruments, but Papá said they were not *that* kind of group: rather, they wrote letters to the press, left missives on the radio, and took credit for car bombs and kidnappings. Papá said the only thing los Extraditables feared was going to prison in the United States, where nobody spoke their language and they would let them die like dogs. Papá said they had a motto: *We prefer a tomb in Colombia to a jail in the United States.*

Cassandra had one earphone in, the other she was holding in her hand, rock music quietly buzzing from it. She explained that Pablo Escobar was the president of the narco-paramilitary — to me — *as if I didn't already know.*

"Yes, but did you know he's a *baron*?" I asked.

"Yes, but did *you* know he's a judge killer?" I didn't have a comeback and was forced to remain quiet as Cassandra nodded with her eyebrows raised long after she had spoken.

The road out of Bogotá climbed between buildings with bay windows and marble surfaces, then snaked through the cold moor of Suba, where rainwater puddled in the grasslands and mirrored the sky. There were cows and horses eating the valleys.

Papá said, "In all the history of this country, there hasn't been *one* newspaper that has printed a map with safe routes before now. Not *one.*" I could see him in the rearview mirror. Earlier that morning, Papá told Mamá he wasn't sure if he was fired, having left the oil site in such a hurry, but he had paid vacation days and would find a job in the meantime if need be. Now, he seemed at ease. He ran his fingers over the wiry, thick fur of his mustache. I felt anxious not knowing if Papá had a job; then I remembered Petrona wearing Mamá's slippers. I leaned forward to the middle between the front seats to ask if anyone had noticed. I opened my mouth, but then I realized I could get Petrona fired. Everyone stared. "Did we buy Petrona a Christmas present?"

Papá glanced at Mamá.

"Oh, no, we forgot!" Mamá said. "Let's get her nice perfume though. I'll bet she'll like it."

I sat back thinking I was right in not sharing what I had seen Petrona do. It was possible after all that Petrona slipped on Mamá's house shoes at the last minute to go out to the garden to see why the car's headlights were on and nobody was coming into the house. But why had she been in our house?

Papá said, "What in the world would a girl like Petrona do with perfume?"

Mamá rolled her eyes. "You never understand anything, Antonio."

Either way Petrona had fixed my arm and stayed with me during Galán's funeral when Mamá and Cassandra left. Telling my family about Petrona would only cause them to judge her unfairly.

All in all I liked the attention I got from my sprained arm. I liked the way everyone talked to me now: softly, like I could break. I got a lot of attention at school too over what had happened in Soacha. I had two versions. The one I told teachers blurred over important details and ended with what I thought they wanted to hear — "And it was at *that* moment, when I realized how *fragile* life really is." It was the kind of rubbish teachers pointed out in the stories we read, and, if we were asked to write a reading response it was that same rubbish that, if quoted, got you the highest grade.

The other version I told was hushed and energetic, and delivered with every other word emphasized: "Right *up* until the *gunshots* the *band* played *merengue.*" That one I told to my classmates, who surrounded me under the trees by the playground. "The *news* didn't say *this* — but *Pablo Escobar* was there, *in flesh and blood.* I saw his *face* lit up by the *fire* of his own *machine gun.*" Kids from the higher grades came to listen. Girls I didn't know bought me candy, and different classmates volunteered to take notes for me because of my bandaged arm. On the last day before Cassandra and I left, the Principal singled us out at the general assembly and gave us a diploma. *Bravery,* it said, and underneath there was her squiggly signature in blue ink. Everybody sang the national anthem, but I sang it loudest of all.

Both versions of the story I told were lies, probably because the truth was more difficult to tell. What was the truth? Something horrible had happened. A man had been killed.

Maybe it wasn't so difficult after all.

"You know there *were* safe routes during the time of La Violencia," Papá said. Mamá placed her black swooping hat over her face and we descended the great mountain Bogotá is on. When the road flattened, the air was so hot we nearly couldn't breathe. We begged Papá to turn on the air conditioner but Papá yelled that driving with air-conditioning cost more money. We rolled down our windows and the wind pummeled against my ears. Papá was nervous.

He was driving, glancing at the little newspaper map, mumbling directions to himself. His lower lip unglued from his mustache and flashed his lower, coffee-stained teeth; then he glanced at the road. The wind shook the map in his fingers.

Mamá awoke as if from a dream. She

158

lifted the rim of her wide hat and studied Papá. Then reclining, resting her small feet with red nail polish on the dashboard, she said, "Either you pull over, Antonio, or you keep your eyes on the road."

Papá pushed the map into Mamá's hands, "We can't pull over, Alma, use your head!" But Mamá didn't help. She opened the glove compartment. She fingered the door pockets, then the sleeves behind the front seats. Papá was yelling. Mamá was searching under her seat when she sat up triumphantly, a roll of clear tape in her hand. She taped the map above the steering wheel on the windshield. Papá shook his head and exhaled. He sat back and turned on his music while Mamá got out her red nail polish, and seeing everything was all right again, I lay down on the seat and fell asleep, the wind pounding hotly on my face.

During our two days of travel, the corners of the little map yellowed and hummed with wind. At the roadside stops I sat in the driver's seat to study it. It was printed in black and white. The areas populated by guerrillas were colored in black and were lorded over by men of different sizes holding rifles against their chests. The men had sunglasses on and wore berets on their heads. There were two small men just outside of Bogotá in the heart of the country and a medium-sized one next to Cúcuta. The bigger men clasped their weapons in the Amazon jungle and along the coastline of the Pacific Ocean.

I traced my finger along the safe route from Bogotá to Cúcuta in the upper eastern shoulder, and read aloud the towns on the way: *Chía, Tunja, Paipa, Málaga, Pamplona.* The route was the eastern highway. All around it, small roads ebbed in dashes. The dashes stood for danger. Just underneath the map a legend read, "Never take an unfamiliar road. Guerrillas could ambush your car. Please take care of your loved ones."

Cassandra was biting her nails. She said she could outsmart the guerrillas if they ever tried to kidnap her. She was, after all, first in her class. She shook her head importantly and settled again in her seat, black hair feathered out over her chocolate shoulders. "My history teacher says most guerrilleros haven't gone past the fourth grade, and *I'm* in fifth." Her white sneakers squeaked against the vinyl seat and her thigh muscles twitched.

My eyes widened as I turned to look out the window. *I* was in third.

Papá must have seen my horror because

he said that if I wanted to be helpful, I could keep a lookout for roadblocks, which were often guerrilla fronts. I nodded, thinking that if I spotted them before they did us, we could escape them. I scanned the rushing, snaking roads ahead and craned my neck at the curves to see past what was hidden by the palm trees and giant rocks.

"Even if something happened," Papá said, "your papá can take the guerrillas. Or didn't I tell you girls about the day I killed a boa constrictor with my bare hands? Eh, chicas? You were too little to remember."

We nodded, but Papá told the story anyway.

Mamá, Cassandra, and I were five steps behind him when he saw a snake sliding into a bush. He held the tail, pulled the snake out, and swung the boa against a tree.

According to Mamá, it was true that Papá had spotted the snake, but it was the hiking guide who killed it. He happened to shoot it with a rifle. All Papá had done was slice the boa's head off with a machete after it was dead. *Just in case,* he had said.

What neither of them said is how Papá hung the snake body on a tree branch and made Cassandra and me squeeze it. It was the only part of the story I truly remembered: the ribbed, hard skin of the boa, pat-

161

terned in tan circles and dark brown diamonds, warm like a bag filled with soggy dough when you pinched it, but eerie when you took your hand away and the skin bounced back in place.

At night Diomedes Díaz played on repeat in the car cassette player. Diomedes Díaz over accordion, piano, congas, and a back chorus, singing "My First White Hair," "The Soul of an Accordion," "Womanizing," "The Cow and the Bull," "You Are the Queen," and "The Fault Was Yours." Papá was the only person in the car who liked Diomedes Díaz. He said he needed the support of a man even if through a cassette player, in order to deal with the woman-viper Mamá had turned out to be.

In the back of the car, I looked for roadblocks on and off, but on our way from the gray, sleek city, through the mountains heavy with fog; to the roadside cliffs with rivers and wet grass bobbing in misty beds; to the plains with dry wind and yellow weeds; to Abuela's home in Cúcuta in El Salado, the Salted Place, we never encountered a single one.

11.
EL SALADO

Abuela's house stood at the end of the dirt road as if a portal between two worlds: the forest hills rose behind her house, and in front the dirt road zigzagged down, lined with adobe houses and dingy auto shops. The people of El Salado sat in plastic chairs all along the road and stared after our car: rust free, shiny from rain and sun, city license plates. When we pulled up to Abuela's, men who had been playing a game of chess at the corner froze. As we got out of our car, the men rose to their feet. Papá waved and the men flexed their muscles in return. I was dripping in sweat and faint from the heat. I kicked my shoes on Abuela's door. Mamá bent down to fix her kitten-heels and said, "The invasión is more and more respectable, no? One day this will all be condominiums!" Cassandra lifted her brows like she wanted to say something snarky but then she kept quiet. She was

163

probably too hot and tired. Papá was staring the men down.

The invasión hadn't actually changed since last year when we visited, but maybe it seemed that way to Mamá because she remembered El Salado when it was just people in huts. El Salado wasn't named that because of luck; rather there was a salt mine nearby. You wouldn't know it was there, but Papá said some streets were sinking because of the underground tunnels.

Mamá's family was the first to settle in El Salado. They had been forced to abandon their farmland just to the north because of the paramilitary. Abuela hated the paramilitary. They burned down good land for no reason. And she had seen them bury bodies underneath the cement of roads so they would never be found. Mamá said Abuela packed their mules crying and together the family walked south until they found unoccupied land. Abuela and Abuelo did what they knew how to do — they cleared a spot, planted seeds, built a shack out of cane. They started to keep chickens and hunt for food. There was no mail, electricity, or water, but Mamá said it all felt like an adventure, like they were the only people on earth. Then more people came. Some of the new people were criminals, but mostly they were displaced families.

To me, El Salado had a beauty all its own. The chipped paint, the adobe houses, the land filled with people's gardening. I wasn't allowed out but I wasn't interested anyway. The building next to Abuela's was a brothel and there were leering men along the dirt road, and, besides, Mamá said there was a chance I could be mistaken for a prostitute. Once, a man tried luring Cassandra behind a bush, telling her there was a baby bird on the ground. But Cassandra is no fool so she yelled for Papá and the man took off running.

There was a sign painted on the front of the brothel. It read *Food and Dine* in fading cursive, but there was no doorway — only a garage door that rolled up. Cassandra and I had once seen women in rushes of blond hair and stilettos galloping out of the garage door into army-green jeeps. *"Those are prostitutes,"* Cassandra whispered. It was New Year's Eve and Papá and the tíos were setting off fireworks and everyone on the street was dancing. The women climbed into the jeep and settled in the arms of shadowy men and Abuela, who was standing behind us, said, "Women down on their luck, that's all they are."

At Abuela's door, I heard the metal click

and clack of the locks, and then the door peeled back and there was Abuela trembling and grinning. "Mis niñas," she said, bringing us deeply into her arms. Abuela was short and stout, seemingly fragile, but her body was sinewy and strong. She patted our heads, then walked to Mamá and Papá, reaching her hands to them, her whole body vibrating. Cassandra tapped my shoulder and signaled with her head toward Abuela's open door. Together we made little noise and took single back steps. Papá had an arm around Mamá. He was counting on his fingers, saying, ". . . the insecurity, the taxes, and the changes of the neighborhood." When Cassandra and I took the last back step into Abuela's house, we ran in circles and howled and hooted.

Mamá yelled, "Cassandra! Chula! Have you turned into beasts? Don't touch Abuela's things!"

"And don't let the dogs in the garden!" Abuela called. "They'll kill my chickens!" We heard Papá's voice resume, his tenor swift and steady, accompanied by Abuela's croaky, slow voice.

Abuela ran a store out of the front room of her house. She hung a curtain over the hallway that led to the rest of the house, so that her living quarters could not be seen

166

from the store. Abuela's store changed with every New Year. At the beginning of the year products were sold at a discount and new ones were bought, organized, and priced. I wanted to investigate, but Cassandra wanted to look for the baby rabbits. We went through the curtain into the main room, ran past the kitchen, and outside into the garden.

Abuela's garden was like a jungle. There was a clearing and a footpath, and we had to fend off the overgrowth of trees and bushes and step over tree roots. Mosquitoes swarmed our heads, and when my skin flared with the feeling of them biting I ran back inside. Abuela's dogs barked and leapt around me. I worried Cassandra was being eaten alive by the mosquitoes, but then I realized there was no one around and I could snoop freely.

All over Abuela's house it smelled like air that had been trapped for years, even though there were open doors and windows everywhere. In the main room the walls were bare except for two painted, old pictures. One was of Abuelo and the other of Abuela. We were not allowed to talk about Abuelo because he had left Abuela for another woman, but nobody could stop me from studying his portrait. His hair was black and he wore a high white collar. He was handsome, but what I couldn't believe was that Abuela had once been so beautiful. She wore rouge on her cheeks and her hair came up at the ends and a purple top with pretty pearl buttons closed along her throat. It was shocking to think of Abuela's face now in comparison: wrinkled and pockmarked by time, her eyes tough and flat. You could really appreciate the portraits from Abuela's rocking chair. That's where Abuela sat in the afternoon. Mamá said Abuela sat there only to curse Abuelo and the woman he left her for, blaming them for taking her youth. Mamá said Abuela liked to gaze at the paintings when she was in pain from her swollen feet — the more she could behold Abuelo in disgust. Cassandra said Abuelo had another family, but it never really mattered to me, because it's not like I could miss what I never had.

Mamá had recently told me that Petrona's father didn't live with them in the invasión. Maybe Petrona's father left her family too. I was about to lower myself into the rocking chair when Papá, Mamá, Cassandra, and Abuela came into the room.

Abuela wagged her finger. "Don't you sit there." Mamá pulled me to her and wouldn't let go of my wrist. Cassandra stuck out her tongue. We went down a hall of closed doors. Abuela had built the hall herself, making the bricks out of adobe, one room for each of her five children. Mamá's sandals slapped on the concrete floor and the sound of Papá wheeling our two suitcases grumbled on behind us and echoed. Abuela had ended up owning the land not because she bought it but because if you lived anywhere for longer than twenty years, it automatically became yours, or at least the government didn't ask questions.

Mamá pointed to a room on my left. "A man died in that room." Abuela walked ahead, her hands touching the walls for balance. One of Mamá's favorite pastimes was to scandalize Cassandra and me. Papá said it was because Mamá had been a young mother, and young mothers never grew up. "Be a *mother*, Alma!" Papá often said when Mamá started on us with her ghost stories, but this time, he remained quiet. When I looked behind, he seemed absorbed in his own thinking. "A stranger," Mamá continued. "He came a month ago in the middle of the night asking for shelter. He was a traveler. He was dead by morning."

The room Mamá was pointing at had its door open. It was stuffed with old furniture and a hospital bed. Cassandra pressed against me and I pressed against Mamá, flushed with fear. Abuela stopped at the end of the hall and held the door open to Mamá's old room. There was still some furniture from when she was a girl.

"Here, Alma?"

Abuela offered Cassandra and me our own rooms, but we didn't want to sleep alone with the menace of the dead stranger. In Mamá's old room there was a large bed with a mesh canopy hanging over it from a wire-circle at the top. It was there for the mosquitoes. A ceiling fan set the canopy in rolling motion. There were no windows, and an old blue desk stood at the corner. It occurred to me that if the fan fell while we slept, it would chop and kill everyone. At the funeral, I would wear a black veil and stand at the pedestal of the church. Behind me the four coffins containing the remains of Abuela and my family would stand in shadow while I received the mourners with one hand — my *other* hand, dismembered by the ceiling fan blade, would lie wrapped in black tulle inside a small coffin marked, *Here lies the hand of Chula Santiago, courageous survivor.* Petrona would give me a white rose and then we would ride away together in a black limousine.

In the bedroom, Papá exhaled loudly. He

propped up our suitcases and set our backpacks on the floor and said, "Yes, this will
do."

At Abuela's I felt happy in extremes. I sat in
the sunlight until I was burning and then I
ran to Abuela's bathroom and dumped
buckets of cold water on myself. The shower
in Abuela's bathroom wasn't really a shower
but a corner where the tiles sloped down
around a drain, and a tall blue barrel stood
filled with water. In the first shock of water,
I gasped and was unable to breathe. It's
hard to say why such a thing brought me
happiness. Maybe it was the burning sensa-
tion of cold after hot, or the anxious joy
with which I gasped for air, or the feeling of
being very much alive, or maybe it was the
way in which the sensations were a short
circuit to the kinds of things I worried
about: Petrona eating from the fruit of the
Drunken Tree, Pablo Escobar smiling in his
Hawaiian shirt, Galán bleeding on the
podium. My days filled with sensations: hot,
cold, drowning, breathing.

Cassandra and I were not allowed to go in
Abuela's store, but we lifted the curtain in
the living room to look. There, under the
single lightbulb dangling from the ceiling,
we would see Abuela taking money from a

customer, sitting on a stool, organizing her wares, sweeping the floor. I told Cassandra I bet Petrona would have liked to see Abuela's store, and Cassandra blinked several times at me. "Who cares, Chula, get a life."

We felt wild at Abuela's. Our classmates were back home taking finals while we were already on vaction, wearing our swimsuits thin, daring each other to stand in front of the room where the stranger had died. The seconds grew as the days passed until we stood in front of the room for a full minute. Cassandra said she could hear someone breathing. Sometimes she saw eyes that hovered above the dirty hospital bed. They were green.

As always when we visited Abuela, Mamá's sister Tía Inés came to visit with her husband, Ramiro, and our cousins Tica and Memo. Tía Inés lived a few blocks away but we never went to her house, I wasn't sure why. Either it was a worse place than Abuela's, or Tía Inés had never invited us. Cassandra thought it was the latter because she had inferred (from years of overheard hints and insults flung during sisterly fights) that a man had once impregnated Tía Inés and that Papá had refused to recommend this man for a job. What had happened to the man? Where was the baby? Neither of us knew. What we knew for sure is that when Mamá and Tía Inés got together things got tense. "What are those sandals you're wearing, Inés, why don't I take you shopping?" "Aren't you a mother of two, Alma? It's time you start wearing blouses like a lady. You're not twenty anymore."

Cassandra and I dragged our little cousins away. Tica and Memo were a year younger so we played tag. Memo was always stuck being it because we easily outran him. We had so much time between his chasing us we climbed up trees. Memo stood under the tree where Tica straddled a big branch and told her she needed to come down because there was a tick on her leg. I smirked at Memo to let him know I admired his cunning, but when Tica came down he really lit a candle and held the flame to Tica's skin and Cassandra and I watched in horror as a little animal crawled out.

In Abuela's garden while Tió Ramiro and Papá got manly and sumo-squatted around a dug-out hole where they were going to create the perfect conditions for a small fire, Tía Inés made Cassandra and me press our hands on her pregnant stomach. It was spongy and had something like eels moving inside it. We were polite and forced grins onto our faces, but then we kept our distance from her "miracle of life."

We sat under the mango tree. After the fire was roaring, Papá tuned the radio to a cumbia station. The adults danced. They held their glasses aloft, making the aguardiente swirl, swinging their hips side to side. Abuela shuffled her feet slowly and lifted her face to the moon. My head began to drop and bob in place, and I caught glimpses of the circling feet, the sound of the hypnotic flute, Abuela's smiling face as I dreamed or awakened.

Tica and Memo slept over during the weekends with Cassandra and me in Mamá's old room. I was usually the last to wake, but one morning I pushed Tica aside and felt like I would die. My arm was so hot I had to unwind the bandage. When the last of the bandage came away, I was sick: the skin was slick and green like a zombie arm. I ran to show someone but then I got dizzy and sat in the living room sweating under the ceiling fan. Somebody had left the radio on.

"The magnicides of now *three* presidential candidates has escalated the hunt for Pablo Escobar. Meanwhile, the Extraditables have released a statement that they will lay down their weapons." I gasped in surprise and

Papá came in.

"Chula, what are you doing?"

"Papá, I'm dying." I dropped to the floor and put my cheek against the cool tile. I was too hot. He took a look at my arm and told me it was just bruised and I was not dying. He said there was a heat wave and I should do everything he said. "Okay, but what's a magnicide?" I asked.

"What?"

"Are the Extraditables laying down their weapons?"

"Chula —" Papá put his arms up and walked away. He got Tica and Memo and Cassandra and me together and we spent the day sucking on ice and folding fans made out of paper. We wore our swimsuits and got wet and stood directly in front of the fan. Immediately we felt better. Cassandra and I spoke to Tica and Memo through the whirr of the fan. Through the fan, our voices became alien voices. We sang, "Arroz con leche me quiero casar . . . Con una señorita de la capital."

When it got late, we lined up for the bathroom to get wet once more before sleep. Drops of sweat trickled down my neck. I awaited my turn on the couch directly under Abuela's living room fan. I was bored so I picked up the phone and dialed home.

It was something I did when we traveled, knowing that since nobody would pick up it wouldn't cost any money. I listened to the elongated ring, sitting in the dark in Abuela's living room, imagining the cool of Bogotá — the drafty stairs, the dark hallway, the kitchen, the icy cans of orange soda in the fridge.

"Aló?"

I sat up. That was Petrona. But Petrona didn't have a telephone in her home.

"Aló?" Petrona said again, then to someone else, "They're not saying anything. Should I hang up?"

"No, just wait. Maybe it's a bad connection." This last I heard dimly, like the voice came from a can, but I could hear that it was a boy's voice.

I cleared my throat. "Petrona, is that you?"

There was silence, then, "Niña? Niña —"

"Hang up, hang up now," the boy said in the background, but Petrona spoke over him: "Oh my god, Chula! So nice to hear from you! I've missed you! Is there anyone with you? Why are you calling?"

I looked around the room. Abuela's black Labrador was drumming his tail at my feet, but there was no one in the main room. Down the hall in the kitchen I could hear Mamá and Abuela getting Tica and Memo ready for bed. "No, there's no one with me, but —"

"Chula, listen to me. I'm in danger. I mean I'm in hiding. But you can't tell anyone because I have nowhere to go."

"You mean someone's after you?"

"Don't tell anyone. Niña? Not even your sister. Do you swear? Not your mother either." The receiver was hot against my ear. Petrona leveled her voice: "I mean it when I say I'm in danger. You don't want to end up with my blood on your hands. Do you? Niña?"

Her words brought bile to the back of my throat. "But are you okay now?"

"Swear on your mother's life. Niña? For your own protection. I can't tell you more, but I'll be safe as long as you don't say anything."

I swore on Mamá's life. Petrona said she had to hang up because she needed to keep the phone line open and I replaced the phone, thinking what a serious thing it was to swear on someone's life. I wondered what Petrona could be running away from; then it hit me that the boy in the background had not been just any boy, but the guy who Petrona had brought to our house on the excuse that he was measuring the carpet. Maybe he was Petrona's boyfriend, but why had she chosen such a brute for a boyfriend? I knew you couldn't break an oath, there were stories of mothers being struck dead by lightning. I felt the weight of what I had promised to Petrona sinking into me like an anchor. I stretched my shoulders back, but the weight was still there. I began to have trouble breathing, and then Mamá came to tell me it was my turn to get wet in the bathroom. She looked into my face. "You okay, mi cielo?"

"I'm too hot," I lied. I didn't want Mamá to die. I didn't want Petrona's blood on my hands either. Mamá felt my forehead with the back of her hand and said I would feel better once I got wet. She left me alone in Abuela's bathroom, and though the barrel looked nearly empty, I dumped two buckets of cold water on myself.

I was breathing normally again, and I sat on the tiles, relieved. I closed my eyes, thankful for the blood thumping in my body, thankful for Mamá's life, and I imagined Petrona's blood thumping in her body too, and I felt like we were all joined in some way and whatever was wrong in Petrona's life she needed me and I would help her.

PETRONA

When Mami kicked me out I looked for
Gorrión. I zigzagged through the Hills. I
did not know where he lived. Nobody did. I
went to the playground. Kids playing soccer
in the flat patch of dirt did not answer when
I asked after Gorrión. I had nowhere to go.
I stared at the bushes where little Ramón
was found. A little boy appeared next to me.
You know who he is, right? His cheeks were
covered in dust. I guessed he slept on the
streets. I waited for him to see my face and
say he had mistaken me for somebody.
Instead he asked, *You're Petrona, right?* I
widened my eyes. *Terrible thing. About
Ramón. My name's Julián.* He spit on the
ground and dug his hands into the pockets
of his dirt-caked jeans. He stared at the
retaining wall. *You know who he's involved
with, right?* I wanted to say, *Who do you
mean.* Finally Julián touched his finger to
his temple and said, *As long as you know.*

He trotted downhill. He gave a high whistle, and then a three-legged dog came running from under the bushes where Ramón had been found.

Wait! I called. *Do you mean Ramón? Or do you mean Gorrión?* I cringed from hearing Ramón's name in that place where he had been dumped and I stared at the boy and dog running together on the path kicking up dust, and then Julián stopped in his tracks and yelled up, *Come back at dusk, you'll see him then!*

For a wild moment I pictured Ramón would rise at dusk from the dead and I could see him here, but the next moment I bit into my hand. Dusk at the playground was when the encapotados met to walk to the mountain where they had meetings. All of us in the Hills knew because we heard their singing, always the song about the international working class echoing down the mountain. If you wanted to avoid the encapotados you did not come to the playground at dusk, and I knew Julián had meant Gorrión: *come back at dusk and you'll see Gorrión,* and I was once again lost and alone, just me, only me, left to figure out how to keep the rest of the little ones safe and in school, and little Aurora from the path I was following even now.

12.
DEVILWIND

When Abuela turned the knob of the water barrels the next day, not a drop came out. Tica and Memo were the only ones awake so Abuela took up their hands and told them they were going on a walk to the grocery store to order some more. Mamá woke me up and said Abuela and Tica and Memo should be back in a few hours. She took me to the cement tank in the garden to cool down. It was rectangular and rose up to my neck. I stood shoulder-deep inside the tank. It was filled with rainwater and Abuela's orange fish. Before the drought Abuela had used it as a laundry tub (it had a cement-cast washboard on the side), but now she washed her clothes in the river.

Mamá sat on the washboard, pouring water over my head with a blue plastic cup, telling me her dream, but I wasn't listening. I was watching the orange fish. They darted underneath my armpits. They circled the bright pink torso of my swimsuit. They horded around me like small gelatinous mice, tapping my skin, then scattering. On the ground there were ants traveling over the cobblestones in two highways: eastward to Abuela's kitchen, westward carrying crumbs. The cobblestones led to Abuela's overgrown garden and, past where I could see, to a metal door that led out to the hot forest hills of Cúcuta. Far away in the hills there was thunder; but it was early.

I took in a big breath and went underwater. I curved my back and waded past Mamá's legs into the space underneath the washboard. I could touch all the walls, but not the ground, dropped at an angle. If I pushed my hands against the underside of the washboard the tips of my toes did not catch. The only light came in beams from the opening by Mamá's legs, where fish swept their tails back and forth and fanned their fins, swimming through the bright columns of green, murky light.

I gathered up my legs and I let my back bounce lightly against the underside of the washboard. It was a magical, lonely feeling.

I was the eye-center.

The beat of my heart thumped thickly in my ears, like an old sound, floating.

When I opened my eyes, Mamá's legs had

disappeared. The fish, too, had scattered. I came up and gasped for air and saw Mamá running down the cobblestones to the back of the garden, the blue plastic cup dangling stupidly in her hand.

We didn't fully know what had happened that day until many years later, when Abuela told the story. Abuela said it began with slow walking, with Tica and Memo taking her hands in theirs and supporting her as they went.

Once, Mamá had taken Cassandra and me through the footpath. It was thick with trees that buzzed with animals like in a jungle. The air smelled like overripe mangoes. The footpath led to a valley of yellowing trees and dry cracked earth, and after the forest, it opened to a buzzing highway and a grocery store with a lopsided sign that read *Arabastos.* It was a footpath Abuela had taken for years and as far as she knew it was safe.

Here's how Abuela remembers it happened: they were halfway to the store, and the path ahead was bathed in sunlight, then shadow, then sunlight. She felt the bite of a mosquito on her leg. There was the cawing, whistling, and cackling of birds. And then, a sound. "Do you hear that?" Memo said. The

183

sound of the thing they could not see approached them. It came closer, near, just above their heads. Helicopters. Between the tree branches above them. Two of them swinging into view. Flashing their landing skids and tossing the leaves of palm trees like loose tongues. Air thundered in the trees and Abuela's dress flapped with wind.

Abuela watched as Tica and Memo followed the helicopters with their fingers, drawing lines and arcs in the sky. It was a good thing for children to laugh. When the helicopters disappeared over the tree-crest, Abuela wondered why there would be helicopters in this part of the forest, but she couldn't think. Then the helicopters appeared behind them. The wind was deafening, and in the distance, at the bend of the path, a group of guerrillas burst out of the bushes. Abuela understood the helicopters were there for these men and women, but she froze. She stared at the first camouflaged man, bounding toward her, machine gun to his chest, the red of his mouth standing out from the dark green painted on his face. He saw her, but then his face lifted, and sparks crackled out of the mouth of his machine gun. The devilwind of the helicopters lifted the leaves from the ground and sent them wheeling in the air as the helicopters dove, firing at the guerrillas. The guerrillas yelled at Abuela, *Get out of the way!* and other things, but Abuela's mind was blank with fear. Abuela felt Tica and Memo pulling at her dress, and then she remembered herself and summoning flexibility and strength from a secret padlock of maternal love, Abuela picked Tica and Memo up and threw herself behind a thorny bush. She landed on top of Tica and Memo and gripped them intensely against the ground. The helicopters flew over the path again and again, firing, wind squeezing Abuela down, grass lashing at her face, Tica and Memo sobbing and covering their ears. Behind the thorny bush, Abuela heard sounds that would never leave her: the popping of machine guns, the helicopters, soldiers screaming. There were sparks kicking up dust around them, shots swallowed by the earth. Abuela cried and prayed to the Virgin Mary for their well-being, their paths rid from evil, their safe return. Then she put her face down.

Even after the screaming and the bursts of artillery faded, disappearing eastward, where the jungle grew thick, Abuela could not move. She breathed the wet scent of the earth. Against the ground, Abuela listened to the cries of Tica and Memo. Beneath that, she still heard the chopping wind, the gunshots, the screaming like it was still coming from the middle of her chest. Time passed with Memo whimpering. Then Abuela pawed over Tica's and Memo's bodies feeling for blood, not knowing if they had been shot. Abuela thought Memo was bleeding. She thought it was blood. But her hand came away clear, and when she smelled it, she understood it was urine that dripped from the crotch of Memo's red shorts to the ground. Tica cried and gasped for air, sucking on her thumb.

Somehow Abuela straightened her legs, stood, and came out from behind the bush. She was sure there would be dead bodies, but the forest was empty. Abuela fell on her knees and called out in gratitude to the Virgin, but she was startled by the shrill sound of her own voice. There were cactus thorns stuck to their bodies. Tica screamed at the lines of red and drips of blood like dew in them. Abuela picked the thorns from her granddaughter, and then her grandson.

Along the walk home there was silence. They huddled and walked as a single being. They startled at the smallest sounds and looked about them, sensing the whites of the soldiers' eyes lunging at them from behind the brush.

Outside her house, lonely palm trees swayed with wind.

Abuela said that it was only when they stepped inside that the sound of things roaring into the sky stopped.

In the back of Abuela's garden, I stood for a moment deaf and out of breath. Abuela's back rose and fell like an embittered sea and Tica and Memo were covered in blood. Mamá had her arms around the three of them and Abuela was saying, "Ay, Alma, Alma. They shot at us, Alma!"

Mamá's voice came out muffled against Abuela's shoulder. "But who, Mamá? Who shot at you?"

"The guerrillas!" Abuela cried. "Dios Santo!" Then Abuela's voice trailed off in a murmured prayer; then audible, then silent, then pronounced among choked wails.

On the grass by Mamá's feet the blue plastic cup lay on its side.

Drops of water ran down my pink swimsuit and rapped against the dry leaves on the ground.

Mamá's eyes lifted. "Chula," she said. "Get Cassandra. Call Tía Inés. Tell Inés to come. Go quickly."

I turned and ran through the flowers and the beds of vegetables that blurred in my vision: away from the sound of Tica's and Memo's crying: musical, fading. I ran past lettuce heads, herbs, tomatoes, dandelions; past the free-roaming rooster perched on a pole; the old turkey, startled, garbling and running to a bush.

I ran onto the cobblestone path and found Cassandra there, kneeling at the corner of Abuela's house, drawing hills and rivers with blue chalk on the wall. She stood up as I came upon her and she grabbed me by the shoulders.

"Chula, what is it?"

I caught my breath. "Cassandra," I said, "hurry. Call Tía Inés. Abuela, Tica, and Memo are bleeding."

"What?" Cassandra shook me. "What happened?"

"They got shot," I said. "Hurry, tell Tía Inés to come."

"Are they alive?"

I nodded and followed Cassandra running to the house. In the living room, the rotary phone winded and unwinded slowly with each number.

Cassandra said, "Tía Inés. Come to Abuela's. Something's happened."

An exclaimed protest echoed from the telephone against Cassandra's ear.

"Tía, just come."

We waited by the window. Cassandra bit her lip. "How bad is it?" she asked, but she shook her head and covered her ears so I wouldn't tell her. Her fingers were stained blue from the chalk. When Mamá came in with Abuela and Tica and Memo we ran to them and they collapsed on the ground. Memo wheezed against my arms and Tica buried her face in Cassandra's shoulder. Memo's tears and saliva dripped down my arm, but I was filled with anxiety watching Tica. Her mouth was hanging open like it was unhinged. Cassandra was holding Tica as she wailed, and Cassandra's face gathered up in sadness, but Cassandra was staring at Abuela, who cried into her own lap.

Two years before the helicopters, after Tío Pieto was put in the ground and dirt was thrown over his coffin, Papá had said Abuela María couldn't cry anymore because she was old. At the funeral, Abuela held yellow carnations and murmured somber prayers. She looked out at me from behind her black veil. She twitched the ends of her lips and tried to smile.

"Tell me, Mamá, try," my mother said to Abuela. Abuela was taking big breaths and letting them out slowly through her thin, pursed lips. Her hands trembled in front of her mouth.

She began slowly, "I took them to come with me to Arabastos."

Then her face shrank. She shook her head of short, gray curls, sucked in air, and began to cry. She covered her face with her wrinkled hands.

At Tío Pieto's funeral, Papá had said that when people became old, they couldn't bring themselves to cry anymore, because they had cried continually, on and off, over a lifetime long with happiness and sorrow. He had said their bank of tears had gone dry.

"For the love of God, Mamá, calm yourself down," Mamá said. She was shaking Abuela's hands. "You're traumatizing the children." I bit my upper lip and looked down at the lap of Memo's pants. His lap was wet. I connected the sight with the smell of urine.

Abuela said, "They ran out of the trees." She took a deep breath. "A helicopter was shooting after the guerrillas. We hid behind a bush."

Then her voice broke, and in a high pitch she said, "Alma, if only I hadn't taken them, Alma!"

That's when we heard the front door open and Tía Inés came running through the curtain and gathered her children to her chest. "What happened?" She inspected their faces and felt with her hands over their bodies. She shook them violently, "What happened to you?" Tica and Memo sobbed, convulsing against her. But they could not answer.

"Inés — you're hurting the children," Mamá said.

Tía Inés took her hands away. There were red marks on Tica's and Memo's skin from her nails, but Tica and Memo were fighting to get close to Tía Inés again.

"They were in the crossfire of guerrillas," Mamá said, "when they went with Abuela to Arabastos."

"Hija," Abuela said, scrunching her face like she was about to cry, but Tía Inés bared her teeth. "How could you, Mamá? After all the rumors?" Abuela was quiet. Tía Inés lifted Tica and Memo up against her waist. "I don't want to hear from you. Any of you." Tía Inés walked out slowly, Tica and Memo wrapping their legs around her pregnant torso, quietly sobbing. We heard the front door close, and then Tica's and Memo's crying faded out.

"Mamá —"

Mamá helped Abuela rise to her feet. "Not now, Chula."

"Cassandra —"

Cassandra pushed herself up. "Chula, be quiet."

I stayed on the floor. I watched Mamá dial Tía Inés. It sounded like a huge commotion, like Tío Ramiro screaming in the background and Tica and Memo crying, then I heard clearly as Tía Inés yelled how come only *her* children were taken to Arabastos, how come not Mamá's. There was the dead sound of the line. Mamá dialed the town store where Papá was sending résumés and left a message with the clerk for Papá to return as soon as possible. I could still see Tica's face without trying. I wiped my eyes.

There were three bloodstains on the cement where Tica and Abuela and Memo had sat. Then I looked at myself. There on the caramel skin of my shoulders was the print of my sister's fingers, pressed on me in blue chalk.

PETRONA

I questioned Gorrión again and again because of what Julián had told me, but Gorrión swore he was not involved with the guerrillas; if anything, he sympathized with the encapotados but *that* wasn't a crime. I cried out and asked if he did not know that was why Ramón was dead, and Gorrión said Ramón was dead because of the Colombian army, who had also shot countless innocent boys in the Hills. *Don't get confused, Petrona.* In Gorrión's presence thoughts went from my mind, things flipped upside down, but I could not be confused about little Ramón. *Ramón was killed by the paras! Why else did we have to call the police! If the army had done it, they would have been there from the beginning, claiming the death of a guerrillero like they always do.*

I was confident in that truth, but then Gorrión's words were like dust that rolled under my doorstep and covered everything with dirt. *Petrona, think. How long did Ramón have — when a country's own army shoots innocent civilians? Wasn't he protecting his own family? Didn't little Ramón think his younger brothers could be shot just as easily as the friend he lost?*

But not this, I said. I meant not this way, another way where Ramón was still alive, but my anger flew from me and then my bones hurt with loss. *What are you afraid of, Petrona, I told you I'm not a guerrillero.* My chin trembled and he fell to his knees, Gorrión saying I was his life, why would he do something to hurt me? Then Gorrión swore on his mother and then my life, which he said he loved: he only liked to go to the meetings sometimes to listen. *Not this,* I repeated in my head, sometimes out loud, until everything drained from me, and then there were no more emotions, I had no more reactions, there was no more fear. I was empty like the Hills at dusk.

I let Gorrión buy me a cup of hot chocolate. Gorrión knew Mami had kicked me out. He blew the steam in my own cup and held it in front of my mouth so I could sip. He said he could ride the bus with me and escort me to the house where I worked and maybe I could stay there in secret until my mother cooled down. *They gave you a key,* right? Gorrión said the woman I worked for would surely offer me her house if she knew the trouble I was in. The hot chocolate was sweet on my tongue. *When we get married, all these troubles won't exist, it'll be you and me and you'll keep the house and I'll go to work, and we'll have dinner and grow old together, and then we'll be abuelos and we'll go to the plaza to feed the pigeons and badmouth the younger generation.* Gorrión was grinning, imagining all this staring into the air, and I took another sip of the hot sweet and pressed his hand and my eyes filled with water. *My sister too?*

Yes, your sister too Petrona. He laughed, looking into my eyes now. *Whatever you want.*

I felt small and fragile, escorted to the Santiagos'. Gorrión must have known how like a thin piece of paper I felt, because he helped me off the bus, he took my hand and pulled gently as we crawled into the gated neighborhood through a hole in the fence by the pines in the park. He rested his chin on my shoulder as I opened the Santiagos' door. We did not turn on the lights. We went to the kitchen and Gorrión and I stood there in the dark. It was nice how quiet the house was, peaceful and quiet as I had only felt in the cemetery. How odd that cemeteries are the only peaceful place. I did not know how much time had passed when Gorrión came near, his voice on my ear, *Let me spend the night with you.* I can't, I said. He whimpered like a puppy, he planted kisses on my neck that were a nice distraction, a nice addition to the peace that was like the silence of a cemetery, and we were in my room then and I stained the sheets a little with blood and we slept, and there was only a moment between closing and opening my eyes.

There was so much space in that house. Gorrión looked at me like men look at women in telenovelas. I knew I did not want him to leave. The light fell on the empty stairs. There was food in the pantry. Hot water relaxed my bones so full of loss. There were the two of us, alone, like we had never been. Gorrión looked at me and I felt things lighting up wherever he set his eyes. Mami would kill me if she knew what I was up to. I left word for her at the corner store saying I was at the Santiagos' and that they had asked me to look after their house. I had left my vacation money at home so I knew they would have enough to eat.

Here, Gorrión admired my body.

Gorrión tuned the dial of the radio. Airy

music came on. He kissed my hand like a gentleman and twirled me around. At the Santiagos' I was someone without a care. A fourteen-year-old with parents away on vacation, I liked to imagine, boyfriend in the house. Gorrión and I lay long on the couch. We put our hands behind our heads. Gorrión massaged my feet. He got frozen peas from the freezer and laid the bag on my head. He called me Reina.

When we prepared food, I thought about the Santiagos. I felt pangs of guilt. They had been kind to me. I felt a growing tenderness for little Chula and Cassandra. But Gorrión said there was a system that took away money from people like us so that people like me did not even have enough to put a family member underground. It hurt me to have Ramón brought up in this way, but then I thought of little Ramón in a box on top of a stranger in a different box and I took the Santiagos' rice and beans. They had plenty, and I had nothing.

For days I slept so well, Gorrión and I cramped in that bed for one. But sometimes I dreamed I was out in the Santiagos' garden. I was heavy on my hands and knees and Chula stared down at me from a great height. She reached her hand out but our hands could not touch. She looked worried

197

at first, then I realized she was afraid of me. I couldn't figure out what the dream was about.

Gorrión found hidden cash and snuck out and back into the neighborhood with frozen chicken. We crowded in the kitchen, cooking it with plenty of oil and onion. We sat in my room, eating with our fingers. We were so happy. Gorrión brought me a glass of water on a tray and it made me cry. But it wasn't just happiness, just reality catching up to my happiness. Little Aurora was doing all the cleaning and the cooking and taking care of Mami and her asthma and the boys. Gorrión knelt by me, calling me pet names. *Reina. Preciosa. Mi princesa. Don't cry. I love you. Let's get Aurora to call you. It'll be okay.* We left word at the corner store and waited for Aurora's call.

I want to be normal for once, why can't I?

Shh, shh, Gorrión said. *We'll find a way.* I found shelter in his great neck then the phone began to ring, and I wiped my face and took a deep breath, wondering who it would be this time, whether little Aurora or Chula, for whom would I have to put on a brave face?

13.
WHEN AT DINNER
YOU HAVE FIRE

Abuela shuffled around the house, going about her duties with an air of grave responsibility. Her house ran on her robotic hands and departed mind. She made the kettle whistle in the morning; the ceiling fans whir; the afternoon potatoes gurgle and toss inside the boiling pot; the sheets clean; the floors free from dust. She spent the rest of the day on the stool in her store, clasping her notebook of customer debts and credits, pen in hand, staring faintly at the open door. Her eyes were flat and lusterless as absent moonscapes. Her face was bruised and swollen. When we addressed her, she repeated the same four proverbs with a muted voice. *We shall eat more and we shall eat less. When at dinner you have fire, for breakfast you'll have water. What is left for time, time will take away. It is only death that doesn't have a remedy.* At night she retired to her room and lay on her bed and fell asleep without dinner.

We didn't hear anything about Tica and Memo. Tía Inés was so upset about my cousins being in a crossfire she refused to see us. Cassandra said Tía Inés probably blamed her and me too for what had happened. Papá and Mamá whispered about Abuela's bruises, but when they tried to examine her, Abuela pulled away. Several times they tried to drag her to a doctor, but Abuela screamed and hid. Everyone tried to talk to Abuela, but Abuela only said the same old things: *We shall eat more and we shall eat less. When at dinner you have fire, for breakfast you'll have water. What is left for time, time will take away. It is only death that doesn't have a remedy.*

Cassandra and I spied on Mamá and Papá. They went to whisper in the bathroom. The bathroom had cutouts in the cement along the top of the wall to let a breeze in. We stood on a table in the kitchen by the cutouts, and heard Mamá and Papá discuss awful things: that Abuela was a burden, that her stubbornness against being examined meant she could die, that Abuela was not just a martyr, but a martyr who *enjoyed* being a martyr. Mamá said, "The cash in her box is gone. I think she gave it to the paramilitary." Papá was silent. Then: "I thought she hated the paramilitary." Mamá clucked her tongue. "Well, now she hates the guerrillas *more.*" Papá sighed. "I guess there's nothing we can do about that."

No one paid attention to Cassandra and me. Abuela's house was like a captain-less ship. We redecorated parts of it. We moved vases, straightened her little crochet mantel-pieces, wiped dust from the brow of her little saints. We climbed the mango trees and ate the fruit while sitting in the branches. Cassandra said I was a complete dimwit, because the day of the helicopters I had told her that Tica, Memo, and Abuela were shot. She explained that to be shot and to be *shot at* were two different things. To be shot meant to have a bullet go through you. To be *shot at* meant you were lucky.

We found a box of sparklers and decided to celebrate the Christmas season since nobody else was. We buried them likc blades of grass and lit them, fire and electricity sparkling from the earth. After it was over, the sticks glowed bright red, like long thin embers. We leaned close to look and I pressed the hot metal between my fingers and didn't take my fingers away when it burned. "Chula!" Cassandra slapped my hand away.

The rod left a deep red crease on my

thumb and index finger and I began to cry. We couldn't find Mamá so Cassandra broke a large piece of Abuela's aloe plant and rubbed it on my burn. We sat quietly in the living room, Cassandra rubbing a new piece of aloe on my finger when the one she was using ran out of slime.

I felt guilty about what had happened to Abuela. It upset me that Tía Inés thought Cassandra and I were somehow to blame. Maybe we were. I couldn't bear to think about it, so instead I came up with stories of the danger Petrona was in. Maybe Petrona's father had robbed a drug lord. Maybe the drug lord owned cheetahs with diamond-studded collars. Petrona's father had stolen one, disappeared, and before the family knew it cheetahs surrounded their house. Petrona was the smart one, so she had the family break a wooden ladder into pieces to make torches. They stepped out holding the blazing wood and the animals hissed, and stayed away. Everyone ran in different directions and Petrona and her family had been in hiding ever since.

Papá sat down in the living room not noticing Cassandra and me. He held a little radio to his ear: "— might be negotiating. The details of the drug lord's surrender are not clear —" Then Papá saw the broken stalks of aloe on the ground, made eye contact with Cassandra and me, and turned the radio off. "What in the devil happened here?"

My eyes welled up. "Papá, turn the radio back on. Was that about Pablo Escobar?" Papá did not do as I asked and I felt a deep pang in the pit of my stomach and then it was like a broken valve and there was no bottom to my crying. I cried until I was red in the face and Mamá was kneeling by me, holding a wet towel to my forehead, asking, "What did you do to her?" and Papá said, "Nothing, Madre, she just started crying." Papá carried me to the bed and I sobbed until there were no more tears, just sounds.

Cassandra sat next to me and said it was all tied to my traumatized issues; she had overheard Mamá and Papá say so. "They also said they would find a psychologist who would do pro bono on you."

"What is pro bono?"

"Terrible, terrible, terrible" is all Cassandra said.

The last thing I wanted was to see a psychologist. There was someone like a psychologist at the school who everyone had to see once a year under the Principal's authority, except she was a Counselor, and then afterward you had to see a Priest. I was forced to talk to the Counselor after Galán died. She made me arrange blocks into different shapes, stare at ink stains, and make drawings of my family. The whole thing was very uncomfortable.

I sat up and dried my cheeks. I tucked hair behind my ears and wiped my nose. "I'm fine, see?"

Cassandra leveled her gaze. She squinted. "Maybe. We'll see. I'll keep an eye on you."

I stood up and stretched. In order to avoid the pro bono psychologist, I had to act indifferent. Next time Pablo Escobar came up, I would pretend like it meant nothing to me.

As I continued to play with Cassandra, Petrona and the tragedy of the cheetahs remained in the back of my mind. Cassandra and I kicked balls, chased each other, broke Coke bottles against the wall, but I felt a growing guilt over nothing bad happening to me. The guilt bore into my skin, into my lungs, and before I knew it, I was waking up in the middle of the night, dialing our number, wanting to hear Petrona's voice. When she answered, I wanted to tell Petrona about Abuela and the helicopters, and ask about the cheetahs, but instead I asked for updates on the telenovela *Calamar*. *Calamar* was about a village called

Consolación de Chiriguay where compasses were useless, ships sank at the harbor, mirages appeared left and right, and everyone who arrived developed an alter ego. The British Captain Longfellow was looking for treasure, and his sidekick Alejandro was looking for a lost sister. Alejandro wore glasses and a suit, but when he wore a bandana on his forehead he was known as el Guajiro, a superhero who fought a pirate called Capitán Olvido — who in turn was also hunting for the treasure, and was known as Artemio when he wasn't wearing pirate clothes and was just a nice old man. Everyone was fighting for the love of Claramanta, a stuck-up lady in curls.

"Claramanta got upset at Alejandro and rode off on a horse, she's such a burra because you know, niña, they are meant to be together. Then el Capitán Longfellow almost found the bewitched medallion, but then he didn't. And then, let me think . . ."

It was nice to hear Petrona's voice while everybody slept. Abuela's house was quiet and dark as I lay on the couch, Petrona's giggling filling my ear. I was glad I had been the one to discover her, because nobody else would have understood. As I listened to Petrona talk about *Calamar,* I could feel the tension of her hiding in the air. It was there behind the things she told me: "I don't understand why Claramanta doesn't see that Alejandro and el Guajiro are the same person, you know, niña?" Then again, maybe I was imagining it.

I called Petrona every night. One night Petrona missed an episode of *Calamar.* "I ran out of food and you know, niña, I can't let the neighbors see me, or they might tell your mamá about me staying here, so I had to sneak out really late at night, and then I just waited for hours until the grocery store opened and I bought some canned food and rice. That wasn't all — then I had to wait *again* for it to get dark and sneak back past the guards, into the house. So that's why I missed the last episode. But maybe they'll run the episode again over the weekend and I can tell you what we missed."

We were quiet for a moment and then Petrona said, "Thanks for keeping my secret, niña. I don't know what I'd do if —"

"It's nothing, I'm glad you're safe." I always cut off Petrona when she thanked me, like I was embarrassed by it, but I relished the feeling of having responsibility, of taking care of Petrona in some way, of knowing things that only I knew.

There was something about the amount of

words Petrona said to me, when once she had been so quiet, that made me hate how Abuela sat in the shadows. The same sickness that had taken Petrona's voice now took root in Abuela. I had to break the spell all over again, and I was frustrated because I was just a kid and why wasn't an adult doing anything useful? Abuela herself could fix it, I reasoned. Instead, she allowed the silence to take her over. Maybe she was a martyr who enjoyed being a martyr, as Papá and Mamá said. Abuela was so absent the thought came to me — she might as well be a vegetable. My lip curled in anger. With no one to stop me, I walked through the tattered curtain into Abuela's store. I looked at and hated each old thing Abuela was trying to sell: the stacked notebooks, black and red pens, soaps, marbles, erasers, sharpeners, pencils, incense, packs of sanitary napkins, cologne, shampoo, conditioner, white and black shoelaces, spools of white thread, candles wrapped in crinkly images of the Virgin, corn flour, eggs. I swiped a stained-glass bottle marked with the word luck and hid it in my hand. Then I stole red pens (buried by the chicken coop), bottles of cologne (flushed down the toilet), black shoelaces (thrown up a tree), corn flour (mixed in mud), and shampoo (mixed into the chickens' feed). Abuela never said a word.

The Luck bottle I kept. I turned it in my hands, Luck sloshing against my fingertips. I told Papá I had taken the bottle at the beginning of our stay, and he said he would need to pay Abuela for it. When he didn't yell at me, I asked him if he would tie a string around it so I could wear it around my neck. Then, I went around opening drawers everywhere, looking for more things to steal, but there was nothing but old trash — sepia-colored maps, old notes, blackened coins. The little bottle swung forward and back, tapping my chest when I moved.

Mamá explained to me that you had luck depending on the year, month, day, and time you were born — it had nothing to do with bottles. She said some were born under a lucky star. She pressed a lot of numbers on a calculator and then pressed the equal sign. Luck depended on the number that flashed on the screen. She said it was numerology, *the science of numbers.* Mamá couldn't add Abuela's numbers because Abuela didn't know them. Abuela was born in Chocó, in a field of banana trees, to a mother who couldn't read or write. I had memorized my numbers. They were four, three, and four. Their sum was eleven. It was a lucky number, so you didn't break it down and add one and one, like you did with the rest. Cassandra helped me do Petrona's numbers. They were three, three, and seven. The end number was four, but neither of us knew what that meant.

Cassandra and I climbed Abuela's roof in the middle of the night. Cassandra dared me to count the stars. Counting the stars was forbidden, because Abuela said if you counted your birth star it would claim you and you would die. There were so many stars, there was no way to know to which one you belonged. I always skipped the constellations that felt familiar, because *what if it was true?* Abuela taught Mamá that some things are written in the stars, but others are up to chance. Abuela learned to read the stars from her mother, who learned from her great-grandmother, who had been a weaver in the Sikuani tribe. But Abuela's eyes were milky now, so the stars couldn't guide her, and anyway, she was like a vegetable.

My hand ticked off the twinkling lights in the night sky, *one, two, three, four.* Why did I feel so guilty? *Fourteen, fifteen.* Like every second I felt guilty — but why? *Twenty-six, twenty-seven.*

Petrona always answered the phone so

quickly; what room was she sleeping in? If she had been staying in her room past the indoor patio, the phone might ring three or four times before she picked up. Instead she answered the phone with the speed Mamá answered the phone. Maybe she was sleeping on the living room couch. *Fifty.* I told Cassandra a good way to calculate the number of stars was to count all the stars in one cluster and then take similar clusters and approximate. Cassandra said her method was better: you just looked at the twinkling lights and came up with a number. "For example," she said and opened her arms wide. "The total number of stars in the sky is . . . *one billion's billion.*"

The morning after we counted the stars everything was worse. Cassandra yelled for help and when we ran outside we saw that all of Abuela's chickens were dead and dozens of flies buzzed about. Black flies disappeared down their beaks and did not come out. White, soapy foam drooled out of the chicken's beaks. I had to run away. I threw up on the path. Mamá came and held back my hair. She helped me clean in the kitchen and my hands trembled. When she asked if I knew what had happened to the chickens I told her yes, I told her Cassandra and I had stayed up counting stars. I told her we must have counted the chickens' birth stars.

Mamá lifted her brows in surprise, and then lowered them, deep in thought, and that's when I told her I felt guilt and I thought it was because Abuela had taken Tica and Memo the day of the helicopters and not me.

Mamá hugged me and said against my ear that I shouldn't feel that way, that Abuela, Tica, and Memo being there at the exact moment of the helicopters had all been written, that she had read it in Abuela's stars. I asked Mamá what she had read in my stars, but Mamá said never to ask. There were things better left unknown.

Papá was gone buying new chickens for Abuela and Mamá pulled up a chair wherever Abuela was: the store, the garden, the bedroom, the kitchen. Telling Mamá I felt guilt made me feel better, so I decided to tell Cassandra something else. I found her deep in thought releasing a steady stream of sand from her relaxed fist over the hole of an anthill. She was like an infant god visiting a great disaster upon the ants, her subjects. I sat before her and blurted, "While you and Mamá were away at Galán's funeral, I met Petrona's boyfriend."

My words made Cassandra loosen her fist all the way, and the anthill was buried in a gulp of soil. "What?"

"That's right. They tried to fool me, saying he was some kind of carpet inspector, but it's not like *I* was born yesterday."

"Chula, what?" She shook her head. "What do you mean? Are you saying Petrona let a stranger into our house?" I glanced down and saw the ants that had been on the outside during Cassandra's great avalanche were now frantically swarming their hill, looking for the entrance.

"Cassandra, I'm telling you, he was *no* stranger. In reality, he is like Romeo and Petrona is like Juliet and they could only meet in secret, isn't that romantic?"

"Did he pass her a *note*?" Cassandra was obsessed about passing notes. There was a boy at her school named Camilo I knew she secretly passed notes to. Once I looked in her school bag and found a string of them, but they didn't say *I like you* or *I miss you;* instead they were drawings about comets and great natural disasters, always one school teacher drowning or dying in some horrifying way. I lied and told Cassandra that Petrona's boyfriend *had* given her a note, and I said again that it was like Romeo and Juliet and Cassandra nodded with her eyes closed, which meant she understood.

Romeo and Juliet was our favorite play. Papá had it on videocassette at home and Cassandra and I put it on whenever we wanted a good cry. Cassandra and I *loved* crying — not polite-crying, but tears streaming, yelling, bowled-over kind of crying. We cuddled on the floor with blankets and popcorn and the tissue box. I felt the Friar was a complete mosquita muerta and every time he came onstage, I made a buzzing sound, which made Cassandra laugh. The Friar probably made Romeo and Juliet die on purpose — that's the kind of person he was. I wouldn't be surprised if he had planned the whole thing in order to teach the Capulets and the Montagues some empty-headed moral lesson about loving your neighbor more than yourself.

At night, Papá and Mamá whispered in bed. They thought Cassandra and I were sleeping, but we lay awake with our heads at the foot of the bed. I could smell Papá's spearminted feet. Mamá was shaking her foot.

I heard the guerrillas are moving on. In a few days the paramilitary will be gone too. We should leave.

We can't leave, who will take care of Abuela?

Your mother can take care of herself. We have daughters before you have a mother, Alma.

I had a mother before I gave birth, Antonio. Why can't we take her with us to Bogotá?

She doesn't want to go — what can we do about it?

In the dark, I sensed Papá turning on his side and then the whispering died down. I tried to stay awake in case anything else happened, but Mamá's rocking foot sent me to a lull. It felt like it was only a second later when I sat up, hearing Abuela scream. We ran to her and turned on the light and saw Abuela tumbled on the floor, coiled in a blanket. Mamá was hysterical. "What is it, Mamá? What's happened? Was it a dream?" We saw Abuela's exposed back.

Through the open back of her nightdress we saw how the skin was covered in a bladed cape of cactus thorns like she was a flesh-and-blood-porcupine. Papá yelled he would get aguardiente and Abuela moaned and crawled on the floor. The thorns were on her thighs too, and I ran out.

Everything came out of me in the toilet, fear and water and food and bile and guilt, and then I lay with my forehead on the tiled floor. For an hour we heard Abuela cry, and then a doctor came in, white coat black bag,

214

and the door to Abuela's room was shut. Everything was quiet and Papá said the doctor had probably injected Abuela with something to make her sleep.

When the doctor came out he told Papá that Abuela had been in shock probably since the day of the crossfire; that's how come she didn't feel anything until now.

"But I don't understand," Cassandra said.

The doctor checked his watch. "The mind can do astonishing things."

We were all quiet and then Papá talked to the doctor privately. When the doctor left, Mamá called all of the aunts and uncles. Everyone wanted to help, except for Tía Inés, who yelled on the telephone, *Good! I hope this teaches all of you to think before acting!*

Tía Carmen came from a neighboring town called La Playa. Tía Carmen was a divorcée, and she managed to leave her children behind with a neighbor, but brought along her yapping dog. It was only an hour's drive for her and before we knew it, her dog barked and jumped at our heels and Tía Carmen crooned about Cassandra and me. "Amorcitos! Cassandra, how many boyfriends? Tell me there's many. Remember to keep many candles burning so when one goes out you still have another, eh?"

215

Her teased hair stood three centimeters above her head. "Chula, did you hear? This is important. How is school, cielitos? I want *Excellent* written over and over on your report cards." She lowered her voice. "How is Abuela?" Abuela was on painkillers and she believed herself to be on a cruise, even though she had never seen the ocean. I refused to go into Abuela's room, but Tía Carmen made me. Tía Carmen held fast to my arm as we entered the dark room. "It's good for Abuela to see your face," she said, even though I could see Abuela's eyes were swollen shut. Her whole body was bloated under the sheets. Mamá wrung a small towel over a bowl of water and placed it on Abuela's forehead.

No one knew what to say, so Papá began to talk at random. "Anyone see the soccer match?" He wiped his hands on his pants and said he didn't know why he was asking, the soccer match had been canceled now that he thought about it, how could he forget, Pablo Escobar had detonated a bomb in an airplane and ruins and body parts had rained down over a town called Soacha, which was where the game was going to take place. "Yes, so the match was canceled," he repeated, and Tía Carmen wrinkled her lip and said, "Antonio, this is hardly the time or the place."

I thought about how Soacha was also where Galán had been shot and then I felt like I would cry again, and then remembered I needed to avoid the pro bono psychologist and in order to do that, I needed to keep my emotions off my face. I untensed my brows and concentrated on counting seconds. I counted sixty, then began again. At my third cycle, Abuela sprang up in bed, reaching with one hand. The moment lasted only a second, but it lingered in my eye, the skin on Abuela's arm hilled in abrasions, and her breasts with the air gone out of them dangling over her stomach. She fell back down against her pillow, asleep. This must have been what the doctor had meant when he said the mind could do astonishing things: Petrona eating from the fruit of the Drunken Tree and believing she had misplaced a bowl of soup in her sheets, and Abuela taking the doctor's drugs and thinking herself on a cruise. Maybe the astonishing thing was how much nicer the things they imagined were compared to the real suffering of their bodies.

I closed my eyes and cried so quietly that nobody noticed. I felt so tired. I thought about the ocean Abuela would imagine; maybe the water still and clear all the way through like the water she knew, her boat smoothly making its way, like an ice cube on a table, sliding over the glassy surface, while below strange animals and long snakes coiled about. *I poisoned the chickens.* Had I said that out loud? I looked around the room. Everyone stared. Could my body speak on its own? Mamá looked down at me. "Chula, say that again." The silence was shameful, but then I was speaking — "I didn't know, how could I know?" — and Mamá grabbed me by the hair and dragged me out of the bedroom and threw me against a wall. "Have you lost your mind?"

I screamed to get free, and Cassandra came running to help me but Mamá dragged us both by the hair past the living room. "Mamá, let me go!" Cassandra protested. "What are you doing? I didn't kill the chickens! Let me go!" Mamá hurled us into Abuela's bathroom, and there, Cassandra and I clung to the walls and Mamá flung bucket after bucket of cold water at us. We cried and pressed against the shower corner and screamed from the cold. I covered my head with my hands.

PETRONA

Aurora said they were doing well, and I should stay away because Mami was not done being angry. I wanted to check on my family. Gorrión said we didn't have money for the bus fare. We cuddled on the living room couch. *I know what will cheer you up,* he said. *What if we have some friends over?* I told him I thought it would be disrespectful to the Santiagos. More and more I thought about the Santiagos. More and more I dreamed of Chula looking down at me from a great height. Sometimes I was as if glued to the grass; other times it was burning rocks. One dream, I heard la Señora's voice ordering me to get up.

Just for an hour, Gorrión said, *I want to introduce my friends to my future wife.* Because he called me his future wife I allowed it.

We invited Leticia over and she brought some men that Gorrión knew but I had never seen. She helped them sneak in through the hole in the fence by the park. They wore hooded sweatshirts and clean jeans and looked like they were just some kids who belonged in the neighborhood. I parted the curtains in the Señora's bedroom and waved them on when I heard the woman next door start the shower.

Seeing Leticia made me happy. We held hands as she introduced the men to me — men she herself had only just met. She pointed to each man, *This is la Pulga, la Uña, el Alacrán. Did I get it right?* The men lowered the hoods of their sweatshirts, putting their hands forward for me to shake with such dignity and cordiality, I couldn't quite make fun of their names: Flea, Nail, Scorpion. I smiled at the clean-shaven, perfumed men. They grinned, not moving an inch, and I realized they were waiting for me to offer them a seat. *Please, make yourselves at home,* I blurted, and then Gorrión hugged each man, and they sat together. I was tense in front of the men and I pulled Leticia with me to the kitchen to make tea and arrange crackers on a plate like I had seen la Señora do. In the kitchen, Leticia smiled with her chin tucked into her chest. *Did you guys . . . ?* I elbowed her, *Leticia!* Leticia wriggled her eyebrows. I giggled and admitted we had. *And did you . . . ?* I covered my eyes, laughing. *So you did!* she said grinning from ear to ear. Suddenly she bit her lip: *How are you guys doing with money?* I hesitated. She held my cheek. *If you ever need to do the thing with the envelopes again just let me know.* She pressed my chin lightly between her thumb and forefinger. *You're so pretty, Petrona. I'm so happy for you and Gorrión.*

We went to the living room to join the men. I carried the tray with refreshments but then I had to set it down in a hurry because they were howling and shouting over a game of dominoes, and there were opened bottles of beer everywhere, and I sprang forward on my hands and knees, urging them to lower their voices, and I pressed my dress on the foamy spot where one beer had spilled, and the one they called la Pulga widened his caramel eyes and snickered: *Ay paisan, she must not know we are invincible.*

14.
CLEOPATRA, QUEEN OF EGYPT

Even though it was Christmas Eve, Papá and Mamá packed our things and told us Tía Carmen was going to take care of Abuela and we were leaving for Bogotá. Cassandra was yelling, then Mamá broke a plate, and in the confusion I ran to the telephone to warn Petrona. The line clicked. "We're coming home." I hung up and ran to the garden. Tía Carmen held me in her perfumed arms and made me go into Abuela's room again. Abuela's consciousness went in and out, but Tía Carmen said we still had to feed her. I stood by and watched as Abuela clenched her jaw against Tía Carmen's spoon. The soup steamed in front of Abuela's face. Other times she allowed the spoon in her mouth.

Mamá had once said that when Abuela was young her teeth had been white and full, but when Abuelo left, Abuela ground her teeth until they became short and flat like a deer's.

Mamá came in and spoke in my ear, "Say goodbye. We're leaving."

I approached the narrow bed, bathed in light from the window. A crucifix hung above Abuela on the wall. I wasn't sure if Abuela was sleeping, but I could see the brightness of her eyes through the slits. At the center were the dark globes of her irises. I hugged my arms around Abuela and placed my head on her chest. She was so small. "I'm sorry, Abuela." Then Mamá came in with Cassandra and Cassandra held Abuela's hands and Mamá whispered in Abuela's ear. After some time Abuela scrunched up her face.

Outside, Tía Carmen told us not to worry, she would care for Abuela, but then she added, "Like I *always* do." Her dog yapped at the door and Mamá didn't look at her and we all got in the car. From the backseat I watched Tía Carmen, her arms crossed over her chest, become small as the forest hills rising behind her grew tall. Just like that we abandoned Abuela. Along the dirt road of El Salado, men leaned on lampposts, women threw dirty mop water out onto the dirt road, children zigzagged around colorful streamers, everyone getting ready for the holiday night. Papá didn't seem nervous. I knew this meant we weren't in any danger. Maybe Abuela would be okay. Then I saw we weren't taking the dirt road back toward Bogotá, but were driving deeper into the invasión. "Where are we going?" Mamá was quiet and Papá answered, "To see your Tía Inés. We'll only be a minute."

We parked our car at the bottom of a hill and hiked up. Papá carried a black trash bag. I would have never guessed Tía Inés lived on a hill. The path was steep and pieces of metal lay scattered on the ground. Women knelt scrubbing laundry in plastic tubs. Then a row of corn stood as a fence and there was a small wooden gate at the middle. The gate opened with the flick of a latch. Papá opened it and I saw Tía Inés standing at the doorway of her house. Her stomach protruded far out in front of her. It seemed she should be falling forward from the weight. She watched us go through the gate, then turned around and went inside, her hands resting on the small of her back.

Tía Inés's house was small, and you could see all there was to it upon entering. There were metal folding chairs in the living room, and at the middle over the cement floor there was a small straw mat. There was a kitchen with two burners and next to it two beaten-up bedroom doors: one for Tica and Memo, and the other for Tía Inés and Tío Ramiro.

I was afraid of going in. Cassandra must have felt the same way because she looked at me and offered her hand. We walked into the house together and sat on the floor as Papá brought a rocking chair from outside for Tía Inés. Tío Ramiro was nowhere to be seen. Mamá said, "Cómo estás, Inés?" Tía Inés didn't answer and when we looked up Tica and Memo were standing at their bedroom door.

They leaned against the doorway together, winded, Tica's hair knotted, and Memo's legs covered with streaks of dirt like he had fallen and had not bothered to clean himself. They looked different, but I couldn't put my finger on what it was. Other than to say they were thinner, and they no longer looked like children. It reminded me of how Petrona didn't look her age, but older.

Like they were scratched behind their faces.

Papá said, "Tica, Memo! Look, we have gifts." He opened the black bag he had carried, and Memo and Tica sat on the straw mat by Cassandra and me. The hairs on the back of my neck stood up. Memo unwrapped his gift quickly. It was a toy rocket.

He stood and for a moment he seemed like the old Memo, weaving between the chairs of that living room swinging the rocket on imaginary airways. Tica turned her present around and around in her hands. She rubbed the white ribbon in her fingers before pulling it. It was a wooden elephant. She lifted the elephant to her eyes and ran her finger along the dress on its back. Tica swung the elephant legs on the hinged joints and Papá told her you could make the elephant move on its own by pulling on the strings attached to the crossbeam.

"It's a marionette," he said, taking up the crossbeam and making the elephant lift its legs one by one. Tica cooed as the elephant clomped its heels and lifted its jointed trunk. Papá made trumpeting sounds with his lips. Papá showed Tica how to make the elephant move its ears forward and back, and then Tica learned on her own how to make the elephant lift one leg. The leg lifted and swung in place at the joint and after a time it landed.

Papá said Tica was a natural. "When I was young, Tica, I used to make my own dolls. I carved them out of wood. I made marionettes and I put on shows for my family."

"Really, Tío?" Tica said.

I watched the wooden elephant as Tica

bounced it on the floor. Then the elephant contorted and went into a handstand. I lifted my gaze and saw the whites of Tica's eyes. She was looking to the ceiling. An airplane was passing overhead. Tica scrambled to her feet and grabbed Memo and they ran to the corner and covered their heads.

Tía Inés said, "They've been doing that for days," and then, "I've *told* you those are just airplanes, don't you ever listen?"

Tica came out of her brooding as if out of a cave and loosened her grip on Memo. She focused on her mother's face. She was embarrassed, and Memo tried to laugh. Tía Inés walked out.

Mamá sat them down on her lap. "Your mother's under a lot of stress, but none of it is your fault, okay?" Mamá touched Memo's chin and he nodded. "Soon you'll have a little brother and you'll have to take care of him, and take care of your mom too." Cassandra stared past me at Mamá holding Tica and Memo, and Papá sank into his chair next to Mamá, his mouth covered by his hand.

Mamá caressed Tica's cheek. "Let me see your hand." Mamá pressed Tica's hand open, pushing her thumb against Tica's fingers to make the wrinkles clear. "Here it says you will be beautiful."

Memo leaned over Mamá to see where she was looking. "Where does it say?"

"Right here. This little wrinkle under this finger."

Tica took her hand back and held the finger Mamá pointed at and rubbed it, pressing against the wrinkle Mamá had pointed out.

"It says you will be beautiful like Cleopatra."

Tica pulled at her Lycra shorts on Mamá's lap and said, "I don't know who that is, Tía."

"Cleopatra, the queen of Egypt, Tica. She was beautiful, and she had your same haircut."

Tica wondered at her hand, and held it close to her face as she looked at it. She looked up at Mamá. "What else does it say, Tía?"

Mamá took Tica's hand again and hooked her thumb around Tica's long pinkie and ring fingers and pressed them back. Mamá laughed. "It says here you will marry three times. And you'll have one baby during the last marriage."

I didn't know if Mamá really saw those things in Tica's hand, but I thought it was kind of her to give Tica those words, because

I saw the effect it had on Tica. Her spirits lifted.

Mamá and Tía Inés had a long conversation before we left. When they returned to our side, Tía Inés offered to walk us down to the car, so maybe they had made up.

I could tell that everything would settle. I knew because until we left Tica grinned secretly and walked with her head up. She grinned without showing her teeth or wrinkling her eyes. It was a magnificent grin. Walking us downhill, it seemed like Tica floated on air. As Papá, Mamá, Cassandra, and I got in the car and rolled down the windows to let out the heat, Tica pulled on her mother's dress, and all at once it came out of her mouth; how she had the same haircut as Cleopatra, Cleopatra who was beautiful, Cleopatra who was the queen of Egypt, and how she, Tica, was going to be *just* as beautiful, and was going to marry three times, but she was going to have only one baby, and then Tica closed her eyes and sighed, and her lids lengthened in the sight of her dreams.

15.
GOD'S THUMB

On the way back to Bogotá, Cassandra and I lay on the folded-down seats in the back of the car with our feet tucked in between the luggage in the trunk, not talking. Cassandra played with a string, twisting it in different ways to make figures — a teacup, a chicken's foot, a noose. The figures Cassandra made over and over again told a story — Abuela's tub, the chickens, Tica and Memo — but I don't think she realized. I lowered my lids to rest my eyes and as our car slid us forward, I wondered whether Petrona had been able to clean up after herself. I hoped she wouldn't be found out. I thought to myself, *Good thing she's a maid,* then frowned at how unkind this was. I tried to make up for it by hoping as sincerely as I could for the danger she was in to pass. Then I thought about Tica and Cleopatra and watched as the sky dimmed and the crescent moon came out.

Abuela said the crescent moon was God's Nail. If you looked at it you couldn't be sure what finger it was, or whether it was the white-tipped crescent of a hand or a foot.

I was confident it was the thumb of the right hand.

Time passed with the crescent of God's nail looming over our car — magical, luminescent, suspended in a vacuum of night.

Little by little, as the car rode on, God's nail slipped back and back. It slid down across the black horizontal lines of the back windshield, and disappeared behind a group of gray clouds.

The next night, the gray clouds swelled and it rained and there was no moon at all and I couldn't help but think —

PETRONA

Gorrión got off the bus five blocks before the stop at the Hills so that nobody would see us together. In the hut, little Aurora was starting the fire. I stood at the curtain that was our front door and watched her twist newspapers. She lit them and blew on them like that was all it took for the wood to catch flame. Sometimes we could afford coal and then Aurora had no trouble starting the fire. I felt Mami's eyes on me, but I did not look in her direction. The little ones came in. *Petrona! We missed you!* I crouched by little Aurora and showed her how to stack the wood. We kept the fire late into the night, Mami asleep or pretending to sleep. I had brought us a bag of corn and a block of butter and I speared knifes into the corn so my little ones could hold them to the flame. A Christmas Eve treat. *Petrona is tall like a bear! Petrona is thin like a street post!* Stupid things the little ones said as they turned the golden cobs, and in the flames I imagined Gorrión's heavy-lidded eyes.

I gave Mami a cob of corn and she took it and thanked me and I guess she had in some small way forgiven me.

Her eyes bore into me asking me what I had done. Eyes lunged at me, too, in the outdoor shower at the back of our hut. The light through the thin spaces of the wood like lightning from someone passing by quick, the glimmer of dark eyes, and I pulled on the string that released the bucket so I could wash the suds off my face and I put on my clothes and stepped outside, but there was no one. Chicharras sang in the grass and birds in the trees.

Eyes like quick darts in the small church two blocks east from the Hills. I lit a candle to make up for my sins: *fourteen years old,* I was sure they were thinking, *and already with four young children.* How could I explain, *my Mami has asthma, she cannot come, you idiots.*

Streamers hung from the columns of the street as we followed a parade. There were trumpets and accordions and we held lit candles that had been passed around. We put extra candles in our pockets for Mami. There was a truck filled with nuns. From the truck bed, nuns passed out wrapped gifts. We each got something — little Aurora a new doll, and the boys a fire truck and a heap of small cars with little doors that opened and plastic parts that when put together formed a ramp. I got a teddy bear. I got an extra gift for Mami too, and when she opened it at home we saw it was a scarf. There were lit candles sticking out of small Coke bottles in our hut and we were soft-spoken, asking for permission before we did anything, and Mami smiled over us and said, *This feels just like when we were in Boyacá.*

And it was true, in Boyacá we had this kind of peace, there were chicharras there too. We glowed with our health, we grew strong by our candles, but in Boyacá we did not notice the beginning of the air souring like turning milk, and what if that was the case now. I whipped my fingers in the air. *Don't say that, Mami.* I was afraid, and my siblings said, *What, Petrona, what?* But I could not explain.

You won't tell I stayed with you in that house? Gorrión had asked me in the bus on our way back. I laughed. *No, why would I do such a thing?* Gorrión stroked my hand, sweet and worried. *What if you're found out, mi cielo?* I shifted in my seat. *I'll explain I was*

234

kicked out, I won't say you were with me. He kissed my hand. *Good.* He looked away and added, *Because you know, the encapotados get nervous when people like me, who know who they are, because like I told you I go to listen, just friendly and cool go hear what they have to say — the encapotados get nervous when people like me get named.*

16.
A GRAND SHUTTING DOWN OF THINGS

I couldn't find evidence of Petrona staying in our home. I wondered if I had made the whole thing up. I asked Mamá when Petrona was coming back, and Mamá said she wasn't sure. I stared at the ground, thinking I had no way to call Petrona to find out if she was okay, and Mamá shook me and told me to not make a scene over a maid.

Papá had been hired as a manager at an oil site in San Juan de Rioseco, a three-hour drive from Bogotá. He came back every other weekend and Mamá was once again ruler of our kingdom of women. Cassandra convinced Mamá to let her turn the attic into a bedroom, and I was alone in our old room. It was strange without Cassandra, spacious and clean like a hotel room.

As the new school year started, I wondered at all hours about Petrona — whether she was injured, whether her boyfriend treated her right, what she was eating, what length her hair was.

In January, the drought we had encountered at Abuela's arrived to Bogotá.

The drought came with heat and dry air that sent the rain-bearing clouds away from Colombia and into Mexico and Texas. In Mexico and Texas there were floods. On the television forests burst into fires, the countryside mummified, the rivers steamed up and left behind fish bones and exoskeletons, and the water reserves in the country evaporated to shallow pools of water. In our yard, the grass cracked dryly under our feet and the Drunken Tree didn't bloom.

Mamá rationed our drinking water. She filled four one-liter plastic bottles and drew horizontal lines in red, writing alongside each in cursive, *Morning, Noon, Night.* When it was done, we drove to the grocery store where she struck deals with the workers. She gave them money when no one was looking. Then, even though there were no more water bottles on the shelf, just a paper folded in half that said *OUT OF STOCK,* the workers brought us a three-gallon container of water. They hid it inside a black garbage bag. Mamá took the bag in her hands and pressed the container against her chest in order to bear the weight. She gripped the sides of the container too strongly, and made the plastic crinkle. A few shoppers turned their heads, as if they recognized the sound, and they stared at the black garbage bag and then lifted their eyes to Mamá.

We drove straight from the grocery store back to the house, Mamá speeding a little, checking her rearview mirror, glancing at the water in the backseat — like we were crooks.

Maybe it was loneliness but probably it was the extra work involved in collecting water, but either way Mamá called Petrona and asked her to move into our house and even offered her higher pay.

Mamá had never asked any girl to move in.

Petrona arrived like how she did the first day — with a long dress pausing at the gate to stare up at our house. From Mamá's window between the folds of her lace curtains I saw how Mamá held Petrona's hand in hers as they walked together toward the house. Mamá and Petrona were directly underneath when I knocked on the window. Mamá kept walking, but Petrona looked up, caught in a half step. Petrona shielded her eyes, and her hand cast a shadow on her face. Then she hurried to Mamá. The back of my hand was still brushing against the folds of the curtain, waving at Petrona, when I realized she was gone.

Nobody knew Petrona and I were friends, so I didn't know how to act. I watched Cassandra, who didn't even say hello to Petrona but acted like Petrona had never left.

"Petrona, could you pass me that blanket?"

"Petrona, could you get me some water?" I wasn't thirsty, but I had to say something. Petrona draped a blanket on us, and then she winked at me when she handed me the glass. Her hair was still short, and she tucked it behind her ear as she straightened. We grinned at each other. Petrona didn't look like she was in danger anymore. My grin grew into a smile as I observed her fresh, rosy skin, and her healthy weight. I'd have to find a time to talk to Petrona privately, but for now everyone was watching, so I returned my eyes to the newspaper.

Cassandra and I were studying a colorful diagram of Bogotá, printed on the front page, where different colors had been assigned to a citywide schedule of electricity and water cuts. People in the newspaper called the cuts apagones, which meant *the grand shutting down of things.*

In the diagram, the city was broken up into grids, making trapezoids, rectangles, and squares. A small key by the map said the neighborhoods in the blue areas would have apagones for six hours daily, while those in the red would have apagones for ten. Our neighborhood was in the yellow, meaning we would get apagones for eight hours daily.

I thought the apagones would have the same carnaval feeling as the blackouts, but they were no fun and all work. Petrona went home on the weekends, and Mamá had to collect water on Saturdays and Sundays with our help. The hours of water sent everyone in our house leaping to sinks and showerheads and street pipes in order to collect as much water as we could in our tins and bottles and buckets and cups.

During the week, the commotion around the water made it difficult to find a time in which Petrona was alone. I was stirred awake at five in the morning by the sound of water rushing out of all the faucets in the house and unloading into hard plastic and tin. The sound of water rang like one grand waterfall. In bed, I looked in the direction of the sound, rubbing my eyes and yawning. I listened to Mamá and Petrona walk back and forth between the bathrooms and up and down the stairs where they collected water from the kitchen and the laundry room. The sound of rushing water made its way into my dreams. I dreamed of wetlands where long-torsoed mermaids clung to swamp trees and called and called for me. Their arms were blue and long like snakes. They sang my name, "Chu-u-u-u-la-a-a." Their voices echoed over the thick mud against trees and sky.

In the shower there appeared a big orange tub filled with water that was collected every morning before the apagón. A cream-colored coffee cup bobbed in the tub like a lazy boat. I sat on the shower tiles fishing out water from the big orange tub in the morning, dumping the cold water over my head, gasping and shivering, like I had done at Abuela's. Some days I only pretended to shower and dumped the water down the drain. I felt a kind of thrilling remorse. Mamá stopped taking showers altogether so we could have more water, though she liked saying that wasn't the reason at all.

"It's because I like to bathe like the cats." She dipped her hands timidly in the water and rubbed them on her face quickly and then under her arms. She smiled. Her face was glossy with water and small drops clung above her lip.

We kept big pails of water by the toilet to drop over our waste and make the toilet flush. There wasn't enough water to do it every time someone went to the bathroom, so the waste of the whole family accumulated in the toilet bowls until the end of the day. We tried to save the worst of our waste for later, but sometimes it was unavoidable, and then we pinched our nose and walked away shamefully from the bathroom, saying, "Only go in there if you have to."

I did small things for Petrona so she knew we were still friends. "Look, Petrona, I found the best rock at school and brought it to you." I presented her with cut flowers, pretty bows, apples, until I thought Mamá was getting suspicious. Then I brought presents for Mamá, and stuffed notes with coded alphabets beneath Petrona's pillow. My notes went unanswered, and it dawned on me that Petrona had a hard time reading as it was. I made her a drawing of our home phone with hearts around it, and this one she understood. I found the same note beneath my pillow with a drawing of her own on the back side — two hearts with the coil of a phone connecting them.

I was so busy trying to communicate with Petrona, and Mamá and Cassandra were so preoccupied with the apagones, we all kept forgetting Papá came home every other weekend. He surprised us when we ran into

him in the halls. "Oh!" we said. "It's you!" we said. "When did you get in?"

Papá said now that he was a manager, his job came with some perks. He brought home an extra television we set up in the living room and then he opened a cardboard box like he was a magician uncovering a jailed tiger. Inside was a computer with a black screen that stayed black because of the apagón. Papá and Cassandra spent the next hours setting up the computer by flashlight in Cassandra's room in the attic.

We left all of our televisions on so we knew the exact moment when the electricity came back. The voice of the newscasters and commercial jingles marked the apagones as they came and went. The moment the televisions in the house came on, Papá and Cassandra cheered and ran up to the attic to plug in the computer. While Mamá and Petrona collected water, Papá and Cassandra sat in front of the screen, taking turns controlling a chicken crossing a road. They shouted back and forth, "Look, look at this technology!"

Cassandra spent a lot of time in her new room, which she decorated with Christmas lights and where the computer had a prominent place. Papá got her games on discs and that's what Cassandra did during the

hours of electricity — she led a little pixelated man through a labyrinthine castle, bats and torches hanging from the walls.

While Cassandra played, I looked in on Petrona. I went to her room and sat next to her on her bed, watching her turn the pages of a magazine. We didn't say much. We smelled the perfume samples that came trapped between folds you could peel open. We looked at the fashion spreads, thin white models riding elephants, small African boys leading the way. I didn't bring up our secret. I figured it didn't matter, Petrona was staying at our house now, what difference did it make. Mamá seemed to always be within earshot so I couldn't ask Petrona about the danger she'd been in. We played tic-tac-toe on the white pages of a notebook and I admired her porcelain skin.

During apagones, when Papá was home, he caught up on his reading. He sank in the living room couch and read the newspaper by flashlight. He created a sort of blanket as he read, discarding the thin pages of newsprint all about him; they rustled noisily whenever he shifted.

Mamá taught Petrona with my old textbooks. They sat at the dining table: Mamá pointing at things in the textbook and Pet-

rona twirling the pencil in her hair. There were floor-to-ceiling mirrors by the table, one behind Mamá at the head, and one behind Petrona to Mamá's left. I looked for revealing discrepancies. Petrona looked the same, but one of Mamá's eyes looked bigger in the mirror. Above the table hovered a small, unlit chandelier. Underneath the table an old Sikuani rug unraveled in one corner.

Every other weekend when Papá wasn't home, Mamá had parties. Women in pretty dresses and men in suits sat in our living room playing canasta, drinking, and laughing. Petrona had to make finger food and keep the tables stocked with enough snacks and drinks. The house warmed with candlelight. Mamá's girlfriends lifted me up from under my armpits. "What are you going to do, mi cielo, with this pretty face?" Their breath rolled in the sweet and sour smell of cigarettes and brandy. "Listen to me, preciosa, break many hearts and never marry. Remember that."

Sometimes it wasn't a big party, just Mamá sitting on the couch talking to just one man. The man was whispering some long story to Mamá while Mamá held her cigarette in the air, without smoking, smil-

ing. Everywhere the light of candles flickered.

and singing.

We went to the Oligarch's mansion. The roof looked like a mountain, while the roofs of neighboring houses looked like hills. At the top of the Oligarch's house, there was a floating yellow light going round and round, disappearing at one corner and appearing at the next. We thought it was a Blessed Soul of Purgatory but then I saw the yellow light was only a person holding a candle, pacing around the wraparound balcony. I gasped. "That's the Oligarch."

The light shone eerily on the Oligarch's face. She appeared pale and all kinds of shadows sent her features askew. I couldn't tell if she was old or young. We sat on the sidewalk and watched her globe of candlelight moving about the house. We guessed the woman lived alone. Once or twice I saw the Oligarch's profile when she set her candle on a table and stepped in front of it. There she was now, a heavyset woman wearing some kind of long cape standing by the window. Was she looking out or in? It was very difficult to tell. Cassandra said it was a miracle the woman's hair did not ever catch on fire and then the lights came back on. The sudden light over the street blinded us. I saw Isa reaching her hand to a car for balance, and when I was able to look up at the

house, the woman was gone. We all looked at each other, then Lala said, "Run!" We sprinted without stopping to our block, Isa and Lala breaking off to run into their house and Cassandra and I sprinting until we were safely inside ours.

Mamá took us to the mall. Cassandra and I had not set foot in a mall since the girl with the red shoe had died. Cassandra said, "But Pablo Escobar is setting off bombs in public places! Do you want us to actually die?" Mamá said that living in a prison was worse than dying, and clicked the turn signal of the car on, and added that if we wanted to continue being imprisoned at home she would happily oblige. She waited for us to speak, but neither of us said a word.

I thought the mall would be empty given what Cassandra had said, but there was a long line of cars going into the parking lot. I admired all the people not afraid to die — except everybody looked bored and unaware of the heroic nature of our defiance. When we got to the entrance, a security guard pointed a gun at our tires, and another held a mirror under our car, looking for bombs. Once inside, Cassandra and I ran straight for the indoor skating rink. We rented skates and lapped the wooden pit, dancing along

to the songs they played overhead. Cassandra said it was called disco. Cassandra stopped to fix her skates and two boys pivoted to a stop by her. They leaned against the low wall of the rink and asked where she went to school. The way they asked her made me uncomfortable, so I went to find Mamá.

I found Mamá sitting at a table, drinking coffee, a man next to her.

"So nice to see you," the man said.

"I feel liberated, this air —" Mamá said.

When Mamá saw me, she gave me money to get a milkshake. She was alone when I returned. "Where did the man go?"

"What man? Come here, mi cielo. Sit here next to me, Chula. We can make fun of the kids who can't skate." I didn't know who the man had been, but I wasn't surprised. Mamá was an incurable flirt. Mamá's flirting was the subject of countless fights with Papá, which ended with Mamá saying it wasn't her fault she was an exotic bird. If anybody was to blame it was Papá, because he had known who she was and had married her anyway. Mamá flirted with policemen, waiters, men at parties. But as we left the mall for home, Mamá was serious. She didn't slow down her car for the bicyclists on the road like she always did, and she didn't comment on their muscles as we passed the panting men.

The man I had seen at the mall came to our house the next day to celebrate his birthday. Mamá lit candles on a cake she had bought and even Petrona sang "Happy Birthday" with us. At the end of the song, where you were supposed to say, "And many mooore," Cassandra sang, "And never mooooore," which was completely shocking. Petrona's face reddened with embarrassment and everyone laughed, but I was quiet and confused. When the man unwrapped Mamá's gift, Cassandra was upset and asked why Mamá was giving the strange man the same tie Papá had. Cassandra burst out in tears and ran up the stairs and the man covered his face. I thought he was ashamed, but then I saw he was smiling. Mamá followed Cassandra, calling, "It's not the same, I'll show you." Then the man left.

Mamá sat in the living room with both ties on her lap, saying, "They're *not* the same. They're different." But from the dining room table, Petrona and I could see they were exactly the same; both blue, both with a pattern of golden squares.

"The man has left, Señora," Petrona said. "Should I cover the cake?"

"Throw it out, give it to stray dogs, I don't care."

"Why is Cassandra upset?" I asked Petrona.

"Nobody's perfect," she said, fitting the plastic cover on the cake. At the time I thought she meant Cassandra wasn't perfect, but now I realize she was talking about Mamá.

It was clear Cassandra was upset by the man coming to celebrate his birthday. It was clear from the way she went around our darkened neighborhood, looking for something to destroy, ringing doorbells without preparation, and then announcing to Isa and Lala in front of the Oligarch's house that she and I were going to walk over and shine a flashlight inside. I said I wouldn't do it, but then Cassandra said, "You're a chicken." *Chicken.* There was that word I didn't like. I dusted my thighs. "I'm not afraid."

Isa and Lala said they would stay behind and be our lookouts. The silhouette of the Oligarch's house teetered in my vision as Cassandra and I advanced. I felt and heard grass under my feet. Then the ground changed underfoot but I didn't know to what until Cassandra whispered, "Be careful, it's a garden." I clutched Cassandra's

shirt as she walked with both arms raised, balancing, trying to avoid stepping on the plants. I looked up but could barely make out the sky anymore. We were completely under the dark shadow of the house. Cassandra stopped abruptly when we reached it.

"Where's the window?"

"I think this way," Cassandra said. "Keep hanging on to me." We stole around the perimeter of the house, and as I let my hand pass over the wall that looked gray I noted the wall was of a rough material. Cassandra said, "This is something." She grabbed my hand and placed it on a darkened spot on the wall. I let my hand roam and discovered it was wood. When I slid my hand up there was a series of wooden slats. "It's a window shutter," I said. "Yes," Cassandra said. "Here's the knob." I heard the creaking sound of the shutter opening. I came closer and pressed my fingers forward into the blackness framed by the window. My fingers came up against glass.

"Okay, now shine your light inside."

"Me? Why me? You do it, Cassandra, you're older."

"No, you do it. You're younger."

I grabbed my flashlight hanging from my belt loop and unfastened it and lifted it up

until I put it against the window. The plastic of the flashlight tapped against the window. "Shh," Cassandra said.

"Well, you do it, Cassandra, you're older." My heart was pounding.

"Don't be such a baby, just turn it on."

When I pushed the button on, I closed my eyes. I was afraid that when the light clicked on, the Oligarch, snarling, staring, would be right there at the window, expecting us, waiting to shine a light on our faces to see once and for all who we were.

Cassandra sighed. "Wow."

I opened my eyes. The light of my flashlight fell over the living room. It was like a museum. The room was spacious and sprinkled with old paintings and single armchairs and pretty tables and so many crystal trinkets that bounced back the light from my flashlight like diamonds.

We heard Lala's lispy whistling.

"What does *she* want?" I asked. Cassandra snatched at my wrist, "Turn it off, turn it off," pulling me across the lawn. I struggled, trying to find the button. When I found it and clicked it off, we heard the Oligarch calling, behind us, maybe from her front door, "Who's there?"

I saw the beam of her flashlight sweeping across the grass, and that's when we took off running. It's a wonder we didn't fall down. We lost Isa and Lala, but we found a hiding spot two houses away. We walked into some pines and came up against a gate. If we climbed the gate, we could see the slight silhouette of the largest house, and the Oligarch's flashlight beam, sweeping back and forth across her front garden, illuminating corners and behind bushes.

Cassandra was panting. "She'll never find us."

"Do you think she saw us?"

"No."

We made our way home with some effort, not feeling safe for a few blocks to turn our flashlights on. When we got back, Isa and Lala were waiting by the curb in front of our house. "What happened?"

"Did she see you?"

"Are you okay?"

We told Isa and Lala about everything we saw. Cassandra said she had seen a fireplace with a bear's fur in front of it like in the movies, and that there was a red rug under every table. I described all the trinkets that bounced light back to us — a glass cabinet filled with tall stemmed glasses, the globes of a chandelier, the dangling decorations from golden lamps, thin vases with no flowers inside — and how because all those objects glittered under the passing beam of our light it made it seem like the whole room was set with jewels.

"It probably *is* set in jewels," Lala said.

"Enough about the house, did you see the Oligarch?" Isa wanted to know.

I was about to say no, but then Cassandra said yes.

"She was wearing a desiccated toad as a necklace."

"Not only that," I said, "but the toad's eyes shone green even though it was dark."

As soon as I said that, a neighborhood guard riding a bicycle entered the circumference of our flashlights. He was passing by slowly, looking at us askance. He wasn't a guard I knew so I was polite and said good evening and the guard doubled back. He circled us on his bike.

"You girls been out here long?" His cap was pushed back on his hairline and he was pale with a big nose and a matching big Adam's apple. His bike made a lilting, clicking noise as he coasted around us.

"This is my house," Cassandra said. "My mom's having a party, so we came out for air." I turned to look at our house, and registered for the first time the gleeful chatter, the soft music. Something was up with Mamá.

"Why, what's the problem?" Isa said.

The guard stopped his bicycle. "We got a call about some hooligans sneaking around a lady's house. Have you girls seen any gangs or juveniles whom you didn't recognize or haven't seen around?"

I was peering into his face, noticing a bump at the middle of his nose, when he noticed me looking, so I turned to Cassandra. "Didn't you say you saw someone running past here?"

The guard turned to look at Cassandra.

Cassandra stammered, "I couldn't see at all if they were boys or men or what, but yes, I did see three people running. They went that way." Cassandra pointed toward the park.

The guard looked thoughtfully in the direction and set his foot on his pedal. "You girls go home and stay inside, okay? No more breaks for fresh air." He winked at us and rode off.

Lala covered her mouth with both hands as soon as the guard was gone. "God, that was close."

Isa elbowed me. "Why did you have to go and say hello, Chula?"

Cassandra said, "Did you see that? He didn't even suspect us."

18.
THE HILLS

School had started again and Cassandra and I were tired all the time — then the government announced that Pablo Escobar was in jail. Cassandra jumped up and down screaming and Mamá shook my shoulder. "Chula, do you realize? We can go to the movies! We can go out wherever we want now and we won't have to fear being blown up!" I couldn't show any emotion that Mamá could later use as a reason to take me to a psychologist. "We can?"

Cassandra was running down the stairs, then she was cheering outside, her yelling growing dim and loud as she ran up and down the block. I was frozen in place because Mamá was studying me. She was calculating something on my face. I tried to appear as natural as possible, like I was posing for a picture. After a while Mamá cleared her throat and declared she was going to give Petrona a holiday to celebrate

Pablo Escobar being in jail. She was going to drive Petrona home. Did I want to come? I said yes, and Mamá said good, she would have forced me anyway. Cassandra stayed behind.

In the car, I sat in the back with Petrona, her backpack and things bunched up in the front passenger seat. We drove toward the mountains that looked orange like desert sand in the distance. Petrona wore tight jeans she had to pull up before she sat and a small black shirt she kept pulling down over her belly button. Her lips were bright red, her eyelids colored blue. I had never seen Petrona in her street clothes before. I rested my head on her shoulder and asked her if she would put blue on my eyelids like she had done with hers, but Mamá said something about germs and how you shouldn't use other people's makeup but your own, and that she would buy some for me later if I wanted.

I pulled away from Petrona and rested my chin against the pane of the window, watching the street rush under us in a blur of gray. Then I heard the name Pablo Escobar on the radio. A reporter was saying that on top of there being rumors about Pablo Escobar blackmailing the Assembly so that they would make extradition unconstitutional, there was also a cloud of suspicion on his whereabouts the moment he had turned himself in. Pablo Escobar had turned himself in at the exact moment the law making extradition illegal had passed. Some believed he had been inside the Government Palace, the reporter said, begging the question: who, *really,* is the president? Petrona was blowing a bubble of pink gum.

Mamá pointed to the passing cars and noted that everybody was smiling. Mamá said it was because people were happy Pablo Escobar had turned himself in to jail, and then asked Petrona whether where she lived the people would be celebrating. "In the Hills? No, Señora Alma. People like el Patrón where I'm from."

I had never heard someone call Pablo Escobar that. I turned my eyes to the street, unable to imagine how someone could actually like him. At the stoplights I watched the people sitting together on the green hill between highways. One family crowded together around a sign that read, *Displaced by the guerrillas. Lost wife and three children. Hungry. Unemployed. Help.* The wind sprang waves across the man's cardboard. Two children crowded at his feet and looked at the passing cars.

Then we turned and Mamá drove down

the street I suddenly recognized as the place where the car bomb had killed the girl with the red shoe. Mamá must have turned on the street by mistake, because she cleared her throat and pretended like nothing was happening. The bomb had happened more than a year ago, but still I looked all along the length of the street for the dead girl's leg wearing the red shoe. I looked for the exact spot I had seen on the screen where there was a crater flaming out of the pavement, but the sidewalk was clean and filled with people speed-walking and chatting and laughing.

Then the walls of storefronts and buildings became dusty and black. My heart was racing. Behind the pedestrians, yellow tape cordoned off a large area where construction workers stood in yellow hats and large machines broke up the ground.

It was obvious where the center of the explosion had been. The gutted building was in ruins, without front walls and half a ceiling. The crater, half blown into the street and half on the sidewalk, was black. Mamá honked her horn. In front of her traffic had stopped. I turned again to the building. At the center of the crater there was a pile of white roses. Our car started going again and I got on my knees and watched through the back window the pyramid of roses shrinking in the distance, thinking how that must have been the exact spot where the girl had her last thoughts. I looked out the side window in amazement as the walls and stores lightened from charcoal black back to bone white. As the blocks went on, the colors of the houses and buildings changed to more cheery colors: sun yellow, parrot green, flamingo pink. There were high-rises with security guards sitting inside behind tall desks. Then the sleek gray surface of the pavement disappeared, the trees died out, replaced by a dirt road that kicked up dust. Mamá avoided my eyes in the rearview mirror.

On one side of the road, children walked barefoot in a line behind mothers carrying baskets on their heads. One by one, they turned their heads and dropped their things on the road and ran after our car. There were so many of them Mamá had to slow down. I watched the children and the mothers as they cupped their thin palms against our windows and banged their fists against the glass, their mouths shaping around words I couldn't make out.

"Mamá, do they want change? Give them change," I said.

"No, Señora Alma," Petrona said, leaning

forward. "That's how they rob cars. I've seen them do it. That's why there's so many of them." She leaned against the headrest of the seat and turned to look out her window. "I bet those aren't even their mothers."

Mamá looked at Petrona through her rearview mirror and nodded, her hair and eyes nodding firmly with her. She returned her gaze to the road and kept it there, as if the children and the mothers didn't exist. She held her chin high and let the car slide forward, slowly making her way through the crowd. Past her I could see a mother holding her hands open like a book, pleading soundlessly.

There was knocking on my window. I turned and saw a boy my age surrounded by many boys, but I only looked into his eyes, the one pressing most firmly: there were dirt stains on his cheeks. He glanced at his cupped hand streaked with sweat and dirt, and then looked up at me. He pressed his hand on the window, the light of his eyes turned off.

"Niña," Petrona said, "don't feel bad, these children have been turned wicked." She put one hand on my shoulder and stared ahead. Her eyelids flashed steely blue.

Slowly our car slipped through the crowd of children and mothers as if through a forest, and then Mamá sped up.

We were coming closer to the orange mountains. The pavement had appeared again under us. We were amidst tall buildings decorated with gargoyles and lions, with big apartments and balconies and iron railings. We took an exit and the road curved up behind the new buildings and the hill took us higher until we could look down at the buildings' garden roofs.

"Tell me, where do I go?" Mamá said.

"I'll tell you when. We're near," Petrona said.

Opposite the new buildings was the orange mountain. There were huts made from scrap wood, tin, and old advertising signs climbing the slope of it, built, it looked, one over the other. The huts climbed the mountain like stairs. There were houses here and there, except they looked like a house does at its earlier stages of construction: poured cement floor, door and window frames without actual doors or windows, blankets hung from the inside. Everywhere there was orange dirt and the huts and houses blended with the ground like a sunset.

"Aquí," Petrona said. "This is where I live."

I guess I was expecting an invasión like Abuela's, with pretty handmade clay houses and corn and cane growing in small plots. But what I saw was a mountain of city leftovers with people living inside. I tried to imagine what it would be like to wake up and see Pepsi logos and old plywood, the walls between you and your neighbors paper-thin.

Petrona opened her door and briefly patted my back and got out, going around the back of the car to the front in order to collect her things. I went out my door too, ready to take the seat by Mamá, but instead I had to wait behind Petrona, who was still bent at the waist with her torso halfway in the car, talking to Mamá about getting some extra money for vacation time. As I waited, I looked over the car to the mountain to see if I could guess which was Petrona's house — but there, not too far, at the exact spot where my eyes just happened to rest, I saw, leaning on a shack and smoking, the same afroed young man Petrona had said was a carpet guy, who I suspected had stayed at our house, who I suspected was her boyfriend.

"Hasta luego, Petrona," Mamá said. "Have a good vacation!"

Petrona was smiling when she emerged from the car, but soon the smile fell from her face. She must have seen him too, because at once she turned and blocked the car door so as to not let Mamá see me, even though Mamá was examining her nails and not paying attention. Petrona grabbed my wrist and peered into my face. She hadn't figured out I already knew he was not a carpet guy. Small rocks came tumbling down the mountain and when we looked, Petrona's boyfriend was giving us a signal: forming his hand like a gun, three times he discharged it against us, mouthing the words *bang, bang, bang.* When I looked at Petrona, her face was pale and her chin trembling.

It surprised me to see that she was scared. Wasn't this someone she loved who loved her back? I looked intensely at her, trying to let her know I had no intention of betraying her.

Mamá leaned over the passenger seat. "Are you coming?"

I stammered, "Yes. I am," and got in. I didn't look at Petrona and when I climbed into the front seat, Mamá smiled. We waited until Petrona made her way around our car and together we watched as Petrona climbed the hill, crawling and holding on to rocks, then climbing upright between the shacks by the middle of the mountain. She made it past the shacks, but she never turned around to wave.

PETRONA

You know how to wash properly, little girl?
With soap and water, right?

Those were the things la Pulga, Uña, and Alacrán said to little Aurora when they thought I had played them. They wanted me to see that they could talk to my little Aurora this way, with their rifles nearly grazing her face.

I didn't look at them. I stared at my hands. They had seemed so civil at the Santiagos'; but I had misjudged. I pulled the husks off the corn. I listened to the tearing leaves. Something happens when you're scared. Your mind goes off and your body doesn't follow. It happened just this way to me. Suddenly I was not sitting there, powerless, in our hut.

I am in the valleys of my father's farm in Boyacá. I am a little girl. The trees hum. Mangroves and mango trees and the coffee bush. I am crouching. I have found a bird's nest. They are learning to fly. If one falls the mother will leave it but I will save it.

I hear the crack of a stick. The birds become silent.

Before I can turn, a man is on me, gripping his hand on my mouth. I bite. I taste the dirt. I yell, *Papá, Papá, they're here!* He hits my head with something hard and metal. I think, *My father, my mother, my brothers, my sister.*

I wake up and it is dark already. The sky is starred and the chicharras are singing. The chicharras are loud. I see the tops of trees. I am outside. The air smells like burning. I sit up and see my brother Umberto beside me, bashing his head into the trunk of a tree over and over again.

I try to get up and stop him, but I am held back. It is Mami holding me back. More brothers and sisters behind Mami. We are all sitting on the dirt and I wonder why we don't have mats. Some of my little brothers are crying. My brother Umberto is still bashing his head.

Mami says, *They took all of them, Petro.*

I look around to see who's missing. My eyes are adjusting. Terrible for the eyes to adjust and see that it is my father who is missing, it is my oldest brother, Tobias, and the second oldest, Ricardo, who are missing. My eyes sting. *Who took them?* I say, but I know. I don't need anybody to tell me and nobody does. The little ones sob — little Ramón, Fernandito, Bernardo, Patricio, Aurora — all of them at once. Umberto throws handfuls of dirt at the trees around us. Uriel, one year younger than Umberto, looks away into the night, stoic, or in shock. I know it's the paramilitary who have taken my family. It's the paras who have come to our farm, day after day, harassing Papi.

Mami begins to wheeze. *Lie down, Mami, lie down,* we tell her. We don't know what to do. We are so stupid we fan her with leaves. Umberto says Mami is wheezing because when the paras burned down our house, the smoke of the house carried a spirit. Mami has swallowed it, that's what the wheezing is. He calls me Petro. This is the last night anybody in my family calls me Petro.

You sure you know how to wash? Should we show you?

The rifles hovered just by Aurora's mouth and I knew exactly what was meant by it and they knew that I knew. Little Aurora had no clue. This was all a show for me. If I did not raise my eyes, maybe it would delay

271

their violence. And so I dug my stare into the ground, and so my mind went off again.

Now I am staring into Fernandito's eyes, just before he becomes an addict. Fernandito tells me he is the man of the house as little Ramón once did. I am trying to think of what words to say. *Trust me. I can take care of you.* Fernandito tells me he is tough and he will kill. Twelve years old, he spends his time collecting sticks and rocks, playing like they're AK-47s and machetes and grenades. He says he'll become a soldier, policeman, guerrilla, paramilitary. It makes no difference to him. When Fernandito discovers glue, I am relieved.

I tell Mami, *Better that, than the other thing.* Mami slaps my face. She clings to a corner gasping, and spends the money I make on candles. She lights one candle for the Virgin, one each for Papi, Tobias, and Ricardo who may or may not be dead, and one for little Ramón whom we know is dead. Little Ramón who lies under *Diana Martínez, beloved wife.*

One day Fernandito disappears. When he comes back he is an addict. Little Bernardo, then Patricio disappear with him.

Then it's just Mami, Aurora, and me in the hut. I can't stop thinking, *Better that than the other thing.* Mami blames me and I try to explain that I am just fifteen. *Why is everything up to me? Why don't the older ones help? Ask Umberto! Ask Uriel!*

Mami wheezes. In between breaths she says, *How — can you be — so useless.*

Mami thinks Umberto and Uriel are good sons. They got married and forgot us. They drive trucks and promise Mami that if the younger ones make it to eighteen, they'll set them up with a truck. Getting them to eighteen is my job.

Relax. Pulga gripped Aurora's hair. Alacrán jumped on me and pushed my face against the dirt. Uña picked up the corncob that had flown out of my hands and started to eat.

I just want to check behind her ears, Pulga went on, breathing on Aurora's neck. *See if she knows how to keep herself clean.*

I spat into the ground. If they were as close to Gorrión as he said, Gorrión must have known they were coming. He had allowed it. Stupid Petrona, I thought. Stupid Petrona played like a violin.

Then Pulga pulled the top of Aurora's ear down and she squirmed but she couldn't get away.

No! I yelled, *Stop!* when he lowered his

273

tongue on the groove behind her ear. Little Aurora sobbed. He threw her on the ground.

Yes, she's clean.

They walked away then, left us shaking in the dirt. I covered my ears, but I still heard Mami's voice, commanding me, *Fix this, Petrona. Fix this.*

19.
BLACK AND BLUE

Papá got home late at night, but we went out as a family anyway to celebrate Pablo Escobar being in jail. We put on nice clothes, Mamá put on lipstick, and then we went to a restaurant in an area of the city with electricity. There was a steaming plate of pasta in front of me, then tea and a slice of chocolate cake — but all I could think of was, why had Petrona been afraid of her own boyfriend? Why had Petrona's boyfriend threatened both of us? The weekend went by as I mulled over these two questions and when Papá left on Sunday, almost immediately there was an urgent knocking on the door. I ran back to see what he'd forgotten. "What is it, Papá?"

But when I lifted my eyes there she was — Petrona, standing at the threshold of the door, her left eye puffed shut and the broken skin by her mouth in a great swell. I widened my eyes in mute astonishment. I noted how the skin of her swollen eyelid ebbed in shades of black and gray and red, but worse, how the expanded flesh of her lid had not only grown out and swallowed up the slit of her eye but also her lashes. Not even the points of her lashes were visible.

Mamá ran from behind and put her arm around Petrona and ushered her inside. "Close the door," Mamá said to me and sat Petrona down in the living room. "Petrona, Dios mío, what happened?"

I went to the kitchen to get sliced potatoes and plastic wrap because that's what Petrona had done for me the night Galán was shot. In the kitchen, I thought of Petrona's boyfriend pointing his hand like a gun, and then I imagined his hands into fists hitting Petrona. Had she left him? I held a potato trembling, took a breath, and steadied my hand and sliced through it six times.

When I returned, Petrona was trying to smile, but flinched as her lip pushed into the bruise by the corner of her mouth, "Really, it was nobody, Señora. I fell getting off the bus." She held the bruise lightly with the tips of her nails.

Mamá's eyebrows went up. "A bruise like that, Petrona? Can only come from a man's fist."

"Honestly, Señora, I fell." Petrona glanced at me with her one eye then back at Mamá. "Could I spend my vacation here? There's no one to care for me at home."

Mamá regarded her without blinking. "Of course." She turned to Cassandra, who was sitting on the steps, and asked her to get some medical tape from upstairs. I didn't know how long Cassandra had been sitting there for, hugging a banister, baring her teeth. Cassandra sniffed and went up the stairs quietly, and when she was gone Mamá explained Cassandra was afraid of blood, and I didn't even bother to point out that nobody was bleeding. Instead I asked, "What bus were you on?"

"What?"

"You said you fell from a bus. What bus were you on? You weren't coming here because you were on vacation, so where were you going?"

Petrona thought for a moment. "I had an errand." Then Cassandra was back and Mamá said it was time to take care of Petrona's wounds. Mamá made Petrona recline her head back on the couch and then the three of us orbited around her, like moons around the face of a planet. I held a sliced potato over her eye, careful not to push. Mamá put a patch of plastic on the potato and then Cassandra and Mamá moved about taping over the slice until it was held in place. My hands trembled. But if I watched Petrona's eyebrow, thin and delicate following the bend of her bone, then I could breathe. I followed the curve of her hairline next, noting how her scalp was the whitest thing I had ever seen. Her hair was feathery and damp, like she had recently taken a shower, and the shirt she was wearing, three sizes too big, was a men's shirt and had a turnover collar that had been ironed.

I had to run up for some peroxide. Mamá had me pour it by Petrona's lip, as Petrona reclined her face, and Cassandra dabbed at the dribbling liquid with cotton balls. Petrona didn't scream like I would have. She didn't make a sound. But I knew it was painful because the small muscles under her eyes flinched and tensed together. The bruise by her mouth, ballooning out in black and gray, appeared sleek under the peroxide, except where the skin was broken and blood had dried out, the liquid foamed. When it was done, Petrona found my fingers and squeezed. I held the potato in place with my other hand. Mamá and Cassandra worked on securing the potato in a way that would allow Petrona to eat. Petrona had to mime eating. Her lower jaw moved in the smallest of half circles and then clenched up. As Mamá and Cassandra secured the slice, Petrona continued opening and closing her mouth, slowly then quickly, then open, then closed, revealing her pink tongue, her white teeth. It looked like she was talking but her voice was muted, like Petrona was really telling us what had happened but none of us could hear.

The electricity came on just as we finished. The television and two radios boomed and blasted from upstairs. Mamá and Cassandra ran up to turn things off and even though they were gone just for a moment, Petrona turned to me and squeezed my fingers in her fist. "Chula, I think you imagined you saw someone when you and your mother dropped me off, but I think you made a mistake."

I tried to pull my hand away. "I wasn't going to tell anyone."

"You don't want bad things to happen, do you, Chula?" She pressed my fingers down into the seat of the couch, making me lean closer.

"Like your eye?"

"Exactly like my eye."

I stammered, "I told you, I won't say anything." Petrona let go of my fingers. She caressed my cheek. "That's my good girl." Petrona reclined back and patted my knee with her extended hand. I massaged my fingers. If Petrona was protecting some guy who had hit her did it mean she had not left him? Unless he hadn't. Unless he had pointed his hand like a gun at us to warn her about some danger coming her way — in which case, it would explain why she was protecting him. I wanted to hug Petrona, but I was afraid of her — her face swollen and black, one eye buried completely beneath her flesh. It was mean to be repulsed by the way she looked, so I lay back into the nook of Petrona's arm and snuggled against her.

When Mamá and Cassandra came back, I sat up. We wiggled the slices of potatoes on Petrona's jaw and eye to make sure the slices wouldn't fall off, and then they took Petrona to lie down in her room.

The question of Petrona's boyfriend kept me up at night. If he hit her, maybe it was because he was in need of money and the prospect of Petrona losing her job was the worst thing that could happen. I thought of all the huts made out of tin. If Petrona and her family couldn't afford to build real walls, how much of her money could her boyfriend be getting? If he was innocent, then the danger Petrona had been hiding from when we were at Abuela's had finally caught up with her. But what could Petrona have done to provoke a beating? Once or twice I got out of bed, thinking I would go down to Petrona's room and just ask her, but then I remembered how she had twisted my fingers against the couch. I held the knob of Mamá's door next, but if I talked to Mamá, Petrona would get fired. I sat before Cassandra's closed door. But I would not tell her either because she would just tell Mamá, and then I'd be the reason for Petrona getting fired — or worse.

Cassandra and I had to go to school before the sun came up now because there was no electricity at the school and we had to make the most of daylight hours. It felt wrong to be out so early, or so late, waiting for the school bus. At school I napped through the morning classes. Then it was time to go home again.

Each night Mamá, Cassandra, and I re-dressed Petrona's bruises with more slices of potato and each night we saw how her bruises changed. One day we discovered that whole blotches of skin had turned deep wine red and yellow, with vivid tones of green and purple in between. It was almost pretty, like a firework.

All of us felt bad for Petrona. When Papá came home the following weekend he brought soft ice packs we could put in the freezer and then give to Petrona to hold over her swollen, broken skin. Cassandra and I gathered pillows for Petrona so she could be comfortable and then we went door-to-door asking for used magazines. Once, as we were putting the alcohol and cotton away, Mamá stood up, struck with an idea. "Petrona — how old are you?" Petrona said she had just turned fifteen, and then Mamá said that was perfect. We should give Petrona a First Communion and a First Communion party. Petrona's jaw dropped. Mamá said Petrona had always wanted one; Petrona had said so herself. Petrona said, "No, Señora, I really don't want to impose." Mamá waved the air and was already leaving Petrona's bedroom saying it was no trouble at all, and then she was in the living room dialing numbers on the telephone. I turned to Cassandra to ask what was happening, but Cassandra put a finger on her lips, and we heard as Mamá said hello to someone and asked for a donated wedding dress.

I turned to Petrona, confused. "Wait, are you getting married?" I was hurt she hadn't told me.

Cassandra fell back on Petrona's bed, cackling. "Petrona! Getting married!"

Petrona wrinkled her brows and hid her face with her hand, mortified. We heard Mamá saying loudly into the receiver: "I *know,* she's *fifteen* years old."

"So you're *not* getting married?"

This sent Cassandra into hysterics and she rolled from side to side laughing and kicking her legs. We heard Mamá say, "Any white dress will do; it's for a good cause." Petrona told me she was having a First Communion party, apparently. "Oh," I said. I patted Petrona's knee over the blankets and told her not to worry: "You just swallow a wafer and drink some wine, it doesn't mean anything, and you'll get presents."

At night, while Mamá and I sat balling up socks, Cassandra spoke up and asked why the two latest wallet-size portraits of herself and me were missing from the pages of the photo album. She was sitting at the edge of Mamá's bed turning the pages.

"They're gone?" I was looking over her shoulder. It was true. The small rectangular spaces where the portraits had once been stood out in white, while the rest of the page was evenly yellowed in a darker tone. We didn't know what had happened to the portraits. None of us had taken them out.

After looking in the drawer where the albums were kept and finding no loose photographs there, Mamá crossed herself and said spirits were terrorizing us. I was sure Petrona had taken them to look at us whenever she felt lonely.

During the coming week the swollen skin around Petrona's eyes started to deflate, and Petrona's lashes slowly reappeared, then there was a lazy alligator eye, taking everything in. Then her two eyes seemed almost the same size and the dramatic colors turned brown and olive-edged. I took this change in Petrona's appearance as a sign that it was safe to be friends with her again. The next night, I tiptoed downstairs and around the swinging kitchen door to see what Petrona was up to. I was surprised to see Petrona's curtain flashing with the unmistakable light of a television. There was no electricity and I was so confused I didn't think twice about turning Petrona's knob and stepping inside. There, Petrona sat in bed, the smallest television I had ever seen on her lap, her face cast in blue.

In a second she lifted her eyes and the television shut off. Her after-image, pale and her lips contorted, hung in the air as I heard the sizzle of her television.

"It's only me," I said.

Petrona exhaled. "Chula, madre de Dios, I nearly had a heart attack!"

Her television came back on with a great flash. Petrona squinted and reached her hand toward me. "Come watch, Chula." I climbed next to her in her bed. "Look," she said. She switched the channels by pressing on two buttons at the side of the screen; then she turned the little machine upside down to show me where the batteries went.

We got under Petrona's blankets and hugged the small television between us and Petrona explained the new telenovela she had started to watch. It was called *Escalona* and it was the true story of a vallenato composer who had an accordion duel with the devil and won. But the real story was about how Escalona was a womanizer. There he was, serenading a curvy blonde from Brazil, singing to her on his knees. The next scene he was running after some gaunt, big-nosed woman, down narrow cobble-stone streets, until he caught her hand and kissed it. As the credits rolled, Petrona said, "Men are so stupid — in the town where I grew up, in Boyacá, there was someone like Escalona. He was such an animal."

I had never known where Petrona was from. I called to mind what I knew of Boyacá. It was the state right next to Bogotá. I tried to recall the safe route map. We had driven through Boyacá on our way to Cúcuta. I thought I remembered many little men with berets and sunglasses.

"What happened to him?" I asked.

"He's gone. I don't know what happened to him. They set our house on fire, and we fled."

"Who set your house on fire?"

Petrona tensed and she stared at the window, as if she'd said more than she intended.

"Was that the danger you were in?"

On the little television a comedy show started. Men dressed as women were selling flowers at a bus stop. I sensed Petrona was not going to say any more on the subject. "Petrona, who was the man that Mamá brought over to celebrate his birthday?"

Petrona pressed her lips. Her face changed colors from the screen. "I think he was just a friend, but maybe he is more."

I sat thinking about what the more could mean. Family members were more. Boyfriends were more. I understood then why Cassandra had been angry. Petrona turned off the television. "Come, Chula, time for bed." She led me in the dark to the stairs and then she kissed the top of my head. I hugged around her waist for some seconds and then I let go.

The dress Mamá got for Petrona was from a *divorcée.* I wasn't sure how Petrona felt about it, but the cloth was a pretty shade of white and it was satiny and cool to the touch. Mamá set up her sewing machine at the dining table but the cloth and tools of her sewing took up much of the first floor. They stood together all Saturday in the middle of the living room, Mamá wrapping pliable tape around Petrona, giving Petrona different orders: *Arms up, Belly in, Stand up straight.*

As the lights came off and on, Mamá unraveled the dress. She said it all had to be taken in with Petrona's specific measurements. During daylight hours, as Petrona stepped in and out of the skirt, tried on the disconnected sleeves, put on a veil, held up the bust, Mamá gave short speeches.

"When a boy is interested, always make sure you are the one to remain in power. Men will want to take power from you — that's who they are — but don't allow it — that's who *you* are."

She said:

"When you are in love, you are in lust. And if you are in lust, satisfy yourself, then walk away. Never do anything for his sake, not until you are sure he is committed. Then and only then can you be nice to him — but, be careful. Don't give yourself entirely. Never owe *anybody* anything, least of all the man you are with. *That's* how you'll remain in power."

It was the same stuff Mamá had been telling Cassandra and me for years, but Petrona listened in rapt attention. "What if you're stuck?"

Mamá held the skirt piece around Petrona's waist, fastening it with pins she took from her lips. The pins had colorful heads — violet, turquoise, red. Mamá took a step back to look at her work. The skirt fell from Petrona's waist like a bell. "Then you leave him."

"But if you're stuck —"

Mamá fluffed the skirt. "It's your own fault, Petrona, if you choose to be a fool."

During the hours of electricity, Cassandra downloaded a program and set up an email account in the computer. She sent single sentences to her friends at school — *Have you done your homework yet? What are you wearing tomorrow?* — and sat refreshing her inbox until a reply came in. Downstairs, Mamá sat on her creaky stool and pedaled the sewing machine. Her eyes were absorbed

288

in the rise and fall of the needle, the divorcée's white cloth rumpling prettily before
the *taca-taca-taca* of her machine. The dress
was nearly done. Petrona could step in and
out of the skirt, and all that was left was for
Mamá to attach the skirt to the torso, and
the torso to the sleeves and then as the last
touch, the zipper on the back.

Late at night, when I looked in her room
Petrona was soundly asleep. I heard the tick-
ing of a clock but not her breathing. I waited
until my eyes adjusted and I started to see
the black block of her bed, the dark gray of
the wall, the lump of her body.

"Petrona," I whispered, but there was no
answer.

I went to the living room and listened to
Papá's radio. The drone voice of the news,
low and professorial, was soothing. *It has
been a busy week for Pablo Escobar,* the
radio announcer went on. I stretched out
on the couch and put my hands under my
head and closed my eyes. *The news of the
kidnapping of a senator was closely followed
by a bomb threat to a wealthy neighborhood
in Bogotá. Carrying 850 tons of dynamite* — I
was soon soundly asleep.

Petrona had to take classes at a nearby
church for her Communion and went on

and on about things she'd learned — like the specifics of a *Confirmation*. Cassandra and I had no idea what she was talking about. I watched yellow candlelight flicker on Petrona's face, making the pointy shadow of her nose grow and shorten across her cheek. Finally I asked — getting confirmed about *what*? Petrona was shocked we didn't know. She said we had probably gone through a Confirmation ourselves, because you couldn't do a First Communion without it. She explained that during Confirmation you got *anointed* with holy oil that had been blessed by an *Archbishop.*

"Wow," Cassandra said.

"Wow," I said.

I didn't know what Archbishops did, but I did know all about their pretty hats. That's because I watched Holy Week live from Rome every year. That's because it was the only thing on the television that wasn't a Jesus movie. Archbishops were the ones with tall pointed hats and staffs that looked like something a shepherd might use, except they were made of *gold.*

"Anoint me," I told Cassandra in my bedroom, and she got Mamá's special body cream and sat me under the moonlight and greased up my hair.

"I'm pretty sure you're supposed to say

something."

"I know." She pulled on my hair. "I was getting to it."

She hovered her hands over my hair heavy with cream and exclaimed, *"Dominus, dominus, anno domini!"*

I felt a great chill pass through me, and I squirmed and sucked in air. Cassandra dropped her hands. "Okay, now you anoint me."

At Petrona's Confirmation, the choir sang in Latin, the Father droned on about the same old stories, and then incense fogged up the domed ceiling — that's when the children being confirmed were called to the front and the Father opened his arms and asked for all the kids to be possessed by spirits; some nice, like the Spirit of Wisdom and Intelligence, but some dubious, like the Spirit of Holy Fear. I widened my eyes as the Father sealed the dark ritual by dipping his fingers in a golden chalice, smearing holy oil on each kid's forehead in the shape of a cross, saying to each one, *Pax tecum.*

At home, I paid close attention to see how the spirits the Father had set on Petrona were changing her. What I noticed was that Petrona looked off in the distance for long minutes, and when I asked what was on her mind, it took her a while to respond. The worry lines on her face seemed somehow to be treading deeper into her bruised skin. When she finally told me what she supposedly was thinking about, it sounded like nonsense: "Just thinking I have to tell your mother to get more laundry soap," or "Oh, just noticing that stain on the wall."

One day I asked her directly if she felt changed by the experience of being anointed. "Yes! Can you *tell*?"

She was so excited I told her I could.

"I feel . . ." she said. "I feel I am made of light."

I tilted my head. Maybe it was true. Here and there Petrona began to seem older to me. Maybe it was the dress. When Petrona put it on and breathed, I noticed she actually had breasts. It was impressive. White lace spread below her neck but at the bust white satin was cut in the top shape of a heart. She was impossibly peaceful and serene. But then I ran into Petrona in the hall, and saw there were bite marks on her hand. She had obviously bitten herself, and as I looked at her it seemed like it wasn't the Spirit of Wisdom settling into her but the Spirit of Holy Fear.

I began to see the Spirit of Holy Fear everywhere. It lived in my dreams, in the pipes that didn't bring water to the house, in the television that showed me Pablo Escobar. It lived in the deep sound of electricity leaving our home — the sizzle static of the television, the humming of voltage through walls and floors and ceilings — ebbing, unwinding, pirouetting into silence. It lived in the quiet after the electricity was gone: the dog's bark, a grasshopper's song, the howling wind rustling the leaves of the Drunken Tree. It lived as some kind of imminent sense, some kind of dark wingspan that slowly advanced on our house.

In the days after Petrona's Confirmation, while we awaited the day of her Communion, everything was in disharmony, and things happened as if full of knots and misunderstandings, like the Spirit of Holy Fear was going around our house wreaking havoc. The Spirit made Mamá obsessive. In the dark she noticed Petrona's elbows were dry. "Petrona, come here, you need some cream."

Papá was in turn more gentle, listening to every word we said as if putting his ear to the ground, trying to detect an oncoming train. But he was careless too, taking unnecessary risks. He drove too fast when he was home, and things that would have usually scared him, didn't. We came to know, for example, that at the entrance of Papá's site in San Juan de Rioseco somebody had spray-painted a wall with the words *You are now entering FARC territory.* Papá dismissed it as fake.

Papá laughed at Cassandra and me. "Look at you — you're as fearful as my workers." He told us there was such a thing as common criminals, with no actual ties to guerrilla or paramilitary groups, who earned a living by *impersonating* those groups, kidnapping people, and demanding extortion money. Papá was sure this was what was happening in San Juan de Rioseco, because the usual signs of the militarized groups — random killings, rape, peasants forced to harvest drugs, people kicked off their land — were missing.

Papá explained all this to his workers, but they were a gullible group, and now they were claiming to have seen the FARC patrol the edges of the oil site. "They hear *the guerrillas this, the guerrillas that,* then they see something, and they jump to conclusions. That's called *the power of suggestion.* You would be amazed at what the mind makes up under those circumstances. See, I was there when they saw *quote unquote* the guerrillas. We were all standing by the drilling rig. Then, at the edge of the oil site where there was some fog we saw a group of men walking. Now, according to the workers, *with their superhuman vision,* they saw all kinds of impossible details — the men carried machine guns, they were wearing dark bandanas over their mouths, all kinds of details. Now, *power of suggestion,* right? But since *I* am a man with a clear mind, not prone to being tricked, both eyes wide open, I can tell you that the group of men we saw walking into the fog were not guerrillas at all." Papá waited a moment for effect, then he added, "I think they were ghosts."

Papá said that the townspeople of San Juan de Rioseco had been seeing a particular group of ghosts that fit the description of what he had seen. Sightings dated back to the 1800s, when a group of Franciscan monks entered the mountains to look for a healing herb and were never heard from again. Sometimes the Franciscan ghosts showed up in full robes asking for a glass of water, and if you didn't give it to them fast enough, they revealed to you their skeletal grin. Sometimes they were seen bending down talking to a child. But because they were Franciscan monks, nobody was really afraid of them, except for *the women of the night,* as Papá called them, because the Franciscan monks often hid those women's shoes and purses when they were trying to leave their house for work. I said I thought the Franciscan ghosts sounded very nice. Maybe they would look after Papá. Cassandra told him to be careful.

Papá had to leave on Saturday. He was missing Petrona's Communion. Mamá said we needed the car, so he got Emilio to pick him up. It was late evening when Emilio arrived. He sat at the dining table stirring milk into a steaming cup of coffee — five times clockwise, twice counterclockwise. Seeing he was occupied, Cassandra and I went to explore his taxi. The vinyl seats were a symphony of smells — cigarettes and cologne and something astringent like rubbing alcohol. There was that little window, too, that had a tiny sliding door. Cassandra and I crawled all over Emilio's seats, playing with the radio, counting his change. There was something about a taxi that was unlike any other place on earth. Even the trunk seemed like a new world. We took turns shutting each other inside. In the dark hollow, the curve of the spare wheel dug on my side. I lay there quietly until it felt like it was hard to breathe. I kicked on the trunk.

Cassandra's singsong voice came muffled: "I can't hear you, Chula. What is that you said?"

I kicked harder and screamed. I gasped for air, trying to calm down, but also feeling like I would suffocate; then the trunk door sprung open, slowly and with a wet sound. I saw the dusking blue of the sky and Cassandra in silhouette.

When Papá left, Mamá walked upstairs, crisscrossing the beam of her flashlight to light our way. She told us we needed to go over some things for the next day for Petrona's Communion. She told us we were going to Petrona's house after the church, which meant we needed to wear hiking clothes. "But it's a special occasion," Cassandra said as we entered Mamá's bedroom. "Don't we get to wear anything nice?" Mamá ignored Cassandra and said that in addition, we had to wear our hair in a tight bun. I asked Mamá if I could put my hair in a ponytail since it was prettier, and Mamá said yes — if I wanted to give a criminal the opportunity of having a proper handle to pull me behind a bush with. "We're going to an invasión," Mamá added sternly. "You will both wear jeans, an old T-shirt, sneakers, and your hair in a tight bun — is that clear?"

We said together, "Yes, Mamá." I went to my room and lay on my bed. Through the night I dreamed of my hair in a ponytail dragging long behind me, a levitating knife coming down on it — the rope of my hair in dismembered sections marking the places I'd run.

PETRONA

To protect my family, I dusted my knees. I brushed my hair. I hiked to the playground, past the bushes, up the mountain in search of the men who I knew congregated around a lit fire. I delivered myself to show I had no intention to betray them. I spoke over the noise of the fire. *I can fix it.*

I said, *Hit me as hard as you can.*

I said, *If the family sees me beat up they'll have me stay through weekends, and then I'll be there every second, I'll make sure the little girl doesn't say anything.*

I said, *I'll do it, I'll deliver what you want.*

Gorrión came from the shadow of the fire and put his arm around me. He called to the others, *See? She's a revolutionary through and through, my Petro.*

I did not consider myself part of them. I barely noticed as Gorrión told me I was doing the right thing, as he put his hand over my shoulder. All I could think of was he had called me Petro. I swirled in the past of my family calling me Petro, that last night, Umberto bashing his head against a tree, and then Gorrión was putting in front of me a teaspoon of gunpowder. *Swallow it, it'll give you courage.* Little Ramón in his casket jumped to my mind, his hands perfumed with gunpowder, and I wondered if they had made him swallow gunpowder too. I hated Gorrión and hated the Santiagos too for not seeing what was happening to me, nobody there to pull me from this free fall and I put my mouth over the dust and then Gorrión gave me a bottle of aguardiente to chase it down with. Gorrión took away his arm from my shoulder and walked away into the shadows of the fire again, and I was afraid, and as the men descended on me like a pack of wolves, I held on to the only thing I had left — the sound of my pet name, the one from the time of before, Petro, how nice it sounded to my ears.

20.
THE DRESS AND THE VEIL

Petrona's Communion was not as exciting as her Confirmation; the priest didn't invoke any spirits and he was overall very tame. The boys and girls taking their First Communion (boys on the left, girls on the right) looked bored and fiddled with their starchy, never-to-be-worn-again clothes. Petrona was the tallest among the girls. They each held a long white candle that was lit halfway through the service. I was struggling to stay awake. It felt like I had only closed my eyes for a second when the congregation startled me in one booming voice, *Deo gratias.* I shot up. The pews where the Communion kids had been were empty. Mamá glared at me, and pulled me down to my seat. Cassandra was smirking. I spotted the Communion kids kneeling a line at the altar. The Father dragged the sleeves of his robe on the tiled floor, an altar boy in tow, and he turned and twisted, picking a holy wafer from a bowl and placing it directly on each kid's tongue, then lowering a golden cup and giving each kid a sip.

When it was over, the whole congregation rose to their feet and clapped.

Outside Mamá gave flowers to Petrona. Petrona's cheeks were flushed and there were sweat stains under her armpits. An old woman approached, dabbling a smudge of mascara. She wore a simple black dress, and as I stepped aside to let the old woman pass, I noted the silhouette of her waist broken by what must have been the tight elastic of her panty hose. The fat of her stomach bulged out under and over it. Petrona put an arm around her.

"Señora Alma, girls — this is my mother, Doña Lucía."

I widened my eyes and felt my cheeks grow hot. I didn't know Petrona's mother would be in attendance — what if she had seen me sleeping? Petrona's mother shook Mamá's hand. "You can call me Lucía, I have heard so much about you."

"Where were you sitting, Doña Lucía?" I blurted, thinking that if she sat near the front or back left there was no way she could have seen me. She patted my head. "They have so many questions at that age."

Mamá drove us to Petrona's house. Doña

Lucía sat in the front passenger seat. She and Mamá were saying something but I couldn't hear what because Cassandra had lowered her window. I was stuck in the backseat between Petrona's dress and Cassandra. Petrona's skirt rose in a tall cloud of shiny white and at the other side I was assaulted with wind. Petrona hugged the fluff of her skirt. "You're going to see my home, are you excited?" I nodded. Petrona grinned from behind her white veil. The white veil cascaded down from her crown, which was made of small, fake white flowers and was secured with pins to her smooth, cropped hair.

We got to the invasíon faster than I expected, and as Mamá slowed, Cassandra rolled up her window. Outside Petrona's window was the blur of the orange mountain. "Where should I park?"

"Anywhere," Doña Lucía answered. Seeing Mamá hesistate, she said, "You don't have to be nervous. I've talked personally to the community. There's nothing to worry about."

Mamá gave a nod but puckered her lips how she did when she was worried. We parked under a palm tree next to some trash bins. When I got out, the air was cool on my face. I had been looking forward to coming, but now that we were there, I couldn't wait to leave. The hill looked deserted — not like there were no people around, but like there was someone lying in wait. I scanned the mountain for Petrona's boyfriend. His afroed hair would make him easy to spot. If he were the threat, then we would have strategy on our side. But if he wasn't, then I didn't even know what to look for.

Mamá dug in the trunk of the car for the box with food and used kitchen stuff we'd brought for Petrona and her family. Petrona was struggling in her cloud of lace and artificial silk, and Cassandra and I took her gloved hands and pulled. Then, Petrona held herself in space as Doña Lucía fussed about the skirt of her dress and Mamá came over to right the crown on Petrona's head. Petrona stood contained in the white bell of her dress, smiling, knowing she looked pretty.

Cassandra stared at Petrona's shoes. Petrona's shoes were old, scuffed, and peeling back in brown scratches all over the heels and toes. Petrona shifted and the tops of her shoes retreated and disappeared under the bell of her dress.

We all turned to look to the tall hill. Orange air blew in sheets over the footpath that cut through the middle. There were thinner paths that sprang from it to the left and right. I wondered where they led. Far up, on a horizontal path that cut across the top of the hill, there was a horse advancing along with a rider. A person on foot was leading the horse. I couldn't tell if the person leading the horse was a man or woman, but the person on the horse seemed like a child.

I heard the beep of the car alarm and Mamá came to my side and leaned the box on her hip. Petrona balled up her skirt and hugged it to her chest, and then we followed after Doña Lucía, who led us to an opening between some rocks. Doña Lucía was wearing shoes with low heels. I stayed two steps behind her and as we climbed the dirt path up the tall hill, I expected her to wobble, but she didn't. She was sure-footed and quick. There was nobody around. I guessed as long as we were with Doña Lucía and Petrona we were safe. I stared at the skin-color mesh of Doña Lucía's pantyhose. There was a place at her heels that was rubbed red from her shoes. I looked over my shoulder to make sure we weren't being followed. The orange hill sloped down, empty. Directly behind me, I saw some of Petrona's dress had escaped her grip and was grazing the dirt. Behind Petrona was

Cassandra, then Mamá, carrying the box, hoisting it against her hip. The path evened out, and when I lifted my eyes I saw we were on the first terrace of the hill, shacks packed as far as the eye could see, but also shacks ahead, climbing up the slope.

We paused to catch our breath. Doña Lucía said she would go ahead and take care of a few things. Before we could respond, Doña Lucía speedwalked across the terrace and began to climb the next slope, getting a foothold on nonexistent stones, ascending like those were stairs she was climbing. Soon she was out of view. Petrona rubbed my back and smiled. "You're safe here," she said. "Here, I'll go in front." The tail of her dress slipped from her grasp and dragged on the sand and stones.

I took deep breaths and looked around and tried to relax. I liked how the shacks were constructed out of random parts. Sheets of wood were made into doors, doors were walls, corroded advertisements were ceilings, plastic tarps were windows. Through the gaps I could see flashes of the lives inside. As the path snaked up the mountain, wherever rust ate through the metal, or a breeze lifted up sheets hanging at door and window frames, I saw — a woman's sandaled foot pushing against the dirt to rock herself in a hammock, a man crouched before a fire on the ground, boys playing marbles, a dresser covered in the kind of vinyl paper Mamá used to line her kitchen drawers. "Chula," Mamá called, "stay close." She adjusted her grip on the box. I saw plenty of crucifixes too, worn and desolate, hanging from nails with string or twine or propped against walls or pots.

Then Mamá, Cassandra, and I were bent down, holding on to rocks and trees. "My house is just at the top," Petrona said. I looked up, but couldn't see the top of the hill. I concentrated on the path, planning on where to place my feet and where to hold on in case I fell. I was wondering whether Petrona's house would be made out of discarded metal or poured cement, when we came upon a boy slumped against a rock next to a plastic tarp held up by sticks. He was chewing on a dry piece of grass. My looking made him stir, but it was only when he spotted Petrona's dress that he jumped up and followed us. "Petrona! You get married without telling me, you love me so little?"

He looked at me briefly, then at Mamá, then turned to Petrona again. "At least let me take off the garter, you look so good all made up." He glanced at her chest, then

307

looked into her eyes. "You're so well packed." Petrona snarled. She was sweating. I saw that the gray of her bruises was beginning to mottle through her makeup. Petrona hastened her step. "It's a *First Communion* dress, Julián, what a rotten little boy you are."

"Yeah?" He hurried behind. His teeth seemed whiter and his tongue redder because there was a film of dark dust covering his skin. "I did my Communion *years* ago." I looked at him out of the corner of my eye. He was younger than I was; there was no way he had already done his First Communion. He turned and addressed Mamá, "Mother-in-law! How are you today? You're a friend of Petrona's?" He looked at Mamá's box. "What are you carrying? Need help?"

Petrona turned, her hands gripping the skirt. "I work for la Señora, Julián, now *go* away." The skirt of her dress was now coated in orange dust, but it was actually nice the way it went from brick orange at the rim, lighter and lighter to satiny white.

"What a travesty, Petrona, I thought we were friends."

Petrona kept climbing. He asked, "Are they going to your house?" Then he whispered to Mamá, "Mother-in-law, come say goodbye to me on your way down, sí? Don't be mean."

"Sí, sí," Mamá said, wiping her forehead on the shoulder of her shirt. "I'll come and say hello."

"Your daughters too? You promise?"

"Yes, yes, we'll say goodbye."

The boy stayed behind, and I asked Mamá if she was really going to make us go back and say goodbye to that creepy little boy, and Mamá laughed. "*Of course not,* Chula. The trick with little boys from invasiones is to say yes to whatever they want only you tell them *later* — all the while you walk away. Isn't that right, Petrona?"

"Sí, it's true. La Señora really *did* grow up in an invasión, didn't she?"

As we made it to a peak, we paused. Mamá set the box on the ground. I pinched at my sweater and pulled on the fabric to feel air against my skin. Having arrived safely, a weight lifted off of me. Down the steep, the little boy was standing still, looking up at us. A three-legged dog was panting by his side. "Here's my house," Petrona said, walking up to the shack immediately to our left.

Petrona's shack was constructed in a nice, simple way. The leftmost wall was made out of a series of doors, and the right wall was made out of mismatched slatted wood.

There was a lilac bush next to it. From here, if I looked into the distance, I could see a cluster of shacks and then a small patch of dry land that had been made into an improvised soccer field. Behind that there was a tall retaining wall with barbed wire on top. The wall was about six meters tall and sleek, obviously put there so that the people of the invasión wouldn't climb over. Above the wall to the left I saw the tops of wealthy condos that rose into the clear sky, and to the right, an imperious mountain.

"Come in, Señora, my family is looking forward to meeting you."

"Come, girls," Mamá said, and Petrona and Mamá disappeared behind a faded flower curtain that hung between the wall of doors and the wall of slatted wood. That was the front door. Cassandra and I walked up to the curtain but neither of us went it. Next to the curtain there was a plastic decoration hanging from a nail. I guessed it was one of the Christmas Magi. He wore a turban and held up a golden chest. The colors of the plastic Magus were faded, but deepened in hue wherever the plastic tucked in. There was twine holding up the curtain and this twine was tied to a post, which seemed to be an old city post meant to hold up electric wires but the wires were gone.

The post seemed to be supporting the whole shelter.

Then Cassandra pushed me and I was inside. Petrona's family, surprised by my sudden entrance, started. I knew Petrona had nine siblings, but there were only her two older brothers and a young girl, all of them, I saw with disappointment, with a very distinct face and not a Petrona face as I once imagined. Cassandra snickered at my side and then Doña Lucía picked up Petrona's hand. Everybody stared at Petrona, and Doña Lucía presented her like she was a decorated official: "My Petrona, look how beautiful! Just like a queen." There were no windows, but there were gaps where the roof went from silver corrugated tin to transparent plastic, and the plastic let some light in. There were three plastic tables, a few stones, and many fresh flowers and potted plants. A metal wind chime tinkled in the back corner over two mattresses placed directly on the dirt floor. A small fan, the battery-powered kind, whirred next to the mattresses, setting the top of the sheets rippling like water. Opposite the mattresses, in the corner, there was an altar with lit candles and photographs. I wanted to look but Mamá put her hand on my shoulder. "I'm la Señora Alma, this is Cassandra and Chula, my two girls." Cassandra and I smiled. We waved. Petrona's brothers and sister smiled back. We kept our distance like we were at a border, none of us with papers. After a while, Doña Lucía said to her sons, "Don't you have manners? Come help la Señora Alma with this box."

"Oh, thank you," Mamá said as one of Petrona's brothers lifted the box from the floor. "Put it somewhere nice where you can unpack. I've brought you some dishes, some kitchen stuff . . . Oh, and we picked up chicken and a cake! Be careful with the cake, it's on top."

Petrona flipped her veil back and came over to us, leading her sister by the shoulders. "Chula, Cassandra, meet my little sister."

Petrona's little sister had Petrona's same caramel, almond-shaped eyes, but her hair was long and messy and blond.

"I'm Cassandra, this is Chula, how old are you?"

"Ten. You?"

She was a year older than me, but I didn't want to reveal that. "What's your name?" I said.

"Aurora."

I looked up at the roof. "It must be nice to have a silver roof — like you're an astronaut." I could tell this was the wrong thing to say because Aurora squinted, then looked away. "Where do you go to school?" Aurora didn't look at me.

"What do you do for fun?" Cassandra asked.

"I play in the swings, I see my friends, we go hunt lizards."

"Lizards! Where do they live?"

"We also go to a haunted place," she said to Cassandra.

"Oh, we love haunted places," Cassandra said. "There's a place in our neighborhood where you can actually see the Blessed Souls of Purgatory and there's also a house with a witch."

"Really?" Aurora tucked loose golden hairs behind her ears and thought about this for a moment. "Well, us, in the haunted place here, we took a candle, and the wind was blowing like a Jesus apocalypse, but the candle didn't go out."

Cassandra nodded. "That's definitely the doing of a ghost."

In the kitchen area, where tall aluminum pots stood piled on the ground, Doña Lucía inspected the set of plates, forks, folding napkins, and glasses Mamá had brought.

Petrona cut the cake and Mamá said to Doña Lucía, "Let's use the plates I brought," but Doña Lucía pushed Mamá's plates aside, and fished around her cluttered place, saying, "I prefer to use my own." Mamá smiled, like this wasn't an insult and she turned her attention to Petrona. "What about some soda?"

Cassandra, Aurora, and I sat on small rocks, the adults sat on cement blocks, and Petrona sat in a plastic chair. One of Petrona's brothers didn't have a seat and he was sitting on the ground eating the cake on his plate. "So tell us," this brother said to Mamá. "Does Petrona behave when she's over there?" Petrona's two brothers had the same nose. Or maybe it was the same eyebrows. It was hard to decide which.

I was about to take my first bite of cake when an old man came in. He was pale with black hair styled back and hanging from his neck was a little satchel, rugged and wrinkled like it was carrying a small corpse. I jumped up thinking he was a thief but Aurora pulled me down to the rock again. "That's my Tío Mauricio. He never comes out of his house, but for special occasions. Anything you want — if you like a boy and the boy doesn't like you back — my Tío Mauricio can fix."

"What does that mean?"

Aurora turned her eyes to her plate and

stirred the cake. The old man was staring at me.

Mamá was saying, "You really didn't think we were coming to visit you?"

"Well, you know how city people are, always with their stomachs on their forehead; they wouldn't show their nose on this mountain if they could help it."

"You're prettier than they say," one of the brothers said to Mamá.

"Me? But you're not far behind!" The brothers laughed, and Mamá went on, "But come, come. What happens when it rains? How do you make it up and down that mountain?"

The old man edged closer to me and lowered himself to a crouch. I didn't look at him and held my breath. I was sure he was a witch. I tried not to think about anything. I stared at Mamá. Mamá was tapping her foot on the ground. Maybe she was as impatient to leave as I was.

"Will you give me your hand?" the old man said.

Mamá had told me to never give my hand to a witch, but I was staring at the corpse-shaped necklace and didn't know what else to do.

"I'm just happy you came, Señora," Petrona was saying. "All the neighbors must be

315

so jealous. Nobody believed me when I said you were coming."

The old man returned my hand and when I looked at it, there was the shell of a snail on my palm. Black grains of dirt clung to it. "I found it today, isn't it pretty?"

When I lifted my eyes I was confronted with Mamá's gaze.

"Señora," Petrona said. "This is Tío Mauricio. He wanted to meet you."

"How do you do," Mamá said. The little groove above her lip was tense.

The old man stood. "If you ever have trouble," Petrona said, "Tío Mauricio is who we all go to for help. Isn't that right, Tío?"

Mamá glanced at me then back at the old man. "Trouble like what?"

"*Any* problem." He dusted his palms. "I have great aim. From a roof, I can take down two."

Mamá smiled briefly. "Well, if I would have known you were going to be here, I would have taken a class; my aim is terrible."

"That's why you need *me*. Look, all I need is a photograph, where they live, I have someone who follows them, and then we give them a good scare."

"My uncle is so good," Petrona said. "All

316

the money he makes, he is saving to give my mother a proper house. You know, out of brick."

"Or if somebody hits your car and they don't want to answer," the old man continued. "Easy. We take the car down, we sell it, we divide the loot half and half."

Mamá turned to Petrona. "How nice for you, Petrona, to have someone so useful in your family. My family, on the other hand, is filled with lazy snakes, I have a sister —"

This is how Mamá changed the subject. I didn't know what to do with the snail's shell. I couldn't drop it on the ground because he would see it, so I clutched it against my palm. Maybe it would break. Aurora scooted closer to me. "When I take my First Communion, I am going to wear a dress like Petrona's but it's going to have an even longer train that's going to go on behind me for like two meters."

"That sounds like the *best* dress." I wanted to tell her it was the worst dress because it would get dirty, especially because of where she lived, but I didn't want to say the wrong thing. The shell started to cut my skin.

"I'm going to have shoes made out of glass like in that fairy tale."

"Cinderella?"

"No, that's not the one."

"Petrona, stand up and show us your dress again," Doña Lucía was saying. "Do a twirl so everyone can see. You really made it, Señora Alma?"

"Yes," Mamá said. "My mother taught me how."

I narrowed my eyes, suddenly remembering Mamá had bought Cassandra's and my Communion dresses from a store. I beheld Petrona with a twinge of envy as she twirled, then I was embarrassed. Didn't Petrona deserve a dress made just for her? I looked away, squeezing the snail shell in my hand. Petrona's brothers clapped and when I looked again, the veil was dragging over Petrona's shoulder and her skirt was filled up with air. Suddenly a small boy came tumbling through the curtain, tripping on the empty box we'd brought and left by the door. The little boy laughed on his knees and hands shaking without sound. Then another boy came through the curtain, his hair curled over his eyes. He stopped at the door. "Who the hell are these people?" No one spoke and the shack filled up with the smell of cement glue. Everything was still for a moment — then Petrona's eldest brother rushed at them and the two boys took off, and Doña Lucía was screaming for

Petrona's brother not to hurt them, and then we heard snickering outside, followed by more yelling. Then Petrona's second brother went out.

"It's the bad influence of the invasión," Doña Lucía said.

"Why don't your older sons help?" Mamá said, like she understood what had just happened. "Isn't there something they could do?"

Doña Lucía shrugged. "They have problems of their own. The police don't come up here. If it wasn't for the encapotados, I don't know where we'd be. They're terrible people, but at least they try to keep our kids from getting hooked on drugs." She stared at the ground for a moment, then said, "My Fernandito made friends with one of those desgraciados, drug addicts. And now look at him. He's dragged his other two little brothers with him. Of course, children are so stupid. What can I do? I got gangrene and asthma after they took my husband and my two eldest and we had to flee. I light candles to the Virgin."

She gestured to the corner with the candles. From where I sat I could count four photographs. I did the math in my head: Doña Lucía had said three of her sons were addicted to glue, and three of Petrona's siblings were present. Three photos were for Petrona's remaining siblings — but who was in the fourth photo?

Petrona ran her gloved hands on her forearms, her mind elsewhere. I understood the fourth photo must have been her father. My heart broke for Petrona. I thought about her little brothers. I didn't really understand how glue could make people addicted. I had seen children in the street many times breathing glue in paper bags. There were so many of them in Bogotá. They looked up with glassy, winded eyes. They slumped in the corners of the street, around the gates of malls and restaurants, begging for money. I stared at the curtain, listening for what was happening out there.

When it was time for us to go, we said goodbye to Petrona's family. Petrona's uncle mimed at lifting an imaginary hat from his head, and Mamá mimed at bowing down holding the imaginary ends of a skirt. Outside, we paused to look down at the climb we had ahead of us. Petrona said it would go by quickly. I stared at the roofs of the dwellings in the invasión — silver and clear corrugated roofs not secured I could see from this angle, but weighed down by piles and piles of brick. If I blocked the invasión with my hand and looked straight ahead, the landscape was Bogotá as I knew it: a sprawling, modern place with paved streets and high buildings and decorated balconies knitted with fog.

Petrona came back down with us most of the way. She held my hand firmly, the lace of her glove coarse against my palm. I wondered again where Petrona's boyfriend was. I felt scared. "Did you have a nice time, niña?" Petrona asked.

"Yes." I stared down at the rim of Petrona's dress dragging on the orange dirt. Petrona stopped and told us she would keep watch as we made our way down. I slipped my hand out of hers and and gave her a hug and skipped down. Below, our car was still beneath the palm. When we reached it, I turned and looked up. Petrona was still there, standing at the terrace in the hill where we had encountered the first shacks. The tall orange hill rose behind her and the white veil lifted in the wind and her skirt was rusted at the bottom. Suddenly, I wanted to stay. "Chula," Mamá called. "Hurry up." I trotted up to Mamá and I got into the car. Mamá started the car and put it in gear. The car was not yet in motion when she spoke to me through her gritted teeth, "That uncle of Petrona is a bad man.

Show me. What did he give you? What did he say?"

PETRONA

The bruise on my eye was still there when I did my Communion but la Señora Alma covered it with green paint, then peach. She made me look pretty, with a thin line of black along my lashes, and a pink dusting of powder on my cheeks. I felt like a princess, Chula and Cassandra waiting on me, bringing me water, fluffing my skirt, playing with my veil. There was a brightness I had never felt before. I held my hands, feeling so light on my feet, so full. Then I would catch sight of my dress as my white, gloved hand brushed against it and I'd think, *Everything borrowed. Just a girl from an invasión.* The priest said inner light and peace came from living your life for others. I held on to this thought and quieted. I thought of little Aurora. The way her blond baby hairs came up like airy roots by her temple.

At the church, I was the oldest girl taking First Communion. Nine-year-old girls looked me up and down and sideways and giggled meanly. I stared at the priest, and thought about my Papi long gone, how he would have liked to see me in this church wearing this pretty dress, how he would have liked to tell me, *See, Petro, how honest work pays off.* I lit my Communion candle from the flame of the little girl next to me, thinking about Papi's white eyebrows. They were so thick and wiry. I bowed my candle to the left for the girl there to light her candle. I knew that if Papi was here, I would lie to him too.

My days were filled with cleaning and cooking and pretending to go to sleep. I tossed and turned in the mattress in our hut in the Hills whenever I was home. At the Santiagos' I bunched up my clothes on my bed, a fake body to account for my real body — which was so good at hiding manila envelopes, so good at speed-walking and advancing on all fours through the broken part of the fence, so good at standing in the dark where the streetlights did not reach, so good at holding the manila envelope out over the street for the approaching man on the motorcycle, who sped by and plucked the envelope right out of my hand like a thunderclap.

Once it was done, I returned and pushed

the fake body onto the floor, the purpose of it met, and there it was, just a dirty pile of laundry on the floor. Then it was just me, climbing into bed with my real body, and I fell asleep the moment I closed my eyes, this body of mine so good at pretending to be innocent.

I knew I would tell Papi, *Yes, from the sweat of my brow . . .*

Maybe if Papi was here then I wouldn't have been stupid, I wouldn't have believed everything that was said to me. When I got like this the only thing that helped was pulling out my little hinged mirror to look at my own face. I taunted myself. *Look into the eyes of a true mentirosa.* My two eyes. The pupils small. La Señora's makeup all a magician's trick. When I looked up close, I could still see hints of the gray of the bruise that I brought onto myself. It spotted through the paint. I stood. It was my turn to get in line and swallow the wafer.

21.
GLASS SHARDS

There was the sound of a car alarm when I sat up and pulled the blanket to cover my shoulders. It was Monday. I couldn't be late for school; it was close to the end of the year and we had finals. But then shards of glass rolled down the blanket and piled at the dip of my thighs.

A cold breeze came through the broken window. The sky was black. The wind carried the smell of smoke and the loud sound of the neighborhood. The screaming and the car alarms.

The door opened. Cassandra rushed in, kneeling by my bed, fanning her hands, repeating in a bewildered monotone, "Blood. Blood. Blood." Her pink glasses were lopsided and hung from her ears down her chin.

Mamá rushed in, then after a second. "Chula! Cassandra! Are you okay?"

In the distance, after the empty lot and

the highway, there was a black, thick braid of smoke billowing from a building. I stared at shards of glass sticking up from my palm. I plucked one. I felt a dull pain and then my palm was wet and alarmingly red, deep red like a rose petal, but warm as well.

I looked from Cassandra to Mamá, then I stared out the window. All around the window frame pieces of glass stood up like icicles. Black smoke tunneled up into the sky, turning and turning. I looked to the lot. Where were the cows?

"Este país de mierda!" Mamá threw my blanket to the side. I didn't spot the cows. She took me up in her arms and then we were running. Running below the ceiling, through a door, into the bathroom, her fast breathing, and then I sat on the toilet crying. Hydrogen peroxide fizzled on my knee and hands and down my face and Mamá was screaming, "This is your father's fault, how could he let this happen?" My forehead pulsed and I wondered about the cows and then I couldn't understand what anybody was saying, so I listened instead to the pitch of the voices, Mamá and Cassandra speaking, yelling. I tried to get up, but they rose to their feet and placed their hands on me. "Chula, sit down! What's wrong with you?"

Then Mamá cried into a red handkerchief

and my hands shook. Everything vibrated with color. I was lying down. Cassandra held a wet towel to my forehead and Mamá gave me a glass of water and had me drink from a straw. I was very tired but still I asked Cassandra, "What happened to the cows?" and then I fell asleep.

When I awoke I stumbled down the hall. It was night. Everything was dark. Mamá was standing on my bed with her shoes on, and Cassandra trained the spot of a flashlight on Mamá's hands. Mamá was stretching plastic over the windows. I stared at her shoes, sinking into my blankets with their dust, thinking how Petrona would now have to wash everything before I could go to bed. Then I remembered Petrona was at home. I remembered her veil lifting in the wind in the middle of that orange hill. I remembered the snail shell cutting into my flesh. I remembered the glass shards sticking out of my palm.

The plastic was taped at two corners of the window, but the rest of it lifted up like a sail, catching the beam of Cassandra's flashlight. I sneaked under Mamá and picked at the plastic to look out of the window.

"Mamá, look at Chula."

It was dark and I couldn't see the cows,

but the chill of night was nice on my face, and the sound of traffic on the highway was nice too, constant and rumbling.

"What are you doing up, mi cielo?" Mamá carried me back to her bed, saying I was lucky I didn't need to go to the hospital. I was the only one hurt because I slept by a window.

"Did you see the cows?"

"What cows?" Mamá said. She took my temperature with her hand on my forehead. I went to scratch my cheek and realized it was covered in gauze. My hand was covered in gauze too.

Mamá got the snail shell Petrona's uncle put on my hand from her purse where she had left it the night before. She didn't have to say that the shell was to blame for me getting hurt — it was clear she thought this because she knelt in her bathroom and broke the shell with a hammer and then doused it with alcohol and set it on fire. I didn't want to smell it. I pulled Mamá's blanket over my nose. Cassandra asked Mamá if she thought she was overreacting and Mamá said there was no overreaction when it came to witches. The burning shell left a dark stain on the tile.

I didn't want to stay in bed anymore. I was wide awake. Mamá gave me permission

329

to sleep with Cassandra in her bed. I went to the attic and when Cassandra fell asleep, I got up and practiced my kicks and worked on my splits. I shone my flashlight out on the garden. Finally I shook Cassandra awake. "Cassandra, did you see what happened to the cows?" Cassandra kept her eyes closed and grumbled, "Chula, I'm sleeping."

"Can't you wake up and tell me? Are they dead?"

Cassandra reached blindly to the floor, palming the carpet for her glasses. She lay down on her back and put her glasses on, but kept her eyes closed. "They're not dead. I saw them. They were hiding in one end of the lot."

"Nothing happened to them?" I was ecstatic. Cows were amazing. I got in bed next to Cassandra. "Did you know cows have eight stomachs? They're superhuman."

Cassandra laughed. "They're actually *not* human." I offered Cassandra my cuts.

"Do you want to touch them? It doesn't hurt at all." She pressed her finger on the cut on my arm and then lifted it quickly, grimacing.

"Oh, it's soft like an egg yolk." She stuck her tongue out, disgusted.

"Cassandra. Can you believe glass exploded over me? Not just anyone can survive glass exploding over them."

"Chula, you were all covered by a blanket."

"Well, not everyone can sleep and keep their blanket in place covering everything in case of car bombs, and they wouldn't make it out alive when glass exploded over them — you wouldn't: you kick your blankets to the floor."

"I don't sleep by the window."

"Cassandra, what if, this night, a man is able to climb to the roof and what if at night he watches us sleep?"

"What dumb questions you ask, Chula. No one can climb our roof, it's too steep, haven't you seen? Besides, who would want to watch your ugly face through the window?"

I hit her with a pillow and then we lay quietly. "We forgot all about our emergency backpacks," I said.

"I know," Cassandra said. "It's funny that we forgot." We hadn't packed an emergency backpack for months. After a few moments I felt scared again, like there might be another bombing. I pushed up on my elbows and looked across the dark attic. "Cassandra, do you think we're safe?"

"Yes," she said, yawning. "Very safe. I'll protect you. Now go to sleep."

22.
THE DREAM

When Mamá woke up the next day to collect our water, she opened the faucets but nothing came out. Mamá told us not to get ready for school — then she went out into the street in her pajamas. While Mamá was gone, Cassandra and I knelt on my bed to see what was happening at the bombsite. It was the only place in the house where we could see. Past the roof of our indoor patio, across the empty lot and the highway, amidst the half-there, half-not-there buildings there were rows of police cars and fire trucks and their flashing lights. Through the thin film of plastic we heard echoing motors and sirens.

I spotted my cows in a corner. They were lying together, very still. They seemed peaceful. I smiled looking at them. There was always enough grass for them to eat, but I wondered who supplied their water. I had never seen a person approach them. It only made the cows more special. They were *my* cows, Teresa and Antonio, my companions through all. In some minutes Mamá entered into the bedroom. She knelt by us and said she found out from a neighbor that the car bomb of the day before had ruptured the pipes that brought water to our neighborhood. Mamá gazed toward the bombsite and said the street over there was probably flooding with the water meant for us. I said we would be smart to drive over and collect it, but Cassandra said it would be contaminated. I said it wouldn't be if you could put your cup right up to the source. Nobody agreed this was a good plan.

Mamá said the government was sending an emergency truck to supply us with water, so we went to the attic to watch for it. The three of us stood on various chairs to see out the little window. Holding on to the sill I asked Mamá if Petrona was coming to work. Mamá said Petrona had a few days off because of her First Communion, and I told Mamá I just wanted Petrona to know I was okay. Mamá patted my back and said we could try and call later.

The truck arrived, parking at the neighborhood gate three blocks away. There was no doubt it was the government truck. It was white and had a behind that globed out like a bee's with *Agua* printed on it in blue. Long hoses came out of it like legs. Mamá jumped off the chair and told me she was going to get water with Cassandra. She had me lie down on Cassandra's bed and peeled back the gauze on my face. When she was satisfied my cuts were not infected, she gathered five-liter plastic bottles and buckets for her and Cassandra to carry and they went out.

As soon as they left I stood on a chair again. From the little window, I saw them, making their way into the street, their hands full with containers. Then, in a second, families all along the block came out, house by house, and the street flooded with a river of people. Out of their hands dangled watering cans, cups, pots, bowls, toy water guns, large tubs, flower vases, milk jugs. A large crowd merged from a side street. I lost sight of Mamá and Cassandra, and then someone broke into a run.

The river of people rushed the water truck like a startled herd, and once they reached it, they boiled and pushed against one another to get water first. The truck tossed like a boat at sea. Two men in jumpsuits jogged on the running boards trying to stay balanced. The men unhooked hoses from the truck and dashed back and forth aiming their hoses at the containers held up for them.

I felt so dizzy from watching the tumult of the crowd I had to go lie down.

Mamá and Cassandra were not back for many hours. I found Mamá's agenda and found a telephone number marked for Petrona. But when I called it, it was a pharmacy.

"Farmacia Aguilar, what can I do for you?"

I was lying down with both eyes closed. "Do you know a girl named Petrona?"

"You want to leave a message, or send word for her?"

I opened one eye, impressed. "Send word." It was funny that the pharmacy screened Petrona's phone calls. I thought to ask whether the pharmacy took the phone calls of all the people at the invasión, but then I thought better of it, and added, "Tell her it's from la Señora Alma."

I heard a soft thud, like the phone had been placed on a counter. I heard the muffled sounds of people talking, the dim sound of a cash register. I was in a daze, nearly falling asleep, when I heard Petrona's voice. "Aló? Señora Alma?"

"It's you!" I sat up.

"Chula!" Petrona was silent for a second.

"How'd you get this number?"

"Petrona, listen: there was a car bomb and my window exploded."

"What! Are you okay? Were you hurt? Who's taking care of you?"

"No one," I told her. "There is *absolutely* no one taking care of me. Mamá and Cassandra are out getting water." Petrona sounded worried. I smiled. I felt better knowing I had passed the shock of my recent brush with death onto someone else. "It was a recent brush with death," I continued out loud, like Petrona was privy to the conversation inside my head.

"Chula, when is your mother coming back?"

"I don't know, I'm sleepy now, when are you coming to see us again?"

"Wednesday," she said, and I took the receiver from my ear, saying, "Okay, bye bye, going to sleep now," and replaced the phone on the receiver.

When Mamá and Cassandra returned I learned we had enough water for a day. Cassandra inhaled. "How long until they fix the pipes?" Mamá bit her lip.

Mamá called Papá in San Juan de Rioseco and told him what had happened and asked what she should do. Papá seemed to be yelling at Mamá. From what I could hear, Papá was on his way to Bogotá and he wanted Mamá to go to the grocery store and buy water. Papá talked to me on the phone — "Are you . . . kay, mi . . . ?" *"Are you,"* the second Papá said. I twirled the telephone cord around my finger. "I'm okay, Papá." "I'll be home s . . . Chula." *"I'll be."* I fell asleep again. When I awoke, it was night and Mamá said the grocery store had been impossible. Everyone in the area was without water and people were getting violent. "I only got that much —" There was a gallon on the table.

I was afraid to sleep alone and Cassandra said I could come to her room again. In the attic, we lay on her bed and Cassandra pointed the beam of her flashlight up. I followed the cracks along the ceiling as Cassandra told me that she had been separated from Mamá when they got to the gate, where the water truck was. Getting water on her own was the most adult thing she had ever done. "You know, like a rite of passage?" The cracks on the ceiling looked like thin thunder. They divided in threes then divided again. "I'm a different person now," Cassandra continued. "Do you understand? I went *through* something." She waited, then said, "You don't know what it's like."

"What do you mean." I turned to her. "I

had glass explode over me."

Cassandra turned off her light. "It's not the same."

She shifted in bed and my eyes slowly adjusted; I was beginning to see the silhouettes in the room. I turned on my light and pointed the beam at the wall.

"Cassandra —"

"What."

"After I woke up from my nap I thought of something."

"What."

"You know how the Oligarch is the richest person in the neighborhood?"

"Yeah."

"Well, what if the car bomb was meant for *her.* You know on the television they're always saying the guerrillas left a car bomb in front of this country club, and this building because that's where rich people go? What if all of this happened because of the Oligarch?"

Cassandra was quiet for a moment. She sat up. "Chula, that is the least idiotic thing I have ever heard you say."

"Really?"

When Mamá left early the next day to buy water at more distant grocery stores, Cassanda and I dialed Isa and Lala and invited them to come over. Isa and Lala were also staying home from school because of the car bomb. The glass of their window had shattered as well, and the exploding glass had barely missed their dog. We told them we had business to attend to and asked them to bring their own water to drink. In the attic, we built a tent out of baby-blue sheets and living room cushions and we sat inside in the aquarium-like light cast through the sheets and discussed what we were going to do about the Oligarch. She was clearly to blame.

"It's all the same story," Isa said.

"It's just the rich getting richer," Lala said.

"It's just unfair," Cassandra joined.

"She has no respect for any of us," Isa said.

"Because she's a witch," I said.

The twins and Cassandra looked at me. I knew I had spoken out of turn. To make up for it, I lifted the gauze from my cheek to show the cut I knew was there. I ran my finger along the gash. "This will be a scar because of her." I taped the gauze back, and then Isa said, "We have to take something of the Oligarch's that's of equal value to Chula's scar."

"Yes," Lala said. "An eye for an eye." The three of them turned to gaze intently at me, but I had no ideas. I stared at the lap of my shorts.

Cassandra said we needed to clear our heads. She took us on a house tour where she pointed out where house flies gathered. Hunting flies was a pastime Cassandra had invented, and she was showing us how it was done. In the kitchen, we clapped the air until we caught one fly; then Cassandra held it between her fingers. We crowded around her as she took Mamá's tweezers and plucked a limb off. The leg came off easily, like pulling a blade of grass, but the fly's other five legs flailed in wild abandon, consumed in panic.

Cassandra plucked limb by limb off until the fly was round like a planet.

It vibrated and buzzed in her fingers.

The last thing she plucked was the head.

I looked on at this new side of Cassandra — her detached concentration, cold and clinical.

When she was finished she laid each limb and the head in a line on the windowsill where she said they would grow dry and crackly with the sun. It occurred to Isa we could pluck the wings off too. The wings were pretty and silver-veined. Within some hours, we arranged thirty-six legs on the windowsill, twelve wings, six heads. We displayed them before the sun.

We chewed into cold bits of chicken Mamá had left in the fridge. Mamá did not return when the apagón came, so we decided to go straight to the Oligarch's house. We walked in the dark on that familiar journey, silently pondering what we would take.

Then we saw a glimmering of light.

It was shocking to see electricity when the whole neighborhood was pitch black. We ran toward the blue-lit place and then we stood, dumbstruck. It came from the Oligarch's house. Electric light poured out of every one of her windows and even spilled out onto her lawn. A large machine rumbled on her grass like a truck engine idling. It shook up our feet and vibrated our bones. Cassandra said it was an electric generator. Only people like magistrates and ambassadors had them. We were afraid to approach, but Isa said that if it was really bright inside the Oligarch's house and really dark outside, the Oligarch couldn't see us, it was a scientific fact. Isa said the Oligarch probably couldn't hear us either, her generator was so loud. And so we came right up to the house and Cassandra opened the little wooden doors to a window and all of us looked in. The Oligarch was kissing a man by her fireplace. They were sitting on the bear skin, wineglasses nearby, and an outlet with many electrical cords coming out — two for twin floor lamps, one for her stereo, another for a hot plate heating water for tea, another to a television turned down. The Oligarch kicked over a glass. The wine spilled on the bear fur but also splashed on her pretty pink slipper and I couldn't help but laugh.

We turned to the Oligarch's generator. We didn't have to say to each other this is what we would take. We inhaled its sharp fuel smell, and pushed down on buttons and levers. We poured dirt and sticks and rocks into its crevices. We yanked flowers from the garden and shoved them in alongside more pebbles and sticks. Then, we heard the pitch of the machine change. It shrieked and shook like a boiling kettle, and we ran. We were behind a car across the street when there was a loud pop. The lights in the Oligarch's house flickered and in the flashes we saw a great cloud of smoke rising, creamy gray, from the generator.

All was quiet again. I grinned in the dark. The air smelled like burning. We heard small thudding sounds coming from the inside of the Oligarch's house, the Oligarch and her boyfriend probably bumping a knee, scraping an elbow, palming the drawer (perhaps in the kitchen) where she kept the candles. We ran two blocks to the park, howling and skipping, falling on our knees laughing. "That'll teach her!" We lay back and gaped at the stars.

Mamá was still gone when Cassandra and I returned. We lit candles and had cereal and soda for dinner. High on sugar, we went to Petrona's room to look for the small television. Cassandra was confused. "But do you know how much those things *cost,* Chula? I have a friend in school who got one, but she's *super*-rich. Do you understand, Chula? *We* couldn't even afford it — how did Petrona end up with one?"

"Maybe she stole it?" I was shining my flashlight under her bed, but there was nothing there.

Cassandra opened up the cabinet and trained her flashlight over the piles of Petrona's clothes. "Are you sure you didn't dream it?"

"I'm sure. I saw it."

We looked everywhere we could think of but there was no sign of the small television. The excitement of the day hit us all at once. It was time for bed. Cassandra looked at a clock and told me it was four in the morning.

■ ■ ■ ■

When I opened my eyes, there were clattering sounds. The room was unfamiliar: the ceiling low, the space narrow. I stood up on one elbow and shadowed my eyes with my other hand. The bathroom door stood ajar and bright skylight flooded on the floor. Light came through the semi-sheer curtains of the window too. I remembered we were in Petrona's room. Cassandra moaned next to me and turned to the wall, clapping Petrona's pillow on her head, and I got up and went out.

I cowered at the brightness of the kitchen. Mamá was standing at the counter with several gallons of water. "Look at all this water!" I said. "Where'd you get it?" Mamá's hair was wet from a shower and it stained dark colors into the back of her blouse. "Is there water upstairs in the bathroom too?" I wanted to bathe.

Mamá stared at me, so I explained, "We only fell asleep in Petrona's room because —" Then I realized I couldn't tell her about the Oligarch, nor could I tell her about Petrona's television. "Because we were waiting for you. It was *so* late and we were *so* tired. You know when you get so sleepy —"

Mamá turned from me and wiped her face.

"Mamá?"

When she turned, her black eyebrows pushed together. She held my shoulders. "Chula, am I a *good mother*?"

I stared into one of her eyes and then the other. I said yes, and she let me go. She put water on a burner. She was suddenly irate. Why was Papá leaving her with all the responsibilities? She was only human. What could anyone expect of her? She dropped a cup of rice grains into the water.

Cassandra came out yawning, and saw all the containers of water. "You got water! Good job, Mamá." She got a bowl and served herself cereal and walked out. Cassandra didn't notice Mamá's clenched jaw. She didn't notice Mamá's sudden gestures. Her sighing. Her banging doors, her clattering dishes and utensils. Mamá glared at me and told me to get ready for school.

I didn't argue. I ran upstairs to bathe, but there was no water in the bathrooms. I was in a daze getting into the school uniform, thinking I wouldn't dare ask why Mamá's hair was wet, or maybe I *should* ask why. Why had she come home so late, where had she taken a shower, where had the water come from? When I went into the bathroom to brush my teeth, I was startled by the mirror. It didn't look like me, but some other girl — someone with a bulging patch of dirty gauze on her cheek, red hot scrapes on half of her face. I lifted the gauze to peek and there was the deep cut, and the skin was inflamed and purple. I taped it back. I wanted to change it for a clean one, but I didn't know how. I winced brushing my teeth and when I spit the foam it was tinted pink with blood.

At school I was sent to the nurse during second period. My cut had bled through the bandage and needed to be changed. The nurse washed it and gave me aspirin and then she let me rest in the little office. She turned off the light and left the room. I overheard the teachers having a quick meeting with the Principal just outside, saying the school had no water again, that they would have to send everybody home. I was glad because I had not studied for finals.

On the bus on our ride home, younger kids ran in the aisle between seats howling, throwing paper, boys pulled on girls' hair, and the older kids sang loudly in the rear seats. The driver nearly crashed from trying to keep order. I was glad to get home in one piece. I was exhausted. Cassandra and I walked together on the sidewalk. We opened the front door. We went up the stairs. We looked for Petrona but she wasn't in, though she had told me on the phone she would be back by Wednesday. I checked with Cassandra — it was Wednesday, wasn't it? Then we found Mamá. She was sitting in bed, saying nothing, widening her eyes at the air.

"Mamá?"

She glanced at us and didn't ask how come we were home so early. Instead she urged us to sit, she needed to tell us something important.

It had been night in her dream, she said, and Petrona had been in a plaza, strange men surrounding her, kissing their lips to upright whiskey bottles and sucking the coppery liquid up. Like they were hummingbirds. *Who are these men,* Mamá asked Petrona in her dream, but Petrona avoided Mamá's eyes. The men stretched their lips into smiles, except the lips kept stretching until they reached all the way up to their eyes.

"To their eyes, really, like monsters," Mamá said. "I'm not exaggerating."

"Mamá, it was just a dream," Cassandra said.

"But why did Petrona avoid my eyes?" Mamá went on. Mamá recounted the dream two more times, landing on the same points, like Cassandra and I weren't there. I told Mamá it was just a dream just as Cassandra had done, and finally Mamá said the dream was a warning. "That girl Petrona is running around with God knows who doing God knows what and I don't know if Petrona thinks I'm painted on a wall, I can't see what she's doing, but I am going to find out."

I tried to do my part without making things worse. "Mamá, I think Petrona is afraid of someone." Mamá narrowed her eyes at the air. "Mamá, did you hear me?"

Mamá loaded us up in the car and drove to every guard booth in the neighborhood and leaned out of her window. "You watch that girl Petrona from my house. Tell me where she goes and whom she meets after work." The guard booths were decorated with Christmas lights. The guards nodded. "Sí, Señora Alma."

When we got home, la Soltera was waiting on her porch, leaning over our planters. There was a bouquet of roses on our porch, and la Soltera ashed her cigarette in the air over it. "It's from that man you've been seeing."

Mamá picked up the flowers, and dusted the ash off the plastic cone. "What do you

349

know, you hag?"

"In front of your daughters and everything, don't you have shame?" La Soltera said it was a disgrace Mamá kept lovers, was too busy to tend to her children, was a Bad Mother. La Soltera said it was hard not to think Mamá was a Bad Mother, Cassandra and I roaming around looking like vagrants. "Look at your little one," la Soltera continued, pointing her cigarette at me. "Did she crawl out from under a bus?"

Mamá squared off in front of the planters and looked straight at la Soltera. "Yes, she did," she said. "And so what?"

La Soltera blew out a cloud of smoke. The smoke fogged Mamá's face, then faded. "And nothing," la Soltera said. She turned and went into her house and closed her front door.

"You make sure you keep your absurd concern inside that stuffy, old house of yours. Vieja amargada!" Mamá lit a cigarette, took a few puffs, then threw her cigarette into la Soltera's garden. I didn't know if Mamá had intended for la Soltera's garden to go up in flames, but it occurred to me that if it did, the fire might spread to our house. I leaned over the tall planters and looked at la Soltera's patio. It was overtaken by dead leaves. I swallowed and slid under the skirts of the pines and pulled myself up into la Soltera's garden. I found Mamá's lit cigarette from its smoke and stamped it out. When I took my shoe away, the grass around the burnt cigarette tip wore a halo like a dark saint.

We waited all afternoon and night, but Petrona didn't show up to work and that's when I knew something was wrong.

PETRONA

By candlelight I whispered to Aurora, *Listen to Papi.* Aurora was afraid, looking at me like I had lost my mind: *Do you mean listen to Mami, Petrona? Papi is gone.* I yanked on her arm, *Do as I say.* Her eyes glazed like she was retreating somewhere, the look of them something new, born the day when Pulga licked behind her ear. I held the pinch of tears back. I pulled her close. I rubbed my cheek on her head. *Don't pay attention to me, I'm just an old woman.*

Aurora was quiet. On the mattress next to her, Mami was fast asleep. My little brothers did not come home anymore, but still the three of us shared the one mattress like always. Aurora said, matter of fact, *Are you running away?*

Of course not! I smiled. *And you know what else,* I lowered my voice, *next time when I come back from work, the first thing I am doing is paying for concrete so we can have a real floor. Won't that be nice?* Aurora nodded. *But how will you afford it?* I smacked a kiss on her forehead. *Don't worry your little head! Now go back to sleep, before Mami wakes up.* I waited until little Aurora settled by Mami on the mattress then I carried the bottle with the candle to the altar and blew it out. I made my way down the Hills. The sun would not be out for two hours.

Once I was small. Once I fit all of me folded in Papi's lap. I could stare into the white scruff of his beard like I was staring up at the stars. Already he was an old man. Papi never tired. He bent over the earth, he whistled a tune. We were rich in eggs and meat then, the hens that clucked at our feet, the creatures that roamed in the wildness of the trees. We were rich in our stories: the time Uriel drank the milk instead of churning it, the time little Ramón, tiny as he was, climbed trees and fell asleep in the branches, the time I took rocks from the river and put them in my bed because I wanted to sleep where the fish slept. Then he was gone, mi Papi, and our home gone with him. But the day after he was taken, as we got ready to go, I saw him. My mind playing tricks, I saw Papi in a field of sunlight wearing his wide straw hat the way he did mornings, his back bent and his hands reaching to the earth; then he straightenend and his hat's shadow flew from his face as he lifted his eyes, and he put his hand in the air and waved to me. I saw his face in the light, how bright and loving it was. I grabbed Uriel's arm, *Look.* But when I returned my eyes, the field was scorched and it lay bare next to the ruins of the farmhouse and Papi was not there, had never been. The black staircase of our farmhouse climbed into the sky. We walked by the road and some trucks gave us rides. Our feet hurt and grew a thick covering of skin. I imagined because I had seen Papi reach his hand into the earth, next to that place where the staircase was black, I imagined the paras had taken his life. *How are we going to eat?* I used to ask him when our harvest failed, small in his lap. *Don't you worry your little head,* he'd say. *That's what you got me for. You go play, Petro, go play, go find me a pretty stone.*

23.
THE GIRL PETRONA

Cassandra and I went through the motions of a normal Thursday morning — packing up our homework, brushing our teeth. We tiptoed around the house, hushing at the smallest sounds, listening intently to everything Mamá said. We put on our uniforms with inordinate care. We pulled on the long blue socks and folded them over below the knee, we laced up the shoes, tucked our white shirts inside the gray skirts, threaded and tied the thin blue ties around our necks, put on the school jackets, dusted the school seal. But we had no intention of going to school. Cassandra was sure Petrona would come to work, and then Mamá was going to interrogate her because of her dream. Cassandra wanted to hear what Petrona would say. Cassandra was going to find out once and for all what was going on with Petrona. I was sure Petrona would come to work too, but she'd be bloodied, the danger she'd been in rushing at the gate in our garden. I remembered her words, *You don't want to end up with my blood on your hands, do you, niña?* I was determined to protect Petrona, either from Cassandra or Mamá or whomever.

In Mamá's bathroom, I entertained Mamá with questions, and Cassandra went about the house stuffing our school bags with supplies. "Mamá, were you ever a beauty queen?" My voice sounded even, or at least Mamá didn't notice I was nervous.

She was putting mascara on in front of the mirror. "Me? No. Why do you ask?"

My throat felt dry. "It's just that you're so pretty."

Cassandra walked past the bathroom door, scanning Mamá's room.

"I was *the* prettiest girl in my village," Mamá said. She opened her eye wide and brushed her lashes with the painted bristles of the mascara wand.

I held in my breath. "Were you really the prettiest?"

"Yes!" She put the wand down on the bathroom counter. "All the boys would die for a date with me. They called me Bird of Paradise; I was so choosy. You have to learn to be choosy too, Chula." Mamá picked up the wand again. "Never say yes to the first boy who asks you out."

I stepped close to the door. At an angle, I could see Cassandra was emptying the change jar into my backpack. "Okay, Mamá, I won't."

Mamá was tensing her lips into an O, applying red lipstick. "Be good in school today, okay?" I gave Cassandra a thumbs-up, and she came in and we kissed Mamá goodbye.

Outside, as we walked to the gate where the bus picked us up, I thought of all the stories I had heard about how dangerous Bogotá was. Even while Pablo Escobar was in jail and we were in no danger of men on motorcycles or car bombs, people said ours was a city of crime. One of Mamá's friends said that her aunt and cousin were riding the public bus when a man whispered to the girl to give him her ring. The ring wouldn't come off so the man cut off the girl's finger. Mamá's friend said her niece didn't scream and hid the hand in the pocket of her coat, because the man threatened to kill her mother if she made a sound. When her pocket filled with blood and the blood began to seep out, that's when everybody realized what had happened. The man was long gone. That was a crazy story; I didn't know if I believed it. I did believe one of Mamá's friends who said she had once been walking in Bogotá when a man gripped a random woman's earrings right as they hung on her ears and pulled. The woman's earlobes split in two. The man ran with blood on his hands and in his fists the woman's golden hoops. I took my earrings off and dropped them into my skirt pocket.

When we were close enough to the gate and the security guard spotted us, he folded his newspaper and lowered his feet and stared at us. Mamá had instructed the guards to watch us closely. It wasn't going to be easy to sneak away, but maybe that was a good thing. Maybe it was better that Cassandra and I just went to school and let Mamá deal with whatever was wrong with Petrona. Then again, nobody knew the full story. My heart ticked up and up and up thinking it was up to me to help Petrona. There was nobody else. It was breaking daylight.

Cassandra spoke out of the side of her mouth, "We're going to have to wait until the last minute." We were just outside the neighborhood gate on the corner, where all the other kids in our block waited for their school buses.

"What does that mean?" I asked out of the side of my mouth.

Cassandra rolled her eyes, "Just do what I say. Try not to be suspicious."

Cassandra made me do what we always did when we waited for the bus. We sauntered back and forth on the sidewalk and brought to our mouths imaginary cigarettes and exhaled white plumes of breath, our breath steaming in the cold air, but my heart was hardly in it. I was distracted, expecting Petrona to appear, crawling, I imagined, covered in blood. The boys from other private schools whistled at us, well, mostly at Cassandra. There were six kids from our school and eight others from other schools. Cassandra pretended to ignore the boys, but she was keenly aware. She adjusted the pink glasses that slipped down the bridge of her nose and swung her hips along the gate. Now that Cassandra's attention shifted, I stood aside and leaned on the gate. I was both scared and thrilled. I suddenly wished that Isa and Lala's bus stop was at our corner. I wanted to look into their faces. I knew Isa and Lala would convince me that there was nothing to be afraid of, that going out of the neighborhood by ourselves would be exciting.

The only time Cassandra and I went outside was with Mamá, inside the school bus, or across the street from our neighborhood to buy candy in the shops. Cassandra had memorized our school bus route, so she knew all the streets around us, but we never went further. Who knew what we might encounter? I looked across the street to the great beyond that was the city — past the wide gray of the street, there was a hardware store, a phone booth, a rickety building in need of new paint, the green tops of trees, the tops of more buildings. I stood by a pine and played at running the branch through my fingers. The guard was still watching us when our bus pulled up.

"Okay, stay close," Cassandra said. We went to the back of the line, and the moment the first students from our school started boarding, we retreated and ran near the back end of the bus. There, as we crouched, Cassandra looked into my eyes. "This is it, ready?"

I nodded. The sky was still dim. I was jacked up with anticipation.

"Now!" We ran away from the bus, just then beginning to pull away, and dove behind a city trash can. We waited bundled against the ground. We heard the rumble of the bus travel up the street. Cassandra peeked around the trash can. Then she looked back at me over her shoulder. Her lids lowered and she smirked. "He's reading his newspaper again." We high-fived each other and then I followed Cassandra. We trotted along, staying low, ducking behind a parked car, a lamppost. We ran in a crouch behind a boy pulling trash in a makeshift horse carriage, and then we were able to run across the street. We went beyond the stores we were allowed to go to — the candy store, the liquor store — and panted behind a bakery. I looked at the invisible border that had been the first row of stores. From where we crouched, I could really take in how big our neighborhood was. The row of pines and tall iron fence that enclosed the neighborhood went on for about five blocks.

Cassandra said that we needed a convincing story in case an adult asked us why we weren't in school. We decided to say there had been a bombing. Yes, a car bomb. We had been sent home early. Also, we were traumatized. We had seen a boy's head come cleanly off his shoulders and roll on the ground while his neck sprayed the walls with blood. Cassandra showed the whites of her eyes. "Always one step too far with you." She told me not to say the last part.

Cassandra stood up and dusted her skirt and pulled up her socks. "Now what?" Cassandra said most likely Petrona would arrive at eleven, her usual time, but we needed to keep watch starting at nine. Once Petrona arrived, we would find a way to follow a few steps behind. Mamá would interrogate Petrona right away, so we needed to sneak into our house quickly but quietly and eavesdrop on as much of their conversation as possible. I nodded, wondering just how I would manage to protect Petrona without giving her secrets away and without announcing we were listening behind the door.

Cassandra said, "The only problem is, that's three hours away. It's six in the morning now, the mall doesn't open until seven and the arcade doesn't open until eight, so we have an hour to kill."

"What should we do?"

"Let's just buy a pastry and coffee here," Cassandra said.

"Are you sure? We don't even know who runs this bakery," I said.

"It's a *bakery,* Chula."

Cassandra looked down at her wristwatch and pushed open the door, bells jingling above. I exhaled in relief once I saw an old woman behind the counter. She wore a black apron and was kneading some dough. "Buenos días," she called, then returned her eyes to her labor. In the corner, a couple held hands over the counter. I was adjusting the straps of my backpack ready to take it off, when I saw that the couple was Petrona and her boyfriend. Cassandra put her hand in front of me and we froze. My relief at seeing Petrona unharmed was overshadowed by my alarm at seeing her boyfriend. Why was he here again, so close to our house? We took a step back. If we were leaving, we would have to open the door again. The bells would sound again. I turned to Cassandra to see what we should do, but she was staring at Petrona.

Petrona wore a tweed coat that probably belonged to her boyfriend. I shrank. He was bigger than I remembered. Just his neck was more muscular than my leg. As he held Petrona's hands, however, he seemed sweet. He drank up her face with that kind of boy thirst I had seen before on a man who whistled at me in the street and Mamá had yelled, "Pedophile!"

We needed to get out of there. Cassandra didn't know this was Petrona's boyfriend, and she didn't know he had pointed his hand like a gun at Petrona and me. I reached for the door. I pushed on the handle. The bells jingling made Petrona look up; she twirled out of her stool, gasping, and her boyfriend fell out of his seat too. Cassandra stepped in front of me, blocking me from view. "Who's he?" He shifted from Petrona to us like he was in a boxing match. Everything was going terribly. "There was a bombing in our school," I called. Cassandra elbowed me.

Petrona inclined her head, a question forming on her face, then coming out of her mouth as she advanced toward us: "Are you *skipping* school?"

I snuck a look past Cassandra's side and saw Petrona's boyfriend hold in a laugh and look away. "Who's he?" Cassandra repeated.

"His name is Gorrión," Petrona said. She righted her head. "He's a friend." She placed her hands on the hips of the tweed coat, her arms bunching up with the material. The shoulders of the coat marked the difference between her and Gorrión's body — the coat jutted out in space past the curve of Petrona's shoulders, and the coat sleeves bunched up at her wrists and hid her hands.

"He's Petrona's boyfriend," I corrected.

Gorrión was stern for a moment, but then he broke into a brief cackle. He jumped on his toes. He cackled once more, unable to contain himself. "I'm calling the driver." He planted a kiss on Petrona's cheek and pushed past us and left. The bells jingled at the door. Petrona fell back one step and her face drained and for a second I thought she would faint. I stepped forward to steady her. "Are you okay?" Petrona rubbed her face, then gripped her hand over her mouth. "Who's the *driver*?" Cassandra asked.

Petrona relaxed her hand. The skin on her face where she had squeezed was red. She put her arms behind us, composed. "Gorrión's ride to work. Come, I'll buy you some coffee and sweets."

At the counter, there was a display of all kinds of sweets: classic croissants, tartlets, scones, but there were also empanadas, pan de bono, pan de queso. The air smelled of vanilla and meat. The old woman behind the counter smiled at me. There was a white hair curling from her chin and her silver hair was gathered in dark netting. I ordered café con leche and pan de bono. The old woman's apron had flour fingerprints marked all over it. I smiled at her, then Cassandra found my hand and held on fast to my wrist. "Why are you here so early, Petrona?"

Petrona picked up the cup of coffee sitting in front of her. She set it down again. She tried to smile. She *did* smile. Her eyes remained downcast. "Why did you girls decide to skip school — today of all days?"

The tone in her voice, official, and just beneath, pleading, scared me. "You won't let anything bad happen to us, right? Petrona?" I asked. I saw Petrona's eyes pool with tears, but she turned away almost immediately, and then the old woman behind the counter was placing in front of Cassandra and me two big cups of café con leche, saying, "Never be afraid of consequences, niñitas. They're the great teachers, don't you know." She placed a plate with a single pan de bono in front of me and winked. "Your parents will find out, you'll be grounded, you'll learn your lesson, and you'll never skip school again — see? Nothing terrible about that." She took up her knife and started dicing carrots.

I nodded at the old woman and turned to Petrona, but before I could say anything more, the bells sounded and Gorrión rushed in, panting.

"Petrona," Cassandra urged. "What is *going on*?"

Gorrión put an arm around Petrona. "She's having coffee with me." He smiled widely, revealing straight white teeth. Petrona was tense under the weight of his arm. She stared at the woman.

Cassandra glared at Gorrión. "Excuse me, but *who* are you again?"

"I'm Petrona's boyfriend." He glanced at me. "Like the little imp said."

I stood. "I am *not* an imp."

"Young man, haven't you heard — you don't touch a woman, not even with the petal of a flower?" The old woman paused her cutting, and was waving the knife at Gorrión as she talked. "If you don't want to be kicked out of my store, you will adhere to common decency."

Gorrión smiled quickly. "As you say, Señora. We were just getting together to talk about their father. He just passed away, you see. That's why everyone is so tense. We should probably get them home, poor devils." Gorrión took out from his front jeans pocket a collection of wrinkled bills. He scattered some change on top, and the sound of the coins landing on the wooden counter, one of them wobbling around and around, seemed to echo back and forth in my ears. What did Papá have to do with anything? My chin trembled and Cassandra squeezed my wrist. I could feel my blood pulsing against her fingers.

The old woman put the knife down. "You said they were skipping school, now their father's dead." She picked up the telephone. "Which story is it? I'm calling the police. I want you two gone. The girls stay."

The old woman said, "Policia —"

Gorrión stood up without hurry. He was

smiling. He grabbed Cassandra by the neck of her jacket. Cassandra lifted off the ground.

"Policia, policia! Come quick, there's a robbery —"

I rammed into Gorrión and Cassandra kicked him in the shin and Cassandra took off running and I ran after her. The bells above the door were jingling and I heard Petrona say, "Let's go, let's go, let's get out of here!" As I pushed past the door onto the wide sidewalk, I heard behind me the bells jingling, plates breaking, the old woman screaming, a smacking sound. I didn't dare look back. Cassandra sprinted toward the street. My backpack was heavy, jingling with all the loose change. I looked behind and there was no one and when I turned back, Cassandra was gone. I scanned the perimeter. The streets were empty. Had Cassandra taken a right or a left? I turned left, panting up an alley. I leapt behind a building and kept running, across a street, crying, still running. I was sure that Petrona or Gorrión would appear behind me at any moment. I glanced all around, searching the horizon for the pines and gate of my neighborhood. *Never be afraid of consequences, niñitas,* the old woman had said. How could I get lost at a time like this? I crouched behind a dumpster. I was inhaling but not breathing out.

I bit my arm and tried to think. I had only run for about three minutes from the bakery, and it had taken Cassandra and me five minutes to get there, which meant the neighborhood was within eight minutes of where I currently was. Around me there were tall looming buildings, and streets empty of cars. The sidewalks were deserted.

Maybe if I stayed hidden and waited for someone, then I could ask for help. I looked to the sky. I was panting again. The sun was rising and the clouds were golden. If I stayed in the same spot, so close to the bakery, they would find me. I got up. I started running again. I needed to get further away, then I would hide. I wished I knew my way around like Cassandra. I looked at my feet as I ran, my stomach knotting together, trying to concentrate on running far, fast, ignoring my wheezing breath. I needed to remember the school bus route, then I would be able to find my way back home. I watched, blurry-eyed, the tight butterfly knots of my shoes. First the bus picked us up. Then it went down the street and took a left. The bus went straight for three blocks and took a right, where it stopped by another gated neighborhood.

There was a patch of grass and rainbow-colored monkey bars I could see from the bus window. But what happened after that? I always fished out a book at that point and didn't look up until we had arrived an hour later, at our school. I looked around as I ran. If I found the rainbow-colored monkey bars, then I could find my way back. I broke into a cough. I couldn't run any further. I searched the horizon for anything remotely familiar.

I saw the aqueduct. The aqueduct ran four meters deep, in between streets to drain the rainwater. Here and there as I rode the school bus, I would catch glimpses of the city aqueduct. I knew there was a place where it ran close to my house. But which way was the right way? Close to my house someone had spray-painted on the slants of the aqueduct *Cuando te violen, relajate y disfruta.* I remembered, because when I saw it out of the school bus window and then Mamá's car, I asked her about it. The thing that struck me about it was the implied, not *if* but *when they rape you,* and the way Mamá's head hurled back with laughter when I told her the second part — *relax and enjoy it* — and how after she was done laughing Mamá's eyes fixed on me and she said, "That happens to you, you kick and run." If only I could find the one graffiti, then I would know which way was home.

I got on my knees and searched along the open-air slants of the aqueduct. I read *Tomás waz here.* Down the street it read, *Galán Asesinos.* I was about to run back in the other direction, when a car screeched to a stop next to me, Petrona in the passenger seat and a man I did not recognize at the wheel. The man sprinted out of his seat. I saw his sweat pants, his black beard, and I dropped my bag and ran. I neared the avenue, a sharp feeling in my right lung, I would throw myself in front of a car, I would make someone stop and help me. There were no cars. I was crying again. I glanced back and saw Petrona sitting in the passenger seat of the idling car like she was waiting at a red light. Her head was in her hands. *Was she really doing this?*

The bearded man was gaining on me. I cried, running again, the graze of his fingers on my back, the pavement bouncing in my vision, the sharp feeling in my lung digging. There was a taxi in the distance, the white amber light above its hood. I screamed for this taxi, I waved my arms to get the attention of the taxi driver. He looked in my direction, then turned away, the left blinker on. The bearded man yanked me back and

I fell and hit my head. My ears were ringing, but I was still conscious. I tried to wriggle free. I saw the blinking amber light of the taxi disappearing at the corner of the road, and then the bearded man twisted my arm behind me and I went limp and shrieked from the pain.

Everything broke inside me and I understood that Petrona really was going to betray me.

The man dragged me by my leg all the way back to the car. My skin burned against the cement, but I was yelling not from the pain, but at Petrona, "How can you do this? How can you do this?" Petrona standing now, out of the car, her arms gripped against her stomach, her face turned to the horizon, her heaving and crying and shaking and looking away. I tried to hang on to the cracks of the street, I gripped on to blades of grass and stones, but it was no use. The man lifted my body and then I was in the trunk of the idling car. He shut the trunk door and all the light was sucked out and then we were moving and loud cumbia drowned out my screaming.

I remembered, the sky dark, Cassandra standing in profile. I remembered Cassandra's singsong voice, saying, *I can't hear you, Chula, what is that you said?* Everything burned: my skin and my lungs and throat and behind my eyes. The darkness with my eyes closed was the same as with my eyes open. Petrona was riding in the passenger seat in the front of this same car that was now leading me away. I felt like I was running out of air.

The car turned left then; we had gone twenty seconds straight. If I could remember the turns I could find my way back when I escaped. I felt alone, like a lost, undiscovered galaxy. There was a flashing crack of light at the right side of the trunk. We turned left again. Then just barely audible over the sound of cumbia, I heard another car beside us — the hint of the sound of brakes, the hint of the sound of an engine. I kicked as hard as I could on the trunk, I screamed into the crack of light.

I put everything into my screaming. The more I put into my screaming, the more things became unhinged — I gave sound to the things that had no language: the tense groove above Mamá's lips, the snail shell in my palm, Petrona's swollen mutant skin swallowing her eye and the points of her lashes, Abuela's porcupine back. I started to lose track of myself, until there was someone else yelling. Then I heard one loud, long honk. Then another. Then another.

We screeched hard right, then left. I nailed my head against the trunk. We were speeding up an incline, away from the honking. I couldn't breathe. I needed to focus. I had been wrong about Petrona, I needed to get back to Mamá. I pawed around by the edge of the trunk door. I would find a way out.

I wiped tears from my face. I would be who Mamá had raised me to be. I felt around for a weapon. There was nothing. I let my fingers crawl over everything. I found tucked behind the lip of steel a long, skinny cable. It led right up to the lock. It did something, but what? I dug my fingers into the little crevice trying to get ahold of it. I grabbed it and when we took another hard right, somehow the trunk door clicked open. I drew in a sharp breath, and held the door down so neither Petrona nor the driver would see. I laughed. I would be able to get away.

The darkness in the trunk deepened. We were in a tunnel. When the car braked, I pushed the trunk door open and jumped out. I skinned my knee, then I was on my feet again, running. I heard wheels screeching, Petrona yelling, the driver yelling, I was running away. I ran along the tunnel, up some stairs, in the light of the street now. I was out of breath. Everything blurred in front of me and I continued to run.

I was behind a building by a cardboard box. I was wheezing, drowning. My knees buckled. Still standing. I bowed over, holding on to the box. My lungs were drinking honey. I grasped for my breath. Then there was Petrona kneeling by my side crying, telling me in her gravelly voice, "Chula, Chula, forgive me." I couldn't speak. *Get away from me,* I was trying to say. I tried to push her, get up and run, but everything was growing dim — Petrona with her ruined mascara, black on her cheeks, her face ashen like a ghost. "Chula, forgive me." A shopkeeper sweeping the street, another lifting a steel shutter. She was holding my wrist. "You *have* to calm down, Chula, please calm down." Down the street someone was unlocking a chain. My knees against the dirty pavement. "Chula, breathe." My hands on the pavement too, the cracks of the street, a blade of grass, drowning, breathing. Galán bleeding on the podium. My shoe coming off, Mamá's cigarette, the tip wearing a halo like a dark saint. Hot, cold, drowning, breathing. I hoped Cassandra had gotten away and Mamá was somewhere looking for me. My face against the pavement, everything fading, Petrona's voice, "Chula, you have to calm down, we can't stay here, *please,* Chula, calm down," her thin, white fingers trembling over my eyes, Mamá's voice like an outgoing train, saying, "Here, Petrona, let me show you your room."

24.
VOID AFTER VOID

A ceiling fan chopped the air at the top of the room, chopped the light too, falling on Petrona's face. Petrona produced a mirror from her pocket. She fluffed her short hair. Her fingers on the back side of the mirror trembled. She closed the compact and ran her hands over her face. We were on a couch in a strange room that smelled like beer and oil. Petrona was staring at the door. I stirred and Petrona knelt before me tucking strands of hair behind my ears. She whispered, "You're awake." Then, "Everything's going to be okay now."

"Where are we?"

"We're in a liquor store. The owner saw you faint. We're waiting for a cab now." My backpack was on the floor. I thought I had left it by the aqueduct. I stared at it, how strange and out of place it seemed in this dark room where the light was chopped by the movement of the fan. Petrona looked as meek as ever. Her tidy amber eyes poised over me, but now I knew that Petrona had not been hiding from any danger, but was the danger itself.

"I want to leave." I tried to stand up.

Petrona held me down on the couch. "Quiet, Chula, we can't go out there until the cab arrives — he'll see us."

I knew she meant the driver. "How can I trust you ever again?" I asked.

Her eyes were soft, then hard, then soft again. She shook her head, crying. Then a white-haired man came running in, telling us the cab was outside, telling us to hurry and get in before we were spotted and got him in trouble. I clung to the couch, not wanting to get in another car with Petrona. The white-haired man lifted me in his arms, saying, "Get out now, I don't want any trouble." I kicked and smelled the tobacco scent of his hair, saw the beer posters with bikini-clad women hanging over his door frame. He forced me in the cab and closed the door. I reached for the door on the other side but Petrona opened that door and got in beside me and blurted out the address of my house to the driver, and then she held onto the taxi door, covering her mouth, crying. I looked at the taxi driver, who was bewildered and surprised in the rearview mirror, and I understood he at least wasn't part of any plot and I managed to say, "please," and "hurry," and the driver turned his eyes to the road and we sped down the near empty streets, tall buildings, a park, the aqueduct, and after a few minutes we were driving by the gates of the neighborhood and Petrona was inhaling and exhaling into her hands.

The cab halted at the neighborhood gate by our house. Mamá was there and Cassandra next to her. In the time I was gone fear had aged their faces. I was returning to my body now, everything would be okay because we were pulling up to our house, and I lifted my arm to the handle, I was finding my voice, "Cassandra! Mamá!" as they ran to the cab. But Mamá's face was chiseled in anger. She threw the door open and yanked Petrona out of the cab, and raked me across the seat onto the ground. "What were you doing with her? What were you going to do?" Mamá wrenched my hair back and forth. "You little fool!"

"Señora, they skipped school and —"

"NEVER have I given you permission to take my daughters out of the neighborhood." Mamá shook her. "You criminal!" Mamá was crying and her hand inched back and slapped Petrona across the cheek to the ground. Petrona held her cheek weeping and Mamá dragged Cassandra and me by the hair into the neighborhood. "You little fools!"

"Papá!" I cried out. I wanted him to be home.

"Why are you calling for your father, I'm here! And *you*!" She turned to Cassandra. "Abandoning your sister!"

"But I ran back, Mamá, I ran back to tell you."

I heard the cab driver protesting, and I turned to look as the security guard approached him. Petrona trailed behind us, sobbing. As we walked, Mamá gripped our hair and pulled, her fist flashing past our ears. Wrapped in her wrath Mamá called out to God. Her hands rose to the sky, knitted in our hair, asking why she had been cursed with such stupid children. Cassandra and I clutched each other tightly. Mamá yelled on and on, but I couldn't listen, or feel when she came again and shook us around. I didn't see what was in front of me. I was only aware of Cassandra's wet cheek against mine, our hot breath joining together, and void after void opening in my heart. In the house, Mamá shoved us up the stairs and hurled us into our old bedroom and locked the door. My scalp burned

and my cheeks felt hot. We cried and listened at the door, as Mamá yelled at Petrona and Petrona pleaded with Mamá.

PETRONA

I told her, *I saved your girl, protect me.* She took the rings off her fingers and put them in my pockets and told me to escape. She pushed cash into my hands and told me to get away. I said, *There's nowhere, they've threatened my family, who knows what they'll do.* She took a cross from her mantel and pushed that into my hands too. She said, *I'll pray,* and I understood I had risked every-thing for another woman's daughter, and nobody would do the same for me.

I thought I could leave at once. I got on the bus that would take me to the central station. I would buy a ticket and go as far as I could afford. I would clean and sweep houses to make more money. I would put thousands and thousands of kilometers between me and Gorrión. Gorrión who had told me not to fear — the girls would be kept in a nice apartment, a nice abuela would cook their meals, for a week at most, then they would be freed. Then I learned of one girl who was shot point-blank in her forehead. Gorrión argued the little girl was dead because the family did not listen and got the police involved and so the men had had to shoot the girl. *You understand, right?* he had told me. *The men cannot compromise their morals.*

I told Gorrión I wanted out, I would not deliver the girls, I had changed my mind. Gorrión clucked his tongue. *Petro. Don't be foolish. Why say a thing like that now? You know who we all are, see? It's too late.*

I was going. I was in a vehicle with moving wheels and soon I would be far, far away. I would go to the coast like little Ramón. I would get a job selling trinkets and coconuts on the beach. I would wrap my hair in a bandana like the women of the coast and I would continue north to the Pacific. My new name would be Claramanta, like in the telenovela. I had never seen the ocean. Maybe it was as beautiful as they said. Claramanta would sunbathe by the ocean. She would drink coconut water from the round husks.

A young boy sat next to me and I made room in the seat. He was young like my Aurora. Little Aurora, what would happen to her? Maybe in time, once I started to make money, I would send her anonymous envelopes filled with cash. It was all I could do for her now. The trouble would be in how to disguise the money so that it wouldn't be stolen along the way. The little boy next to me was unwrapping a small candy in his lap. Maybe I could put the cash inside a chocolate bar. They said the people that worked in the post offices held every envelope to the light and if they saw it had cash, they stole it, but they wouldn't suspect a chocolate bar. The ears of the boy were dirty, covered in dust. At least he didn't smell. Maybe I could hide the cash inside toys instead. Maybe Aurora would figure it out, maybe she knew I would want to write her letters. She would think to look inside. The little boy lifted his hand up to his palm, bringing the sweet to his mouth, and just then someone sat in the seat in front. The man in front had a mole at the back of the neck in the same place Gorrión did. How many people, going around, with identical moles. The little boy opened his palm, and I turned to look at him. He blew on his palm like he was blowing me a kiss and white dust flew on my face. I tried to get up, and the man in the seat in front who not only had Gorrión's mole but also, I could see clearly now, his face, was telling me, *Stay, Petrona, stay,* and so I stayed, thinking, that's Gorrión's voice too, and the other voice, the voice in my head, telling me to get up and run quieted now. It died down. I waited for whatever else this man would tell me to do, and then I was swimming in a black dark.

25.
RAINFALL

"Cassandra?"

"What?" Cassandra's eyes were red and bewildered. She rested her head against the bedroom door.

"But she brought me back."

Cassandra's nostrils flared and her eyes grew red and moist and some seconds passed before she answered. "I know."

I rested my face on the carpet, listening. The house was quiet now. Petrona had gone. I rubbed my head on the carpet. "She changed her mind."

We crawled into my bed. Nobody had cleaned it. The grit of dust prickled my skin. The house was eerily quiet. The wind rippled the plastic-covered window and the light waned. There was no electricity and in the darkening room, I felt the skin on the back of my legs burning. I did not move. Cassandra said, "But when she offered to buy us coffee at the bakery? Her boyfriend said he was going to get the driver — Chula, remember? *She knew what that meant.* She was keeping us there until —" Cassandra didn't finish. Then she said, "She could have told us to run then. She could have made something up. But she didn't, Chula. She didn't."

"You left me behind," I interjected.

I wasn't sure why I needed to make Cassandra feel bad at that moment. I didn't really blame her.

"I ran to get help," Cassandra explained.

"You left me," I repeated, and allowed Cassandra to sit with her knees drawn to her chest, quietly wallowing in guilt. When it was night, we heard faint crying. It was Mamá. I couldn't sleep and neither could Cassandra. Cassandra said Papá was probably on his way home and once he got home everything would be all right again.

Some hours later, our door unlocked and we thought it was Papá, but it was just Mamá, carrying a tray with burning candles, two glasses of orange juice, and bowls with cereal. She set the tray on the floor. She drew her fingers from the tray and said, "I kicked her out, I don't know what's going to happen to her now. We can't worry about her, we have to worry about us now."

"But Mamá," I said. "She brought me

back, doesn't that count?"

There was hate in Mamá's eyes. "You almost disappeared, and you're asking me whether Petrona bringing you back *counts*?"

The bowls of cereal Mamá had brought sat on the aluminum tray, spoon handles sticking out, the milk snow white, the bits and pieces of sugared wheat softening, unraveling, as time passed.

We heard a soft tapping against the plastic of my window. Then there was drumming. Then we understood. "It's raining."

We hadn't seen rain in so long, all three of us got up and went downstairs. We opened the door, and walked out into the street with our flashlights. The rain streaked long lines of silver. There were other people on the street too — a man in his pajamas walked under an umbrella, chuckling in amazement; small children ran pulling up their rain boots, parents looked on smiling.

The wind picked up and then it began to pour. I stayed on the porch, but Mamá went to stand in the garden. I saw her in silhouette, lifting her face to the sky. I listened to the rain tapping on roof and street. I thought of Petrona. I pushed the thought of Petrona away. I could smell the Drunken Tree, instantly revived by rain, releasing its sweet scent like overripe vanilla and molasses, and then there was a flash of thunder and in the light I saw Mamá: her hair was wet and her robe, soaked, stuck to her skin.

26.
THE HOUR OF THE FOG

All the next day we waited for Papá. There was hail falling from the sky. It bounced on the pavement and the roof of our house. I could barely hear anything anyone said. Mamá yelled he was on his way, stop asking. Alone in Mamá's room, I dialed Petrona at the pharmacy. "Farmacia Aguilar," came the familiar voice. I hung up. What if I found out she was dead? I observed the front garden where globes of hail bounced and lay glistening in the grass like round jewels. I turned on the television. I allowed the senseless noise to wash over me. There was the weatherman taking up the screen, his voice a consistent stutter under the roar of hail.

"What's this?" That was Mamá touching the red inflamed skin at the back of my legs, startling me with pain. Mamá gripped my chin with her hand, forcing a bend into my neck. "Did you bump your head too? What happened to you?"

I imagined myself telling Mamá about the bearded man, about being dragged by one leg on the pavement, about rattling like fancy luggage in the trunk of that car that would have taken me into increasingly darkening compartments — or so I imagined. What happened when they took you? Was there a jail cell? Were there handcuffs? Or was it more like a hospital waiting room with the glare of fluorescent lights and a magazine and a clock and a receptionist?

I knew that if I told Mamá about the trunk of the car she would never forgive Petrona, and it was important to me that Petrona be forgiven. "I skinned my legs when you dragged me out of the cab."

Mamá released the tension of her brows and raised her hand to her mouth, shocked at what she was capable of.

Mamá cleaned my scraped skin in the shower. My legs burned in long ruts wherever she touched. Mamá blew on my skin to make it bearable. Cassandra held my hand. I knew they felt guilty. For the first time since the bombing I felt relief. The ways we failed Petrona was a bitter pie and I had divided it in three and maybe now it would be easier to bear.

When we came out of the bathroom,

everything on the television was about Pablo Escobar. There was a banner of text running at the bottom of the screen — *Breaking news: The biggest manhunt in history.* We turned up the volume to hear over the hail. A reporter was saying Pablo Escobar had escaped, and that he had not been in a high-security prison as the government wanted the country to believe, but he had been living in a high-security mansion.

"He's free? He can come to Bogotá?"

"Chula, hold on a minute, I'm trying to listen," Mamá said.

Every channel on the television was showing specials: reporters stood inside the high-security prison, showing off the waterbeds, Jacuzzis, fine carpets, marble tiles, the sauna, the bar with a discotheque, the telescopes, radio equipment, and so many weapons — grenades, machine guns, pistols, machetes. He had been running the cartels from prison.

Finally we found a channel that was talking about the details of the escape. There was an animated map of the prison. The prison was nested in the hilly mountainside. Little army men swept to surround the building. The reporter said that since the prison guards were all Pablo Escobar's men, the escape was easy. They helped capture a few hostages and used them to hold the Colombian army at bay. The reporter said Pablo Escobar and his men were thought to have escaped at the hour of the fog. That's because they slipped unseen past the battalions surrounding the prison, and since up in the hills a heap of women's clothes was later discovered, it was thought that Pablo Escobar and his men went out into the mountains, in disguise, a row of ladies walking into the clouds.

I lay on my stomach since I couldn't sit on my scrapes. As the news went to commercial break, I imagined Pablo Escobar making his way, with each step transforming things: that was *narco-grass* he was stepping on, *narco-fog* that rolled by his hair, *narco-silence* that fell upon the mountains.

Mamá locked herself in Petrona's room with a phone, saying she had some things to take care of, and Cassandra and I went out into the garden. We hid under umbrellas to shield us against the pelting hail and set plastic cups on the ground. We waited an hour and then retrieved our cups and ate the hail with a spoon. There were white-etched spiders inside each globe. They tasted like dirt and mercury.

Cassandra and I ate cereal and watched television for hours. When it was dusk and the storm passed, Cassandra and I went to find Mamá. She was sitting in the living room, the telephone at her feet. She said Papá was late because of traffic. Then she said maybe there had been a landslide, which happened sometimes on the winding cliff roads leading back into the city, small pebbles and rocks loosening with rain but collapsing only later, when it was sunny, filling the roads with the mountainside. I thought of car accidents, hospitals, women in distress, hitchhikers.

Then Cassandra asked, "What did he say exactly when you talked to him, Mamá?"

Mamá shrugged. "He said he was leaving right away, he was going to get his bag and drive home."

The television droned on in the background: Pablo Escobar this, Pablo Escobar that. I huddled with Mamá on the couch. Night fell. It began to rain again. The drum of rain banged on our roof and windows and the howling wind crept through the bottom of the front door. I was falling asleep when Mamá rose to her feet and went about the house moving things from one table to another. Her bathrobe ballooned about her as she bent and picked things up from the floor. She dropped the dictionary into a cabinet drawer and said, "His car probably broke down on the highway."

Mamá scrubbed her face with her hands. For the first time I noticed the color. Her forehead was white but her cheekbones and overlip glistened in a sickly green. I tried to imagine Papá's car breaking down. Maybe there had been a nail in the middle of the road. I imagined Papá cranking on the cross-shaped tire iron as neon orange triangles flashed by the car, reflecting passing headlights. Then I imagined Papá bursting through the front windshield of his car in an accident. I averted my eyes, but the image was there. The tips of my ears tingled.

"Go to sleep," Mamá said. "I'll wake you when your father comes."

"I want to wait, Mamá."

"I'm sure he's fine. Go and I'll wake you."

I went to the attic and crawled into bed next to Cassandra, the patter of rain over the world of our dreams. I tried to remain awake, thinking about Papá as I waited. I saw him walk by the attic door and went after him. I ran after him across halls and mirrors, and then I realized I was dreaming. I awoke from dreams of waiting into other dreams of waiting.

When I awoke Cassandra was gone. I ran to Mamá's bedroom but didn't see Papá's suitcase and the bed was still made. Downstairs, Mamá was smoking in the living room, and the television was emitting a loud continuous beep, showing a static image of color bars.

"Mamá," Cassandra was saying, shaking her shoulder. "Mamá, did Papá come?"

Mamá narrowed her eyes until they closed. She sucked her cigarette, swallowing the smoke, then it came forked out of her nostrils. Cassandra shook her again.

Her eyes broke open. "What is it?"

"Did Papá call?"

"What time is it?"

"It's seven."

She sat up and put out her cigarette in the ashtray. She picked up the telephone, and then held it in her hand. The telephone buttons lighted fluorescent green and the dim sound of the dial tone filled the room.

"Mamá, why don't you dial?"

"I'm thinking."

"Mamá, dial! What are you waiting for?"

But the color drained from her. She was looking into the distance as she replaced the receiver, then she was on her feet braiding her fingers at the nape of her head and then she was sitting against a wall hiding her face between her knees.

"It will be okay. Your Papá is okay," she called after a while. Her voice built a new

396

anxiety in me.

The police in Medellín found a Pablo Escobar hideout. The reporter was standing fully
dressed in the shower, showing how a young
cop, who for no reason wondered whether
the apartment bought with laundered
money had running water, had turned the
shower knob. What happened next was that
the shower wall swung out like a door, and
there, below a few steps, was a small apartment. The reporter motioned for the cameras to come in. He flicked on a switch.
Everything was in disarray. There was a bed.
"Here, you may imagine, the subject of the
biggest manhunt in history peacefully slept
while the police searched the apartment."
The reporter lifted a coffee cup left on the
nightstand. "When police first entered, this
coffee was still warm. The room was empty
and the police left to search the vicinity, but
little did they know," the reporter said, walking to a wall where he pulled on a cord,
"there was another hideout within the
hideout." A small door swung out from the
wall and revealed a tight crawlspace. "Pablo
Escobar probably sat here, literally a hair-
breadth away from the authorities, biding
his time to sneak away."
The telephone rang all day, but Mamá was

holed up in her bedroom with her door shut so I stayed with the television. On other channels reporters followed the police in Medellín. They stood in front of normal-looking buildings, giving the same kind of updates, "The police in Medellín were seen earlier today taking over this building. The area is crawling with Secret Service agents, as authorities try to hone in on Pablo Escobar's hideout."

At night Mamá turned into a black widow. Her bed was stripped and the pillows and blankets on the floor. I found her sitting on the mattress. The firelight of the candle clasped between her thighs threw a satin sheen on her hair and her contorted fingers radiated orange shadows. Her cheekbones and forehead glistened, but her eyes hung back. She was braiding the air with her fingers, mumbling prayers. When I touched her, her body crumbled under my fingers as if it were ash. She curved by the candle, crying.

Bowled over, she rocked on her thighs and howled.

It was a pained, low, guttural howl. It washed through my entire body. Everything was terrible. I howled as well. My eyes sprang with tears and my sight doubled: Mamá with four hands covering her face, saying, "What are we going to do, Chula? What in the world are we going to do?"

I fell on my knees and cried on the lap of the scratchy mattress.

"What is happening, Mamá?"

She kicked her legs. "The guerrillas have him!"

"So give them what they want, Mamá, what do they want?"

"I don't *know*!" Mamá pulled her hair. "I don't know! They just called to say they have him."

Cassandra came in running. She shook Mamá until she understood what was happening. Then together Mamá and Cassandra screamed back and forth, Cassandra crying, "Mamá, do something!" and Mamá screaming, "I can't!"

Late at night, there was a sharp pain in my stomach, and my hands trembled as I stuffed them under the pillow. Mamá said that the oil company didn't want to negotiate with terrorists because they were an American company, and Americans didn't negotiate with terrorists, but said they would do everything to get Papá back. They would help us get to safety. In my bed I kicked my feet in sudden anger and my voice stuck in my throat, then tears ran down my cheeks.

One policeman turned on the knob of a stove in an apartment and almost fell through the floor as it slid away revealing a staircase. Secret tunnels led from each hideout into a neighboring house, which meant the people of Medellín were all conspiring to keep Pablo Escobar safe. Nobody seemed surprised though, because Pablo Escobar built and gave free homes to his community and he drove around invasiones handing out stacks of money to the poor. Meanwhile, Pablo Escobar was making car bombs explode in public places all over the country, because he wanted the government to call off the search.

I stared at the walls and sat next to Mamá, overhearing her conversations on the telephone. Sometimes the voices on the phone, echoing dimly against Mamá's ear, were prim and elegant. There was a policeman, someone from the American embassy, a lawyer. There was a plan to get us American tourist visas, but I did not understand how in the world that would help anything. I did not ask because at other times the voices were short and alarming: "We've got that hijo de puta, we'll send you his balls in the post." Mamá had to put it on speakerphone to record the voices on a little tape. When they hung up, she spoke the time and date. Mamá didn't notice I was there, sitting on the floor by the bed — just as Petrona used to. The guerrillas wanted all the money we had. Mamá wired all our money to an account. Cassandra said we were destitute, but it didn't feel like anything had changed. We still had our house and car, food in the kitchen, and a closet full of clothes.

There were stories of how the kidnapped were never returned. You gathered the money, you paid the ransom, you gave them what they wanted; but the kidnapped never returned. There were many kids at school whose family members had been kidnapped. They didn't come to school for days and then one day they showed up with grim faces and bags under their eyes. Once, the Principal provided buses for our class to go to the funeral of our classmate's father. Her name was Laura. Everyone was afraid to talk to her. At the funeral, I handed Laura a single red rose and said what everyone said on those occasions. You said, "Mi más sentido pésame." And then you bowed. Standing at the altar, Laura collected a bouquet of flowers in her hand as each classmate handed her a rose and bowed, saying, *My*

*most heartfelt condolences. My most heartfelt
condolences. My most heartfelt condolences.*

They aired a message on the television
from Pablo Escobar's daughter to Pablo Escobar: "I miss you, Papi, and I am sending
you the biggest kiss in all of Colombia!"
Her voice was so cheery. Maybe she was
trying to sound upbeat for him, so that he
wouldn't worry, or maybe she was used to
this now, her father perpetually running
from the police.

Mamá turned off the television and
dragged Cassandra and me downstairs.
"Come with me, we're cleaning out her
room." She didn't have to say whose. I
didn't want to go near Petrona's things, but
still I obeyed. I watched myself walking
behind Mamá like it was somebody else going down the stairs, through the kitchen,
the indoor patio. "I just want the room
clean," Mamá said to no one, and opened
Petrona's door.

It was somebody else in Petrona's room,
then, as Mamá whipped large trash bags in
the air, making them unfold — somebody
else noticing the dust that had collected on
the sill that used to be her window, staring
at the bed that used to be her bed, gazing at
the empty shelves where Petrona used to
keep her clothes. Mamá was shoving the

bedding into the black plastic bags. Mamá lifted the mattress to pull the old sheets off, but she dropped the mattress. *"Jueputa!"* She jumped away and clung to the wall.

Her cursing brought me back to myself. I crowded around Mamá. "What's wrong, Mamá, is it a mouse?"

Her eyes fixed on the mattress, half the sheet taken off. "Help me," she said. Under her direction, we pushed the mattress up until it was propped against the wall. Then we saw what Mamá had seen. A rifle. It sat on the box springs. A black long rifle with a wooden handle. It vibrated with power on top of the flower print of the box springs.

Mamá dropped her hand from her mouth. "God," she said. Then, "We can't tell your father."

"We can't trust anyone," she added, and she put the rifle in a black trash bag. She put us in the car, drove to the police station, and dropped the rifle off. Mamá told us the policeman said the rifle was loaded. Cassandra looked worried. A nervous nausea settled in my throat.

I wondered what Petrona had planned to do with a loaded rifle underneath her mattress in our house. Maybe she had planned to attack us at night. Maybe the guerrillas were going to storm our house and she was going to join them.

Maybe Petrona was planning to defend us.

Maybe she was planning on defending herself.

27.
THE MOUTH OF THE WOLF

It was early morning when Mamá shook us awake; Cassandra and I still in our pajamas, Mamá urging us into the car, "Get in, get in." She hurried down the avenues, sped through the red lights, rounded the corners with screeching tires. We asked, "Mamá, where are you going? Where are you taking us?"

It was only when we exited on the dirt road where the boy had pressed his hand streaked with dirt on my window that I understood. We advanced now on the orange hill, which grew in size in the windshield until everything began to seem like a dream. The hill looked different: wet and rust-colored, and in the air the scent of burning. What would we find on this hill with its melted face? Maybe Petrona in pieces on the mattress in her shack. Maybe Papá tied up against a tree. Maybe no sign of either of them, just Gorrión burning the carcass of an animal.

Mamá said, "There are guerrillas here, so we'll leave soon." We were driving parallel to the hill now. "Mamá, think this through," Cassandra said. "What if Petrona's boyfriend is here?"

Petrona's boyfriend, large as a boulder, roasting a pig.

Mamá stopped where we had parked before. Uprooted trees and washed-out debris littered the hillside. There were large rocks and pebbles on the road too. "Her boyfriend, yes." Mamá opened her car door. "That's who I hope to meet."

We stared at Mamá standing outside the car, sizing up the wet incline, pulling up her sleeves. "She's lost her mind," Cassandra said, but it didn't seem that crazy to me. I wanted answers too. I got out. There were broken planks of wood and pieces of plastic chairs and car tires scattered all over the road, all of it washed down from the top of the hill. Mamá found the opening between the rocks where Doña Lucía had taken us and she began to climb. I went after her. Cassandra yelled, "Mamá, don't be stupid." The mud slid from under my steps. Then I heard Cassandra behind me, "Ugh, all of this is mud."

We hadn't gone that far but already my

pajama pants and arms were covered in mud. I looked up to see Mamá kicking her shoes into the hill, then stepping up, like she was making a staircase. If I stepped into her steps I could ascend quicker. Little bits of plastic trash emerged from the mud like roots. We flung ourselves against the hill, advancing and slipping like we were climbing the slick insides of a living thing. We came upon a destroyed shack that had slid down, stopped halfway on the steep. Its posts were broken and the tarp that had once been a roof now flapped in the wind, tethered at one point to a post. This is what happened when the hill, that was the long throat of an animal, swallowed — you were washed down and stuck to it forever.

The smell of burning was more intense now. I was sure it was burning. When we got to the terrace where the first shacks still stood, I saw that a great hill of trash with drawers and broken furniture and sheets and plastic had been set on fire. The smoke burned black.

"Chula, cover your mouth, it's toxic," Cassandra said. She held the neck of her pajama top, worn and streaked with mud, over her nose. I did the same. Many shacks were still standing, but they had gathered debris around them. People bent over cleaning, picking up plastic and wood and rocks, clearing the way around their homes. For a while nobody noticed us. I saw shacks with broken roofs, half melted into the ground. An old woman sat inside the tent of her half-collapsed shack organizing plastic forks. A group of people roasted corn around a great fire. Suddenly everything was quiet. There was only the crackling sound of the fire. The people of the invasión watched us walk by. At the edges and corners of door-ways, window frames, behind tatters of cloth, I saw eyes that flashed then hid as soon as they were seen. Mamá called out, "I'm looking for Petrona Sánchez, or infor-mation on her whereabouts. Anybody who comes forward I will pay." Mamá slowed down to see if anybody would come. Ripped sheets lifted in the breeze. We were at the point where the boy with the three-legged dog had mistaken Petrona's Communion dress for a wedding gown, but the tent that had been his was gone, nothing in its place.

We rushed behind Mamá, digging toward Petrona's house, balling up the orange hill in our hands and against our shoes. We arrived at the ridge and I saw Petrona's house, too, had been destroyed. The post that held the structure still stood in place but every-thing else had collapsed. There was the triangle of the roof right up against the dirt, an opening like a small cave. I turned around and looked down the hill. The houses that had once stood on the steep were gone. Maybe that's what had been burning. I could see from this height there were broken planks of wood in the fire, pieces of sheets, the legs and backs of dismembered chairs.

Petrona's house was so quiet we knew it was empty. Neither Mamá nor Cassandra could fit through the opening, but I crawled inside. What if Petrona was on the mattress? Maybe there was a note. Maybe something would explain where Papá was, where she was. I pulled myself forward on my stomach, sliding under the collapsed ceiling of corrugated steel.

"Chula, what do you see?" That was Cassandra's voice.

Ahead, there was light. I crawled forward. Above the mattresses, the roof was halfway in place. Beams of light fell on the tossed beds, small puddles collected in different places on the mattresses. I stood. "Everything's destroyed," I said. The potted plants lay in pieces on the ground. One wall had slanted in and on the ground there was a broken table with a drawer half open — inside broken sunglasses, a nail, a small plastic soldier.

"Señora Alma!" I heard outside. It was the voice of Petrona's mother. I turned and hurried to crawl out. "Have you seen Petrona? She's missing! Did you see her yesterday?" I crawled on my stomach toward the light. If Doña Lucía had not seen her, then maybe Petrona was with Gorrión. My elbows dug into mud. "Señora Alma? Did you hear me?" My head grazed the corrugated steel that had once been Petrona's roof, my eyes stayed on the glare of light at the opening. "Señora Alma?" My knees slid on the mud, my hands nearly at the light. Mamá's voice rang out: "Where is Petrona's boyfriend?" It was crisp and cold like the corrugated steel I was escaping, then Doña Lucía's voice, like the quicksand of mud on my feet: "You know, don't you! You know where she is, but you won't tell me, vieja despiadada, tell me where she is!"

In the light, Mamá stood tall over Doña Lucía, who was just an old woman on her knees, mud on her shins, gray gathered hair tangled in a braid. "Have compassion for a mother who's lost her child," she begged. Then she spoke into the back of her hand, "You've always been a patilimpia," and she jumped to her feet, tearing at Mamá's shirt, "Tell me what you did with her!"

410

Doña Lucía pulled her own hair and screamed and dry heaved, and I held on to Cassandra. Petrona was missing, and this woman was broken. *If Petrona was not on the mattress, was she in pieces somewhere else?* Doña Lucía straightened, and it was like somebody had yelled cut and action and next scene, because when she rose all her aggression was gone and she pushed a triangle into her wrinkled forehead with her brows, and her eyes became soft. "From one mother to another — go to the police. Tell them what happened to Petrona. They'll listen to you, a woman from the city. They'll have no choice but to look for Petrona. The police don't listen to me." Doña Lucía patted Mamá's hand, now gazing down the hill, now pulling Mamá's hand. "The station is a short walk away, come Señora Alma, just a few steps this way. Come."

Mamá stayed rooted in place. "Where is Petrona's boyfriend?"

Doña Lucía grasped at the mud, "I don't know where he is, stop wasting time! Let's go to the police!" and for the first time Doña Lucía looked to us, Cassandra and me in our pajamas, clinging to each other, covered in mud, and she pointed a finger into Mamá's face. "I don't know what happened to you, but Petrona had nothing to

411

do with it. Can't you hear me, Petrona is missing! Why in the hell are you wasting time looking for that man?"

Mamá swept her eyes over the hills, the rust-colored mud, the black smoke rising into the air. "When there's a tempest, it comes down on all sides equally," she said. And then she pulled us and we walked away.

So many times before I had interceded for Petrona, defended her, protected her. Now, my feet sank into the mud behind Mamá, her cold hand over mine, pulling me forth down the steep, and I understood that Papá was missing just like Petrona was missing. I walked away knowing I was leaving Petrona behind. This was us, walking away from her. When I had been in danger, Petrona had chosen me over herself. I was not in danger and now we wouldn't lift a finger to help. I was choosing myself over Petrona. My body was heavy with this knowing as we hurried down the hill. The mud was a wet pillow that sucked at our feet, made us trip, welcomed us as we fell, wanting us to remain fallen, to make a house there in the dark belly of the earth. We slid down the hill in a controlled fall, gliding down great distances, slowing ourselves down by grabbing on to rocks, digging our hands into the mud, or sometimes the mud accumulated beneath our feet in such a way as to give us a foothold. At the terrace of the hill, where most of the invasión dwellings were, where the burning was, I thought, *I can still ask Mamá to turn around and help Petrona,* but I did not. We ran across the stretch of land without a word and continued to slide down the polished mud. *Was Petrona taken like Papá? Would I switch places with Petrona if I could?* Mud squished even inside my shoes.

At the bottom of the hill, the boy Petrona had called Julián leaned on our car. His three-legged dog panted at his side. Julián didn't bother straightening up when we got to him, though his dog tapped his tail quickly on the ground. He saw our clothes and chuckled. "It really is true, you come to the invasión once, and you're muddied forever." He smiled archly, enjoying the fear in Mamá's eyes, how she clutched the car key, her fist nearly white, enjoying how Cassandra and I went around to the passenger side away from him. He glanced at me and then stared at his nails in feigned boredom. "Seño, I heard you're looking for Petrona."

"Tell me what you know, I don't have time."

Julián yawned and stretched up his arms. "Birds in the Hills have it that you're willing to pay a good price." Mamá looked over her shoulder to the hill. It looked desolate, but then a man appeared. He had a black beard. He looked like the man who had taken me, but I wasn't sure. He was holding the leash to a burro, staring down in our direction.

"Mamá, hurry," I said.

"I know what happened to her," Julián told Mamá, sitting on his haunches and petting his dog. "How much is that worth?"

I looked to the hill. There were five men now, standing in a group, staring down. They pointed at us. "Mamá —"

He stood. "Is it worth a minute with your daughter?" He looked at me. Mamá looked to the hill and took out a bill from her pocket and handed it to the boy. Julián held it up to the light, then scrunched it up in his fist. "I was here when they brought her. Poor Petrona, all burundangueada. That boyfriend of hers was with her. He brought her here."

Mamá said, "Tell me now, where's the boyfriend? What's his name?"

Julián touched Mamá's hair. "Listen, Seño, hand over all the money you got in that nice purse of yours and I'll tell you."

Cassandra said, "Mamá, I know his name, what are you doing, we have to go." The men were climbing down toward us. Mamá

414

looked over her shoulder and saw.

"But do you know his *real name*?" Julián said. "His street name is Gorrión, but that won't help you any."

Mamá fitted the key in the driver's door, and all the doors unlocked. Cassandra and I got in, but Mamá grabbed Julián by the collar. "Tell me his name, what am I giving you money for."

Julián smiled at Mamá. "Well, I'll tell you now that we are so cozy."

The men were at a short distance. We could see their faces; one of them had blond hair, two others had beards, but none of them was the one that had taken me. "Mamá, hurry." Cassandra wiped at her face. "What are you doing, Mamá, let's go!"

Mamá pushed against Julián. "His name."

"Seño, he put her in a car with five others. Who knows, they probably killed her."

Mamá sighed in anger and released Julián and got in. "Cipriano," Julián called, "but I don't know his last name," and then Mamá was reversing the car and our tires spun in mud, then caught, and we lurched forward speeding away. I turned and looked through the back windshield as Julián slinked away, his three-legged dog following close behind, and then the five men ran into the middle of the road, watching us get away, then the orange hills shrank in the distance, and we were among the city buildings again.

At home none of us could eat. We sat in front of our plates of beans and rice, stirring the food with our forks, all of us still covered in mud. Things were so complicated I could hardly think. Petrona drugged. *They probably killed her,* Julián had said. I wondered if she recognized what was happening to her, since she had eaten from the fruit of the Drunken Tree before. Cassandra said, "Maybe we should go to the police."

Mamá stared at her pale hands clasping the dining table. "We can't go to the police. They have contacts there. No. We are selling everything and we are going away."

"What? Go where? What if Papá comes home? We have to wait!"

"Maybe we can drive to San Juan de Rioseco. That's where he was last seen."

"To the wolf's mouth, Cassandra? They will kill him if we do that."

"But is the company going to pay, Mamá? They have to pay, how else are they going to let Papá go!"

"We are going away and we are selling everything," Mamá said. "Your father will know what is happening and he will meet us. You can each pack a suitcase."

"Mamá, you can't be serious."

"Mamá, he won't find us!" I cried.

"Pack everything you want tonight." Mamá stood and walked calmly to the telephone. "Because tomorrow, everything that is not packed we are selling. We will buy tickets to wherever and we will get out of here. Your father will find us."

"Mamá, we can't leave!"

Cassandra cried out, "Mamá, I'm *not* going!"

Mamá lifted the telephone and called everyone she knew and told them we were having a sale; we were leaving the country and we were getting rid of everything we owned.

Mamá pulled out two small suitcases and put one, unzipped, on each of our beds. I packed some clothes, but then I went about the house snatching treasures: a small hand radio, pastel plastic bracelets, a small crystal elephant, a wooden spoon, Mamá's black eye shadow, Papá's red wool sock. When my suitcase was full, I went downstairs and hid the small television from the living room in Petrona's shower. I didn't want Mamá to sell it. I didn't know what I would do without it.

In the attic, Cassandra picked at the clothes in her closet. She packed her clothes and a chessboard, and then packed the contents of her drawer crying. I felt very tired of everything and I crawled underneath my bed and slept.

I dreamed of Papá again. Cassandra and I waltzed together in an empty ballroom. Papá watched us from outside the window. He banged on the glass, but we didn't turn our heads. Papá stood in the garden of our house, frowning in sadness under the shade of the Drunken Tree, but then I noticed that he wasn't in our garden at all, but in the middle of some field over which the stars shone brightly and black firs stood tall.

28.
GHOST HOUSE

The neighbors arrived at dawn. They perused our house with their noses in the air as if it were a smelly market. They brought big shopping bags and deep wicker baskets. Close to the wall, with a discerning look they turned our table lamps off and on, blew the dust from Papá's records, rolled up our Sikuani rug, rattled the paintings hanging on the wall, questioned the authenticity of Mamá's porcelain teacups. In the kitchen women bickered over Mamá's stainless steel.

One woman threw her money at Mamá as she went out the door with a stack of Papá's books — I saw the book spines: *Arabian Nights, Twenty Love Poems and One Song of Despair, Motorcycle Diaries, Plato* — and then I saw Mamá bend down to pick up the roll of pesos from the floor like she herself had dropped it. The looking-down-their-noses at us was partly because we had fallen from grace but also because it fitted with their idea of who we had always been. They knew Mamá had grown up in an invasión and that we had Indian blood, and they had always suspected we didn't belong in that nice neighborhood with them.

Cassandra and I sat on the living room couch, watching the neighbors hoarding our belongings, depositing them into piles to be guarded by their children. "Don't let anyone take anything from this pile," they said. The children — kids who had once ignored us on the playground — ignored us now in our own house. They stared over our heads at the crowd of adults, snapping objects from under each other's noses and hiding things under their arms. A man hooked our umbrella on his arm and pointed at a painting depicting a storm. "This one would look good in our hall," he said.

"That ugly thing?" his wife asked. Mamá's Indian tapestries were rolled under her arm.

"Let's ask about the price, anyway," the woman said.

Isa and Lala came by. They looked just how I felt, damp. They told us that their parents were getting a divorce and that they, too, were moving: they were going to live with their abuela.

"But how did this happen?" I said.

Isa frowned. Lala shrugged. Isa and Lala didn't mention Papá and I understood this was what you did for the people you loved. You sat with them in their pain. Isa and Lala said nothing as women descended the stairs with boxes filled with Cassandra's and my toys. We hugged. *Good luck, Have a nice life,* we said, *See you.* Not yet understanding the finality of goodbyes.

La Soltera came to see what she could buy. She paused at our front door and gasped in delight when she saw us sitting on the living room couch. "Pobrecitas," she said. "So young and already dragged under the mud." Then she clicked her tongue and widened her eyes as if she was struck with a thought. She looked down and caressed the couch. "Lovely," she said. "Run along, girls. Go sit on the stairs where you can't damage anything." Cassandra pulled me away and made me sit on the stairs and I had to bite my tongue. Cassandra even called Mamá so Mamá could negotiate the price for the couch la Soltera so obviously wanted. I looked on, counting to one hundred, the details of our lives disappearing. At some point I saw la Soltera exiting. When she saw me she bowed exceedingly, then turned on her heels. She seemed to float out the front door, touching the white, pointy tops of her ears. Later a few men came to carry all the furniture away.

"I can't believe all our things will be in other people's houses," I whispered to Cassandra. The house felt cold in its emptiness. "It's like we're dead." It was like Petrona's house, I didn't say out loud, everything gone and ruined, except we at least were getting something back for it.

At five in the afternoon, Mamá sold our car. I didn't understand how we were supposed to escape if we had no car. As the day darkened, our few remaining belongings made their way out through the front door. Slowly the house emptied.

On the bottom floor, one of three things that still belonged to us was an amulet. It was the four aloe leaves strung together, hanging above the door. It twirled, even though there was no wind. The aloe plant was supposed to absorb the bad energy that came to our doorstep, but it must have been useless all along.

The second thing we still owned was the small television I hid in Petrona's shower. I dragged it back to the living room and turned it on. I don't know if Mamá didn't notice the television or if she didn't care, but she didn't yell at me for hiding it. On the television, the reporters were still talking about Pablo Escobar, but now they were saying that Pablo Escobar had so much money, he probably had altered his appearance. Posters took up the screen for minutes at a time. There were grids of Pablo Escobar faces — with mustache, without it, with head shaved, with nose altered, with the beard of a pilgrim, with the chin thinned out, with the cheeks deflated, with the cheekbones pulled up. I sat by the television learning the black and white lines of the Pablo Escobar faces on the posters: the parentheses by his mouth, the fat nose, the sideways commas of his eyes, opposing each other, as if they were bulls getting ready to charge. Only the sepulchral black, beady eyes repeated themselves down past rows and sideways past columns. Pablo Escobar eyes.

I asked Cassandra, "Can Pablo Escobar change his eyes?"

"Pablo Escobar?" she said. "Pablo Escobar can do *anything.*"

The third thing we still owned was the telephone. Mamá kept it in her room and it rang and rang. She picked it up mid-ring and then she was quiet and breathless as she listened into the receiver. The telephone cord coiled around her toes as she rotated her foot in circles.

■ ■ ■ ■

I thought about how Papá kept small portraits of Cassandra and me in his wallet, so he could look at us with just the flick of his wrist. If anybody found his body, they would find our portraits and then they would know that this dead man had once belonged to two young someones. Papá kept our portraits behind the clear plastic meant for ID cards. Mamá had taken our portraits in the park when I was seven and Cassandra nine. In her portrait, Cassandra appeared without her glasses. It was striking how similar we looked. We could pass as twins if it weren't for some minute differences: my eyebrows were messier, Cassandra was lighter-skinned, her forehead was grander, my lips were smaller.

Papá had once said that he showed the pictures to his workers so often, he wouldn't be surprised if his coworkers could recognize us if they saw us walking down the street. Papá was always showing our pictures to everyone he met: the elevator man, the guards, the guy at the grocery store. Anyone could have noticed how much he treasured us; the way he faintly ran the tip of his fingers on the face of the portraits, the way his eyes fell back into memory, the way he enunciated, *"Mis niñas."*

The hard, possessive hum of *Mis,* the misty aspirated vaporousness of *ñasss;* how the *s* trailed behind like the tail of a long snake.

"I present to you *mis niñas.*"

My loved ones, my pirates, my queens.

I was sure now that Petrona had taken the portraits that were missing from our album. She had taken them to give to the guerrilla group. I wondered where our portraits had ended up? In the grubby hands of the driver perhaps, or maybe they were with Petrona's body too.

I sat in the garden and watched the wind turn at the gate. At any moment, Papá could turn the corner past the pine trees and finally come home. At last, at long last. I sang a song Mamá taught us:

Mambrú se fue a la Guerra
Qué dolor, qué dolor, qué pena
Mambrú se fue a la Guerra y no se cuando
   vendrá
Do-re-mi, Do-re-fa
No se cuando vendrá

Papá would turn the corner into our yard, walk down the stone steps, and look up.

Forever changed.

Even though Pablo Escobar was on the run, he gave an interview on the radio. They played snippets in the news. He had called from an undisclosed location. The television screen went black and then I heard the voice of an interviewer: "For you, what is life?"

Pablo Escobar's voice rang out: "It is a space full of agreeable and disagreeable surprises."

The calm, bored quality of his voice surprised me. I blinked thinking how I had imagined dark things happened when someone like Pablo Escobar spoke — thunder, disembodied snickering, the sound, far off, of clashing cymbals. Instead, he spoke with the rote boredom of someone passing the time, as if he was reclined, too, in a hammock, and, I imagined, squeezing a stress ball.

"Have you ever felt afraid of dying?"

"I never think about death."

I raised my brows, impressed. I thought about death all the time.

"When you escaped, did you think about death?" the interviewer continued.

"When I escaped I thought about life — my children, my family, and all the people who depend on me."

"By temperament are you violent and proud?"

"Those who know me know that I have a good sense of humor and I always have a smile on my face, even in difficult moments. And I'll say something else: I always sing in the shower."

I was astounded. What song could Pablo Escobar possibly sing in the shower? The news show moved on from the phone call then, and went on to talk about a beauty queen.

The sound of the announcers and reporters filled my days. The hours shortened and lengthened, sagging and tightening like strings. I stared at the black gate past the garden. The gate swayed with wind, mourning metallically. I gagged from imagining Papá's return. I didn't want to picture what I suspected was not possible. Better to imagine the worst. At least then you could be prepared. The phone rang and rang and the four aloe leaves twirled. Time was, I agreed, a space full of agreeable and disagreeable surprises.

PETRONA

Between dreams, there was white powder floating into my face. Someone saying, *This is what we do to traitors.* I saw Aurora's face. She stood in sunlight on a hill of sunflowers. Her cheeks were red from giggling. She lowered herself among the stalks, calling, *Petrona, here I am! I am napping now.* I went to search for her and there wasn't a trace. Her body was gone.

There were men between my legs.
 I think I was dreaming.

Gorrión held my hand as we took a walk to the top of the Hills. He stared intensely at my face, *Petrona, how can you stand to be so pretty.* This had all happened before. It was like watching a film. His friends who I previously thought to be dangerous smiled at us. They called, *There go the lovebirds,* and, *Look how cute they look together.*

Gorrión waved them away like they were teasing children and the men turned from us, laughing, still teasing. I wasn't afraid when I was with Gorrión.

Gorrión brushed a rock before I sat on it like I could not get dirty. I laughed at him because it's like he forgot where we lived. We didn't say much. We stared at the skyline of Bogotá. There were mountains so large and so blue, the city looked unimportant.

Gorrión brought a handkerchief from his pocket and when he unfolded it all the way there was a small green stone resting on the fabric. It looked like glass, but he set it on my palm and told me it was an emerald like me. Would I be his girlfriend?

I looked at Gorrión, and smiled. I said yes. His face melted then regained its shape. I was dreaming. The me in my head wondered, *Where is my body?* while dream-me didn't know where to put the gem. Gorrión pulled out a round small plastic pillbox. It was see-through with a bed of cotton. He unscrewed the top and placed the emerald inside, saying this way I can always look at it.

I shook the little emerald in the box but it stayed put, pressed against the cotton and the lid. Dream-me said, *Wait till I show Leticia.* Head-me said, *If I concentrate I can open my eyes.*

Gorrión said, *Don't you* ever *show Leticia.*

Dream-me was telling Gorrión that Leticia was like my sister, that when I first arrived to work for the Santiagos, I had felt so alone. She recognized me from the Hills, and offered me a cigarette.

Then I was walking next to Leticia in the Santiagos' neighborhood. Leticia asked how my employers were, then told me she hated hers. She told me she made herself pretty and paraded around in front of the man of the house to make that woman cancreca who acted like she was a duchess angry. Then, when she knew she could trust me, she told me she also gave information about their bank accounts and whereabouts to the guerrillas. I could do that too, if I wanted, in addition to passing the manila envelopes into which neither of us peeked. I fingered the little round pillbox in the pocket of my maid's uniform. I remembered having that conversation with Leticia, but I didn't have the emerald at that point. I was definitely dreaming. Head-me was weighted down by something. Head-me said, *Wake up. Wake up.*

There was a dirty white room. I was on a mattress low on the ground, Gorrión

430

screaming *Enough!* from the doorway. A man mounted on top.

I was gone again, in the Hills at first, and then I didn't have a body or a name. I was in a garden of sunflowers. I was blades of grass pushing up against dirt.

29.
GOD'S NAIL

Pablo Escobar's family was trying to leave the country too. The police apprehended them at the airport when they were trying to leave for the United States. The news cameras were there to capture the embarrassing scene — the police pulling Pablo Escobar's wife and his two children from the passport control line, Pablo Escobar's wife protesting, arguing, and then the camera focused on Pablo Escobar's young daughter, a nine-year-old girl wearing a kerchief, who seemed unaware of anything that was happening and was playing on the floor with a fluffy white dog. I knew she was nine years old because the reporter said so, speaking over the footage, adding that the little girl's hearing had been damaged in a bomb blast when a rival cartel made an attempt against their lives, and that was why she was wearing a kerchief.

I sympathized with Pablo Escobar's family. If you forgot for a minute about Pablo Escobar, they were just a mother, a boy, and a girl, going from embassy to embassy — American, Spanish, Swiss, German — begging for refugee status.

Nobody wanted to take the family in. The embassies said that Pablo Escobar's children were underage and they needed a notarized letter from the father in order for them to leave the country. A notarized letter meant that Pablo Escobar needed to turn himself in. Because to get a letter notarized you had to show up at a public notary, stand in line, give your signature and thumbprint, swear an oath, and only then would the official press a series of seals on your document and glue down some stamps and sign it. Everything had to be notarized in Colombia. Who came up with the system? When Mamá needed to open a new bank account, she had to get a letter notarized confirming that she was who she said she was.

When Mamá said we had applied for refugee status and were going to Venezuela to wait for our papers, I was suddenly short of breath. "We need a notarized letter, we're underage."

"Chula, what are you talking about?"

"But what about Papá? You can't seriously leave him here!" Cassandra cried.

"What good are we to him dead?" Her lips turned down. "We're leaving Friday night." That was in two days.

Thinking of Papá, my breath thinned in my stomach. I rushed to the bathroom and vomited. I could barely keep anything in my stomach. I ran out of breath often. I hid in Petrona's old room and held my head in my hands. If Mamá was taking us to Venezuela we were in immediate danger. But at least it wasn't that far. We didn't know anybody in Venezuela, I could not imagine where we would go.

I ran outside. I wanted to say goodbye to somebody, but Isa and Lala were gone. I kept running down the street, everything blurred, and then I was catching my breath at the Oligarch's door ringing and knocking desperately, and the Oligarch was asking me what was wrong. She was wearing a long cotton dress, black to her ankles, and her feet were barefoot on the tiles. Her arms came over my shoulders and then I was sitting on the couch, in that plush room I had seen only from the window and being there was all I had imagined, as I blurted out, "My father has been kidnapped." I cried, not inhaling.

The Oligarch covered me with a blanket. "Where is your mother? What is your name?" She touched my chin and pulled tissues from a golden box on the table to dab at my wet cheeks.

"Mamá wants us to leave the country, without Papá.

"Please," I added, but I didn't even know what I was asking. All I wanted was to be in the proximity of someone whose life was going according to plan. All I wanted was to cry in that well-ordered living room, with the heavy yellow curtains matching the tasseled pillows on the couch, to cry and look into the face of that woman who seemed so well-put-together, so balanced and poised. She stared at me patiently.

"My own mother was kidnapped. I was a little older than you," she said. "Is this why you've come?"

I shook my head no. The Oligarch went to a table and pulled on a little drawer. She brought a small cedar box and opened it on her lap. Inside there was a brown braid of hair and a rosary. The hair and rosary were all the things she had left from her mother. The Oligarch hugged me close and crossed herself and took up the beads. *Creo en Dios, Padre todopoderoso, Creador del cielo y de la tierra . . ."* She prayed the full Rosary as I nestled against her chest, soothed by the sound of her voice, staring at the braid of her mother's hair sitting in that box. When it was done, we sat together for a while longer and then she walked me in silence to my house. She kissed the crown of my head and knelt and looked into my eyes. The whites of her eyes were filled with red little veins, but her pupils, dark brown and large, were steady.

I went back inside the house and when I turned, the Oligarch was gone. I ran to my bedroom and I ripped the plastic off the window. I searched the empty lot for the cows. They stood by each other, near each other maybe because of the cold, chewing grass in the close distance. I bit my lip and mooed at them. There were so many things I wanted to tell them. I was leaving. My father was kidnapped. Petrona was gone. I would miss them. I tried to get across the fact that Antonio needed to be a good cow, and honor my father's name. I mooed, trying to tell them everything through the lonely sound. The cows looked up in my direction and threw their heads back, then they lay down on the grass. Maybe they were saying goodbye. I fell on my knees and I did not wipe the tears that came.

At night the walls ran high and bare to the ceiling, and the mirrors throughout the house multiplied the emptiness.

The mirror in Mamá's bedroom, facing the bare wide windows, reflected the slate clouds. The windows were open.

I sat in the space where Mamá's bed had been, and when the storm came, instead of getting up to close the window, I watched the surface of the mirror trembling from the wind. If I looked at myself in the mirror, my face shook as if I were in an earthquake.

I looked into the mirror for a long time. For a while, I started to believe I really was in an earthquake. But when I looked away, everything was still. I was still. Great huffs of wind lifted my hair and I listened to the howl of the storm. The air always smelled sweet in the rain from the scent of the Drunken Tree.

The rain reached me and I got up to close the window. But I could not bring myself to close it and I stared at the bruised and bulbous sky. My shirt was wet. The Drunken Tree was blowing in the wind up-skirted. I reached for the window handle.

"What are you doing?" Mamá asked from the bedroom door.

"Closing the window," I said.

"We have nothing to save from the storm," she said. "There's no reason to close the window. Let the storm come in if it wants."

I turned to Mamá. She was leaning on the door frame and her eyes were closed against the handle of a broom. My heart was beating fast. I walked past Mamá, swallowing everything, and then tiptoed around the empty house. There were no runners in the hall, no tables, no paintings, but I pretended they were still there. I walked through the house sidestepping the imagined dotted outlines of our furniture: the paintings, the vases, the lamps, Papá's books. I visited each bedroom and traveled up and down the stairs.

The air around the ghost objects felt charged and solid. Space held in place compact over ghost tables, chairs, and bed frames. In the dining room, the carpet dipped in creamy light circles where the table legs used to be. That was how I knew where the ghost table was, the sofa chairs, the glass cabinet.

I thought of all the objects in relationship to Papá. The chair Papá had sat in. The runners his feet had walked on. The rails he had rested his hands on.

Then, I found the last of Papá's belongings in the house hiding in the dark corner by the refrigerator, overlooked, forgotten, dusty.

It was a scarlet-tinted bottle of whiskey sequestered in the darkness. I reached for it and holding it against my breast, I ran and took it to the indoor patio.

Papá's whiskey.

When I uncorked the top I breathed in the scent greedily. The smell was bitter and churned in my throat. I took a small sip, imagining I was Papá. I remembered Papá's wooden-scented breath laughing over his whiskey. It was a gagging feeling, but I continued to take sips until I felt the floor rising up to meet my feet. I couldn't think straight, but there was nothing to think. I left the bottle behind the fridge, and I staggered up to my room crying, crawling to avoid the ghost objects.

I imagined Cassandra couldn't help but feel the ghost objects like me. When I came into my bedroom, a chill of wind came through the uncovered window and Cassandra was sleeping in the rectangle that used to be her bed when we shared a room. Her chest heaved, snoring quietly; Papá's black wool coat, which Mamá had saved, wrapped around her legs, and her hair tousled and knotted around her. She looked so peaceful sleeping: her shiny black hair in waves about her head, and her skin with twitching, muscular secrets underneath. I walked around her ghost bed and I went to lie down in mine.

I spun lying down. I stared at the night sky through the window frame. The rain had stopped and now the sky was clear. I stared at the stars shining in the black sky. Like brilliant pearls. I sped forward but they vibrated vertically. They popped and popped.

Only the crescent moon stood in place.

The crescent which Abuela said was God's nail. His hand or his foot.

30.
TWO FINGERS

When it was morning, Cassandra lifted her head from the floor and she looked toward the bedroom door. Her eyes opened in tired slits, the pattern of the carpet printed on her left cheek. She yawned, closed her eyes, and dropped her head heavy on the cross of her arms. I went downstairs and sat in front of the small television. There were cartoons, then an image of a man facedown on a roof took up channel after channel. Blood pooled underneath his body on the roof tiles. Then the reporter was speaking over the images, saying, "The police are preparing to take the body to the medical center for an autopsy." I couldn't breathe, thinking what if it was Papá, but policemen came and when they turned the body to place it on a stretcher, I saw it wasn't Papá. It was Pablo Escobar. On the stretcher, Pablo Escobar's hair fell long over his ears, and his face was wet with sweat, but his body was so still I immediately knew he was dead. This man I had feared, dead.

There were crowds of people on the street, waiting in a hush, as the stretcher was hooked onto ropes and lowered from the roof. Even as the stretcher came swinging at street level, people remained quiet and only reached their hands to touch the body and then they traced a cross over themselves. The policemen escorted the stretcher through the river of people, allowing the people to touch Pablo Escobar, his hair, his bloodied shirt, his arms. There was the sound of women crying.

Television specials, expert interviews, press conferences — the sun fell then rose in the background of the same information rearranged then said anew. I stayed near the television. I didn't tell Mamá or Cassandra that Pablo Escobar was dead. We each hid in separate corners in the house, dealing with our own horror. Watching the television is how I dealt with my grief, seeing the unfolding event of Pablo Escobar's death — experts gave their opinions, witnesses gave their statements, then the president congratulated the police snipers who had shot Pablo Escobar, decorating them with medals, speaking to a crowd, "Colombia's worst nightmare has been slayed." In Medellín people were in mourning. There was live footage at the cemetery, rivers of people chanting *Pablo, Pablo, Pablo!* They pressed against each other and the pallbearers carrying the silver casket, trying to run their fingers on the wood, trying to capture the feeling of the wood that carried the last of Pablo Escobar. The thousand mourners called together: "Se vive, se siente, Escobar está presente!"

The camera caught a few seconds of Pablo Escobar's widow, crying behind a black veil, and then her children. I only saw Pablo Escobar's daughter for a second, but that's who I wanted to see the most. She looked down, pale and bewildered, staggering next to her brother. Then the camera showed the scene from above. The casket was being lowered. Many hands held on to the casket. Someone flipped open the lid, and for a moment the news camera caught Pablo Escobar's face. Red roses framed that pale face, his eyebrows splayed themselves at rest over his swollen eyes, and a thick beard grew out of his chin. He died fat, another man. Then the silver casket clicked shut and was lowered. A tractor dumped a mountain of fresh dirt over it.

It was dark when Emilio's taxi arrived. Emilio was haggard and he put our suitcases in the trunk and then he held Mamá. I cried against his shoulder, his wide shoulders like Papá's shoulders. I cried incessantly. I rocked, sure that Papá would show up at the last hour, the last minute, the last second. Now he would be lost to us forever. It was raining. We were on the highway, streaks growing long on our windows. I saw Pablo Escobar waiting at a streetlight in a dripping wet trench coat. I jolted up and pressed my hand to the window. Pablo Escobar stared at me, frozen, then he spit and turned on his heel, burying himself in the shoulders and umbrellas of pedestrians.

Then I saw Pablo Escobar holding a wet newspaper at a different corner, I saw him crossing himself in front of a church, saw him struggling with an umbrella that had turned inside out, saw him running with his chin tucked close to his chest and a book under his arm. Rain fell all over the city.

I remembered Cassandra said that when Pablo Escobar found out someone had betrayed him, he sliced the person's throat and pulled the tongue out and left it hanging out the slit. I got the pressing desire to touch my tongue then, squeeze it in between my fingers. I wondered what not having a tongue would be like. You would probably forget you didn't have a tongue, and would try to move the red, lean muscle, but there would be nothing to move. Just the empty dark hall of your mouth. You would be alone with your thoughts.

At the airport Mamá tried to give money to Emilio, but Emilio wouldn't take it. He pressed money of his own into Mamá's hands, telling her it was his savings, telling us to be careful. I puked in the bathroom. When we boarded the airplane it was night, and my chest congested with tears. The air lengthened in long, stretchy strings inside me. I couldn't breathe. There were terms for what we had become: *refugees, destitute.* I clicked my seat belt on and from the airplane window I saw the bright blinking lights of the city. I ran my fingers along the scar on my face from the car bomb. The skin imperceptibly tucked in a long line across my cheek. It was cloudy, and the shimmering lights of Bogotá disappeared behind the clouds. I didn't care where we were going anymore.

From the airplane window, when the clouds cleared, I saw how red and blue fireworks exploded throughout the city. They opened like glittering umbrellas over the dark. People were celebrating the death of Pablo Escobar.

Beneath the clouds, far below was our

deserted house, with the ghost imprints of furniture on the carpet and the television left on.

Beneath the clouds, far below in the garden of our house, was the Drunken Tree shivering in the wind.

Beneath the clouds, far below, the Oligarch was lighting her fireplace.

Beneath the clouds, far below, Abuela María was in bed, her white hair loose upon her pillow.

Beneath the clouds, far below, Petrona's body weighed down like a stone in an empty lot in Suba, mud on her clothes, her panties over her jeans.

Beneath the clouds, far below was San Juan de Rioseco.

Beneath the clouds, far below, were Papá's two fingers traveling in the mail, proof of his capture by the guerrillas. Papá's fingers would be left at our doorstep in a cardboard box, waiting, nobody there to receive their homecoming.

31.
THE TRIBE WHOSE POWER
WAS FORGETFULNESS

We were a number: *Case 52,534.* We were a
paper in a file in a metal cabinet in an office. We were the same story, told over and
over again, in tents, in quiet rooms, before
recorders in front of officers from Venezuela,
the United Nations, in front of immigration
officers to the United States. In the beginning they were called Credible Fear Interviews, then they were Prescreening Interviews, Eligibility Interviews, Security
Clearance Interviews. It did not matter what
they called it: everything we had to say
always came down to that crackly voice
coming from Mamá's little recording device
with the little cassette tape; it came down to
the whirr of the rewinding, the way the cassette kicked into motion when she pressed
PLAY, the same spot of the tape growing thin
each time Mamá played it for a new audi-
ence, the voice becoming more tinny and
inhuman: *We've got that hijo de puta, we'll*

send you his balls in the post. We know where you are at all times, we'll get your girls too. In the camp, we were afraid of other Colombians. We didn't know who had ties to what and so we didn't get close. We slept in our tent. We gave the interviews.

We were hungry at the refugee camp, but we did not mind because Papá was being held and it was somehow decided, without discussion, that none of us would enjoy anything from now on. I kept salt packets, which we stole from fast food restaurants, open in my pocket so I could wet my finger when I felt hungry and suck the salt.

With Emilio's money we bought a telephone card to call Abuela María. We stood all three of us under the shelter of a public telephone. Mamá held the phone out so we all could listen. Amidst the rush of cars, the city murmur of people walking and talking, and distant music, we heard the dim sound of the phone ring. I imagined Abuela's house — the living room with the yellow couch, the bathroom with the barrel of water, the breezy hall that led to the kitchen. It was so long since I had thought of that house. I wondered how Mamá would explain what happened to us. "Aló?" The sound of Abuela's voice brought tears to my eyes. Mamá said, "Mamá." Abuela was surprised. "Alma? Dios mío, where are you? I've been calling you —"

"Antonio's been kidnapped, Mamá." Mamá told Abuela about how we had sold everything, how Papá was being held, how we were in Venezuela. Mamá didn't tell Abuela about Petrona, and she did not tell Abuela we were in a refugee camp either. I guessed it was because she did not want her mother to worry. They were both sobbing, and I closed my eyes because it was one way to go away. Abuela said, "Why didn't you call me sooner?"

Mamá said, "I didn't know who was listening."

The telephone began to beep and an elegant woman's voice told us we only had a minute remaining. I asked Abuela for blessings, but Abuela was already praying into the telephone, asking God to protect us. She prayed until her voice was cut out.

When we received our first mail, we knew what it was as soon as we laid eyes on it. It was the Styrofoam box Papá's company had said would arrive. It was small and white with the word *BIOHAZARD* printed on its sides in blue. Seals and signatures and acronyms had been hurriedly scrawled and stamped on all different sides of the box, but nothing betrayed the fact that inside lay Papá's two fingers. There wasn't a skull and bones for example, no frowny faces, no outline of a casket, no outline of a cross.

For days the package with Papá's two fingers had waited at our door in Bogotá. La Soltera called the police because of the smell and then Papá's company undertook the challenge of acquiring the fingers from the police and sending them to us.

We were quiet as Mamá picked up the box from the main refugee camp office, a little trailer with a small antenna hooked on top. We brought the box into our tent. Mamá didn't like to make terrible things linger, so she ripped it open immediately. We crowded around the box, not knowing how the fingers would look — I imagined they would be on a bed of ice — but as the shock subsided, I saw that among several clear pillows of air, there was a small clear bag filled with gray ash.

"It's better that they burned it," Mamá began to say. Cassandra ran away in tears.

I wanted to be alone but I couldn't, so instead in that place crowded by need I kept my eyes down. I wondered if there had arrived to our abandoned house Petrona's fingers too, a sign that she was being held somewhere. Maybe in the unmarked box lay her ring finger and the long, thin pinkie, the one with the always too-long nail.

It seemed unforgivable that the sun still rose in Venezuela, that others in the refugee camp could laugh together. I thought we heard the distant sound of waves, but maybe it was just the nearby freeway. Cassandra fought with Mamá, asking her how come we didn't just go to Abuela's, and Mamá said she had never imagined we would be sleeping in a tent, but now we were here and had to wait it out. Every day Papá's coat that Mamá had saved was still there in the suitcase, even though I believed that it would disappear just like Papá. Mamá kept the little bag of ash that were Papá's two fingers stuffed in her pillow and slept, soundly, on it.

When we were told our application to go to the United States had been accepted, we cried all night, holding our knees, our hair, each other. I only knew a few things about the United States. I knew that sometimes it was called America, even though America was also the name of our continent. I knew everything would be clean. Everything would be organized. But how could we start a life without Papá? I did not want to go further from Papá, but I did not want to stay either.

We went to the airport in Caracas early, afraid that this, too, could be taken away from us. Everything seemed like a miracle — the ticket agent giving us our tickets, the official at emigration stamping our papers, the flight not being canceled, the plane not crashing, our arrival in Miami, the drug-sniffing dog not barking at us, the American immigration not sending us back, and even as we crossed into the regular part of the airport, nobody trailed us, nobody questioned us, nobody blocked our way. I should have wanted to be sent back, because it would mean being home for Papá when he was released. Instead every fiber of my being wanted to escape — to escape and to survive — and I realized I was a coward not only when it came to Petrona, but also when it came to Papá. There were Americans everywhere: standing in lines, asking the time, trailing small suitcases, checking the arrivals and departures. The airport was one big murmur of American English, that garbled metallic noise.

It was up to Cassandra and me to find the baggage claim at the Miami airport. The flight attendant who came with us from Colombia told us there would be a sign hanging from the ceiling and all we had to do was follow the sign. She drew the sign on a napkin so we could be sure. In black ink she traced a circle and inside she drew a briefcase. We couldn't find the sign anywhere, and Mamá didn't want us to ask anyone in case we drew the wrong kind of attention to ourselves. Cassandra walked up and down the hall of the airport, holding the napkin in the air with her trembling fingers, comparing the flight attendant's drawing to every sign she saw. Finally we found our way. It was my job to remember the words *U.S. Committee for Refugees and Immigrants* and *USCRI* because that's who was meeting us. I repeated the phrase under my breath, and even as we walked up to the baggage claim and the man from the Committee walked up to us holding a paper with our last name on it — because we alone were the obvious refugees, pale, and tired, and terrified — even as he introduced himself, over his own voice I was asking, "U.S. Committee for Refugees and Immigrants? USCRI?"

The man was Colombian, like us, and his name was Luis Alberto. His wife had been kidnapped by guerrillas too, and so we clung to this man who wore an echo of our face, who talked in an echo of our voice. We hung on to his arms as he delivered us to our hotel room. Luis Alberto rented a movie for us, put our suitcases up on a stand, and set our alarm for the next day. But we could not bring ourselves to enjoy anything. How odd it was to be in a place with walls. I had forgotten how quiet it could get. There were no crying children, no arguments overheard, no deafening sound of wind making the tent flap. Luis Alberto told us to rest, he would come back early in the morning to drive us to the airport. Mamá turned the air-conditioning off. I had water without ice. None of us changed into our pajamas. I slept without a pillow.

Luis Alberto knocked on our door at four in the morning, five hours before our flight — Mamá wanted to be sure we would have enough time to board. She was afraid — but we all felt it, the notion that everything could at any moment evaporate. Luis Alberto stayed with us as we collected our tickets and walked us to the gate and explained to Cassandra where we were boarding and when we said goodbye he looked deeply into our eyes, and pressed our hands in his for long seconds.

When our plane arrived in L.A., an African woman was waiting for us. Her name was Dayo and she was kind and old. She grinned with half-lowered lids and talked slowly in an English Cassandra and I could understand. She helped us find our suitcases and then drove us to our apartment, rented and paid on loan to us by the United States government. Dayo ambled about the two-bedroom place explaining the appliances, turning the lights on and off, opening the fridge, igniting the stovetop, operating the air conditioner — like we had lived in a cave. There were things we had never seen before though: the dishwasher, the fire extinguisher, the fire alarm blinking a red eye at us from the ceiling.

Cassandra and I translated for Mamá even though we were exhausted.

"Ella dice que hay comida en la nevera para estos días," I said.

"Para toda la semana," Cassandra corrected.

When Dayo left, Mamá sank down against a wall. Cassandra lay down on the couch. I walked to the kitchen sink and opened the spout. The water was a perfect cylinder, silver-edged and transparent. I rested my chin on the counter. I stared at the endless stream of water like it was a holy thing.

None of us unpacked, but after some hours Mamá brought out Papá's coat and brushed it, saying this is how it would be ready for when he returned. She hung it in the tiny closet by the door.

Dayo had given Mamá a little key to recover our mail. Mamá didn't want to check it, but I liked to open the little door to see what was inside. There were advertisements for credit cards and catalogs, addressed to no one, but all bearing the name of our street — Vía Corona. *Way of the Crown.*

We still hadn't unpacked when a crowd of people came to our door. Dayo and her family were there, but also a Cuban family and a couple from Chile. They held heavy trays of food and told us the community was having a potluck, did we want to go?

We had never heard of a potluck before, but we went anyway. We crowded into Dayo's small living room, people and trays and dishes covering every surface, and there, we were told of the rules of the tribe: every person shared their story one time, then you were forbidden to talk about it again.

In that room that steamed with the mingling scent of jollof rice and apple empanadas, cassava and pupusas, Mamá told our story. The Cuban father translated for her. In Spanish and in English it was a story I barely recognized — Papá's dismissal from the Colombian oil company, his hiring by the American oil company, his slow rise in position, his kidnapping, and our fall into destitution. Nowhere in Mamá's story was there a mention of Petrona, though that's where the story would begin and end for me. All the same Mamá cried. Dayo rubbed Mamá's back and raised a glass, and we toasted to new beginnings.

We pulled together some of the money we had received from the U.S. government on loan and bought a little space at a cemetery, a grave meant for babies. We commissioned a stone to be carved with the words, *Sus dos dedos. His two fingers.* We put the bag of ashes that was Papá in a little box and we buried it.

On Vía Corona, we all lived together — the Cubans, the Salvadoreños, the Chileans, the Colombians, all packed inside the buildings with paper-thin walls. The landlady knew who we were, she knew that we were refugees escaping some awful reality but she never asked us for personal stories like most people.

Cassandra thought being friends with other refugees was painful. She said she had tragedy enough, and she didn't need to add to it with other people's problems. But I couldn't speak, and I was happy in that tribe

457

where my silence finally had a function. I could listen. I was a vessel for all pain, all stories. I burrowed into the safety of Vía Corona, that corner of the world where we had started anew, that tribe whose only power was that of forgetfulness.

Mamá had only a month to find a job but she didn't have any trouble. She walked into a South American market and in a few days she was stocking vegetables. In a few days more, she was doing nails at a beauty salon. Mamá's boss at the beauty salon was a fierce woman everyone called Señora Martina. Señora Martina was short even in heels, and I towered over her in my tennis shoes. I could stare into her hair, dyed red, and see little speckles of white hiding here and there between the dark strands. When I went to see Mamá, Señora Martina told me Mamá had a specific talent — clients would arrive to get their nails done, but Mamá had such a tongue of gold, clients stayed longer, getting their hair done, their haircuts, getting facials. Mamá could talk about anything, for any length of time, with anyone — wasn't it amazing? When I didn't answer, Señora Martina furrowed her brows, "Alma, what happened to this daughter of yours? She's a mute."

I thought again about Pablo Escobar cutting off people's tongues. It made sense to stop speaking, to say only what was necessary and nothing beyond. It was a way to survive. I sat in corners at home saying nothing until I realized it alarmed Mamá — then I sat in corners with almanacs, flyers, discarded books. I sat staring at the pages without reading, listening to the *swish swish swish* sound of Mamá brushing Papá's coat.

Because the coat was kept in the little closet by the front door, we hung nothing else there. I brought pretty stones and shells from outside and Cassandra made paper confetti and plastic flowers. We lit candles. We knelt before Papá's coat. We didn't even know where he was being held. I couldn't even picture his face. I repeated *Our father who art in heaven.* I prayed for Petrona too. Kneeling before the shadow of Papá's coat, I tried to imagine her safe, but it was no good — I couldn't picture her face either.

PETRONA

I was a woman without a name, lying still, in an empty lot.

The night was clear.

I was lying perfectly still, quiet as a mouse.

I was a woman without a body.

Maybe my body was cold.

I didn't know because it did not shiver.

Fireflies flashed about the field.

I could see through the swollen slits of my eyes — the night was blurry.

Someone, an abuela, checked if the body was breathing.

I didn't think it was breathing, but the abuela must have decided it was, because she began to drag the body on the grass.

I was a woman without a name, dragged earlier too. Two men abandoned the body on a patch of grass where it would be hidden from view, at least for some days.

Now there was the abuela, dragging.

The body came to a rest in a dim hut,

where I was still a woman without a name, but sometimes I awoke, sitting on a bed, drinking a foul-smelling soup, I was throwing up, no name for this woman who was ill, whose breasts were tender, whose belly would soon start to grow, whose feet were cut, who wore abrasions on her thighs and arms and back, whose insides burned like a live gash.

32.
THE LIST

Mamá enrolled us in public school and told us we were to become the best students of our class. This is how we were going to honor Papá — with above-average report cards. Cassandra listened to Mamá, and she threw herself into catching up, learning the new system, getting good grades. She was energetic and upbeat. I couldn't participate. Every time something was asked of me, in the blur of that grid of seats, I couldn't find my voice. I felt my tongue stick to the roof of my mouth.

I was put in a smaller class filled with immigrants who couldn't speak English. I did inordinately well on the exams and the teacher realized I already spoke English. Then I was put in a Special Needs class. The students in the Special Needs class didn't do as we were told, and the woman running it didn't seem to care. She was happy if none of us had outbursts. She allowed us to read and write what we wanted. She allowed me to sit on the floor under my desk. I wrote and wrote and wrote.

Every once in a while there was a list of recently released kidnapped persons published in the Colombian newspaper. Scanning the list of the recently released was painful, and Mamá would have done it alone, but the list was published online and we had to go to the public library to use the computer. Cassandra refused to go, so it was just Mamá and me, signing up for a computer and waiting for the appointed hour. Mamá couldn't read the names on the screen because she was afraid she would miss a name, so I had to feed a collection of coins to a machine that spit out a card, and then I took this card to the librarian, and the librarian counted our printed pages and punched holes into our card. I took the pages to Mamá and then Mamá sat on a table with a ruler she had brought from home. She slid the ruler down the page, so that she could be sure she was reading each name correctly.

I waited for it to be done.

So much of my life was waiting.

I had developed different strategies for waiting. One involved counting to eleven, then counting to eleven again. In another strategy, I followed the patterns of the walls, carpets, ceilings. If there were other people around, like in the library, I counted other people's movements — the seconds until somebody flipped a page, the number of words until somebody paused in their speech, the rhythm in the drum of some-one's fingers against the table.

How many breaths did Papá take in a minute? How many times did Petrona scratch her arm during the same length of time? I chose people in the library to answer for me. The rhythms of strangers were a prayer for what I did not know.

At home Cassandra was always planning for the things she would accomplish and Mamá clapped her hands in praise. Cassandra's was a different type of waiting. Exciting things loomed on the horizon and her waiting diminished as she got closer to her goals.

My waiting anticipated a black future where nothing existed but more waiting.

I spent a lot of my time sitting on our stoop. I thought about Papá — his black mustache, his large hands, the incessant heat radiating from his skin, the protuber-ant veins running up and down his arms that I liked to poke. I tried to picture his hand without two fingers, but I could not.

Which hand would it be — the right or the left? I thought about Petrona, then, imagining scenarios where I was brave for her. I saw myself lying still in the trunk of that car the day that I was almost kidnapped, which was also the last time I saw her. I saw myself in the darkness of that trunk burning in silence like a sacrifice — but then I realized that in this daydream I was not trading myself for Petrona: I was trading the torment of not knowing where she was with physical danger, which I thought more bearable. In fact, the only constant was my cowardice. I watched the palms shaking in the sea breeze. The sky was impossibly clear. The weather was hot and balmy. I watched children hang on the hands of their mothers, sucking on lollipops, asking for toys. I sank in blackness.

When no one was looking I went to the phone booth at the street corner and dialed collect-call the number to our house in Bogotá. I lost track of time listening to the ring, the way it sounded underwater and faraway and lost. I imagined our deserted house, maybe now filled with the moving boxes of new inhabitants, the signal of the incoming call traveling through the cables in the wall of our old house and out into the outlet, except there was no physical sound because no phone had been left connected to the wall.

Then I'd hear the automated voice say in English *Your call cannot be completed as dialed; please check the number and dial again.* Listening to the phone ring was a way of coming home.

One day the line did not ring at all and a man's voice said: *El número llamado ha sido desconectado; gracias!*

There was a name for what had happened to me in the streets of Bogotá after I escaped from the trunk of the car. The same thing would happen at school for no reason, other than the cafeteria had too many people and the ceiling felt too low. I collapsed with my tray unable to breathe and was rushed to the nurse. The nurse explained it was a panic attack, and that I could stop it from happening if I imagined calming things — I could picture the waves of the ocean, she suggested, or the faces of loved ones. I could count imaginary grains of sand.

The things she suggested made me anxious. But I learned to tell the signs of an oncoming attack. My hands tingled, my breath became shallow, and little things — a closed door, a sudden stare — made me inexplicably nervous. Then, I went to the library. Somehow the library calmed me. There were a lot of things to count in the library, and everything followed a pristine order.

I made sure to never be too far away from a library. I came to know the school library, the public library, and the small branches throughout East L.A. quite well. There were books in the library, about the experiences of people held captive by guerrillas, but I couldn't bring myself to touch them. One day I discovered there was a section for international newspapers in the main branch. Day-old issues of every major world newspaper were stacked in that room. I read the national newspaper of Colombia.

Reading about Colombia calmed me. I paid close attention to any article that mentioned Pablo Escobar. I got a notebook and copied out words I liked. In *El Tiempo,* a journalist named Poncho Rentería wrote, "Remember the death of Galán, the bomb to *El Espectador,* the kidnapping of Diana Turbay and Pacho Santos? Ugly days when adrenaline spread from the feet to the head and you had to write, even if it was with fear."

Hours passed as I transcribed things. I went to the library so often, scanning the newspaper for the same subjects, the librarian began to set aside the newspapers before I got there, leaving paperclips on the pages where there were articles on Pablo Escobar. I called him Mr. Craig and greeted his frequent question, "What's your interest in all this? You related or what?" with what I thought Papá would say: "Me? I'm a student of history." Sometimes I answered how I imagined Petrona would, rattling off, "No, Mr. Craig," the same way Petrona had said *No, Señora Alma,* adding a curtsy to my step.

In Colombia, several journalists doubted Pablo Escobar was dead. The government's refusal to release photos of the autopsy to the public was a clear indication that things were not what they seemed. Journalists theorized about body doubles.

One journalist who did not doubt Pablo Escobar's death wrote about a prayer found in Pablo Escobar's wallet the moment he was shot. I transcribed a fragment I liked of the prayer —

Multiply me when necessary,
make me disappear
when warranted.
Transform me into light when there is
    shadow,
into a star
when in the desert.

There were reports of citizens spotting Pablo Escobar all over Bogotá after his death. A common story was that late at night a public bus stopped and picked people up at a few stops. Then the bus sped and got off the route and began to drive in circles around the city. People said that the man driving was Pablo Escobar.

I nodded to the paper, thinking this supported my own experience of seeing Pablo Escobar the night of our departure. I was sure I had hallucinated most times, but maybe one of the times had been real. But which?

Had the real Pablo Escobar been the one waiting at a streetlight, the one crossing himself in front of a church, the one struggling with an umbrella, or the one with his chin tucked close to his chest and a book under his arm?

I memorized the prayer they had found on Pablo Escobar's body. I repeated it at odd times when I felt anxious: *Multiply me when necessary. Transform me into light when there is shadow.*

Mamá decided that we would spend every weekend at the Colombian consulate until Papá returned. She said it was the proper way to be with him in his struggle. What was his struggle? Mamá wouldn't say. Amidst the leather couches at the consulate, the Colombian flags, the aquarium filled with tropical fish, the people in the waiting area chatting amicably one second and cutting in line the next, everyone sipping coffee, I felt at home. I smiled at an older woman. She bowed her wide hat with flowers. "What a nice young woman." On the weekends Mamá brought flowers and fruit to Ana, the consulate's secretary, who let us spend our free days there as we waited for news of Papá. She gave us water and coffee in paper cups.

I saw the Drunken Tree all over L.A., but here it wasn't a tree, it was a shrub. I took clippings and put them in a plastic bag. I took the clippings to the library and in the biology section Mr. Craig found a book for me that had drawings and a small entry. I discovered it was a less poisonous type than the one Mamá had in our garden in Bogotá. The shrub all over L.A. was called *Datura arborea,* and it was sometimes used for recreational hallucination, though some kids died from the poison. There was an entry on *Brugmansia arborea alba,* the Drunken Tree from our garden in Bogotá. The entry said indigenous people called the tree *The Breath of the Devil* because when you were exposed to it, it snatched away your soul and you became a shell of a person.

The newspapers printed the autopsy photos of Pablo Escobar, but they were grainy and it didn't look like him. People wrote to the newspapers: *A man like Pablo Escobar, if he could fake a prison, why not an autopsy report?*

Ana told us about a radio program that aired from midnight until six in the morning in Colombia. It was called *The Voices of the Kidnapped* and the signal could be picked up in the jungles. Ana said there was a radio host, but the program was taken up by the voices of the families of the kidnapped, who talked to their loved ones directly, like nobody else was listening. They chatted about love, courage, the future. We had no way of listening to the radio program, but Ana told us that if we recorded cassette tapes they would be broadcast and there was a chance that Papá would hear us.

My mind stayed with the beginning of what she'd said: Papá was in a jungle.

One Friday every month Ana waited for the consul to leave and then she allowed us to use the consulate's cassette player to make recordings for Papá. When we were done she sent the cassettes to Colombia using the consulate's mail service:

This is a message for Antonio Santiago: Hello Father! We love you so much, from here to the sky! We are doing well. We miss you! We pray to God for your release.

Hola Papá, it's Cassandra, I cannot wait to see you!

Hola Papá, every day we remember you —

It was difficult not to break into tears. I was supposed to sound upbeat, but Cassandra had asked about all the *if*s and now it was all I could think about. If the signal made it to the jungle where Papá was held, if a guerrillero had a radio, if the guerrillas felt benevolent, if Papá happened to be listening. She did not say, if Papá was alive. But I knew we all thought about it.

I remembered the sound of Pablo Escobar's daughter on the news, sounding so cheerful. "I miss you, Papi, and I am sending you the biggest kiss in all of Colombia!"

Hola Papá, every day we remember you —

We sent twelve cassettes that year. Each time, I was better and better at sounding happy and hopeful. I learned to sound hopeful by imagining Papá staring at a fire, roasting marshmallows, perking up his ears upon hearing our voices, closing his eyes in remembrance of us.

Papá, Merry Christmas!

Papá, happy birthday! We blew candles for you!

Dear Papá. How I miss you! This year I am getting Cs in school. I am on the volleyball team. Every time I score a point I dedicate it to you.

I started to talk to Papá in my head. *Papá, which lettuce head would you choose? What bus should I take? Do these socks match my shirt?*

In that small, cramped place where Mamá did nails, which sported a Puerto Rican flag hanging over the mirrors and mariachi hats hanging on the walls to reflect the dual citizenship of Señora Martina, I washed people's hair.

I handled all different types of hair — wavy, curly, springy, straight, blond, brown, black, red. No matter what kind, all hair looked beautiful when wet. Under the spray of warm water hair was silk, pressing against the silver basin. Sometimes there were men, but mostly it was women who sat in my stool. I asked them to sit back and relax. I placed carefully folded towels at the lip of the sink to support their neck. Almost all people closed their eyes at the touch of warm water on their scalp. I massaged soap into their hair, feeling how tender and soft heads are, startled at how the bones are so nearly palpable. I felt I wasn't handling hair but small universes.

It reminded me of Petrona. I'd see Petrona in my mind's eye, all those years ago, reclining her head the day she was beat up, Mamá, Cassandra, and I orbiting her bruised, sweating face like we were three moons and she the planet.

At the library I noticed that the journalists stopped writing about Pablo Escobar. I had to turn to old newspapers. The old newspapers were recorded on microfiche. As I read, I discovered that every year there was a national tragedy. It was like clockwork. Headlines were our funeral song.

When I was two, they killed the minister of justice — *A DEATH FORETOLD.*

When I was four, they murdered a newspaper editor in chief — *STAND UP!*

When I was five, a presidential candidate — *THIS COUNTRY HAS GONE TO THE DEVIL.*

When I was six, a politician negotiating peace — *CARAJO, NO MÁS!*

When they murdered Luis Carlos Galán, the journalists didn't know what to say. There was no headline — just a larger-than-life photograph, and his name printed above

474

it in bold.

When they killed Pablo Escobar, the year Papá disappeared, the headline read: *AT LAST, HE FELL!*

The rules on Vía Corona dictated we break free of our past, but every month we made cassette tapes and every month Mamá bought a phone card and called Colombia. Cassandra recorded the tapes for Papá, but she had no interest in the phone calls, our past, or the tribe. Cassandra thought Mamá and I wasted too much time whining. It was ironic that Cassandra complied perfectly and automatically with the rules of forgetting and moving on, but had no interest in counting herself a member of our community that struggled to forget and move on.

When Mamá dialed Colombia, Cassandra made herself scarce. Mamá prepared tea and sat on the couch with me. She pressed endless numbers from the back of the calling card into the receiver, and finally the phone rang through. Mamá put her calls on speaker so I could listen, but I rarely spoke. She called Abuela first. Abuela updated Mamá on the news of the family, the well-being of her dogs and plants, the ups and downs of her store. Mamá in turn told

Abuela about Cassandra's grades, how many books I read. They never talked about Papá, except in code, using words like *peace of mind.* Abuela said, "I put another candle, Alma, for your *peace of mind.*" Mamá said, "One day I will recover *my peace of mind,* I have to believe that."

After talking with Abuela, Mamá dialed a friend of hers who still lived in our old neighborhood in Bogotá. Her name was Luz Alfonsa and because she was a nurse, she came and went at all hours and saw more secret things than the guards ever did. I liked listening to Luz's gossip. She told Mamá about la Soltera. La Soltera had finally entrapped a suitor, Luz said, *who knew what hole he crawled out of.* She told stories about the loud young couple living in our old house; how they drove a jeep, how one night they had a screaming fight, how they were letting all our garden plants die. I wondered if that meant our Drunken Tree was dying, but now that I only said what was strictly necessary, I couldn't just begin voicing whatever came to mind. I thought of Petrona. I understood her silence in a way I never would have been able to when I was a little girl and nothing had yet gone wrong. My quiet grew from the coils of my stomach, and stopped frozen at my throat. I wondered if there were children who thought I was a witch or under a spell, who counted the syllables of what I said when I was forced to speak.

One month, Luz said she had the gossip of the century.

Mamá picked up the phone and turned up the volume of the speaker and laid the phone back down on the living room table, "Tell me immediately." She smirked, sipping her tea.

"Well," Luz said. Her voice resounded in our small apartment. I was lying on the floor by the low table, staring at the ceiling. Luz said she was friends with a woman who was friends with the employer of a girl who knew the last girl we had. "The girl you were asking for a Communion dress for? *That* girl, do you remember?"

Mamá was quiet.

My fingertips tingled and I began to feel short of breath. I counted to eleven and counted to eleven again.

Luz said the poor girl must have fallen on bad steps, because rumor had it that she'd been found in a lot with her panties over her jeans, raped. I pushed up on my elbows and stared at Mamá. Mamá said, "Are you sure — raped?"

Luz said, "Well, you explain how else a

young girl's underwear ends up on top of her pants."

I saw the play of emotions on Mamá's face — the furrow of her brow, the twitch in the corners of her mouth, the flinch in her lids. Her hand slipped down her cheek, and when she met my eyes, I smiled. I don't know why I smiled. In my heart I was broken, and there was no healing beyond this brokenness.

When Mamá told Cassandra, Cassandra was hysterical, covering her ears, yelling for Mamá not to tell her anything else, ever. She was done hearing about Colombia. She needed to concentrate on excelling at school. She needed to attend events for all the different clubs she belonged to. She needed to apply herself, and be smarter than everyone else in order to take cracks at a system that was not made for her so that the system yielded what she wanted: scholarships, travel, opportunities, a life of her own.

Mamá took me on a bus to the ocean. She held my hand as she bent by the shore collecting stones. "Have you ever wondered why the ocean is salty?"

I pushed the hot sand on top of my foot.

"See how royal," Mamá pointed. We stood staring at the lull of the waves, then we sat.

The white of the ocean was hallucinatory. As we sat there, sea salt coated the flesh of my lips, my hair, my lashes.

"The secret is to carry what you were given with grace." She pointed to the horizon. "Like that. What do you see?"

I stared where she pointed, but I didn't move or answer. I saw that the ocean was inhuman.

I started stealing salt packets again like I'd done in Venezuela. I snapped them up from the condiment station at McDonald's when the workers weren't looking. I wet my finger, coated my finger, and sucked. The salt was something I could feel.

Another year, another twelve more cassette tapes to the radio.

Just before I turned fifteen and Cassandra turned seventeen, Cassandra said she didn't want to make any more recordings because it hurt her too much to have one-sided conversations with a ghost. *Papá was gone, we needed to admit it.* Mamá slapped Cassandra. I glared at her, her downcast eyes visible through the strands of hair that had flicked across her face. *Who did she think she was?* I wanted to slap her too. Cassandra was calm and said she was done living in the past, she couldn't keep living two lives at once, and I yelled, "This is the present, Cassandra! Papá is alive —" and Cassandra said, "Are you sure he's alive?" She waited a moment and added, "You don't know, do you?" And Mamá was stabbing at her chest saying, "*I* can feel it, I can *feel* it."

Cassandra had won a scholarship to attend college across the city, and that summer she got a job as a secretary at a dentist's office to make extra money. In our recordings to Papá, Mamá told him Cassandra was going to business school, he would be so proud of her, and I told him I was washing hair at the beauty salon where Mamá did nails. I told him Mamá was everyone's favorite because they loved to hear her stories. *Remember her stories?* I asked Papá. *Remember all those nights we stayed up hearing her tell her stories?*

Every night without fail, Mamá brushed Papá's old coat, muttering, *He is not gone, he will return, any day now,* and I thought about how I'd had no answer when Cassandra asked if I was sure Papá was alive. The truth was I wasn't sure. But I couldn't assume him dead. How could I do such a thing?

Two weeks went by and then Cassandra ripped the coat from Mamá's hands and threw it on the ground. "What about when we were all together and you betrayed Papá with *that man?*"

I was speechless and silent, and stricken tears fell down Mamá's face. Her hands lay frozen as if she were still holding the coat and I ran to the bathroom with pen and paper. Fifteen is how old Petrona was when she betrayed us. And I needed to know whether Petrona had been raped, and whether she had been raped because of me. I turned on the shower and thought: *Probably this letter won't reach her. Her family's shack collapsed. I saw it. I am writing a letter to a place that does not exist. Unless it has been rebuilt. What if I am writing to a dead woman? And even if, by some miracle, she does receive my letter, won't Petrona tear it up upon seeing my name?*

I felt guilty about writing to her, because it was in violation of the rules of my tribe — *Better to leave the past in the past, let sleeping dogs lie* — but as I wrote to Petrona, locked in the bathroom, mirror fogging with steam, I was only aware of the drum of my age in my chest, how it connected me to Petrona, across distances, across time.

33.
A HOME FOR EVERY DEPARTED THING

It's strange how you can forget a voice. After a few years, the tone and quality of it just goes. You can't recall what it ever was. In idle moments, I stared up as if I was looking up the library of my brain, looking for the right aisle, the right call number that would lead me to the record of Papá's voice. Was Papá's a low baritone? Was his cadence slow? I didn't understand how I could forget this central detail.

I was trying to remember Papá's voice as I waited for Mamá to be done reading the list of the recently released. But this day was different, because she pointed at the list unable to talk. Her hair was a frizz about her face as she motioned for me to read. The letters jumbled together and I read then reread the list, then Mamá read it again, and not being able to prove to ourselves that that was indeed Papá's name printed on the paper, we called Cassandra at work and she rushed to us on her bicycle and when she arrived, some ten minutes later, she read the whole thing out loud, "In exchange for guerrilla prisoners, the biggest guerrilla group has released . . ." then she skipped to the bottom. "S-A-N-T-I-A-G-O, A-N-T-O-N-I-O."

"Is that him?"

"Maybe it's not him."

"Is that how you spell his name?"

"It could be a different person."

We called a taxi even though we couldn't afford it, and we cried as we rode to the consulate, "What if it's him?" "It's not him, don't say that!" We could only speak in exclamations, and that's how we paid the driver, how we burst into the office of the consulate, how we cut in line, how we came up to Ana, yelling that we needed help figuring out if it was really Papá who had been released, what if it was a different person with the same name, how many people in Colombia named Antonio, how many with the last name Santiago, how many Antonio Santiagos held by the guerrillas? Ana said she had Papá's ID number, she would compare it to the list of the released. She punched numbers into her screen and Cassandra said, "It's not him, it can't be."

Then I was on the floor crying, and Ana

was saying that it *was* Papá, and Mamá was angry with Ana, saying, "Don't dare tell me things you're not sure about, this is not a game," and Ana pulled Mamá behind her computer, showing her, "Look, it's the same ID —" Cassandra was looking too, and then she was talking quickly, asking what we needed to do to get a loan, to buy a ticket for Papá, to get his papers in order, did he need a hotel? Meanwhile Mamá repeated, "I can't read these numbers on the screen, Ana. Print them out for me. They're not the same." Everything was tinged with our grief mixed with our joy.

"You know he might be different," a woman said, but we ignored her. My hands trembled and Cassandra was still asking about tickets and loans, and Ana was in tears too, telling us where to go and what to do, saying she would rush an application for his papers, and then Mamá and Cassandra and I ran — first to the bank, then to buy a ticket, then to our house phone to call Ana. Ana kept us on the line on one phone as she called the American embassy in Bogotá from another phone. We waited, the three of us, barely breathing, clutching different parts of one receiver. Ana came on and said the embassy in Bogotá would get Papá to the airport for the ticket we bought. She told us to wait; she had a surprise. "I'm going to hold this phone to the other phone, okay?" I imagined Ana sitting at her desk, holding the two telephones, ear to mouthpiece, mouthpiece to ear.

"Madre, hijas" we heard Papá say.

I blurted out a sob at the sound. Papá's voice fit into a groove in my ear, deserted for so many years, now full of his timbre. How easy it was to recognize this once lost detail. There was a home for every departed thing.

"Antonio, it's really you," Mamá said.

"Papá —" I couldn't say more.

"Papá, you're coming home!" Cassandra said.

"After all these years."

I could barely stand my own skin. Papá's flight would arrive the following day. I didn't understand how we were supposed to survive these hours of waiting. Mamá poured us shots of whiskey and then we tried to eat and then we tried to sleep. We sat staring at our television screen, without seeing what was on. Every once in a while one of us blurted, "What if we don't recognize him?" I don't know how time passed, how night came, how the sun rose.

On our way to the airport, I panicked every minute, wondering what if the guerrillas changed their mind, what if they recaptured Papá, what if the airplane fell, what if he never made it?

We watched many arrivals: one crowd from Mexico, another from Brazil — there were people who were native to those countries and arrived looking downcast and nostalgic after their visit home, but there were also American women arriving from vacation, their skin red, on their hands and heads other peoples' cultures.

I asked the same question again, "What if we don't recognize him?" but added, "What if he doesn't recognize us?" Cassandra was brave and said, "He'll be the same, you'll see."

I felt again like a child, waiting for Papá to return from a trip, dreading the moment of seeing him get out of the taxi, open the gate, and look up. *He would be thin,* I told myself. *Old.* I sat down, staring at nothing, minutes passing, trying to prepare myself. I stared at the tiles of the airport, not knowing what else to do. Was time passing or was I in the hell of an interminable minute? Cassandra told me it was time but my legs were asleep. I struggled to get up as a small crowd trickled out of the arrival gate. I hobbled behind Mamá and Cassandra, arrivals brushing past me. There was a tall blonde with two small boys, a stout man. I tried to shake my legs, but I couldn't put my weight on them. A crowd of teenagers brushed past me, to my right and my left, and then Mamá and Cassandra squealed and jumped into the arms of a stranger, and suddenly I was holding the thin, frail frame of this man in borrowed clothes.

Everything was sharp. "Papá?"

The man was laughing out of a prodigious black beard. Was that what Papá's laugh was like? I withdrew, frightened. Unlike when I had heard his voice on the phone, his laughter now, in person, didn't fit anywhere in my memory of what Papá was supposed to sound like. *Transform me into light when there is shadow, multiply me when necessary.* The black bushy eyebrows were the same, but the skin around his eyes wore deep wrinkles and his cheeks sank in against the arc of his teeth, and his hairline had re-treated revealing skin that looked soft and mottled. I struggled to put together the old features of the Papá I knew to this new, rav-aged face on which even the eyes were dif-ferent. I remembered how as a girl Cas-sandra had assured me that Pablo Escobar could change his eyes. I held on to this man's forearm, wondering what if they had switched him, what if the real Papá had died. Cassandra with wet cheeks reached her hand into his pocket.

She pulled her hand out with his — it was his hand with the index finger and the middle finger gone. I stared at the stumps, the skin where the fingers had been severed smooth and glistening as if wet. It was his right hand. This awful answer to an old question.

I wondered, *How easy would it be for the guerrillas to just cut another man's fingers?*

The ravaged man allowed Cassandra to envelop his hand in hers and Mamá buried her face into his chest, "You're home now, everything will be okay." I searched Mamá's face, then Cassandra's, and I didn't see any doubt, but relief. I was in a daze when we got in a taxi, thinking how was it possible that I was the only one that had doubts? I looked up and the man was staring into my face. It was a look Papá had never given me; in his eyes a flash of such suppressed desperation, or suppressed need, it took my breath away. Cassandra was biting her upper lip. Mamá was gripping her hands over her own knee. Nobody knew what to say.

If it were the old days, we would have talked about the driver in Spanish knowing he wouldn't understand us. Papá would have told us something about history.

Maybe Mamá would have said, *What does this remind you of? Remember our old road trips to see Abuela?* Maybe Cassandra would have said, *Who cares about the past? What's for dinner? What do we want to eat?*

Sitting in the back of the cab, the four of us sandwiched together, I felt the weight of time. The years and strain of our lives of waiting. If the man was not Papá, there would be more waiting — I would have to gather DNA evidence, and save money for a test. People got paternity tests, I knew, as a regular thing, so maybe I could do the same. If the man was not Papá, we would submit the evidence to the consulate, and then we would have to wait for the government to recognize that the guerrillas had lied, and then there would be an investigation over what had obviously been an unjust execution. Maybe the real Papá had been shot and his body left in the jungle. I needed to know Papá's final resting place. L.A. ran across my window. I showed the man the tall palm trees like the ones in Cartagena, the hot balmy weather, the pretty mansions, the clean streets. I wanted to make him comfortable; maybe he would slip up. The man rubbed his stubbed fingers with his thumb as he listened. It was a gesture Papá never had made. I stared at the man pressed against me in the cab, thinking what if we never recovered Papá's body.

At home, Mamá served what had been Papá's favorite dinner — arepas fried to a crisp, steak, cabbage salad, and rice. The man had a difficult time eating. I stared at his fork pushing the food on his plate and noted there were mosquito bites on the arms of the man Mamá and Cassandra believed to be Papá. There were random cuts and scratches on his thighs and a red marking along his wrists and also around his ankles where he must have been bound, the dark brown skin bare, hairless, and raw. There was no doubt in my mind this man had been a captive too.

Mamá remembered the coat she had been brushing for years and she retrieved it from the little closet by the door. She presented it to the man. "Every night you were gone, I brushed it so that it would be ready for you."

The man looked at the item of clothing, I thought not recognizing it, and he caressed it as he placed it over his lap. "Thank you, Madre." That's what Papá used to call Mamá, but maybe that would be an easy detail to find out. Anyone could have known that.

In our apartment that night, we heard the

only things the man would ever say about his kidnapping.

He said, "I was making my way back to the car in San Juan de Rioseco, I saw the peak of the Sierra Nevada; then seven guerrilleros stepped out of the fog.

"They said: 'Freeze or we'll piss you with bullets.' They said, 'We have your girls, cachaco — better come with us.' "

The man said he was blindfolded. The guerrillas shoved him through the jungle until they reached a guerrilla camp. He was put in a hut.

There was the smell of jacaranda flowers in the air, that bitter honeyed smell, as a guerrillero aimed at the man's fingers with a machete.

When his fingers were gone, gone because the guerrillas deemed the man a traitor — once a communist and then a capitalist — the man thought of Emily Dickinson. He thought, "I must go in; the fog is rising." He was a prisoner for 2,231 days. He moved camps sixty-eight times. He heard us four times on *The Voices of the Kidnapped.*

When they told him they would let him go, three boys escorted the man through the mountain to the exchange site. They pushed aside the plants and trees with the point of their guns. The man thought to the very last minute they weren't going to release him but shoot him.

I wondered if this man pretending to be Papá had been Papá's cell mate. The Emily Dickinson quote was something I could absolutely picture Papá thinking as he lost his fingers. It rang true, but Papá wouldn't have told that detail to just anyone, so maybe the pretender had been Papá's confidant.

I tried to ask the man more, specifically about what he had heard us say on *The Voices of the Kidnapped,* because this was something that could prove he was who he said he was, but Mamá told me to be quiet — *let your father forget, Chula, leave it alone.*

I wondered who the man's real family was. Why had he agreed to come to us to fake a life he didn't know anything about? Was it for the prospect of living in the United States? Possibly it was the American citizenship, which was not easy to get and not cheap either.

That night as I lay down to sleep I wondered if the guerrillas often sent a pretender to the families of the kidnapped. I had to admit it was clever. Papá had been missing for six years, and kidnapped persons were often gone for decades, so if ever anyone wanted to take over a person's identity, pretending to be a kidnapped person was the perfect circumstance. By the time a kidnapped person was released, after the horror they'd been through, it was believable that their faces would change. Anyone remotely similar could pass for the real person.

If the pretender gained the trust of the family, it was a way for the guerrillas to renew their blackmail. The guerrillas had given us a man with similar build, similar skin color, similar shoe size, but had failed in the thickness of hair, the posture, and the expression in the eyes. Where Papá had been able to emanate an effortless command, this new man was skittish, and insecure. The man now living in our house was afraid of large spaces. If he was outside, he was nervous and on edge until he was able to go inside a building. At night, the man didn't want to sleep in Mamá's bed, which I thought made sense, since he was a stranger to her. He took a blanket to sleep in a corner of the living room. He lay down between the wall and a table holding Mamá's vase filled with potpourri. I couldn't sleep at night and sometimes I wandered out of the small room I shared with Cassandra and looked for the man. The dining table hid him from view. I wondered what each object was meant to substitute. The wall of a shack, the trunk of a tree, the open air of the jungle, the soft bed of dead leaves.

The man spent a lot of time cooking. He made little stands out of tin containers and put large chunks of meat on top. He stared at the flames licking the flesh. He turned the slab of meat every five minutes, waiting for some specific color to emerge. This was something Papá had never done.

The man refused to meet the other refugees, so Mamá asked me to bring the man to the library with me, but when he saw any South American, he tensed up and wanted to get out of there. I guessed he was afraid of getting captured again. We found him a psychologist and I bided my time to share with Mamá my suspicions. We all took extra shifts so that the man could go talk to the psychologist about what had happened to him.

It occurred to me that a pretender couldn't be a pretender with everyone. The pressure of faking would eventually beg for release. I was sure if anything, the pretender would say something to the psychologist. As I waited I spent my days at the library, trying to discover the ins and outs of DNA tests. I read about how saliva could be tested — there were remnants of a person's saliva on postage stamps, the rims of coffee cups, and these could be isolated and tested for a match. But most hospitals did paternity tests with blood.

A month after the man had arrived, I went to see the psychologist. I didn't want to make a formal appointment, so instead I went to her office and sat in the waiting room. As she greeted diverse clients, opening her door just a crack, I saw she wore kitten heels and a skirt suit, and her hair was dyed red and curled tight. She never seemed to break a sweat even though it was warm. Mamá said she was Cuban. It was the end of the day when she came out and saw me sitting there. She was startled and held on fast to her keys. I told her not to worry and told her who I was. I said I just wanted to know if the man called Antonio Santiago had revealed to her that he was a pretender. The woman gazed at me with a mixture of concern and pity and she let the hand holding the keys fall to her side. She reached out her hand to me. "Let's go in my office, I can make you some tea."

She told me to call her Ms. Morales and in her office, with the big palm growing out of a pot, she heard all the instances in which the man had revealed himself to be someone else. She heard all my proof and theories, and when I was quiet, she was quiet too. She regarded me, and then she leaned against her lap. She told me she wasn't supposed to, but she wanted to satisfy my doubts. She took out a file and opened it. "Here is the first day I talked to your father — is it true he once killed a boa?" I didn't answer, so she retold to me what he had said to her: she described his feelings of powerlessness when Galán had been shot, his feelings of failure when the crossfire with the helicopters had taken place. I told Ms. Morales those were stories the pretender could have easily gotten off the real Papá when they were both imprisoned by the guerrillas, and Ms. Morales asked if I knew that Papá had been kidnapped by a few of his workers, that the oil site where he worked had been infiltrated and he hadn't realized it until the last second.

Ms. Morales said, "He knows you stole that Luck bottle you took when you were little."

I opened my mouth, wanting to say something, but not knowing what, and then Ms. Morales was pulling out a calendar, saying she thought I should start seeing her too, and then I was crying, telling her I wanted a DNA test, and in response she wrote me a prescription for a drug.

Ms. Morales made me sit in her waiting room as she called Mamá to come and get me. After some minutes, Ms. Morales opened her door a crack and told me Mamá would be there to pick me up in an hour; I was free to sit in her waiting room or in her office. I thanked her and stayed put. I picked up a magazine. I thought Mamá would be angry at me, but when she arrived her face was blank. I thought we would be going home, but instead we rode a series of buses to a hospital, and there Mamá told a nurse she wanted a paternity test.

I was silent as the nurse took a swab from the inside of my cheek and Mamá gave her a comb that belonged to the man I said was a pretender. When the nurse disappeared behind a door, I told Mamá I had saved money for the test, and she told me to be quiet, she did not care how many payments it took to put this to rest.

I took the little pills Ms. Morales prescribed for me. They made me sleep and when I was awake they made me groggy. It was hard to pay attention. Ms. Morales gave me another prescription and this time the pills hurt my stomach, but they didn't slow my thinking, which I liked. Two weeks after I changed pills, the hospital called to say the paternity test had been a positive. I held the phone speechless and when the woman on the phone asked if I was there, I just hung up.

I sat down. I cried, knowing that what I had wanted was a return to normal, but there would never be a return to normal. Papá was gone. In his place was this man whose cheekbones cut hard into his skin, whose burnt-dark color and malnutrition were still present even though he no longer lived in a jungle. This man who allowed me to hold his hand and sob onto his shoulder, even though it made him anxious to be so close, so near to anyone. I needed to learn how to live with this new man, to negotiate a relationship with his body that was not the body I knew.

When Mamá saw Petrona's letter, she told me to get rid of it before Papá saw. That's the only thing she said after we sat in silence staring at the photograph on our stoop. Papá was inside doing what he always did in the afternoon — staring at the television without actually seeing.

I nodded. Ours was such a small space I couldn't burn the photo inside; everyone would smell, everyone would see. I waited until it was late at night. I got out of bed and put on my sandals. I went to the edge of the parking lot, and behind random cars I crouched down and brought out the envelope, the letter, the photo. I rolled my thumb on a lighter until it sparked and then I dipped the envelope and letter into the fire. I watched Petrona's words disappear. *There's a paved road to the invasión now. I am growing cabbages, let —*

As I watched her handwriting disappear, I thought about the date I knew was printed on the back of the photograph. I calculated that the baby had to be five years old now.

I took up the photograph and fed it to the small flame. Gorrión, Petrona, the baby, fading into the orange-dark, curling paper.

What would our lives be like had Petrona remained just another girl with fleeting appearances in our family album, whose name we couldn't recall? If I had said something to Mamá or Papá back when I could, could I have spared Petrona the choice that was forced upon her? Maybe if I got Petrona fired earlier, she would have escaped being drugged with burundanga as Julián told us she'd been. She would have escaped her belly being filled with bones. Now the same silence that had been her undoing was the only thing I had left that I could still bestow upon her, whom I loved. I daydreamed of her cabbages, and my silence about her was like an eternal burning.

I didn't tell Papá that Petrona was raped.

I didn't tell Cassandra I had written to Petrona and that she had written back.

I didn't correct Mamá when she assumed the photograph Petrona had sent was a new photograph. I didn't tell her it was actually printed the year we fled Colombia.

I didn't tell Mamá that the man in the photograph was Gorrión.

I was the only one with all the pieces. I was the only one that knew that Petrona had made a home with a man who had betrayed her, that she had chosen to keep the baby, that this new life she had fed from her breasts was something I had to make up to her and the only thing I could do was keep silent about what I knew. After all, who am I to judge? As her photo burned, I thought: *even oblivion is a kindness.*

PETRONA

Only three times in my life did a letter arrive bearing my name.

One time it was a letter from the city morgue.

It was a photocopy of a form with typewritten information, signatures, and city seals.

Name: Ramón Sánchez.
State: Deceased.
Age: 12.
Occupation prior to death: Guerrilla member.

There was a note in the envelope too. *Dear Petrona Sánchez, Our most sincere condolences for the loss of your loved one.* It was signed by a policeman. It felt important that I was being addressed by a policeman. Mami tore the letter to pieces. *Asesinos all of them.* She flung the paper in the air, my name printed on that nice paper gone.

Another time, it was a Christmas card from Aurora. The card was decorated with red glitter that came off on my finger when I rubbed it. Aurora could have given the card to me in person the year she went to live with Uriel and his wife, but she wanted to give me a surprise. She bought an envelope and paid for the stamp.

The third one was this letter from the United States. Nobody in the Hills had received a letter from the United States so the mailman didn't leave it with the rest of the mail at the pharmacy. Instead he climbed the Hills to give it to me. Along the way he showed it to a few women washing clothes by the path. *Look, ever see an international letter? See how many stamps.* The women were curious. *Who's it for?* they asked, then they ooh-ed and ahh-ed when they saw. Or that's what Julián told me later.

The mailman found me crouched doing laundry by my hut. I had reconstructed it from the heap Mami had left before she disappeared into the streets, the heap that people in the Hills refused to throw out or burn because they thought a curse would come down upon anybody who touched it. I built a nicer home.

The mailman rapped his knuckles on a

nearby tree to get my attention. He widened his eyes and fanned a thin envelope in the air. *This came for you from the United States.* I wiped my hands dry on my dress and took the envelope. I stared at the name. *You have family over there?* It was Chula's handwriting. *It's a girl I used to know,* I told him. He took a step closer, averted his eyes but creeped his ear toward me. *And what could she want?*

I went through the curtain inside my hut without another word and out the back door to the garden. I sat down on the rocking chair. What would Gorrión do if he saw the letter? I was thankful I was alone. My son, Francisco, named after my father, was at school, and Gorrión was driving a truck to the coast for my brother Uriel. I could destroy the letter before Gorrión returned. I still had some weeks.

I had expected such a letter for many years, and now that it was here, I couldn't bring myself to rip the envelope open. For days I left it tucked in the band of my underwear. I wasn't sure if I wanted to know what Chula had to say.

One day after dusting the hut I sat on the floor of my kitchen. I took the envelope out. Chula had used a series of stamps with a picture of a man swinging a bat. The ink with my name had begun to run. The envelope was wrinkled and thin from being so close to my skin. I took the letter out. I didn't understand anything the first time I read it, and had to go over the same words many times. Slowly I pieced things together.

In the Hills we had code words. We called the guerrillas encapotados. We spoke of la situación. *Cómo está la situación?* and if somebody said *Mal, muy mal,* we knew to stay indoors because there was something underfoot with the encapotados or the paras or the army. Salt was Chula's word for the aftershock. I knew her father had been let go. The people in the Hills said as much.

Everyone remembered the day the mother and the two girls who had come for my Communion came looking for me after I disappeared. *They were covered in mud,* the people in the Hills said. *Serves them right.* The people in the Hills told the story like it was a folktale. *When there's a tempest, it comes down on all sides equally — can you believe that's what the rich woman said?* The people in the Hills loved that part of the story, where they could let their derision for la Señora Alma really come through. *The rich woman said this to a mother who had lost three children and whose house had just fallen down. Of course, the rich only see their own pain — aren't they living outside the country now, with their health, with a job? And where's Doña Lucía? In the streets, lost her mind.*

I knew what the people of the Hills said about me too. *Poor Petrona. Poor woman without a memory.*

It's true that after Doña Fausta found me abandoned in the lot, I didn't remember who I was. Doña Fausta named me Alicia and told me the story of how she had found me, like it could help me remember the before. As I flinched with a fever from infected wounds, she told me how she was on her way home one night, when she glanced into the empty lot by her house. There were fireflies that night and she was watching them light up the grass when she saw a body. It was a bruised, dead body. The girl was beat up and her panties were soiled and had been pulled on over her jeans. Within three steps, she saw the chest was moving with breath.

Doña Fausta dragged me to the road and then she got a wheelbarrow and carted me to her house. She liked to say the fireflies were God lighting her way to me. She got me a little pendant made of tin in the shape of a firefly that she bid me to wear even

505

though it stained my skin blue. I didn't like the pendant. I thought the fireflies were filthy animals, little flying specks attracted to the smell of men on my crotch.

I was four months pregnant when I remembered the Hills. I saw in my mind the orange hills, the path up the steep. I knew how to get there, but nothing more. Doña Fausta and I went together. We climbed and climbed and I asked everyone we came across, *Do you recognize me? Do you know who I am?* People stared. Nobody answered. *I know this is where I lived,* I told Doña Fausta. We got close to a ridge. We stood in a playground, staring at a tall retaining wall, hearing the sound of cars on the other side, waiting and hoping for something to return to me, but nothing did. I cried in frustration, thinking, *I know this is where I lived, how come I couldn't remember;* then a black man ran up and hugged me, sobbing. I froze in his arms. *Petrona, thank God,* he said against my neck.

I stared at the slope of the hills, wondering if Petrona was really my name.

When he let me go, I searched his face, *So you really know who I am?*

He pulled on his nose. He said, *Petrona, yes, of course, yes.* He looked into my eyes. *You don't know who I am?*

I shook my head no. He told me his name was Gorrión, that he was my boyfriend, that he'd been taking care of my family, and he'd been searching for me everywhere. I looked at his face and wondered if this was a face I could love. His eyes paused on my stomach. He glanced at Doña Fausta. He lowered to his haunches, staring at my stomach.

Is it yours?

He stood, staring at me, staring at my stomach, and then he nodded. *Yes,* he said. *You were pregnant. We were going to have a baby,* and he held me again. I felt the thump of his heart when he hugged me, that's how astonished he'd been.

There was one photograph of me holding my newborn, Francisco, Gorrión standing behind me. In this photograph I had no memory of the before. My home was a hill of rubble, so I stayed with Gorrión's mother, who made me teas and broth. She was a small woman, startling white hair gathered in a knot at the nape of her neck. Gorrión said we got married just before I went missing, though when I first met him in the Hills he had introduced himself as my boyfriend. I guessed since we were newlyweds, he wasn't used to calling himself my husband. His mother cried bitterly, *Why*

507

would you keep such a thing from me? I was sad I couldn't remember our wedding. Gorrión proposed we have another ceremony. *You and Mami can make new memories and we can leave behind your being mugged and turning up in a lot in the past, where it belongs. We can become a happy family.* Gorrión's mother smiled through her tears. *You would really do that?*

Gorrión took me to my brother Uriel's house. I didn't remember Uriel. I didn't remember Aurora, who was young and said she was my sister. I didn't know what to say. I looked at the walls. There was a guitar in a corner. Finally little Aurora stood up and left. She brought back a dirty white bundle. When she unfurled it she looked steadily at Gorrión, then at me, then she said it was my wedding dress. I stood. *It is?* The empty dress held my shape. It was like the shell cicadas shed and leave behind. I touched the soft material. Dust came away on my fingers. *What happened to it?* I asked. Little Aurora said, *It got buried when our shack fell. But I found it and saved it for you.* Little Aurora cried in fits. I didn't know how to comfort her. She was a stranger to me.

At the church, little Aurora carried the baby and threw rose petals on the floor. I stepped on the petals Gorrión had bought specially for the occasion. My wedding dress had been so dirty it took hours to get clean. We'd paid for it to be altered to my new shape. In the dressmaker's living room, just a few blocks from the Hills, when I stepped into the dress, I saw flashes of another woman who took my hand. Her eyes saw through me. Who was she? I felt naked when she looked at me. I didn't ask anyone who she was but I thought of her on my wedding day, my small steps echoing in that church, little Aurora with my baby, softly sobbing to the altar where the Father waited on us. I knew something was trying to speak to me, and I looked to the tall ceiling of the church feeling shame, because there was this woman with her eyes sinking like daggers into me and then there were clouds with changing faces of men hovering over me. I shook my head and let all those visions drop from me and I knelt before the Father. Where did the visions come from? Maybe they were just dreams.

In time the difference between a memory and a dream became clear.

I remembered the things I was not supposed to.

I understood Aurora's fit of tears after she handed me my Communion dress, once given to me by la Señora Alma. I understood

509

Aurora's sobbing that echoed in the church as she walked ahead of me to the altar. She had chosen to lie to me to protect me. But I couldn't tell her that I knew.

And I didn't tell Gorrión.

I needed a father for this son, who I knew was not his.

I took his guilt.

His guilt that got him out of bed, to go to work, to bring back money from an honest job, to get us food. I demanded a house of brick from him. I demanded proper schooling for my growing boy, Francisco. I thought about Chula, daily, especially now that Francisco was almost the same age as she had been when I first arrived to work at her house. Some nights I thought of the body out of clothes I used to make in the bed the Santiagos had provided for me. How it lay still in the darkness. It waited out the night. It was deaf and dumb and without memory.

When Gorrión got home, after weeks of driving, I imagined myself that pile of laundry. Gorrión liked to feed Francisco his dinner, and tell Francisco things that were more for my sake than his: *I fell in love with your Mami because she was beautiful. You were on your way to us when we got married in the Hills. She wore a white dress, and a crown with a veil that was so long it lifted in*

510

the wind. I was a pile of laundry smiling at Gorrión, doing dishes, making the beds.

When I was alone or just with Francisco, I felt peace. Other times I saw features on Francisco that were not mine and belonged to that terrible night. I loved Francisco above all. I wanted to tell Francisco, *Once there was a little girl I took care of.* I wanted to say, *I once outsmarted the encapotados. One day you and I will go away. Far from all this.* But I could not tell him, not yet, because he was young and had a loose mouth and I didn't want him to repeat anything to Gorrión.

Once I thought that when you have nothing your life stretches toward nothing. In our farm in Boyacá, when the paras started to come, Mami instructed us to not see, to not hear. If we did it right, we would come out of it alive.

We made ourselves deaf and dumb, but still we lost. The story repeated itself, and we lost some more. We had no other choice.

I wanted to tell Chula everything, but I was afraid of my letter being intercepted or read. I didn't have a word to give to Chula to let her know how I felt, like she had done for me. I did have a photograph, and in this photograph was everything I lived. Sometimes the less you know the more you live.

511

AUTHOR'S NOTE

Fruit of the Drunken Tree is a novel inspired by personal experience. Kidnapping was a reality for many Colombians until 2005 when the practice really began to decline. If they had not been kidnapped themselves, every Colombian knew someone who had experienced it: a friend, a family member, someone at work.

There was once a girl like Petrona who worked as a live-in maid in my childhood house in Bogotá. Like Petrona she was forced into aiding in a kidnapping attempt against my sister and me, and like Petrona in the face of this impossible choice, she did not comply. I have thought of her throughout the years, along with all the women I have met who are stuck in hopeless situations in Colombia.

My father, too, was once kidnapped. He described the day he was captured as the longest day and night of his life. He spent the time in darkness, bound in a crude shelter. The next day he was taken to see the head of the guerrilla group, and then, he was lucky — the head of the guerrilla group was a childhood friend. The guerrilla boss slapped my father on the back, happy to see him, and in the way of long-lost friends, asked him what he'd been up, how he'd been, how his family was doing — all the while my father was still bound. He was let go. An uncle was not so lucky. He spent six months captive.

I write this at a time when the biggest guerrilla group in Colombia, FARC, has demobilized and the former members are attempting to go back to civilian life. For years the violence in Colombia has been a landscape of victims, corruption, and desperate choices, where the perpetrators are often perpetrated against. In writing this novel, I was inspired by the political born into the lives of children. I remember my little cousins who were afraid of any man or woman in uniform — even the police — because they had no ability to discern between all the armed groups in the country. Pablo Escobar was larger than life to all of us.

While the story told in this novel is fictional, the historical details and political

events are factual: the assassination of Galán, the drought, the hunt for Pablo Escobar, his prayer, and his last interview. This
historical timeline between 1989 and 1994
was used sequentially, but time was com-
pressed as the emotional timeline of the
book required. A girl was tragically killed by
a car bomb near my neghbohood in Bogotá
when her father went inside a building to
buy tickets to the circus. I don't know for
sure if the television showed the girl's leg
still wearing her shoe, but that's what I
remember. That year I would go to the
circus. My sister and I were picked from
among the kids in the crowd to ride atop
the elephant. My sister held on to me and I
gazed down at the great wrinkles of the
elephant's head, people cheering in the
pews, but all I could think was that the girl
was gone, no longer with us.

MIL GRACIAS

When you are an immigrant your successes are a direct result of the sacrifice and toil of your family, so I would like to begin by thanking them — Mami, Papi, and my sister, Francis. I would like to thank my agent, Kent D. Wolf, for his luminous reading and suggestions, and for his unwavering support. A thousand thank-yous to my editor, Margo Shickmanter, whose unstinting passion and vision were a guiding light.

Thank you to Sam Chang, who sat with me under the shadows of trees and gave me advice on writing and the writing life. To Leslie Marmon Silko, who was a veritable life force and from whose pure heart I learn even now. To Tom Popp, Andrew Allegretti, Patty McNair, Megan Stielstra, and John and Betty Shiflett.

Gracias to all who read this novel: my dear friend Mike Zapata with whom I exchanged letters and writing for years, the incomparable Tiana Kahakauwila whose wit and range and kindness showed me a new way, and to the talented Jacob Newberry who gave his honest advice. Countless others read parts of this book and their thoughts helped me polish this story and gave me wings to continue. Thank you.

I am grateful for all the places that opened their doors to me and gave me a desk with a view to write: Djerassi Resident Artists Program, the Camargo Foundation, and Hedgebrook, as well as the National Association of Latino Arts and Cultures, and the San Francisco Arts Commission, whose support allowed me to make time for writing.

In the writing of this book, I consulted many Colombian news sources. Thank you to all the journalists who are no longer with us, who risked their lives to tell the suppressed stories of Colombia, and to the journalists who survived and kept reporting even though they knew the risk.

My good friend Ken Lo, who is very hard to impress, talked with me about this book many bar nights over cocktails. To him, a special thank-you.

Without my partner, Jeremiah Barber, this novel would have not been possible. You are my moonlight coyote.

ABOUT THE AUTHOR

Ingrid Rojas Contreras was born and raised in Bogotá, Colombia. Her essays and short stories have appeared in the *Los Angeles Review of Books, Electric Literature, Guernica,* and *Huffington Post,* among others. She has received fellowships and awards from *The Missouri Review,* Bread Loaf Writers' Conference, VONA, Hedgebrook, Camargo Foundation, Djerassi Resident Artists Program, and National Association of Latino Arts and Cultures. She is the book columnist for KQED Arts, the Bay Area's NPR affiliate.

The employees of Thorndike Press hope you have enjoyed this Large Print book. All our Thorndike, Wheeler, and Kennebec Large Print titles are designed for easy reading, and all our books are made to last. Other Thorndike Press Large Print books are available at your library, through selected bookstores, or directly from us.

For information about titles, please call:
(800) 223-1244

or visit our website at:
gale.com/thorndike

To share your comments, please write:
Publisher
Thorndike Press
10 Water St., Suite 310
Waterville, ME 04901